We hope you enjoy this book. Please return or renew it by the due date.

You can renew it at www.norfolk.gov.uk/libraries or by using our free library app.

Otherwise you can phone 0344 800 8020 - please have your library card and PIN ready.

You can sign up for email reminders too.

D0755050

NORFOLK ITEM

30129 086 188 803

NORFOLK COUNTY COUNCIL
LIBRARY AND INFORMATION SERVICE

Also by Beth Good

Available in paperback

Winter Without You
All Summer With You

Available in eBook

The Oddest Little Beach Shop
The Oddest Little Book Shop
The Oddest Little Chocolate Shop
The Oddest Little Cornish Tea Shop
The Oddest Little Romance Shop

A Very Cornish Christmas

BETH GOOD

Quercus

First published in Great Britain in 2020 by

Quercus Editions Ltd
Carmelite House
50 Victoria Embankment
London EC4Y 0DZ

An Hachette UK company

A CIP catalogue record for this book is available
from the British Library

PB ISBN 978 1 78747 743 8
EB ISBN 978 1 78747 744 5

10 9 8 7 6 5 4 3

Typeset by Jouve (UK) Milton Keynes

Printed and bound in Great Britain by Clays Ltd, Elcograf S.p.A

For my father, Richard Holland

CHAPTER ONE

Sitting on her sofa, Caroline clapped both hands over her ears, groaned loudly, and wished for the umpteenth time that she hadn't moved in next to green-haired Cruella de Vil and her fanatic boyfriend. The constant thump-thump-thump of their music – if it could be termed music, which she seriously doubted – through the thin walls of her ground-floor flat was giving her a headache for the third morning in a row.

'So much for a quiet week off work,' she muttered, perversely wishing she was at work, despite having taken a week's holiday over the Halloween celebrations.

She could go out, of course, and give her poor ears a rest.

But although this Halloween had dawned bright and sunny, it still felt chilly. Besides, she'd gone out yesterday, and the day before, and frankly, her budget wouldn't stretch to lunching out every day just to escape her neighbours.

The music from next door abruptly shifted tempo, now an unbearable thumpity-thumpity-thump, accompanied by some kind of strange shrieking.

Caroline frowned.

Was the green-haired goth girl singing along to the music?

No, she realised, with a sinking feeling. Her volatile nineteen-year-old neighbour was having yet another argument with her boyfriend, who was at least twenty years her senior and a tattoo fanatic, no flesh visible that wasn't colourfully decorated. Caroline had nothing against tattoos, of course. But more was not always better. And Malcolm was a surly beast too, though that could have something to do with the fact that Caroline kept going round to their front door and complaining. About the music, about the constant rows, about their two huge German Shepherd dogs, who barked and howled whenever left alone for more than ten minutes. Which happened most days.

Jumping off the sofa, she buttoned her cardigan and thrust both feet into leaf-covered wellies, the nearest footwear to hand. 'I've had enough of this,' she muttered crossly, flinging the door open, and stopped dead at the sight of a sports car purring into her cul-de-sac. 'Oh!'

The sleek and shiny Aston Martin stood out among the aging hatchbacks and estate cars parked outside the flats.

As she watched, the driver's window rolled down and a tanned arm waved at her cheerily, gold bangles jangling on its slim length.

'Hello!' a familiar woman's voice called out. 'Surprise!'

'Jennifer!' she yelled back in delighted amazement, forgetting all about her infuriating neighbours, and running down the leaf-strewn pathway to the car parking area. 'Oh my God!'

Jennifer parked and climbed out of the mind-blowingly

expensive car, all legs and chic designer clobber. Caroline hugged her before examining her stepsister critically, her fashion senses on full alert.

It had been a little over two years since Jennifer had met film star Alex Delgardo and been swept off her feet by his taciturn good looks and impressive bank balance. The happy couple had married nearly a year and a half ago, in a lavish show-biz wedding ceremony that had left Caroline feeling just a teensy bit envious of her younger sister. Still, it had been the most amazing experience to precede the bride to the altar, treading through rose petals strewn around the outdoor church in California, clad in clinging pale silk with satin pumps and clutching a gorgeously scented bouquet as the maid of honour.

Barely eighteen months of marriage to a film god, yet already Jennifer seemed at home with her multimillion-aire status. Which was odd, given that she'd been part-goth when she left, constantly clad in gloomy black or draped with occult pendants and hippy-style cardigans.

'Happy Halloween!' her stepsister said with a wink, and a slight American drawl. 'Trick or treat?'

'What on earth are you doing here, Jenny?' Caroline gasped.

Jennifer abandoned the fake accent. 'Visiting you, of course, in good old Pethporro. I see it's freezing as usual. But at least it's not wet, I suppose.'

'I mean, why aren't you in LA?'

Jennifer looked her up and down, her lips quirking. 'Nice wellies. Not your usual style, but I like the look.'

'I wasn't expecting company.'

'I tried to ring first but your mobile's off.'

'That's deliberate, so nobody can ask me into work for emergency cover. Oh my God, is that Chanel?' Caroline plucked at her sister's pretty woollen jacket, rendered speechless with envy.

'Um, possibly. Alex bought it for me.'

Caroline shook her head, disgusted by Jennifer's complete disinterest in fashion. 'Fabulous wealth is wasted on you,' she complained, but smiled, looking her up and down. 'It's wonderful to see you, Jenny. I had no idea you were back in England. How is Alex?'

'He's exhausted, poor pet. We only flew in yesterday from LA.' Jennifer made a face. 'Jet lag, you know? I left Alex sleeping it off at Porro Park and drove straight over.'

Porro Park was the gorgeous country house her filmstar husband owned and where Jennifer had first met him. She had been his tenant, living in Pixie Cottage in his huge grounds, and had made friends with his late grandmother, Nelly.

'I had to talk to you. I stopped at the clinic first, but they told me you'd taken a week off.' Jennifer raised an eyebrow, glancing oddly at the block of flats, its once whitewashed walls – now grimy and grey – pulsating with rave music. 'Is that *your* music?'

'My neighbours, Savannah and Malcolm.' Caroline pursed her lips, keeping her voice down, though she doubted the couple could hear anything through that din. 'Savannah is nineteen and has green hair. Malcolm is a forty-something self-employed painter and decorator. They have lively disputes that go on for hours. As for that unearthly din, I was just going round to complain.'

'Good idea. Don't let me stop you.'

'Oh, those two can wait. You said you needed to talk to me. What about?'

'Let's go inside first.'

Caroline grimaced. 'What, with that hideous noise thumping through the walls? We won't be able to hear ourselves think. Look, why don't we go into town instead? There's a posh new coffee shop slash bistro.'

'In Pethporro?'

Jennifer was not bothering to hide her disbelief.

'You won't have to lower your Hollywood standards too much, trust me. They do everything from macchiatos to salad lunches.' Caroline laughed at her mock-impressed expression. 'Give me a minute to change my shoes and lock up.' She ran back to the flat while Jennifer waited by the car, swapped her wellies for smart tan ankle boots, grabbed her coat and purse, and then hurried back. This time, she gave her sister a more critical once-over. 'Seriously though, what's up? You look tired.'

'I told you, it's jet lag.' But Jennifer sounded deliberately vague, and Caroline knew there was more to it than that. 'You're right, though, I could do with a caffeine hit. Come on, let's visit this posh new coffee shop.'

Getting into the passenger seat of the gorgeous Aston Martin, Caroline knew a moment's glowing satisfaction as she glanced back at the dingy flats to see both Savannah and Malcolm framed in the window next door, peering out at her in wide-eyed disbelief.

She pulled the door shut with a blasé air and a flick of her blonde hair, as though she regularly rode about in madly expensive sports cars.

'Good God. Is that them?' Jennifer had seen the staring couple too.

'How did you guess?'

'I bet they look forward to Halloween. The one night of the year when they won't look out of place in Pethporro.'

'I would laugh, but I've run out of humour.'

'Better give them the full treatment, then.' Jennifer put her foot down hard, revving the Aston Martin so that it roared wonderfully, then accelerated out of the car park, engine growling under the bonnet. 'What was that appalling racket they were making, anyway?'

'Rave music.'

'It sounded horrific. And insanely loud.' Jennifer headed for the town centre, apparently oblivious to the considerable attention she was attracting from the good Cornish citizens of Pethporro. 'How on earth do you put up with them as neighbours?'

'I've been asking myself that question a lot lately.'

'You poor thing.'

Caroline studied her profile suspiciously. They were good friends, of course, as well as stepsisters. But they'd always enjoyed a cat-and-dog relationship, frequently sniping at each other and making sarcastic comments. It was true that Jennifer had mellowed considerably since marrying her film star – and who wouldn't mellow, spending most of the year in sunny California in a fabulous mansion with swimming pool and tennis courts? – but this sudden solicitude was a bit too much.

'I don't usually have to put up with them much,' she admitted. 'It's only because I'm off work. Normally, I'm out most of the day, and they tend to go out partying in the evenings. Though the early hours can be fun.' She bared her teeth. 'Sometimes, they come home at two or three in the morning, both off their heads, and start yelling at each other like banshees. I sleep with a pillow over my head those nights.'

'You should move out.'

'Love to, but I can't afford it. Have you seen the rental prices around here lately? Pethporro has become even more popular since you left, especially with owners of second homes. And I don't qualify for council housing. Not as a priority case, anyway. So I guess I'm stuck there for now.' Caroline shrugged, enjoying the luxurious feel of the leather seats. She ran a hand along the smooth dashboard. 'Maybe they'll move out instead.'

'Not knowing your luck.' Jennifer's brow was knitted in concentration. She weaved her way carefully between a parked taxi and an oncoming tractor. 'So, who are you dating these days?'

'Nobody.'

'Nobody?' Jennifer swivelled her head to stare at her, then flicked her glance back to the road. 'That's not like you.'

Caroline hesitated.

Lately, she'd been going through a dry patch, boyfriend-wise. She'd had a few offers over the past year, yet somehow couldn't get up the enthusiasm to bother dating. There was no obvious reason why not. Or none that she could pinpoint. Work just seemed more interesting right now.

But she didn't particularly want to share that thought with Jennifer. It sounded a bit self-pitying.

'Too busy at work, I suppose.'

'Heard anything from Mum and Dad lately?'

'I spoke to them on the phone last week. They love their new art gallery in St Ives. I promised to drive down and see it as soon as I can.' She grinned. 'Very generous of you and Alex to buy it for them.'

'Yes,' Jennifer glanced at her guiltily, 'I probably should have mentioned that. Their lease on the old gallery had run out, and they'd found this great new exhibition space. So I said I'd buy it for them. But it was Brodie who handled the sale, so it slipped my mind.'

'Brodie's still with you and Alex then, is he?'

Caroline tried to keep the judgemental note out of her voice. Brodie was Alex's personal assistant, and highly protective of his superstar boss; the two men had been best buddies for years, ever since they'd met back in their army days.

Caroline had found Brodie quite attractive on the few occasions she'd met him during Alex and Jennifer's courtship. He had a faint Scottish tinge to his accent, and the kind of rugged good looks that made it hard not to look twice. But she'd been less impressed with the guy since discovering that he'd been against Alex and Jennifer's relationship at first, though he'd changed his mind after realising that Alex was absolutely smitten. Anyone who could diss her lovely sister was not worth knowing, Caroline thought.

'Need you ask?' Jennifer shook her head. 'Those two are inseparable!'

'That must be difficult for you.'

'Not at all. I know we had a few problems in the beginning, but I get on okay with Brodie now. He really looks after Alex well, does everything for him. Which means I don't need to, of course.' She bit her lip. 'Though I probably shouldn't have asked Brodie to organise that art gallery purchase. He's not *my* personal assistant, after all. And they're not Alex's parents, they're mine.'

'It's the same thing. You married Alex. What's his is yours, et cetera.'

'I'm not sure Alex would always agree with that.' But Jennifer laughed. 'I'm glad they're enjoying the new gallery space. I wanted to give something back, and Alex agreed. Mum and Dad did a pretty good job of bringing us up, don't you think?'

'Given the material they were working with, I suppose so.'

Jennifer's eyes sparked dangerously. 'Sorry?'

'Hey, I was only joking. Of course they did a good job as parents. Seriously, you should see some of the teenagers I have to deal with at the clinic. Never been within a mile of a baby, and suddenly they're going to be parents.' She grinned. 'The nappy-changing workshops are hilarious. Especially with the boys. Their faces!'

Jennifer was quiet for a moment, then said abruptly, 'Do you think we were badly behaved as kids?'

'No worse than any other Cornish teenager, bored out of our skulls all winter and then working three jobs every summer.' Caroline shook her head, bemused by Jennifer's question. 'What put that into your head? Did Mum and Dad accuse you of being a brat?'

Caroline called them Mum and Dad, though Debbie was her stepmother. But Debbie had always been 'Mum' from the very beginning, as though there was no difference between Caroline and her own daughter, Jennifer, from her first marriage.

In the same way, Jenny had always called her stepdad 'Dad' even though Jim was no blood relation.

It had been an unspoken convention, and both girls had fallen in with it quite naturally, perhaps because their respective parents had married while they were still both in primary school. But while Jennifer had kept in touch with her real father, and even invited him to her wedding a summer ago, Caroline hadn't seen her birth mother since she was five. All she knew about her, in fact, was that her name was Topaz. Though that seemed such an unlikely name; she always suspected her dad had made that up. He was an artist and a bit vague at times, so anything was possible.

'No, nothing like that.'

'You were a bit wild at times, it's true. You remember that coven you started? You had to break it up when you melted Mum's potpourri dish during a full moon ritual.'

Caroline laughed, and Jennifer joined in with obvious reluctance. 'But I was the one who was always slapping on the lippy and sneaking out to meet boys. *Crafty Caro*, that's what you called me.'

'I'd forgotten that.' Her sister shook her head. 'They gave up so much to look after the two of us, that's all. I just wanted to say thank you.'

'With an art gallery.'

Jennifer shrugged. 'It was what they needed. And we have the money. God, we've got money coming out of our ears. I don't know, maybe I was just feeling nostalgic and homesick . . .'

'Slow down, you've passed the coffee shop!'

Jennifer hit the brakes and backed up along the high street in a slightly precipitous manner, having spotted a parking space near the chemists. Luckily, the traffic was light, the season having finished several months ago, so they didn't collide with anyone.

Jennifer glanced up at the sign as they went inside. 'Kornish Koffee?' She cast Caroline an ironic look. 'Very klassy. With a K.'

'Hey, come down a notch or two, lady. This is Pethporro, not LA.'

'Sorry.'

The coffee shop was decked out in spooky décor in honour of Halloween, with witches' hats suspended from the ceiling and black candles burning on each table. They found a table for two in the window, just vacated by an old couple and still covered with a fine sprinkling of cake crumbs. Nothing loath, Caroline dashed these to the floor and wiped the table with a leftover napkin. She then piled up the used crockery and shifted the entire heap to another table.

Jennifer watched all this industry with a slight smile on her face.

'That's better.' Caroline plonked herself down by the window and peered out through the Halloween display of cottony spiders' webs and black netting. The church clock chimed softly out of sight, and she counted them mentally. Twelve bongs. 'Oh, it's lunchtime already. How did that happen?'

'So let's have lunch.'

'What a good idea.' Caroline grabbed two menus from the condiments tray, handed one to Jennifer, and then studied the laminated list herself without really seeing it. Something was nagging at her, deep down, but she couldn't for the life of her work out what it was. 'I can't believe I'm eating out for the third day in a row.'

Jennifer lowered her own menu to look at her questioningly.

'Savannah and Malcolm,' Caroline explained briefly. 'Savannah's not started back at college yet, and Malcolm's home a lot. I find it less stressful to go out than sit and listen to their ruckus next door.' She rubbed a little porthole in the steamed-up window, trying not to dislodge a large plastic spider attached to the glass at nose level. 'The weather's been holding up since the summer. Not too much rain yet, for all it's nearly November.' She glanced wryly at Jennifer's smooth coppery tan. 'Though I suppose having come from sunny California, it must feel like the Arctic Circle here.'

'Cornwall is a trifle nippy in comparison,' her sister agreed with a theatrical shiver, keeping her jacket firmly buttoned up.

The waitress arrived, looking flustered and distracted, order pad in hand. 'What can I get you ladies?'

They both ordered traditional Cornish pasties with side salad and a pot of tea, without having consulted each other.

'Great minds think alike,' Caroline said after the woman had gone, grinning with appreciation.

'Well, we are sisters.'

'*Step*sisters.'

Jennifer frowned. 'I thought we'd agreed to forget about that. That's what Mum and Dad always wanted, wasn't it? For us to be a proper family. Like we're blood, not steps.'

Again, Caroline felt an odd jangle of nerves. There'd been something unexpectedly pointed behind that remark. Was something wrong with Jennifer? It wasn't very likely. She seemed happy enough with Alex, or had never complained of any issues in her marriage. But she knew from her job that women rarely did complain, at least not openly.

'Quite right,' Caroline said with a smile, deciding not to push the point. 'I was only pulling your leg. You know, the same way we used to tease each other as kids, always saying we were *step*sisters.'

'I know.' Jennifer leant forward abruptly, touching her

hand. 'But we're not kids any more. And I'd like us to be *sisters* now.'

'Of course.'

They talked easily for a while about their parents, and the art gallery in St Ives that Alex and Jenny had bought them. Jennifer laughed and smiled in all the right places, but Caroline could tell she wasn't entirely there. Her sister's mind was elsewhere, nagging away at something she didn't want to share. But what?

Their large shared metal pot of tea arrived, courtesy of the now smiling waitress. It seemed someone in the kitchen must have recognised them.

'There you go, *Mrs Delgardo*,' the waitress said breathlessly, placing Jennifer's cup carefully in front of her while slapping Caroline's down without so much as a glance in her direction. She had even brought an unasked-for plate of ginger snaps. 'We're honoured to have you here at Kornish Koffee. Please, help yourself to these courtesy biscuits.' She put a hand to her flushed cheek, her voice even more tremulous. 'The cook and I ... That is, we were wondering ... Will your husband be joining you for lunch?'

'Not today,' Jennifer said politely. 'Maybe another time.'

'Oh, well ...' The waitress nodded and bustled away to make her report, somehow managing to look both disappointed and exhilarated at the same time.

'There goes your anonymity. By now, the Pethporro gossip machine is already cranking out the news that you and Alex are back in town. Next time you drive past this place, they'll have a plaque saying, "As visited by the Delgardos" over the door. I get my fair share of questions too, you know. Asking how Alex is doing, and when his next film is out, as though I had the inside scoop on his career. Which obviously I haven't,' Caroline added pointedly, 'given that you and Alex are as close as clams about stuff like that.'

In an excellent impersonation of a clam, her sister didn't say a word.

Caroline sighed and busied herself stirring the hot water, sorting out the cups and picking up the milk jug. She hesitated. 'Shall I be mother? If that isn't too confusing, now we've established I'm your sister.'

Jennifer was staring blindly out of the window. 'Hmm?'

Definitely a problem there.

'Here you go.' Caroline poured two steaming hot cups of tea and pushed one towards her sister, trying not to let it slosh into the saucer. 'Okay, enough chit-chat. Tell me to mind my own business, but I can't help noticing you're not yourself. Is it really jet lag, or is something actually wrong?'

'Wrong?' Now she had Jennifer's full and rather unnerving attention. 'Why do you think something's wrong? Do I look different?' Pushing a hand through her short dark hair with an impatient gesture, Jennifer met her sister's gaze frankly. 'Be honest with me, please.'

Caroline frowned. Her sister had not only been a well-known folklorist before her marriage to Alex, but a witch on the side too. Had she continued practising witchcraft while out in the States? Not that Jenny had ever been the type of witch who went round turning people into frogs – if that was actually a thing, which she doubted – but she wasn't someone you wanted to offend. Not if the scary jars she'd kept in her kitchen back then were anything to go by. Mandrake roots, devil's dung and the like . . .

'Not at all,' Caroline said politely. 'But you mentioned having something to talk to me about. Wasn't that why you drove over today?'

Slowly, Jennifer nodded. 'It's probably nothing.'

'Tell me.'

'You were right. I've not been myself recently. I've had headaches, and funny moods, and . . . Well, I don't think I'm well.' Jennifer hid her face in her hands. 'I think it's serious.'

'Have you seen a doctor?'

'God, no.' Jennifer looked horrified. 'Alex would be bound to find out, and he's been so stressed out with work recently. I don't want to worry him. And it might be nothing. Just a tummy bug, you know.'

'You've been feeling sick?'

'Vaguely.'

'And out of sorts?'

'You could describe it like that, I guess.'

'But headachy?'

'Definitely.'

Caroline sat back as their Cornish pasties arrived with a lavish salad, the waitress once again beaming with pleasure, and the cook accompanying her this time, his funny white cap bobbing up and down as he practically bowed to Jennifer like she was royalty. But Caroline's mind was working fast.

Because she'd heard all those symptoms before.

Many, many times.

She'd finally qualified as a midwife about a year before Jenny met Alex, after long years of study on top of her original training as a nurse, and now absolutely adored her job. There was a wonderful roundedness to the process of seeing a woman through from that exciting first clinic visit to post-natal check, the birth itself being the highlight of her work, though also the most stressful. The pay wasn't wonderful, but it was graded, which meant she might actually be able to buy her own place one day, especially if she rose to senior level.

Midwifery was a vocation rather than a job, she'd always felt. But the idea of becoming a homeowner through her own hard graft meant a great deal to her. It would demonstrate that she'd finally arrived in a state of adulthood, after several decades of prolonged adolescence. Also, she needed the security of her own place. Mum and Dad had been good parents, yet somehow, she'd never felt perfectly right at home, as though a part of her was missing. Which was a ridiculous notion, of course.

More importantly at this moment though, she was an expert on the classic early symptoms of pregnancy.

When the waitress and cook had finally gone, she leant forward across her plate and whispered, 'Jenny, when was your last period?'

Cutting into her pasty, Jennifer stopped to stare at her, wide-eyed with astonishment. 'I beg your pardon?'

'You heard me.'

'That's a bit personal . . .' Slowly, comprehension dawned on her sister's face. 'Bloody hell. Are you kidding?'

'Is it possible?'

They were still both whispering by instinct, aware of other people seated nearby in the busy bistro. People who might be eavesdropping like crazy, for all they knew, given Jennifer's celebrity status as wife of a film star.

'Of course not.'

'Because you both played it safe.'

'Exactly.'

'No contraceptive is one hundred per cent safe. You know that, right?'

Jennifer hesitated. 'Well, there may have been one time when . . .' Then she stopped dead, biting her lip.

'Go on.'

'It's none of your business.' Her sister's cheeks had flushed pink, and her voice wavered. 'Honestly, I can't believe we're having this conversation. That you're asking me such embarrassing questions. And over lunch, too!'

'I'm not embarrassed. It's part of my job.'

'It's *not possible*,' Jennifer hissed.

'Anything's possible. One time is more than enough. One tiny mistake.' Suddenly peckish, Caroline picked up her pasty and dug her teeth hungrily into it. After swallowing the first tasty mouthful, she shook her head at her sister's horrified expression. 'Trust me, I've seen enough shell-shocked teenagers to know that ten seconds of carelessness can change your life forever.'

'No, no, no. Oh no.' As if in a dream, Jennifer cut her pasty into quarters. Gingerly, not looking at Caroline, she nibbled on one quarter. 'I may be a bit impulsive at times. But I'm not a teenager.'

'Have you and Alex been bonking like bunnies?'

'Caro!' The flush in her sister's cheeks hadn't faded yet. She peered about the coffee shop in obvious consternation. 'For God's sake, lower your voice.'

'So, basically, the two of you have been going at it like jackhammers, and now you're surprised that the inevitable has occurred.'

'Good grief, you're incorrigible.' Despite herself, Jennifer was laughing. 'You make us sound . . . sex-mad.'

'That's a yes, then.'

'Maybe a bit.'

Squirting a dollop of tomato ketchup on to the side of her plate, Caroline dipped her pasty into it, then took another large bite. The pastry was melting and delicious. 'Let's pop over to the clinic after lunch,' she said indistinctly, 'and you can take a pregnancy test. Fifteen minutes, tops.'

'I have no idea what you just said. Finish your mouthful. And use a knife and fork, would you? I'd forgotten you eat like a savage.'

Swallowing her food, Caroline said more clearly, 'Come back and pee on a stick for me. Or in a pot. Whichever you prefer.'

'Christ, shh!'

'Sorry, that came out a bit louder than intended.'

'I know this is only Pethporro out of season, but even at this time of year, you never know who's listening. Everyone's got a camera phone these days. And the last thing we need is for the media to get hold of this.' Jennifer looked down and seemed to balk at her tasty Cornish pasty. She put down her knife and fork, shaking her head. 'If there even is a "this". Which I still don't believe, by the way. Alex and I have been careful. Mostly.'

Mostly.

Caroline studied her sister's face, which was suddenly pale again, then returned to eating her pasty with her hands, unfazed by Jenny's disapproval.

'What is it the Americans say? Don't bet the farm on it.'

CHAPTER TWO

It was a perfect autumn day, cold but bright. Brodie swung the Land Rover up the cliff road, his attention drawn by the cool grey swell of ocean to his left.

He had missed his daily views of the Atlantic since following Alex and Jennifer to the States. Even now he wasn't sure how long they'd be staying in Britain, let alone this remote corner of Cornwall, tucked away on the west coast of this sea-locked land. But that was part of the job. Never stopping too long in any one place, always moving on without looking back.

It had been the same in the army, where he'd served with Alex long before his friend became an international film star, and Brodie took on the role of his personal assistant. A nomadic lifestyle had become second nature to him now, and it hardly bothered him these days to pack up and leave friends behind.

What would it be like to settle somewhere for good?

He shrugged off the question as the car dipped out of sight of the sea, transferring his gaze back to the coastal road. It was unanswerable. Besides, settling down was unlikely to be something he needed to think about anytime soon. Alex had a new film role under negotiation, and his wife had only come back to Cornwall to see her sister for a few weeks.

'I'm homesick,' Jennifer had said out of the blue, and Alex had immediately suggested a trip back to Cornwall.

Alex doted on his wife, that was clear. And Brodie had come to see, over time, that Jennifer was not the problem he had at first feared she would become. His first impression of her had been of a highly strung young woman, with secrets in her past and a way of dominating Alex with a look.

Totally unsuitable for a man whose psyche was still in pieces – in other words, a man recovering from a nervous breakdown.

But, after a shaky start, Alex's nerves had shown signs of improvement as their relationship blossomed and deepened. And his late grandmother had taken Jennifer into her heart too, Nelly perhaps sensing in her last year that here was someone who could take her place in Alex's life.

Eventually, Nelly had sadly passed on. In his grief, Alex had first tried and failed to forget Jennifer, then had come back to Cornwall on some ridiculous pretext or other – something to do with his grandmother's goats, Brodie recalled – in a shamelessly transparent attempt to forge a relationship with the woman.

And it had worked.

The couple had decided to get married, and Brodie grudgingly accepted Jennifer as a part of their tight-knit unit. It hadn't turned out badly so far. The film roles had started to come in, and Alex had been working full-time again, on location and in the studio, with no obvious signs of strain.

Recently though, Brodie had become aware that something was bothering Jennifer. He didn't know what, but he was worried it might spell trouble for their marriage. And his first concern always had to be Alex.

He slowed for the next bend, of which there were rather too many for comfort. The road was insanely narrow in places, and its high grass-bound hedgerows hid oncoming traffic as well as the rough green fields on either side, seen only in flashes through occasional five-bar gates. Shaggy sheep peered at his passing vehicle or paid him no attention, cropping the grasses. On the far horizon, tempestuous-looking clouds were rolling in across the Atlantic, perhaps threatening rain to come. But it was still sunny here on the coast, the inland hills and valleys steeped in cold, golden light.

Suddenly, a long-tailed pheasant burst out of the under-growth and dashed in front of the Land Rover.

Brodie braked instinctively, but the bird was gone in another instant, stampeding through the hedgerow with a mad cry and flapping wings.

'Bloody hell!' he muttered under his breath.

His mind was still clinging to the hot dry hills of California they'd left only two days before. There he'd still been in shorts and T-shirt most days, enjoying the relaxed Hollywood vibe and kiss of sun on his skin. Only the nights had been cooler.

Though he'd probably continue wearing shorts here in Cornwall, even in winter, as they were so much easier than wrestling trousers over his artificial limb. He'd pulled on bootleg jeans for today's expedition, unsure how Lizzie would feel about his prosthesis being on show, but it was an inconvenience he didn't need.

In truth, this Cornish landscape was not so very different from the place where he had grown up: a dark farmhouse nestled amidst misty green hills and fathoms-deep lochs, a few miles from Inverness, at the farthest ends of Scotland.

He hadn't been back to Scotland for years though, his parents having left there now too, and no siblings. All he had left of that time was the faintest hint of a Scottish accent, which grew stronger, according to Alex, whenever he was deeply moved or excited, such as when watching a football match . . .

But his heart sometimes yearned for the peace and tranquillity of the highlands, its bleak loneliness in winter, the heath lightening in early spring when the first buds broke and the skies softened to a mild blue. And California, while undoubtedly sophisticated and seductive, was not for him. Something inside him needed the cool, rainy landscape only to be found on home shores.

He came to a crossroads and paused, grinning at the new sign erected in the field opposite, next to an open gate, the track leading away through trees and meadows. LIZZIE'S ANIMAL SANCTUARY, the sign announced in large, uneven, hand-painted letters, with a rough sketch of a goat and donkey underneath, alongside a mobile number.

It had shocked Alex to receive a text from Lizzie last night, less than two hours after arriving back at Porro Park.

Welcome home!! Come see your goats. They miss you!!! Lizzie xxxxx

Firstly, it was clear that news moved quickly in Pethporro. They'd barely started to unpack and already the locals knew they were back. How was that possible? Secondly, none of them could quite believe that Lizzie had a mobile phone, crowding round Alex's mobile to stare at the unexpected text message.

'Lizzie has a mobile now?' Jennifer had seemed astonished. 'I wonder what else has changed since we've been away?'

'I guess we'll find out soon enough,' Alex had said, then smiled at his wife fondly. 'Shall we ask her to bring Ripper home to see you? Or do you think that would upset him too much? We may only be here a few days, after all.'

Jennifer had been tempted, missing her aptly named Siamese cat, his chief skill being ripping people's fingers to shreds when they stupidly attempted to pet him. They had chosen to leave Ripper behind when they flew out to the States, but one of their friends, Lizzie, who had a special affinity with animals, had happily offered to look after him during their absence. A bit of an eccentric, she'd also agreed to take their goats, which had relieved Alex's mind greatly.

But Jennifer knew it was probably a bad idea to uproot the cat for such a short spell. 'Perhaps we could visit him instead. If Lizzie doesn't mind.'

Brodie hadn't been sent to check on the goats. But he

had fancied a drive to clear away the last vestiges of jet lag, and visiting the goats gave him as good an excuse as any to escape Porro Park.

Carefully, he turned into the gated entrance and made his way down the dirt track, his vehicle bumping up and down over damp mud ruts.

A mobile phone did not sound like Lizzie's style, he thought, remembering the friendly but eccentric local woman, habitually clad in tracksuit and trainers, with springing grey hair under a bobble hat, who seemed to spend most of her time outside.

Within a quarter of a mile, he reached the main enclosure, passing fields of skipping goats, some of whom he definitely recognised, plus several grazing donkeys, a couple of ragged sheep, and even what appeared from a distance to be a llama, wearing a tartan jacket.

Beyond the enclosure stood the ancient barn and outbuildings she'd acquired from an animal-loving old lady. But the ramshackle premises he recalled from their first visit had been completely transformed, presumably with some of the large sum donated by Alex when she agreed to rehome his late grandmother's seven goats.

The gaping hole in the barn roof was gone, and the grim farmyard with its weed-infested, broken-up concrete had become a flat rectangle of gravel marked out – with another of Lizzie's hand-painted signs, by the look of it – as 'Visitor Parking'. Altogether, he counted seven or eight individual animal pens, comprising an indoor shelter with outdoor run attached, plus the main reception area, all brightly if rather garishly painted in yellow and neon blue. Through the trees he could see smoke rising from the old farmhouse, where presumably the old lady still lived who had donated her outbuildings to Lizzie's enterprise.

He parked near the converted barn and got out, studying the glass-fronted reception area with a raised eyebrow.

The whole place had changed beyond recognition, in fact. But Alex's donation, substantial though it had been, could not possibly have covered all this development work. It seemed the animal sanctuary had other backers, including some very generous ones.

The reception door flew open and Lizzie bounded out, bobble hat still in place, though her grey hair had been cut to a surprisingly neat bob. She was also wearing wellies, so thickly mud-splashed the green rubber beneath was barely visible.

'Hello, hello, hello, erm . . .' Seconds later, Lizzie threw her arms about him, enveloping Brodie in a tight, breathless hug. 'Can't remember your name. But hello, it's wonderful to see you!'

'Hello,' he said, staggering backwards in surprise. She had never been physically demonstrative before. 'It's Brodie. And good to see you too.'

'Sorry about the hug, Brodie. That was from the goats, not me.' Lizzie released him with an awkward smile. 'I told them you might be visiting today, and they wanted me to do that. Funny creatures, goats.' She peered over his shoulder at the Land Rover, clearly disappointed that he was alone. 'No Alex? No Jennifer?'

So she could remember *their* names. But not his.

His mouth quirked in an ironic smile.

'I'm afraid not, no. Not this time, anyway. Jennifer's gone into Pethporro today to see her sister.' Brodie hesitated. 'And Alex has a touch of jet lag. I'm sure he'll come by soon enough though. To see for himself how the goats are getting on.'

'But you're here.'

She waited, looking at him expectantly, head cocked to one side. It seemed some kind of explanation was in order.

'Yes.' Brodie felt a little self-conscious. He stuck his hands into his pockets, shrugging. 'I felt like a drive out, I suppose.'

The truth was, he had felt restless and anxious on waking this morning, for no obvious reason he could think of. He had dropped in on Alex first thing, hoping to drag him into the home gym for a blistering workout, only to find his boss too groggy to get out of bed, let alone lift weights. Not surprising, perhaps. Alex had been working hard for months, only grabbing a few hours' sleep most nights, and the lengthy plane journey from LAX must have knocked him sideways.

'I love what you've done with the place,' he added, turning on his heel to survey the buildings and land. 'You must be very proud, Lizzie. It was just a load of tatty old sheds last time we were here. But this is really impressive.'

'Thanks.' She grinned, seeming embarrassed, and dragged her bobble hat down to the level of her bushy eyebrows. 'Penny and Bailey helped. And we got money from the council. And a few other people.'

'Well, it looks fantastic.' He nodded back up the dirt track. 'Shall we walk out to the enclosure and visit the goats?'

'You okay to walk that far?' She cast a dubious glance down at his jeans, as though she could see his prosthesis through the thick fabric. 'Gets bumpy in places. And there's boggy bits too.'

He felt an unexpected flash of pain at the question, however innocent on her part, and was surprised at himself.

It had been a long time since he'd considered himself 'sensitive' to the issue of his prosthetic leg. He'd lost half the limb, from the knee down, his foot and ankle blown off during a terrorist hotel bombing in the Middle East, and the rest amputated soon after. It had been several years now, and he'd reached the stage where he no longer felt so self-conscious in shorts, and could even joke about it with close friends. But he could still get blindsided by people staring or asking difficult questions.

'I can manage.'

Lizzie peered at him, her expression suddenly careful. 'Oops. Did I say the wrong thing?'

'Of course not. Forget it.'

They reached the goat enclosure. There was a gate, tied shut with some tatty rope, and a wooden stile to one side.

'One of our goats has a falsie,' she confided.

'A what?'

'A false leg, just like you.'

She ambled cheerfully over the stile into the goat's enclosure and stood watching him on the other side. There was something unnerving about her intense scrutiny, Brodie thought. But he swung himself over the stile with perfect ease, which seemed to satisfy her concern.

'Strawberry, we calls her,' she continued, heading up the boggy field at a quick march without waiting for him. 'Vet said it was gangrene or some such. But he fixed her up with a falsie, and now she's good as new.' She gave a laugh. 'Well, it don't stop her a-munching on everything in sight, leastways.'

After some initial difficulty around the stile area, Brodie soon caught up with her. The field was indeed sodden from recent rain and difficult to navigate, especially as it began to slope upwards. But his pride had been wrung now and he was determined to match her stride for stride.

Though the terrain had other ideas.

'I should have worn wellies,' Brodie said ruefully, pausing to drag one trainer out of some particularly glutinous mud with a squelching sound.

'Townie,' she said with obvious glee.

The goats had seen them. The herd came charging over the brow of the hill like a small hairy army, hopping and skipping. And there was the llama in the tartan jacket again, bringing up the rear like a super-sized goat.

Of the donkeys there was no sign. No doubt they disdained hanging out with goats. And he couldn't say he blamed them.

'They think it's lunchtime,' Lizzie said, stopping to wait.

He hadn't brought any treats with him.

'Oh dear.'

'S'all right,' she said confidently, digging into the bulging

pockets of her tracksuit bottoms and producing two generous handfuls of seeded snacks. 'I got it covered.' She passed
him some sticky odds and ends. 'Don't let 'em grab. Bad
manners, this lot.'

As the first goat reached them, he started to say authori-
tatively, 'Now, no jumping up, or else—'

Next thing, he was on his back in the mud, surrounded
by a posse of warm, smelly goats nosing at his jacket and
hands. Their breath steamed into his face, lips drawn back
and big teeth exposed, as though snickering at him.

'Bloody hell!' he exclaimed, flailing his arms at them.
'Get off me, you . . . you . . .'

Lizzie bent over and held out a hand, helping him back to
his feet. 'Tsk, naughty goats!' she chided her charges, though
without much heat, as though nothing unusual had happened. 'How many times do I need to tell you? We don't treat
visitors like that. Especially nice visitors like, erm . . .'

'Brodie,' he supplied again croakily, then cleared his
throat. 'Brodie Mattieson.'

'Sorry, not good with names.'

'It doesn't matter.'

The goats were nudging him violently, apparently uncaring that Lizzie had told them off. He tried to take a step
back and nearly fell again, his feet stuck firmly in the mud.

'They want the snacks,' Lizzie pointed out calmly. 'Best
give 'em, before they have you over again.'

Sucking in a deep breath, Brodie held out both hands
and let the goats lick and nuzzle his palms, wrists and fore-
arms, and even tug on his pockets with those huge teeth.

Nelly's goats.

He felt a jerk of nostalgia, recalling how Nelly used to wander out in the milky dawn most mornings to feed her 'babies', as she'd called them, often in her long white nightie, like a smiling ghost crossing the lawns with seven goats skipping after her . . .

He missed Nelly, he realised. But then, he'd never had a grandmother of his own. Both sets of grandparents had passed on by the time he was born to middle-aged parents, a late 'miracle' baby. So it had been easy to adopt Alex's nan as his own pseudo-grandmother, and she had certainly been happy to play that part for him, always there to give him advice. Even if it had mostly been cryptic and difficult to decipher.

But that had been Nelly, her utterings often mysterious and yet somehow full of wisdom that felt just out of reach.

'Is that . . . Bananas?' he asked, trying to recall the name of each goat as they milled about him. 'And this one is . . . Fruitcake?'

'Other way round.' Lizzie gave a guffaw of laughter. 'Goodness, don't you know their names?'

'Of course I do. More or less.' Brodie frowned. 'I thought Bananas was the yellow-looking one. Hence the name.'

'She *be* yellow. Can't you see?'

He looked more closely at the goat she was indicating, its rounded sides caked in copious amounts of black and grey mud. 'Underneath all that dirt, I suppose . . .'

'How about him there?' She pointed to a goat with an idiotic expression, lips pulled back from his teeth as he tried to nibble at something on the ground. As soon as he'd succeeded, the goat limped away up the field, no longer interested in them. 'What's his name, d'you think?'

Oh, God.

'Erm . . .' Brodie struggled for a name. 'Hoppy?'

'Full marks!'

'Ah, and I know this one for sure,' he said with relief as one very small but persistent goat butted his arm with her bony forehead and bleated, no doubt in hope of another treat. 'That's Baby.'

He stroked her head and ears, and then watched with a grin as Baby nibbled the last sticky snack off his flattened-out palm, licking until every trace of sticky goodness was gone.

Baby was the goat who had brought Jennifer and Alex together. She had a tendency to wander and had run away to Jennifer's little cottage on the edge of Alex's estate, so that Jennifer felt obliged to rope the goat and bring her back home. Whereupon, she had encountered Nelly and Alex, and later Brodie too, who'd seen the look in his boss's face and known something very special and powerful must have occurred.

Even though he'd feared the relationship with Jennifer would bring an already vulnerable Alex to his knees, he had reckoned without Nelly's almost supernatural influence and understanding.

It all felt rather a long time ago. Though in reality it was only just over two years. But so much had happened since that day . . .

'There, see?' Lizzie beamed as the goats skipped away together, sated and seeming to lose interest in the humans once all titbits had been devoured. 'They be good little things, really.'

He wiped a sticky hand on his jeans. 'Oh yes, saintly.'

'I done a proper job, caring for them?'

'Absolutely. You deserve a medal.'

Her eyes widened. 'What's that? I'm going to get a medal?'

'Not an actual medal, I just meant ... You've done a great job with the animals and the sanctuary.' He gave her a reassuring smile. 'I'm sure Alex and Jennifer will be thrilled when they see how well Nelly's goats are doing.'

'I bring the goats back to you at the big house, then?'

'God, no!' Brodie grinned at the thought of Alex's face, waking up to the sight of seven goats running wild about the place again. His boss had loved his grandmother: her mad goats not so much. 'We're not staying that long. Besides, the goats seem happy here. Let's not disturb their routine.'

'If you say so,' she said, sounding uncertain. 'And the cat, Ripper?' She paused. 'I likes Ripper. He be a good mouser, all right.'

He considered the question. Ripper was Jennifer's volatile Siamese cat. She would want to see him, having constantly missed her 'familiar' while out in the States. But she'd reluctantly decided there was no point bringing the cat home to Porro Park. Not when it was only to be a flying visit.

'Is he still living with you at Hannah's place?'

When they left Cornwall, Lizzie had been staying in an old farmhouse out on the cliffs belonging to Hannah and Raphael Tregar. Lizzie was nomadic by nature though, and he knew she might have moved on by now, taking the cat with her.

'That's right,' she mumbled though. 'Kernow House.'

'If Hannah doesn't mind the intrusion, maybe Jenny could come and visit Ripper at Kernow House for a few hours one day soon.'

'I s'pose.' But it was clear she was troubled.

'Don't worry, Lizzie.' He patted her shoulder gently. 'Nothing's going to change just because we've come back to Cornwall, I promise.'

CHAPTER THREE

'It's impossible, I don't believe it,' Jennifer said in a horrified whisper, staring at the result of her pregnancy test. She sank down on to the plastic chair beside Caroline's workstation, visibly shaken. 'Can it be wrong? I mean, we were so careful. What are the odds against it being right?'

They were in one of the nurses' rooms in the small local GP practice where Caroline worked as a midwife.

'The odds of a false positive?' Having washed her hands with antibacterial soap, Caroline dried them thoroughly on a blue paper towel. 'Staggeringly low. False negatives happen all the time. Too early testing, not enough hormone present to trigger a positive result, that kind of thing. But it's very rarely the opposite.'

'Bloody hell . . .'

'So you're pregnant. Congratulations!'

Her sister glared up at her, clearly unimpressed with the news. 'Caro, could you at least try to be sensitive to the situation? I . . . I'm pregnant, for God's sake!'

'And I don't see what the problem is. You're happily married, which isn't the case with some of the women who

come through my clinic doors. You're wealthy. Or your husband is, at any rate. And you're healthy too.' Caroline paused
in her task of closing the equipment drawers and looked
round at her with sudden alarm. 'I presume, anyway.'

'Oh, there's nothing wrong with me,' Jennifer said, then
added bitterly, 'except for a bun in the oven.'

'Jenny, don't get me wrong, but everything feels perfect
here. You couldn't be better placed to have a baby. So, why
the long face?' She paused. 'Shouldn't we be celebrating?'

'You don't understand.' Jennifer buried her face in her
hands and gave a plaintive groan. 'Oh God, what am I going
to do?'

Caroline, used to her sister's odd moods, had not been
worried before. She'd thought maybe she needed time to
adjust to the idea of becoming a mum. Women often did
when it was their first. But there had been a note of genuine fear in Jenny's voice. Had something gone wrong in her
marriage? There'd been no hint of it before.

Perhaps Alex didn't want a child. That often turned out
to be the case when a woman confided that she hadn't told
her husband or boyfriend yet, fearing he would be livid
about the pregnancy. But she was pretty good at reading
people in her line of work, and Alex hadn't struck her as
that kind of man. Despite being a global film star, he was a
surprisingly humble and emotional man, whose difficult
past had made it hard for him to fall in love with Jenny.
Once in love though, he had behaved like a man completely
smitten. There was no way Alex Delgardo would not move
heaven and earth for his wife, whatever the situation.

She sat down next to Jennifer and patted her shoulder awkwardly. They had never been very demonstrative with each other, but this seemed like a moment for pushing boundaries.

'Look, Jenny, I can see this has been a bit of a shock. But there's no need to get upset. I'm sure everything will be all right.'

But Jennifer only groaned again, still covering her face.

'Jenny, come on. What . . . what's wrong?' She hesitated, unsure whether to wait or keep pushing. 'This is to do with Alex, I'm guessing?'

Oh God, was it possible the baby wasn't his?

As soon as the dreadful thought popped into her head though, Caroline dismissed it. Alex and Jenny were deeply in love, there was no chance of infidelity.

Besides, the only other man Jenny ever mentioned on the phone or in her emails home was Brodie, her husband's taciturn PA.

Like Alex, Brodie was an ex-soldier, and good-looking enough, in a gritty sort of way. He had a prosthesis, an artificial limb, though it was usually hidden under jeans or trousers, so you would never know looking at him. Not from his army days, ironically. He and Alex had been at a hotel in the Middle East during location filming for one of his action films when a bomb had gone off, killing one of Alex's entourage and gravely injuring Brodie. Alex had survived relatively unscathed, though not without terrible mental scars. It had been his love for Jennifer that had brought him out of that dark place, he had said during their wedding vows. That, and Brodie's constant care and companionship.

But though she could imagine some women falling for Brodie's quiet charm, she did not think Jennifer would ever have looked twice at any other man. Not with Alex at her side.

'Alex has only just got his career back on track,' Jennifer whispered from behind her hands. 'After the bombing, he came out here to hide. And he would have stayed here too after the wedding, for my sake. But I persuaded him to take on new work. Alex tried to hide it from me, but his acting career is deeply important to him. And he's about to negotiate a new film role.'

'So?'

'So once he knows I'm pregnant, he'll want to slow down.' Jennifer lowered her hands, her face pale, her eyes red-rimmed. 'Give up acting for a while and settle down instead. That was always the plan. That he would work in the States for five years or so, then we'd try for a baby.' She shook her head, staring at the pregnancy test. 'This has ruined everything.'

'Don't be silly. He'll be over the moon.'

'Oh yes, Alex will be pleased.' Jennifer's smile was sad. 'That's not what I'm worried about. Alex is already a household name. But I truly believe he could become a great actor. And I want him to realise that ambition. But this baby . . . It'll stop him taking on any of the new roles he's being offered.' She sighed. 'I never wanted our marriage to interfere with his acting career. Now this . . .'

'How did it happen, do you think?'

'I've never got on well with the pill. So I had a cap fitted in the States. But there were times when I . . . I forgot. We were so busy, and constantly moving about . . .' Jennifer jumped up and paced about the small clinic room, looking distraught. 'This is all my fault. I ought to have been more careful. I should have—'

'Hey!' Caroline got up and gave her a tight hug. 'Quit stressing out. Everything's going to be fine. You'll see.'

'I wish I could believe that.'

'Don't be such a pessimist. Alex will be delighted, and you won't need to change your lifestyle for months yet.'

'Honestly?'

'Cross my heart and swear to die. I'll organise a scan while you're here, but from what you've said, you can't be more than seven or eight weeks gone. Which is early days.'

'Brodie will blame me, all the same.' Jennifer's voice sank to a whisper.

Caroline was instantly outraged on her sister's behalf.

'What on earth has Brodie got to do with it? He's not your husband.'

'No, but Alex listens to him. He's not just a personal assistant, he's Alex's best friend too. They've known each other forever. And Brodie was the one who put the idea into my head in the first place. To wait before starting a family, that is. We'd been talking about other stars with young families, and the choices they'd made, and it started me worrying about the impact on Alex's career.'

'But that's nothing to do with him!'

'Maybe.' Jennifer sat down again, and unconsciously wrapped her arms about her lower belly, as though already protecting the tiny life growing there. 'Or maybe not.'

'What do you mean?'

'Brodie only has Alex's best interests at heart. And in a way he's right. Alex will probably insist on stopping work once he knows I'm pregnant, and taking another break could derail his acting career. He already took a year off after the bombing. To drop out again could be disastrous for him.'

'What's done is done.' Caroline shrugged. 'And if that Brodie gives you any hassle, you send him in my direction. I'll soon put a flea in the man's ear!'

Jennifer laughed, but without much humour. 'Honestly, I doubt you'll get the chance. As soon as I tell him the glad tidings, Alex will probably insist on cutting our visit short and flying straight back to the States.'

'Why's that?'

'The hospitals there are amazing, like nothing you've ever seen. He'll probably want me to be examined by some high-powered obstetrician, to make sure the baby's okay.'

'That doesn't sound very relaxing.'

'No,' Jennifer said ruefully, and bit her lip. 'Oh dear, having a baby is going to change everything, isn't it?'

Her sister was scared, of course. All this was new to her. But while she might have no idea how to handle an international film star and his entourage, this was a familiar reaction that Caroline knew only too well how to address.

'Hey, relax. Everyone thinks like that, first-time round. And there are a few minor adjustments you'll need to make, it's true. Watching what you eat, being careful how you exercise, and no more alcohol.' Caroline opened the drawer where she kept the maternity folders and began to gather together the information sheets and brochures for new mothers. 'But there's no need to panic. You'll soon get used to being pregnant, trust me.'

'You think so?'

'I know so, Jenny.' Caroline gave her sister a reassuring smile, though deep down she suspected that Jennifer might have a rough time of it, given the circumstances. Worse still, if the couple did decide to return to the States for the baby's birth, she would only be able to give advice down the phone, not be there in person to give hands-on help. 'Look, wherever you choose to have this baby, you're going to be fine. So try not to worry.'

Though things weren't exactly perfect for Jenny, were they? A husband whose career might be derailed by becoming a father, and his best friend who seemed determined to meddle in their marriage. She had once thought Brodie rather attractive, but when she'd tried her luck with him at the wedding, he had brushed her off like an insect on his sleeve. As though she was not worthy of his attention. Horrid, stuck-up man. And now he was probably going to make Jennifer's life a misery for having fallen pregnant at an inconvenient time.

I'd like to give that nasty Brodie a piece of my mind, Caroline thought crossly, suddenly very protective of her sister.

Though, as Jenny had said, it was unlikely she'd ever get the chance.

CHAPTER FOUR

Stunned by what he had heard, Brodie stared from Alex to Jennifer, and back again. His friends' faces revealed nothing. Yet surely this had to be a joke? And a bad joke at that. He felt like he was going mad. Or was about to.

'Excuse me?' He could hear a sudden Scottishness behind those two words, and saw Alex grin.

They were seated in the large living room at Porro Park, the one with huge sofas and elegant French windows overlooking the lawn and woodlands. *The room where Nelly died*, had been his first unhappy thought on entering it again. When the fascinating old lady passed away on the day of her ninetieth birthday, the pain had been almost as great as if she'd been his own nan.

'I said, I'm pregnant.' Jennifer squeezed Alex's hand, and then quickly corrected herself. '*We're* pregnant.'

Brodie did not know what to say.

We're going to wait to start a family, Jennifer had reassured him early on, when he'd asked about their plans as a couple. *At least until Alex's career is back on track.*

It hadn't been his business, of course, but he'd approved

that approach: waiting had been the most sensible option for Alex. His film career had already taken a bashing due to his long absence from the industry, recovering from the hotel bombing and its appalling aftermath. So for the next four or five years he needed to be available to take on film roles at a moment's notice, which meant starting a family would be awkward timing, to say the least.

Now this . . .

His boss seemed equally dazed by the news. Alex must have only just heard it himself, Brodie realised. Jennifer had come back from Pethporro with her sister Caroline, looking mysterious and secretive, then gone upstairs alone to wake Alex, who was still sleeping off his jet lag.

Left alone in the living room with Caroline, Brodie had made small talk for a few minutes, then lapsed into silence under her narrowed stare.

Caroline Enys was tall for a woman. Almost as tall and willowy as some of the languid models Alex used to date before he met Jennifer. When not in her midwife's uniform, she even dressed like a model, elegantly turned out and with perfect ash-blonde hair that would not look out of place in a Vogue fashion shoot, though her conversation was surprisingly blunt and offhand. 'Caro likes to speak her mind,' was what Jennifer had said more than once of her outspoken sister. But, in his view, that was merely shorthand for rude and insensitive. And he preferred to keep people like that at arm's length.

She had grimaced at him as soon as he appeared. Had he done something to offend her? That seemed unlikely. All he'd done in the hallway was say hello and shake her hand. Hardly offensive behaviour. But he often found it hard to read women, so decided he must be imagining her bristling air of hostility.

Except Caroline did look pretty annoyed with him.

Perhaps she objected to his shirt, which was steel-grey, buttoned-down at the collar and probably too severe for her tastes, or his blue denim jeans, which still sported a few dried patches of mud from the goat field. He sniffed himself surreptitiously, but smelt nothing untoward. No lingering stink of goat.

So why the accusation in her glaring eyes?

To his relief, Jennifer had then reappeared with an ashen-faced Alex in tow, and requested him and Caroline to come into the sitting room, because she had something to say.

Everyone had sat down facing each other on the two large sofas like a scene from a murder mystery in some English country house, where the detective gathers everyone at the end to explain whodunnit. Only a few minutes and one stammered confession later it seemed clear who had done it.

Jennifer was pregnant and Alex was the culprit.

Well, Brodie thought, aware of a sinking feeling inside, this was certainly going to change things.

Meanwhile, everyone was looking at him expectantly.

'Good God,' he said at last, clearing his throat before adding with a belated smile, 'Congratulations!'

'Thanks,' Alex said faintly.

'Yes, congratulations,' Caroline agreed, her voice far warmer than it had been when talking to Brodie. 'I couldn't be happier for you both.'

Alex gave her an uncertain smile. 'Thank you, Caroline.'

A short silence followed.

'It wasn't planned,' Jennifer said suddenly.

'But it is very much wanted,' Alex declared, then blinked and corrected himself, gazing at his wife as though speaking directly to her, 'I mean, he or she is very much wanted.'

'Yes,' Jennifer said in a high, breathless voice, gazing back at Alex. 'Absolutely.'

The couple clearly had some stuff to work out, Brodie thought. Alex looked as astounded by the news of a pregnancy as he himself had been.

Perhaps it was time to make himself scarce.

Brodie glanced sideways at Caroline, meaning to suggest they go for a walk while the other two talked, and was surprised to see an almost feral look on her face. What on earth was wrong with her now? It was almost as though she were blaming him for Jennifer's pregnancy. Which was absurd. Not to mention a little unnerving.

She wasn't looking particularly surprised though.

'You knew,' Brodie said.

It wasn't a question.

But her sister jumped in hurriedly before Caroline had even opened her mouth to reply. 'Actually, it was Caro who guessed what was going on. After lunch, she took me over to the clinic to make sure. All those odd symptoms I've been experiencing . . . the headaches, the light-headedness, the nausea, and . . . a few other things. It was because I was pregnant.' She sucked in a swift breath. '*Am* pregnant.'

Alex said nothing. He was listening to his wife as though he couldn't quite believe his ears, an air of strain about him, his eyes oddly blank.

Brodie watched him, carefully keeping his emotions out of his face. But he hoped Alex wasn't going to have a relapse. Since finally deciding to make a go of it with Jennifer, his boss had clawed his way back from the brink of a second nervous breakdown. The last thing anyone wanted was for Alex to plunge back over the abyss into that dark nightmare world he'd been trapped in for months after the hotel bombing.

'Well, I think it's wonderful news,' Caroline said loudly, and glared at Brodie. 'Don't you agree?'

'Of course.'

'You don't seem too happy about it.'

'Don't I?'

'Nope.'

'I'm maybe a little surprised, that's all.'

'Why? They are married, you know. It happens.'

'I know that.' Brodie was taken aback by the venom in her words. 'I'm not an idiot.'

'So why are you "surprised"?'

'No reason, I guess. Except . . .' Brodie hesitated, suddenly uncertain, aware that a trap was being laid for him but not understanding why. 'I thought they were planning to wait before starting a family, that's all.'

'Aha!'

He frowned. 'Aha, what?'

'Aha, that's all.' Caroline pointed a finger at him. 'Aha!'

Bemused by what was clearly meant to be an accusation of some kind, Brodie looked towards his friend for guidance.

But he got no help there.

Alex was tracing a finger round and round Jennifer's upturned palm with a gentle rhythmic motion, his head bent towards her as she whispered something meant only for her husband's ears.

Brodie sighed. He doubted that either of them had even heard his bizarre exchange with Caroline. The couple were still wrapped up in their own little world, as they so often had been in the States, not having been married long enough yet to have lost the special cocoon of intimacy that newly-weds always seemed to inhabit.

'Let's go,' he said abruptly, getting to his feet and gesturing Caroline to follow him. 'Come on.'

But she stayed where she was, sunk into the deep cushions of the sofa like she was planning never to move.

'Sorry?'

He had intended to suggest a walk in a friendly fashion. But something about the acid note in her voice stung him.

'I want to talk to you. Privately.'

'Tough.' Caroline glared at him, a mulish look on her face. 'I'm not going anywhere. My sister needs me.'

'What your sister needs,' he said carefully, 'is some time alone with her husband.'

'Is that so? Mind reader, are you?'

Brodie bit back his angry response, smiling back at

Caroline with as much patience as he could muster. It wasn't obvious what her problem was. But no doubt she would share it with him soon enough. And he was used to dealing with difficult people in the film industry.

'Sorry?' Alex had stirred at last, finally realising perhaps that other people were in the room with them. He glanced up vaguely at Brodie, then gave Caroline a strained look. 'Actually, that's not a bad idea. Jenny and I . . . we do need some space to talk things through.'

'Jenny?' Caroline said pointedly, waiting for her sister to say something.

'Yes, Alex is right. It's probably for the best if we have some time alone. Just an hour or so.' Jennifer's voice was husky, her head still bent. 'Thanks, you two. You're being very patient.'

'No problem.' Brodie held out a hand to help Caroline out of the luxurious depths of the sofa cushions.

'I'm fine,' she snapped, struggling inelegantly off the sofa on her own.

Bloody-minded woman.

Last time he'd seen her, Caroline had been quite friendly. A little too friendly at times, in fact. Had he offended her by not responding to her interest? This new smouldering dislike seemed a bit of an overreaction. But perhaps that was just her style. He barely knew the woman, after all.

No, she definitely didn't like him.

Before he could be tempted to respond with something equally impolite, Brodie stalked out of the living room and into the atrium-style hallway.

Above his head, through the glass roof, the afternoon sun was already beginning to dip low, the sky a pale water-colour blue wreathed with soft, scudding clouds. It would be a cold night, he thought, once those clouds had moved away. The house was warm though, despite the autumnal chill outside. Alex had sent his super-efficient housekeeper on ahead to prepare the house for their arrival, and it was clear that Françoise had been busy since her return to Pethporro; everything was spotless, the bedrooms warm as toast, with no indication that the house had been standing empty for months. She really was worth her weight in gold, Brodie thought.

'What was all that about?' Caroline demanded in a hiss at his back. 'You've got some bloody nerve, do you know that?'

He turned, surprised. 'Sorry?'

'Why did you drag me out of there?'

'Because I thought they needed some time alone before everyone started piling in with their advice.'

'By everyone, I take it you mean me?'

'If the cap fits.'

As soon as the words were out, he sighed inwardly, aware that she was offended by the way her eyebrows had risen steeply. And he hadn't meant to be so rude. Indeed, it was unlike him to be rude at all. But something about her aggressive manner had him sniping back at her.

'She's my step—' Caroline blinked, then continued, 'Jenny's my sister. I have every right to talk to her about this baby. Plus, I'm a midwife. Who better to advise her?'

'But she's not about to give birth, is she? So your advice might be a little, shall we say, *premature*?'

'Well, really . . .' Her cheeks flushed angrily.

'I'm going for a walk around the grounds,' he told her, heading towards the kitchen and the back door out on to the lawns. 'Want to come?' He didn't look back to see if she was following, but called laconically over his shoulder, 'Unless you'd prefer to stay there and listen at the door?'

After a few seconds' delay, he heard Caroline come stalking after him, muttering various expletives under her breath.

Brodie smiled to himself. So what if she was annoyed with him? It didn't matter what she or anyone else thought of him. His primary responsibility here was to Alex and his wife. Not to Jennifer's sister. And he had got this busybody of a sister-in-law away from them, so the couple could have some precious time alone at what was clearly a delicate time in their marriage.

Nonetheless, he couldn't deny there was something about Caroline that didn't quite sit easily with him. She needled him, and very few people were able to do that. But at least their stay here was only temporary, so he wouldn't have to put up with her disturbing presence very much longer. Or the peaceful beauty of Cornwall, which frankly allowed him far too much time to think and brood about his own problems.

Yes, the sooner they flew back to the constant bustle and excitement of Hollywood, the better.

CHAPTER FIVE

Following Brodie out of the kitchen on to the back lawns, Caroline found it hard to keep her temper under control. She was fuming. She could not believe how high-handed Brodie had become. Or maybe he had always been like this, and she was only just noticing. After all, she hadn't seen that much of him when they were in residence at Porro Park before, except to observe that he was rather sexy in a detached, keep-your-distance way. Which had been the only encouragement she needed at the time, bored and between boyfriends, to flirt with the man.

They had danced together a few times at the wedding reception, but she'd been rather drunk at the time and couldn't remember much except pressing closely against him, and then . . .

Had Brodie helped her up to bed afterwards? She wasn't sure, but recalled waking up in the cool dawn light, still fully dressed but with her high heels removed and set neatly beside the bed, as though someone reasonably sober had put them there.

Now though, after more than a year out in California

with the happy couple, Alex's personal assistant had grown even more distant. Like he was on another planet, in fact.

What on earth gave him the right to behave like he was so much better than her? It made her temper rise, just looking at the dark back of his head, the severe straight-backed way he was walking ahead of her on the path towards the woods.

And if he looked down his nose at her one more time . . .

Brodie stopped by the edge of the woods, as though waiting for her. He turned his head, studying her face. 'Okay?'

No doubt she looked flushed and annoyed. Which she was. Well, no point hiding the fact that she found his interference intolerable, was there?

'Of course I'm okay,' she snapped.

His brows shot up. 'Sorry.'

There was that thickening of his accent again. Just a touch Scottish. Jenny had told her that he came from Inverness, but hadn't lived there since he was a child, so had almost lost his accent. But not quite.

This was a fine time to realise she found that husky accent attractive.

'I'm a bit cross, that's all. I'm . . .' She paused, her head suddenly woolly, her thoughts jumbling together. 'I'm . . .'

'Confused?'

She glared at him. 'I'm not confused. I'm just . . .'

Maddeningly, her brain seized up again.

Something about him made it difficult to gather her thoughts coherently. Which was strange, as she was known for being cool under pressure. Cool and able to deal with the worst emergencies with complete unflappability.

He waited, a faint smile on his lips that made her want to bash him round the head with whatever was closest to hand. Which was a few damp clumps of fading fuchsia in the nearby flower bed. Hardly an effective weapon.

'You had no right to speak to me like that back there.'

'Like what?'

She caught up with him, and raised her face to his, her cheeks hot with temper. Goodness, he was surprisingly tall, up close. How had she forgotten that?'

'Like a child.'

'Then perhaps you shouldn't behave like one.'

'How dare you?' She was finding it hard to breathe, her heart thumping. 'You don't know the first thing about me.'

'Maybe. But I know you're overreacting.'

'Oh, my God!' Caroline stared at him, feeling the blood pounding in her temples. 'You are so bloody . . .'

'Right?'

'Please!' She could not help stamping her foot, both hands clenched automatically into fists. 'Stop finishing my sentences for me.'

Again, his brows rose. 'I rest my case.'

Caroline ignored his mocking tone and walked hurriedly past him into the woods, trying to calm herself down before she said something she might regret later. The man was Alex's assistant, after all. So he wouldn't be going anywhere in a hurry. It would be better if she could get on with him, not keep sniping at him.

But her head was whirling, her thoughts still hopelessly confused. She had no idea why his gently ironic comments made her blood boil, nor why she was finding it so hard to stay calm in the face of his provocation. He wasn't being rude, as such. But he was being annoying. It was like being teased, but not in a nice way. They were back in the school playground, she thought wildly; any minute, he would yank on her hair or stick his tongue out.

Brodie caught up with her under the cool shade of the trees. 'Hey,' he said, the mockery gone from his voice, 'hang on a minute, would you?'

She stopped, but didn't look round, still infuriated.

'I'm sorry, okay?' He sounded genuinely apologetic. 'I can see you're upset. I just don't know what I said to make you so . . .'

When he hesitated, Caroline couldn't help turning back to him with an ironic smile. 'Mad?'

'Grouchy,' he finished at the same time.

She sighed. 'I'm not angry with you. Though I am frustrated.'

'I'm sorry, I don't understand why.'

'You shouldn't be interfering between those two.'

He was frowning now. 'This is about Alex and Jennifer?'

'Of course,' she said impatiently. 'I know you work for Alex. But this is none of your business.'

'Forgive me for stating the obvious, but it's my business to make sure he has a career.'

'And how does Jennifer having a baby interfere with that?'

Brodie looked at her with disbelief in his face. 'You think he's going to waltz off and leave her to have a baby on her own? There's no way. And he won't want her travelling with him while he's filming on location, not even once the baby's been born. It's no life for a pregnant woman or a young baby. Living out of trailers and buses, getting up at four and going to bed at six in the evening, eating canteen food the whole time. It's gruelling, arduous, and totally antisocial.' He shook his head at her. 'Jennifer falling pregnant. That's serious. That's a deal-breaker, right there.'

'You seriously believe Alex will give up his film career because he and Jenny are going to have a baby?'

'I do.' Brodie nodded, his face completely serious. 'And if you knew him at all, you'd understand that.'

'I know Alex.'

'Not like me. And not like Jenny does. Ask her if you don't believe me. Alex is very private, deeply emotional. He's a family man. This baby . . .' He gestured back through the trees to the distant glass walls of the house. 'This is everything he's ever wanted. A chance to settle down and raise a kid. To feel normal again, not always out in the glare of publicity. Alex would give up anything to have that dream.' He looked at her sombrely. 'Even the big film career we've all worked so hard to get back for him.'

Caroline knew Jennifer had said something similar, but she'd assumed her sister was panicking. She'd been so sure that Alex would leave Jennifer at home while he went off on location. Or perhaps take her with him, as he'd been doing for the past year.

'I didn't realise he was so serious about starting a family.'

'Why should you?' Brodie shrugged. 'You're nothing like

Jenny. You're really into your career, I can see that. You've probably never thought about settling down.'

Her eyes widened, but she didn't contradict him.

'That's perfectly understandable,' he continued. 'I'm not judging. A woman needs a career every bit as much as a man. But perhaps it means you don't really *get it*.' His sharp blue eyes lingered on her face, and for all he'd said he wasn't judging her, Caroline felt good and judged. 'The need for a baby, I mean. For the whole family-dream thing.'

'Of course I get it,' she said crossly. 'I deliver babies for a living. I know better than anyone how strong that urge is, to start a family of your own. I've seen it hundreds of times … the look on a woman's face when she finds out she's pregnant, or first sees her baby on an ultrasound scan. Of course I understand.'

'I'm sorry, I didn't mean to offend you.' Brodie hesitated. 'But you must see that I need to keep Alex on track. He's got a great talent, and it would be a shame to let him waste it on an ordinary life. His choice, I accept that. But you can't expect me to rejoice that he's planning to push his talent aside to play happy families with Jenny instead.'

'Because *you* would never do that.'

'In his place, probably not,' he said grimly, pushing his hands into his jeans pockets. 'But then, something tells me you wouldn't either, Caroline. So maybe we're both as work-obsessed as each other. Or self-obsessed, depending on how you look at it.'

There was a long silence between them. It suddenly felt quite chilly out here under the trees, she thought, unable to suppress a shudder. A solitary red leaf spiralled slowly to the woodland floor, and Caroline stared at it, her face averted.

Self-obsessed.

Brodie wasn't the first man to call her that, was he? And she imagined he wouldn't be the last. But that didn't lessen the sting.

'I've offended you again,' he said abruptly.

Caroline raised her gaze to his, careful not to let that odd little prickle of unhappiness inside her show. Besides, he was partially right about her love of career. Looking after other women, bringing their babies into the world, that meant everything to her. But if he thought she had never considered having babies herself, he was wrong . . .

'No,' she said. 'It's just a bit nippy out here.'

'Let's head back to the house.'

'It's not been an hour yet.'

'We can wait in the kitchen. The range is on; it'll be warm in there.' He started to walk back towards the house, glancing at her over his shoulder. 'Come on, you're getting cold.'

'No, I'm not,' she fibbed, chin up.

Stupid to lie about it, really. It was a little cool under the gloomy shade of the trees. But she hated people seeing beneath her armour even for a second. Men, in particular.

Relaxing her guard with a man only ever led to trouble. Especially a man she found attractive. She'd been hurt in the past by doing that, more times than she cared to remember, and her studied air of independence was all she had left to protect her. With it, she could sail through casual dates and even enjoy a sexy flirtation without risking her heart. All the fun of the ball, but none of the consequences!

Besides, she wasn't about to risk seeming vulnerable in front of this man. Not after he'd caused so much pain for her sister, however much he might say it was for Alex's benefit.

'It's my job to notice things, and you're cold.' His grin surprised her, smoothing out the stern lines of his face so that he looked almost friendly. 'Hey, have you ever tried black tea with brandy?'

'Sounds disgusting.'

'It is disgusting, actually. But it warms you up in about ten seconds flat. I'm going to make a cup for you as soon as we get back to the house.'

'No, thank you,' she said primly.

His grin was still in evidence, but it looked a bit forced now. 'You're pretty hard work, Caroline. Did anyone ever tell you that?'

'Oh, only a few dozen men.'

Brodie said nothing in response to this airy quip, but his mouth tightened, his blue eyes sharp and assessing.

He waited for her to follow him, then fell in beside her. His limp was less noticeable over the uneven ground of the forest path, his stride covering the terrain with easy strength.

Studying him covertly, Caroline wondered what Brodie thought of her, deep down inside, behind that polite mask. Nothing good, she guessed, after their recent discussion.

But his opinion didn't matter to her.

Not one tiny bit.

As they crossed the lawns that bordered the house, Brodie heard the distant beep of a car horn. Surprised, he walked a little further until he reached the path that overlooked the main road. Down the long driveway, outside the imposing iron gates that kept everyone out but the postie, local delivery vans and carefully arranged visitors, someone not quite visible was sitting inside a battered old truck, alternately beeping the horn and waving a pale, slender arm out of the window.

'Who on earth is that?' Caroline had followed him silently across the grass and was now standing at his shoulder. They were almost the same height, he realised, or would be if she were wearing her usual high heels instead of tan ankle boots. 'A friend of yours?'

'No such luck. A crazed fan, I suspect.'

Brodie's first thought was for Alex's safety, as usual, but now he had to consider Jennifer and her unborn child too. The pregnancy complicated an already difficult picture, but he felt confident that the high gate and fencing that enclosed the large estate was probably enough to keep out all but the most hardened fanatics.

'Sorry?'

'Someone came to the gate a few days ago,' he said slowly, recalling what Françoise had told him on their arrival at Porro Park. 'Some woman who wouldn't give her name on the intercom but wanted to come up to the house. Apparently, she was quite insistent. Kept saying the spirits had sent her.'

'The spirits?' Caroline grimaced. 'Right, I see.'

'Exactly.' He frowned, studying the truck, which was now parked across the closed gateway, effectively blocking the drive in both directions. He didn't like the look of that. It was an aggressive act, and one designed to prevent exit as well as entry. 'Françoise told her to go away or she'd call the police, which seemed to work. But this could be the same person. Probably some fan desperate for a selfie with Alex.' Abruptly, he came to a decision. 'I'd better get rid of her myself this time. And if she won't go, it's the police next.'

At that moment, Françoise appeared round the side of the house, slim and smart in her stern black uniform. There was a determined, no-nonsense look about her. He had to admit, he hadn't approved of Françoise at first. But he'd been wrong about the Frenchwoman. She had a sensible head on her shoulders, and she shared his concern for keeping security tight.

'Ah, Monsieur Mattieson,' she called out urgently, 'it's that woman again on the intercom. I tell her, no, she cannot come in. Not without an appointment.' Swiftly and impatiently, she came striding across the lawn. 'I tell her, nobody gets into Porro Park without an appointment. Still, she refuses point-blank to go away.'

'Is she still saying the spirits sent her?' Brodie asked, grinning.

'*Ah, non.*' Françoise gave a frustrated Gallic shrug. 'Now she says she is your mother!'

'My mother?' Astonished, Brodie stared down the drive at the battered old truck. 'That's not my mother's car.' Then he blinked, shaking his head at his own gullibility. It was clearly not true. Just one of those unlikely stories fans sometimes came up with in a desperate attempt to gain admittance and get closer to their idol. 'Why on earth would she be here, anyway? Completely absurd.'

'Not *your* mother.' To his surprise, Françoise looked past him at Caroline, an accusing finger jabbed in her direction instead. '*Hers.*'

'Mine?' Caroline seemed equally stunned by the suggestion, shooting him a confused look as he turned to study her. 'No, you're right. It's absurd. My mum and dad live in St Ives now, miles away. Besides, she would have rung first, not just turned up out of the blue.' Her voice rose on a note of outrage. 'And Mum wouldn't be caught dead in a filthy old truck like that.'

Brodie felt sure that was true. Caroline was always so elegant and well-turned-out, rarely a hair out of place; it stood to reason her mother would be the same. He was not normally given to fanciful thoughts, but he had frequently thought she had the face of an angel. A spoilt, outspoken angel who knew how to rub him the wrong way, it was true. But Caroline was undeniably poised and beautiful, and unlikely to be related to whoever was driving that truck.

The woman inside had stopped waving her arm, and

seemed to be leaning on the horn instead. Its long unwavering blast scared pheasants out of the undergrowth and birds out of the trees in all directions.

Definitely a job for the police.

Though he knew there weren't too many police officers going spare in Cornwall, so it might be a long wait for the cavalry.

Perhaps he should walk down there meanwhile and have a persuasive chat through the gate, rather than relying on the impersonal static of the intercom. Maybe all the woman needed was a little face time, and then she would go away.

'Did she give a name?' Brodie asked.

'Oh yes, sorry, monsieur.' Françoise blushed, obviously having forgotten that little detail. 'She says her name is Topaz.'

CHAPTER SIX

Topaz?

Caroline's head was a hot mess. There was no point pretending otherwise. Not to herself, anyway. But she kept a politely frozen smile pinned to her lips, the kind she used when a supervisor or doctor was talking to her in a condescending way. It was a smile that usually meant, *Go to hell.* But silently, internally, privately. Only today this smile was for the world in general. *Don't look at me, I'm in pieces.*

She stared ahead to the gate, her heart beating hard.

Topaz.

That was such a familiar name. And yet a stranger's name too.

Her mother's name.

Not Debbie, the woman who'd married her dad and brought her up as her own child, alongside Jennifer. Topaz was her birth mother's name. And that name was all she knew about the mother who'd abandoned her at age five, the woman who'd walked out on her husband and left her child behind too.

That was what she'd been told, anyway. And she'd never

pressed to learn more, seeing her dad's automatic flinch whenever she dared mention that name.

Topaz.

'What's the matter?' Brodie had been heading for the gate too, but stopped now, looking round at her. His blue eyes narrowed on her face. 'Caroline?'

She'd been trailing in his wake, half considering an undignified bolt back to the safety of the house. But his question shook her.

'Nothing's the matter.' Her voice was light and devoid of significance. Had he seen through the fake smile to the pain beneath? If so, he would be the first to do so, outside the family. 'I just thought—'

'Do you know the name?'

'Sorry?'

'Topaz,' he said patiently, and it was hard to repress the shudder that ran through her, hearing it aloud again. 'You know that woman, don't you? You know who she is.'

Her smile felt utterly stuck. Like the wind had changed and this was her permanent expression now. A stupid grin, like the Joker in those cartoons. She couldn't unsmile it even if she'd wanted to.

Brodie glanced at Françoise, and without a word the housekeeper melted discreetly away, leaving them alone on the gravelled path leading to the driveway. But no doubt she was used to making herself scarce during privileged conversations in a celebrity household.

'Tell me,' he said calmly.

She hesitated, but knew there was no point trying to

hide the truth. If this 'Topaz' was who she thought, it would all soon come tumbling out. 'Well, you know that Jennifer and I are stepsisters . . .'

'So you're always saying.'

'Because it's important. My dad married her mum when I was seven, and Jenny . . . she would have been about five, then. Debbie brought me up as her own kid. But I always knew she was my stepmother, not my real mum.'

She paused, aware of Brodie watching her intently, his arms folded across his chest. The man had a way of seeing right through her defences, as though he could read everything she was trying so hard to hide. His military training, perhaps.

'Go on,' he said.

'Jenny had her real dad around too. He used to visit most weekends when we were young, take her to the park and so on. But my real mum . . .'

She felt her throat dry up and couldn't go on.

There was an awkward silence. The car horn sounded again, and now she could hear a woman's voice, trying to get their attention.

Brodie helped her out, his voice gently prodding her. 'She didn't want to see you?'

'No, she . . .' Caroline shook her head, swallowing. 'That is, nobody knew where she'd gone.' Her voice was thin and scratchy. 'She just walked out one day, my dad said. And never came back.'

'Why?'

'I have no idea. Dad refused to talk about it. All he ever

said was, she'd walked out on us both. And that she didn't deserve to be in my life.'

He nodded, his face carefully expressionless, giving none of his thoughts away. 'And you think this woman at the gate, this Topaz, might be her? Your birth mother.'

'Maybe. I don't know. Probably not.' She sucked in her breath, hearing the blast of the car horn again. 'I mean, why now? And why here?'

He said nothing, then gave an abrupt nod, and held out his hand. 'Come along,' he said coolly.

'Sorry?'

'Only one way to find out for sure.' He raised his eyebrows when she didn't move, still holding out his hand. 'You're coming down there with me to find out exactly what Topaz wants.'

Horror filled her. 'No, no, I can't do that.'

'Yes, you can.'

'I couldn't possibly. You don't understand.'

He dropped his hand, sighing. 'What on earth do you think she's going to do, Caroline? Shout at you? Demand that you love her? Maybe leave you all over again?' His slightly weary tone made her hysteria feel ridiculous and overblown, though still she couldn't order her feet to move. 'There's a large iron gate between you and her. You'll be perfectly safe.'

'But—'

'You're not a little girl any more. And even if that woman does turn out to be who you think, she hasn't been your mother for a very long time. Besides, don't you want the answers your father wouldn't give you?' Brodie turned his back, shoes crunching on the gravel as he started to walk towards the main road. His voice floated back to her, soft and mocking. 'Don't be such a coward. It doesn't suit you.'

By rights, she ought to have gone back to the house first. To tell Jennifer what was happening, and to share her fears with the one person who could possibly understand them.

But the woman had seen someone coming down the drive at last. She climbed out of the truck and stood in the road, hands on her hips, as though waiting impatiently for them to arrive.

Topaz.

Caroline drew a deep breath and began to walk after Brodie, her steps quick and uneven, her gaze fixed on the stranger by the truck.

It was a torturously long walk to the gate.

But she was glad of that; it gave her precious minutes to study the woman as they drew nearer, and to rehearse a few lines in case this Topaz was indeed her birth mother.

Something polite and restrained that would not give away the agony seething and throbbing in her chest, the decades of unexpressed hurt and resentment, the anger and, yes, even the hatred she had felt at times for her unknown mother. Something that would sound forgiving, perhaps even gracious, if she could manage that.

The woman had a slim figure and looked to be about Caroline's own height of five foot eight. But that was where the similarities between them ended.

She was wearing a long-sleeved men's white shirt under

faded blue dungarees, a pair of deep red Doc Martens on her feet. The shirt sleeves were rolled up to her elbows, despite the cold, and the top few buttons were undone, revealing a pale throat. No jewellery, no make-up that she could see. The combination ought to have looked masculine or clumsy, yet on this woman it was somehow cool and elegant.

Her striking white-blonde hair defied what her true age must be, but it didn't hang straight like Caroline's – instead, a careless riot of shoulder-length curls was held in place by a cheerful red-and-white checked bandana. She had frank blue eyes, a smiling, generous mouth, and a bold nose. Her wrinkle lines suggested someone who laughed and smiled a great deal, but although she was clearly in her fifties, the overall impression was of a much younger woman.

Brodie reached the gate first.

'Hello,' the woman said, thrusting a hand through the iron bars, her gaze moving past him to Caroline's silent figure so that she seemed to be addressing them both. 'I'm Topaz. But I imagine you know that already, from the woman I spoke to on the intercom. Your housekeeper, she said.' She looked Brodie up and down. 'And who are you? The film star's muscle, I'd guess. Come to send me packing?'

Her voice was light and musical, yet somehow deep at the same time, a wealth of experience and knowledge behind every word. Caroline thought she sounded vulnerable too, as though fully expecting to be sent away.

Brodie hesitated, then shook her hand. 'I'm Brodie. I work for Mr Delgardo, yes. I believe you were here a few days back?'

'That's right.' Topaz gave him a hopeful smile. 'There was an article in one of the fashion mags about Jennifer Delgardo. Some kind of interview. It mentioned her sister, Caroline. That's my daughter. I was in London at the time.' Her voice softened. 'Her name brought everything rushing back, and I ... I just suddenly decided I needed to see her.'

'So you came here.'

'First port of call. The housekeeper warned me off. But I've been staying locally, hoping for better luck. And today, I was told you were all back in residence. So here I am.'

'It's a good story, but I can't promise you better luck, I'm afraid.' Brodie glanced over his shoulder at Caroline, presumably noting her stiffness and silence. 'I have a suspicion your daughter doesn't want to see you.'

'I hope that's not true.' She dropped his hand, which she'd been clasping all that time, and smiled past him at Caroline. 'Hello, darling.' Her voice was tentative. 'Do you remember me? Do you know who I am?'

'You're ...' Caroline's voice failed her. She swallowed, and licked dry lips, then tried again. 'Are you my birth mother?'

'Bravo, yes!' Topaz looked delighted, her eyes bright. As though Caroline had passed a test of some kind. 'I knew you couldn't have forgotten me. How could anyone forget their own mother?'

Her smile seemed to suggest that they were going to be friends. That the past would be forgotten, while their future would hold nothing but love and puppies and balloons.

All thoughts of polite, mature forgiveness fled in a sudden upsurge of hurt and confusion.

'I'll tell you what I remember, Topaz,' she said, dredging up a hazy, partial memory Caroline had always filed away under Do Not Disturb. 'I remember my mother walking out on my father when I was little.' Unexpectedly, her voice wobbled, on the very edge of tears. 'And leaving me behind.'

'Oh!' Topaz looked horrified. 'It wasn't like that, darling, honestly.' She bit her lip. 'I expect your father only gave you *his* side of the story. You need to let me explain what happened.'

'I don't want to hear your explanation, thank you. If it had been worth hearing, you'd have come back sooner than this to tell me.'

'Darling, please.' Her mouth twisting in frustration, Topaz rattled the iron bars with both hands, then gave Brodie a pleading look. 'I can't do this through a prison gate. You look like a reasonable man. I haven't seen my daughter in ... oh God, too many years to mention. And I can't talk to her properly through these horrid bars.'

Brodie glanced back at Caroline, who shook her head. His face gave nothing away, but she felt instinctively that he was on her side. Much as she still disliked Brodie for interfering with Jennifer and his damn boss, she was glad to have him around at this particular moment.

'Sorry,' Brodie told Topaz flatly, 'that's a no.'

Topaz peered through the iron bars at Caroline, her lower lip trembling, tears in her own eyes. 'Darling, I know I'm too late to be forgiven. Yes, all right, decades too late.

But at least hear me out. Or you'll never know the truth. And, deep down, I think you want to hear what happened between me and your father. The real story for grown-ups, not the fairy tale he spun to a little girl.' Her mother tipped her head to one side, white-blonde curls falling elegantly on to one shoulder and across her high temple. 'Don't you?'

Caroline believed her, instinctively. There was something about her quick smile, the turn of her head, the dishevelled curls. Something . . .

Familiar.

Yes, that was the word. Something about Topaz was deeply familiar, so that she felt tugged towards her by an invisible cord.

At that moment, a huge, hairy, white-grey dog sat up in the passenger seat of her truck and yawned, showing an alarming set of teeth.

As though sensing that they were both looking past her, Topaz glanced back too and gave a shaky laugh. 'That's Bouncer. Everywhere I go, he goes too.' She looked at Caroline. 'Would you like to meet him?' She paused delicately. 'And me?'

The dog stared at them through the dirt-flecked windscreen with an air of bemusement. No doubt he was wondering what on earth was going on, and why it was taking so long. He had deep-set grey-green eyes shrouded by bushy brows, and an appealing air of mischief.

Caroline liked Bouncer at first sight. But his mistress was a different matter entirely.

CHAPTER SEVEN

Brodie could tell by the softening look in Caroline's face that she had decided to speak to her mother properly. Perhaps it was the mountain of a dog now standing up and wagging his tail in the front seat of the truck that had swung it for Topaz. A mongrel, by his shaggy, nondescript appearance. But charming with it. And he hadn't barked yet. Not once.

He approved of dogs that didn't bark. Unless they were trained to do so in the pursuit of some professional duty, like bomb disposal or drug searches.

'He does look like a lovely dog,' Caroline admitted.

'So come and play with him.'

'This is all so sudden. I need time to think first.' Caroline took another step towards the gate, all the same. 'Do you mind?'

'What's there to think about?' Topaz flashed them both another charming smile. She was obviously used to getting her way, Brodie thought, and he could see why. 'It's been years. Too many years. Let's not waste any more time, Caroline.'

In the distance, a car could be heard slowing for the tight corner along the deserted road to Pethporro, and then accelerating towards them, kicking up dust on its approach.

Brodie stiffened, instantly recognising the silver Volvo estate. It belonged to one of the more relentless photographers who hung about Porro Park with his long lens whenever Alex was in residence, hoping for a celeb picture he could flog to the nationals.

'We need to move,' he said quietly to Caroline, who had also seen the car. 'Paparazzi heading this way.'

To his relief, she nodded.

He doubted she would want an impromptu snap of her and her estranged mother splashed across the celebrity columns. Especially once people started trying to guess who this woman was – and why she was visiting Alex Delgardo's private residence.

'Look,' Topaz said quickly as Caroline turned away, 'if you won't invite me in, then why not let me drive you into town? We could go for a drink together.'

Caroline hesitated, clearly torn.

'Jenny needs you later today,' Brodie lied, giving Caroline a significant look. 'Maybe you two should meet up another time.' On neutral ground, he thought. 'For lunch in Pethporro, maybe?'

'What a good idea.' Topaz sounded delighted by his suggestion, which surprised him. He was sure she had come here to try and get closer to Alex, like most celebrity stalkers who came to the gate. But her smile seemed genuine enough. 'Here,' she said quickly, handing a business card through the gate. 'I'm staying in Pethporro. Give me a call when you've decided when and where you'd like to meet.'

Brodie took the card first, glancing down at it.

TOPAZ, the card announced in a bold, dramatic font, with an email address, mobile number and website listed beside the italicised words, *Artist, Designer, Visionary.*

His brows rose.

He said nothing though, merely handing it to Caroline, who gave him a cross look as though accusing him of interfering in her business.

But her private life would rapidly become his business, he thought, if it began to cause trouble for Alex. And he wasn't sure he entirely bought Topaz's friendly demeanour.

'Thanks, I'll ring you,' Caroline told her mother after studying the card briefly. 'I promise.'

'How about lunch tomorrow?'

'I'll think about it.'

With a nod, Topaz jumped into the battered truck and started it up, then turned slowly in front of the gate, tyres grating over the gravel. The dog stared out of the window at them, his pink tongue lolling enthusiastically. No doubt he was hoping for a good walk in the grounds.

Then she waved a slim arm out of the window and drove away, her truck kicking out a few smoky fumes in the cold air.

After a few hundred yards, her truck passed the silver Volvo coming the other way, the car having slowed as the driver turned to stare after her, eagle-eyed in case she was someone important.

Caroline gripped the bars of the gate and also stood staring after the truck until it had disappeared round the bend. Her eyes were wide, but her lips were pursed and there was a high colour in her cheeks.

'Come on,' he said brusquely. 'There's a photographer in that car. Let's get back up to the house before he starts snapping.'

Her arms dropping to her sides, she gave a nod and turned away.

Brodie watched her face covertly.

Despite the long years of absence, all the hurt and bewilderment caused, Caroline had not rejected the woman out of hand. Equally though, she hadn't smiled at Topaz, nor said anything particularly conciliatory. He was usually good at reading people but his skills failed him here. Brodie couldn't work out if she was happy to be reunited with her birth mother or not. She was certainly a hard woman to second-guess. Except where he was concerned. There, her feelings were only too transparent and in his face.

'I liked her dog,' he said.

Caroline shot him a narrow-eyed look, then headed back to the house without another word.

Brodie made a face at her back, then followed, his eyes on her stiff figure all the way up the drive, trying to work her out.

She had been offended by his interference, no doubt. Especially hurrying her away from that first meeting with her birth mother. But right now, a stranger at Porro Park was the last thing they needed. It was a sensitive time.

Keeping the news of Jennifer's pregnancy strictly between the four of them was of paramount importance. God only knows what would happen once the media got hold of that story, he thought grimly. And he wasn't sure Topaz could be trusted.

Jennifer was still struggling with the often brutal and restrictive demands of a celebrity lifestyle. The last thing she needed right now was a whirl of media excitement over her pregnancy, especially when she was only just coming to terms with motherhood herself.

It was late afternoon. The sun was dropping low in the sky, the first hints of burnished orange beginning to streak thin cloud banks out to the west. The huge old trees that bordered the drive were turning colours too, their foliage cheerful yellows, oranges, reds, the gravel littered with bright leaves fallen from their branches. Autumn was his favourite season, and Cornwall was one of his favourite places. He ought to have been calm and relaxed. And he had been happy briefly, out with Lizzie and the goats, and then driving back along the Atlantic Ocean, beside rock-strewn bays and rugged cliffs blanketed in heather, letting the dramatic scenery of the Cornish coast wash over him.

Now, far from being relaxed, Brodie was wound tight as a coiled spring. He was also limping more heavily than usual. His prosthesis had been bothering him today. And he could guess why.

He'd been pushing himself hard for the past forty-eight hours, determined not to let his personal problems get any kind of hold on him, or admit to fatigue after their long-haul flight.

But the past was still needling him, making it hard for him to concentrate on the present. He'd been having those nightmares again, the ones where he was back in the hotel during the bombing, the night he'd lost his leg. He frequently woke to the pitch-black of his bedroom, his skin clammy, heart thudding as though he was in danger.

Was he about to slip back into the gloom of depression? He couldn't allow that to happen, not when Alex needed him to be on full form.

Last year, he'd managed to survive a prolonged bout of depression by keeping busy at work. But that had only pushed the darkness away, not excised it completely. His instincts told him he needed to stop focusing on his career and start living a fully rounded life if he wanted to get better long-term. Which meant starting a relationship with a woman, of course.

But how could he even contemplate a relationship, when he couldn't bear the thought of undressing in front of a would-be lover, tensed for her reaction to his missing limb?

He watched Caroline disappear into the house, and sighed.

She was sexy, he couldn't deny that. But she was damn prickly with it. One thing was for sure, she would never be interested in a man like him and her sharp tongue would let him know that instantly. So there was no point even looking in that direction . . .

*

Once back inside the house, Caroline hurried through the atrium and bumped into Alex, who had just come from the direction of the kitchen, a steaming mug of coffee in hand.

He frowned. 'You okay, Caro? You look flushed.'

'I'm fine. Walking too fast, I expect.' She managed a smile, not feeling up to explaining what had just happened. Not to him, anyway. 'I need to talk to Jenny. Any idea where she is?'

'She insisted on doing an hour of yoga over in the gym,' Alex said, with a wry shake of his head. 'I don't know where she finds the energy. I'm still shell-shocked after our big news.'

Behind her, Brodie could be heard coming into the house. Not wanting to get caught in a conversation about Topaz before she'd had a chance to speak to her sister, Caroline patted Alex on the arm, her smile reassuring.

'I expect it will take a while to sink in. But I'm really pleased for you both. Truly I am.'

Without waiting to speak to Brodie, Caroline made her way straight through to their well-equipped home gym, situated next to the swimming pool. She didn't like to interrupt her sister's exercise regime, but this news was too important to wait.

Jennifer was lying flat on a green floor mat, both legs stretched backwards over her head, following an online yoga class available via a wall screen. A background of gentle music filled the fitness studio which housed several treadmills, exercise bikes and a stepmill, as well as a rowing machine and a bank of free weights beside a huge mirrored wall.

She looked around in surprise at Caroline's entrance. 'Hello, I thought you'd gone home.'

'Not yet.' Caroline perched uncomfortably on the weights bench, aware of her heart beating fast. She rubbed damp palms together. 'There's something I need to tell you first.'

Uncoiling slowly from her yoga position, Jennifer shook herself out, then stood and reached for her towel. Her pregnancy was not noticeable yet, even in the tight-fitting black leotard. But it soon would be.

'That sounds ominous.' She cocked her head at Caroline. 'Go on then, spill the beans.'

'I just met my birth mother.'

Jennifer gaped. 'What?'

'She was down at the gate just now. She wants to meet me. To talk. I . . . I wasn't sure if I wanted to see her, though.'

'Oh my God, seriously?' Jennifer searched her face, no doubt picking up on the raw emotion in her voice. 'Are you okay?'

'I'm dealing with it, yes.'

'You poor thing. But she came here specially to see you? That's promising, isn't it?'

'Maybe.'

'Budge up.' Jennifer swigged from her water bottle, then sat next to her on the weights bench. 'Right, start at the beginning. Tell me everything.'

Hesitantly, picking her words with great care, Caroline told her about the unexpected visitor at the gate, what she'd looked like, the things she'd said. And saw from her sister's sympathetic nods that she understood Caroline's agitation, and even shared it a little.

They'd never discussed Topaz much as kids, perhaps sensing that the topic was too sensitive to broach, but the family legend of Dad's problematic first wife was something they had both grown up with.

'You didn't want to ask her up to the house, then?'

'I didn't like the idea of intruding on your privacy. I mean, Alex is famous . . . I thought it wouldn't be right, letting a stranger come to the house.'

Jennifer absorbed that thoughtfully. 'But you're planning to meet up with her somewhere else?'

'She wants us to have lunch together in Pethporro.' Caroline found it hard not to cry, suddenly overwhelmed by emotion. 'My real mum. After all these years. Never a word from her, and then suddenly she turns up out of the blue.' A little shakily, she dragged the business card out of her pocket and showed it to Jennifer. 'She gave me this.'

Jennifer studied the card, and then handed it back. She ran a hand through her short hair, her face troubled. 'You need to tell Dad about this. You should give him a call.'

'I will,' Caroline agreed. 'Though maybe not yet.'

Jennifer looked surprised. 'Why not?'

'You know how secretive Dad's always been about Topaz. I don't think he mentioned her name more than three or four times when we were growing up. So he'd probably tell me not to meet her, wouldn't he?'

Jennifer shrugged. 'I suppose.'

'What do *you* think I should do?' Caroline pressed her.

'I think you should ring Dad,' she insisted.

'But would *you* ring him straight away, if the boot was on the other foot and it was your birth mother who'd appeared at the gate? Wouldn't you be a tiny bit curious?'

'Curious about what?'

'To find out why she left like that.' Caroline crossed her arms, chilly all of a sudden, though the gym was well heated. 'I want to know the real reason she walked out on us.'

'What are you saying?' Jennifer got up, staring at her. 'Caro, you can't really believe Dad lied about that.'

'I'm not saying he did. But she seemed so friendly. So charming. And it felt like she really wanted to connect with me.' Caroline thought of how fragile Topaz had seemed, handing over her card with that eager smile, begging her to change her mind. 'Now that I've met her in the flesh, I can't believe she left me behind without a good reason. And I'd like to find out what it was.'

'So you're not going to tell Dad?'

'I just want to hear her side of the story, Jenny. Without bringing Dad into it for now. I'll ring him afterwards, I promise.'

Jennifer nodded, and gave her a quick hug. 'Look, if that's what you've decided, I support your choice. She's your mother, not mine. But I'm going along with you to meet her.'

Caroline was surprised by the fierce light in Jenny's eyes, the emotional note in her voice. They hadn't always been that close as sisters, not since they'd grown up and left home. But she guessed Jenny wanted to change all that now she was starting her own family. Perhaps this sudden protectiveness was part of that urge.

'Thanks, I really appreciate it. But I'd rather talk to Topaz on my own,' she admitted, 'at least the first time.'

'You hope there'll be other times?'

'I'd like to get to know my real mother, yes. I mean, why not?' Caroline hugged a secret joy to herself as she imagined the two of them meeting regularly, maybe even becoming friends. 'I've always wondered what Topaz was like, and now I've got the chance to find out.'

'Well, let's meet up in Pethporro straight after your lunch date. I want to hear every detail.' Jennifer gave her a worried smile. 'And to make sure you're okay.'

CHAPTER EIGHT

Caroline walked into town late the next morning, wrapped in a warm coat against the chill autumn air. The wind off the Atlantic that day was sharp, lifting her hair and dragging at her clothes as it swept through the narrow streets of Pethporro. But she paid no attention, merely sinking her chin into the folds of her fake fur-lined coat. She was used to Cornish weather. And it was difficult to push Savannah and Malcom's noisy antics out of her head; the couple next door had kept her awake half the night, hurling abuse at each other over some slight.

Still, she tried to regain some semblance of inner calm, not wanting to meet her real mother in a state of agitation.

Her real mother!

Caroline couldn't believe she was actually going to sit down to lunch today with the woman who'd given birth to her.

The whole thing felt surreal.

But lovely, too.

For years, her only "memory" of her mother had been an old photo she'd managed to turn up while still living at home, depicting a very young Caroline, aged about two or three, cute in a short pink dress, walking through a park with her mum, bright flowerbeds on either side. It wasn't a real memory, of course. She had looked at the photo so often, it felt like one, that was all.

But, in truth, she could remember nothing about her life before her dad married Debbie and Jenny became her slightly annoying instant sibling. Had she blocked it all out? Or was it simply all too long ago? Then, yesterday, a total stranger had turned up out of the blue, claiming to be her real mother.

Back home last night, Caroline had spent a good hour rummaging through storage boxes in the dark cupboard under the stairs until she finally ran her old family photograph album to ground.

Holding the photo to the light, she'd compared her mother then with the woman who had come to Porro Park to see her. And yes, they were one and the same. Topaz might be much older now, but there was no disguising her height, or her slim build, or the high forehead and jutting jaw.

Besides, those were definitely the same hands. The slender, long-fingered hand holding her chubby toddler's hand in the photo was the same one that had passed Brodie a business card through the bars yesterday. As a nurse, she'd been trained to notice physical details, and she was sure of it. And neither yesterday, nor in the old photo, had Caroline seen any hint of a gold band on her left hand.

Topaz had never married Dad, of course, Caroline reminded herself. They had been a common-law couple.

Which had left him free to marry Debbie later on, after Topaz had left him with a small child and a broken heart. That was what Dad had always told her and Jennifer, refusing to elaborate any further on their split, insisting it was 'ancient history' and not worth bothering about. And it seemed Topaz hadn't married since, or at least was not wearing a wedding band.

Today, Caroline might finally discover the truth of why she left.

Arriving in the town centre, under a stormy sky that threatened rain later, Caroline halted outside the steamed-up windows of Kornish Koffee and tried to calm her thumping heart, suddenly too nervous to go in.

'Hello, Caroline,' a woman said in passing, startling her. She was pushing a buggy with a small child in coat and boots, small feet kicking constantly. 'Not at work?'

'Hello.' She smiled automatically at the young woman, who was one of her patients, six months pregnant with her second child. 'I took a week off. Stella's holding the fort while I'm away. How are you, Nancy?'

'Very well,' Nancy said cheerfully, then peered through the café window. 'Having lunch in the new place? I hear it's very good.'

'Yes,' she agreed awkwardly, and exchanged a few words about Nancy's pregnancy before the woman moved on.

She slipped through the bistro door with a jangle of the bell, and looked around, her heart thudding with nerves.

The Halloween decorations were being taken down by a spotty-faced young man, halfway up a ladder with an expression of intense concentration. It was a few minutes past midday, and the place was half-full, upbeat pop music pumping out of several speakers on the walls.

Her mother was already there.

'Over here, darling!' Topaz called across the bistro, standing up to wave.

Heads turned.

Topaz was smiling at her.

Caroline could not help smiling in return. And why shouldn't she smile? Why not make friends with this woman? Jennifer had urged caution, but it seemed the most natural thing in the world to feel pleased at the prospect of growing close to her own mother.

Though she was apprehensive too.

After that brief meeting yesterday, she guessed that Topaz's account of their break-up would be a little different from her dad's. Perhaps a lot different. There was even a chance that her secret fears were right and she herself would turn out to be the one to blame.

Could she cope with that possibility?

Nodding to the waitress, she crossed to her mother's table, struggling out of her coat. 'Hello,' Caroline said breathlessly. 'Sorry I'm late.'

'Nonsense, darling. I've only been here a couple of minutes myself.'

Her mother pleased her by kissing her warmly on both cheeks, then giving her a quick hug too.

Her perfumed smell was vaguely familiar, but the memory was gone before she could grasp at it. One of her curls tickled Caroline's cheek too, impossibly white-blonde, like an aging Shirley Temple. Her mother's restless gaze ran over Caroline, as though looking for something – the small child she remembered, perhaps – and then she sat down again, glancing rapidly about the bistro instead.

'Isn't this a fun place? Though I've never been a big fan of Halloween myself.' Topaz gave a mock shudder as she reached for the menu, gazing up at a forgotten fake plastic spider dangling from the ceiling. 'I prefer Christmas. Much jollier.'

'Me too,' Caroline agreed, taking the seat opposite. 'Luckily, we won't have long to wait until the shops will be full of tinsel and festive music.'

'Is Jennifer joining us?'

'No.'

'Oh.' Topaz smiled. 'Well, two's company, three's a crowd. Did you tell her about me?'

'Erm, I didn't get a chance,' she fibbed guiltily, deciding it was best not to admit she would be meeting up with Jennifer straight after lunch in order to tell her everything that had been said. 'She was still tired yesterday.'

'I'm not surprised, poor love. Those long flights from the States, they really knock it out of you.'

Caroline frowned. 'How did you know she'd just flown in? I don't think I mentioned that yesterday.'

'Didn't you, darling?' Topaz looked puzzled. 'I must have read it online. I've been in Pethporro for days, googling your name like crazy, trying to track you down.'

'Is that why you came to Porro Park to find me?' Caroline

asked, while they were on the subject of Jennifer and Alex. 'I don't live there, you know.'

'Someone told me I might find you there.' Topaz shrugged. 'A woman in the post office, I think. Maybe that's where I heard about the Delgardos flying back too. I really can't recall.'

That sounded reasonable. It was a small town and people loved to gossip. 'But why come to find me now? Why not before?'

'I told you, darling. I was in the waiting room at the dentist, just for a check-up, and spotted something about Alex Delgardo in an old celebrity mag. It was a bit out of date but it mentioned his wedding to Jennifer. That was the first I'd even heard of it.' Bright with curiosity, her eyes searched Caroline's face. 'Such a brilliant catch for your sister, you must be madly jealous.'

'Not a bit.'

'Really?' Topaz looked dismayed. 'Is Delgardo a beast to her? He does look rather big and imposing. Does he throw his weight around at home?'

'No, of course not. Alex just isn't my type, so why would I be jealous?'

Though that wasn't strictly true, she admitted to herself. There had been a time early on when she'd rather fancied Alex. But it had been blindingly obvious the film star only had eyes for Jennifer, so she'd given up. She'd never competed with her sister for a man, and she never would.

Topaz looked at her almost pityingly. 'That's very loyal

of you, I must say. Anyway, this magazine . . . It had a photo of the wedding, and I saw you there too. Her maid of honour.' Her smile became dazzling. 'Such a beauty, just like me when I was your age.'

'So you saw a photo of me in a magazine and decided to come down here. But why now? Why not seek me out years ago?'

'Oh, darling, I wanted to, please believe me. Only . . .' Her mother looked uncomfortable. 'Well, there were reasons.'

'I'd love to hear them,' she said coaxingly.

'Maybe we could order first.' Topaz turned, trying to catch the waitress's eye, but the woman was busy taking someone else's order.

Caroline, studying Topaz up close for the first time, was unprepared for the powerful rush of emotion she felt. There was no doubt in her mind that this was her birth mother: their facial features and physical build were simply too similar. But she was almost overwhelmed by anger and a sense of grievous loss at all the years she had missed with this woman, and had to grip her hands out of sight in her lap, to control her desire to get up and leave.

Her first overall impression was one of raw energy, and an enthusiasm for life barely contained by a pair of candid blue eyes set beneath delicately arched brows. Yesterday's garish bandana was gone; blonde curls clustered loosely about a strong, oval face, only lightly powdered, her lips brushed with pink lipstick. Nothing was overdone, nothing was out of place. And yet, somehow, there was a hint of studied awareness about Topaz, as though she knew she had come here to be watched and evaluated.

Topaz turned back and caught her looking. She smiled a little nervously. 'Having a good look, are you? What do you think? You said yesterday that you remembered me. Have I changed at all?' She grimaced. 'I'm older, of course. But let's not talk about that.'

'You haven't changed much. Not according to this.' Caroline drew the faded colour photograph out of her handbag. She held it out to her mother. 'How old was I in this picture? And where was it taken? Do you remember? How long after this was it that you and Dad …' She paused, correcting herself, 'Before you left?'

'Before our unhappy house of cards came tumbling down?' Topaz took the photo and studied it for a moment, her lashes lowered, hiding the expression in her eyes. 'Yes, I remember that park. It was in Devon somewhere. They built over it later. Such a shame. You would have been about three years old, at a guess. Your father took this photo, of course. One of our few happy days out together. God, I look so young!' She handed back the photograph. 'A summer picnic. So it must have been about six months before the fateful day. Is that what you wanted to know?'

Before Caroline could say anything, the waitress finally arrived, and they both ordered a glass of dry white wine.

Topaz smiled. 'Ah, a girl after my own heart.'

'And to eat?' the waitress asked.

Caroline ordered a local crab salad with warm ciabatta.

'I forgot to look.' Topaz scanned the menu carelessly. 'What's good here, Caroline?'

'They serve proper Cornish pasties with salad.'

Topaz glanced at the waitress. 'Do you do a vegetarian pasty?'

'Spinach and spicy chickpea.'

'Perfect, thank you.' Topaz smiled warmly and handed her the menu. 'And maybe a dish of olives while we wait?'

The waitress nodded, and went away happily.

Topaz certainly knew how to charm people, Caroline thought, studying her mother and feeling again that tug of emotion.

'You said yesterday that you'd tell me the truth. Not a fairy story.'

'Of course, darling. If you're sure you want to hear it.'

'Why wouldn't I?'

'People are strange when it comes to family. Sometimes reality is less important than what they've already decided is the truth.'

'I want the reality, not the dream,' Caroline told her firmly.

'Good for you!'

Caroline waited, her lips pressed tightly together, stomach tight with nervous excitement. Something told her she might not enjoy what lay ahead. But Topaz was right about one thing, at least: it was time she heard the other side of her parents' story, however disillusioned she might feel about it afterwards.

'I was never cut out to be a mother, that's what you need

to understand from the start.' Topaz met her eyes with a directness she hadn't shown before. 'I loved your father. And he loved me. We were so deeply in love, it was crazy. But a baby ...' She winced. 'It's a cliché perhaps, but I couldn't cope. Jim had a job at a design shop at the time. He went out to work every day, leaving me alone with you. And you were such a demanding baby; you needed constant care and attention.'

Caroline felt guilty. 'That sounds awful.'

'Oh, not your fault, darling.' Topaz clasped her hand across the table. 'God, no, it was my fault. All mine. I tried my best, but I'm just not a natural parent.'

'I'm sure that's not true.'

'Bless you for that.' Topaz sat back, sighing. 'In the end, I realised your father was coming home later and later in the evenings, and sometimes working weekends too. I became suspicious.' She bit her lip, looking mistily away as though recalling the past. 'I started to follow him after he left work, while a neighbour watched you. That was when I discovered he was having an affair.'

Caroline put a hand to her mouth, horrified. 'An affair?' she repeated in disbelief. 'But Dad said ... He told me you just left for no reason.'

'Men will say anything to get themselves out of trouble,' Topaz said dismissively. 'I confronted Jim, and he admitted that he was thinking of leaving me. That he'd only stayed with me because of the baby. He said I was a bad girlfriend. That I couldn't cook and was too difficult, and that I was always throwing tantrums.' Tears sparkled in her eyes as she added angrily, 'He even called me a prima donna and blamed *me* for the affair.'

'I don't believe it!' Caroline burst out, unable to control herself any longer.

'That's because you swallowed all his lies, darling.' Her mother looked at her sadly. 'But I don't blame you. He's your father, of course you want to believe him. Just like I did when Jim pretended he didn't believe in marriage. He only meant he didn't believe in marrying *me*!'

Caroline struggled to calm down. 'All right, so you left him. But why not take me with you?'

'Oh, I didn't leave you behind.' Her mother shook her head vehemently. 'That's not what happened.'

Their dry white wine arrived, the waitress glancing from her to Caroline doubtfully as she set down the glasses. Presumably she had caught some of their conversation. But she didn't say anything, hurrying away to another customer.

Caroline knew she had to stop raising her voice. It wouldn't do for anyone to overhear this conversation. Not now that she was Alex Delgardo's sister-in-law. It would be too easy for the paparazzi to get hold of the story and make trouble for Jennifer with it.

She gulped down some of her wine, and then whispered, 'Go on, you were saying?'

'You want to know how it all ended? I stuck with him for a while after that, hoping he would stop straying. But he didn't, of course. Things only got worse. In the end, I wanted to hurt him as badly as he'd hurt me,' Topaz said grimly. 'So I decided to kill myself.' She gave a crooked smile at Caroline's shocked gasp. 'Obviously, I failed, or I wouldn't be sitting here today.'

'My God, that's appalling.' Caroline leant forward, her gaze on Topaz's face. 'Tell me what happened. But you'd better keep your voice down.' She glanced around. 'Walls have ears in Pethporro.'

Topaz nodded. 'After that, I was committed to a hospital,' she continued more softly, an unhappy, faraway look in her eyes. 'For my own safety, the doctors said. Your father never once visited me, or brought you to see me, though I wrote to him every week at first. The letters came back unopened. I was so distraught, missing you, not knowing what was happening to my little girl, I tried to kill myself again. After that, the doctors said it had to be an indefinite stay, as I was a danger to myself.'

'You poor thing.'

'Thank you. It was a hard time for me.' Topaz drank half her glass of wine in one long swallow, then set the glass back down, toying with the stem. 'Though not as hard as for you, perhaps. You must have been wondering all that time what happened to Mummy.'

'Yes,' Caroline agreed, an old pain lancing through her. 'And never getting a straight answer.'

'What a terrible man he is. Though I suppose he had his reasons.' Topaz ran a hand through her vibrant hair. 'After about three years in that ghastly place, the doctors finally decided I could be let out, and that was that. Only your father had disappeared by then, taking you with him. It took me months to track him down. By then, he'd dumped the woman he'd been seeing before and had married Jennifer's mother instead. What was her name again?'

'Debbie,' Caroline said faintly.

'Yes, that awful brunette with the huge teeth. I remember seeing her from a distance and thinking, well, if that's your taste in women, no wonder you didn't want me.' Topaz saw Caroline's expression and sucked in her breath. She was instantly contrite. 'I'm so sorry, do you like Debbie? I shouldn't have said that. Was she a good mother to you?'

Caroline nodded, unable to speak.

'Well, that's something, at least. My baby was well taken care of.' But that sad look was back on her face. 'I found a lawyer as soon as I could afford to. But he said I'd have a hell of a job trying to get custody, given my history. Three years in a mental hospital, getting my head sorted out! Not ideal mummy material, is it? So, I decided it was hopeless. I moved up to the Midlands to find work as a designer. And that's where I've been for the past two decades.' She patted Caroline's hand, tears in her eyes again. 'It was the hardest thing I've ever done, letting you go. But it was probably for the best. Don't you think?'

'I don't know what to think.'

'You're angry with me. Of course you are. You think I should have come back to see you when you were a child. But I was too scared. You have to believe me.'

'You mean, you were scared of Dad?'

Topaz rubbed away a stray tear, a slight flush in her

cheeks. She downed the rest of her wine and peered unhappily into the empty glass. 'I thought I wouldn't be welcome. And that his wife would be a far better mother to you. And she was, wasn't she?'

Debbie had been a good stepmother. But she hadn't been her real mother, and Caroline had always been aware of that absence in her life.

Caroline decided not to comment. There was no point hurting Topaz's feelings over something that had happened so long ago. Their food arrived, and they were both silent for a while, eating their lunch while glancing at each other from time to time.

'Will you go Christmas shopping with me?' Topaz suddenly asked. 'Next week, perhaps? I can arrange to stay in Pethporro a little longer if you like the idea. I seem to recall there are some lovely boutiques in Boscastle, full of the most gorgeous, unusual gifts. I've always dreamt of going shopping there with you. Like a real mother and daughter.'

Tears sprang into Caroline's own eyes at those last words.

That had always been her dream as a child too, to be able to spend time with the unknown mother she couldn't remember properly. Later, as a grown-up, she had occasionally glimpsed women out shopping with people who were clearly their mothers, two women smiling at each other, walking arm-in-arm, and had been struck by the most ridiculous envy ...

'I'd really like that,' she heard herself say, and could not understand why the prospect of a simple Christmas shopping trip to nearby Boscastle could make her so deliriously happy.

After Topaz had left, Caroline paid for lunch and stumbled out into the windy sunshine, feeling distinctly shaky after what she had just heard.

She made a quick phone call and, fifteen minutes later, Jennifer picked her up discreetly round the corner from the bistro – or as discreetly as was possible driving an Aston Martin through a tiny Cornish town – and demanded to know *everything*.

'How was it?' Jennifer asked eagerly before Caroline had even put her seat belt on. 'What did she say about Dad? Did she explain why she left him?'

'Please, let's drive along the coast,' Caroline said briefly. 'I'll tell you everything once we're clear of Pethporro.'

'Fine!' Jennifer accelerated away from the kerb and headed out of town along the coast road, clearly impatient to hear her news. But a few sideways looks at Caroline's hunched figure in the passenger seat made her slow down, frowning. 'Hey, are you okay? You look really upset.'

'I'll survive.'

Caroline suppressed the urge to cry. It hurt inside, but she wasn't a kid any more. Instead, she sat back and stared out at sunlight sparkling on the cold sea, glad to be out of the wind. A dark cloudbank drifting in from the west would probably bring rain later, but it hadn't hit land yet.

'I'm sorry for pushing you,' Jennifer said, sounding chastened. 'You don't need to discuss it if you don't want to.'

'No, I want to talk,' Caroline told her, and closed her eyes. 'I need to talk or I'll probably go mad.'

But how to explain what she was feeling when she wasn't even sure herself?

Once she'd finally got her thoughts in order, Caroline repeated what Topaz had told her over lunch. Including the awful parts about her dad's infidelity, her mother's suicide attempts, and how she'd been too 'scared' to visit her while Caroline was growing up.

'She genuinely claimed that Dad had an affair?' Jennifer was incredulous.

'Yes.'

'Our dad?' Jennifer shook her head. 'Old Mister Boring and Reliable?'

'I know. Incredible, isn't it?'

'And you believed her?'

'She seemed genuine enough. And so sad, Jenny . . .' Caroline felt a rush of emotion. 'It was awful, looking into her eyes when she was telling me how the doctors locked her up for three whole years, because she was depressed and they were worried she would try to hurt herself again.'

'Hmm.' Jennifer looked ahead at the coast road. 'But she still didn't come to see you after they let her out.'

'I think she's really sorry about that now. And she did seem scared.'

'Of *Dad*?'

'I know, it sounds crazy. He's really not that sort of man, is he? But maybe she misread the situation.'

'Or maybe she's exaggerating,' Jennifer said flatly. 'I'm heading back to Porro Park to ring Dad, like we agreed. I want to hear what he has to say.'

Caroline was suddenly uneasy. 'Can we wait a little bit longer before we ring him? I need to sort this out in my head. Please, Jenny? Their stories are so different. It could sound like I'm accusing Dad of lying.' She hesitated. 'Also, I don't want this situation to spoil your big news.'

'Sorry?'

'About the baby?'

'Oh God, yes.'

'How could you forget that?' Caroline managed a shaky laugh. 'They'll be delighted. Their first grandchild!'

'Mum will be thrilled, for sure.'

'And Dad.'

'All right,' Jennifer said, nodding. 'We'll put off telling Dad about Topaz. Until you feel more confident about doing it. Besides, I want to tell them both about the baby in person, not over the phone. And Alex needs to be there. He's the father, after all.'

'So you're going to St Ives to see them?'

'Soon, yes. I'm still thrashing out the details. Alex has been so busy, he never stops. He and Brodie have been making Zoom calls and sending emails almost non-stop since we got back. But he's promised to set aside a day for us to visit Mum and Dad.' Jennifer grinned at her. 'I'll expect you to come along too, of course. Then maybe you can tell Dad about Topaz after I've told him about the baby.'

'I wouldn't miss it for the world,' Caroline said promptly. But she knew it would be very hard to tackle her father face to face about Topaz and her wildly different version of their break-up.

If only she could be sure which of them was telling the truth . . .

CHAPTER NINE

Kernow House was an ancient farmhouse, dating back hundreds of years, perched rather precariously on the edge of the cliffs beyond Pethporro. An imposing residence with big gloomy windows and a dark slate roof, it always looked to Brodie as though the next winter storm might sweep it away into the Atlantic Ocean, which even now foamed and crashed against rocks far below its walls.

'There it is, the big house itself.' Brodie smiled, taking the final bend in the track with care; as predicted, he had remembered the way to Kernow House without needing to turn on the satnav. 'Thank God we finally shook off that photographer. I thought the pest was going to follow us all the way here.'

'You overtaking that tractor on the coast road was what did the trick,' Alex called from the back of the four-door sports car. 'I expect he's still stuck behind it, cursing your name. But he's not driving an Aston Martin Rapide.'

Brodie grinned, then realised his other passenger had said nothing. 'Feeling nervous, Jenny?'

Seated beside him, Jennifer peered at the farmhouse

ahead, her face unreadable. 'I wouldn't characterise it as nerves,' she said, with a touch of asperity. 'It's true I would have preferred to visit Ripper with only Lizzie on hand. But I'm more than up to the challenge of seeing Hannah Tregar again.'

'Of course you are.' Alex shifted in the back seat of the four-door sports car, leaning forward to join in the conversation. 'I'm sure all that business with Raphael has been long forgotten.'

'What business?' she demanded fierily, turning in her seat to glare at her husband.

Alex chuckled, but did not rise to the bait. 'Look, if there was still any bad blood between you two, why would Hannah have arranged to be at home when you visited Ripper? She could have gone out for the day and left Lizzie to deal with you. No, I'm sure you've been forgiven.'

'Forgiven?' Jennifer sounded outraged. 'What on earth is there to forgive? I was there first, remember.'

'You did attempt to warn her off Raphael at one stage, I seem to recall you saying. Even though he was no longer seeing you at the time.' There was a faint note of teasing in Alex's voice. 'Played the witch card and threatened to turn her into a toad or something, didn't you?'

'Oh, well.' Jennifer folded her arms and subsided into mutterings that Brodie only caught in snatches. 'Can't blame a girl for trying . . . man-thief . . . all water under the bridge . . .'

Hannah Tregar had apparently inherited Kernow House from her late grandmother, and had come across from Greece while pregnant with her young son, Santos. The child's father had been her boyfriend out in Greece, but had died tragically in an avalanche.

Raphael Tregar was a neighbouring farmer who had swept a pregnant Hannah off her feet, as local gossip had it, despite being a miserable sod to everybody else. Everybody except Lizzie, of course, who seemed exempt from his bad temper and curmudgeonly attitude. Though word had it, Raphael had only married Hannah to get his hands on Kernow House, which he'd considered as good as his own for some reason Brodie didn't quite understand.

Jennifer had briefly been Raphael's girlfriend before he met Hannah, and though he'd already broken it off by then, she had felt proprietorial towards him and tried to warn Hannah off.

Not surprisingly, her intervention hadn't worked, and the happy couple had eventually married, leaving Jennifer heartbroken and depressed.

Until she'd met Alex, that is.

Since Lizzie lived with Hannah and Raphael at Kernow House, that was where Ripper had been taken, yowling unhappily in his cat box, when Lizzie agreed to house him during Jennifer's time in the States.

Brodie wasn't sure that Ripper would be too pleased to see his beloved mistress again, only to realise when she left that he was not accompanying her home but continuing to live in exile at Kernow House. Though perhaps Lizzie was right, and Ripper preferred running wild and terrorising the farm's rodent population to being an indoor cat back at Porro Park.

It was typical November weather, tense and windy, scudding dark clouds out to sea threatening more unsettled weather to come. There had been a sudden flurry of rain earlier, but it had moved further inland since. On either side of the long approach to the house, vast windswept fields, some of them containing huddled clusters of sheep, were still dotted with puddles from the downpour.

Not a promising day to be driving about the Cornish countryside, Brodie thought grimly, parking in the yard at the back of the farmhouse. But at least further rain seemed to be holding off for the time being, and there was even a sulky hint of sunshine breaking through the clouds.

Alex gave Jennifer a quick hug as she got out of the car. 'Sorry if I teased you back there, love. I know you're preoccupied with Caroline and her birth mother, you probably don't need any more angst.' He gave her a searching look. 'How is Caro, by the way?'

'I'm worried about her. It's clear she's happy to have her real mum back in her life, but she seems confused too. And upset.' Jennifer grimaced. 'The horrible things this woman has said about our dad . . . I'm not sure whether to believe them or not.'

Brodie studied her thoughtfully. 'So you think Topaz is lying about him? Why would she do that?'

'That's the million-dollar question, isn't it?'

Alex stroked her face. 'You think she's after something?'

'I think it's a bit too convenient that Topaz should only have come back to Pethporro since discovering there's a film star in the family.' Alex grinned lazily, but she ignored him. 'Before we fly back to the States, we need to sit down with Caroline and have a proper chat about this. Show her we care.' She glanced round at Brodie, including him in that suggestion. *All of us.*

Surprised by her vehemence, Brodie locked the car and pocketed the key. 'Like a council of war, you mean?'

'If you want to call it that.'

'A council of war?' Alex frowned at him warningly over his wife's head, then slipped his arm around Jennifer's waist. 'Now don't bite my head off, sweetheart,' he said gently, 'but don't you think it's possible Caroline might be offended and rightly accuse us of interfering in her private life?'

'Maybe she will. Maybe she won't. But she's my sister, she needs our support, and I'm going to make sure she gets it before I leave Cornwall.' Jennifer's eyes flashed with defiance. 'Whether she likes it or not.'

The back door to Kernow House opened and Lizzie came bounding towards them. 'Hello, Jennifer!' she shouted, her grey hair restrained under what looked to be the same home-knitted bobble hat. Did she ever take it off? Brodie wondered. 'Hello, Alex!' She hugged them both, then came to Brodie and hesitated, chewing her lip. 'Oh, hello, erm . . .'

'Brodie,' he supplied patiently.

'Yes, hello, Brodie. You came to see the goats yesterday. I remember now. Nice to see you again!' Lizzie beamed at them all. 'Come inside, quick! Ripper's been waiting for you for hours.'

'You've cut your hair,' Jennifer said. 'It looks wonderful. Very smart.'

Lizzie looked embarrassed. 'I got it caught on a barbed wire fence, trying to get a sheep free from a thicket. Hannah said as how I should get it all chopped off.'

'It suits you,' Alex said, and gave her one of what Jennifer called his 'bone-melting' smiles.

'Oh, you!' Grinning wildly, Lizzie closed the door behind them, and then ushered them through the pretty oak kitchen and along a narrow passageway towards the living room. 'Where are you, Ripper?' She opened the door a crack and peered around the wood-panelled room in search of the cat. 'Ah, there he is. Look who's come to visit you, boy!'

Jennifer squealed in excitement as her skinny, cream-coloured Siamese cat sprang out from behind the sofa and stared at her.

She scrambled towards the cat and scooped him up, stroking his sleek head and delicate ears while making soft noises under her breath. Ripper did not struggle but began to purr violently, like an engine had been switched on inside his narrow breast.

'Oh, my darling,' she was saying in ecstatic tones, 'has my ickle baby boy missed me? I'm so sorry for going away. Do you forgive me?' Ripper glared up at her with accusing blue eyes, but kept purring. 'You couldn't come with me, you would have been shut in a quarantine station for months. Better to stay here with Lizzie and stay free, catching tasty mice.'

When they came in, Hannah and Raphael Tregar had been sitting together on the large blue sofa by the window, holding hands, their heads together. But they'd hurriedly dropped hands when they saw who it was, Hannah jumping up with a smile that looked rehearsed and over-bright.

The room was warm compared to the chilly weather outside, thanks to a fire leaping in the open grate. It looked very welcoming, the curtains drawn back to reveal a dull, stormy sky, the lights on to counter that effect, and even a few candles flickering in coloured glass containers on the coffee table. There were two double sofas and a comfortable-looking armchair – more than enough places for everyone to sit, Brodie noted – and soft music was playing in the background. There was a tall oak bookcase along one wall, filled to overflowing with books of every kind, and a huge pot plant dangling green, jungle-like leaves over the armchair.

Alex, meanwhile, was shaking hands with Hannah Tregar, who was still smiling broadly and suggesting that they all sit down together for a nice cup of tea. Raphael didn't say much, but grunted as he too stood briefly to shake Alex's hand, then nodded at Brodie and sat back down again. The Cornish farmer was wearing a flat cap, even though he was indoors, perhaps because it allowed him to peer at them all from under its grey tweed brim in a suspicious manner.

'Good to see you two again.' Alex was at his most charming. 'And thank you so much for housing Ripper for us all these months. I hope he hasn't made a nuisance of himself.'

Raphael gave a guttural laugh, and held up his hands as though checking them. 'Still got all my fingers. Not sure about Hannah though. She does insist on trying to pet the damn thing.'

'Just the odd scratch here and there, nothing to worry about. Cats are like that, aren't they?' Hannah watched with a faint smile as Ripper made a spirited attempt to climb on to Jennifer's head, and had to be removed by Alex. 'Well, he's certainly pleased to see you. None of us get that kind of attention.'

'You planning to take him back to Porro Park now?' Raphael asked straight out, as though profoundly wishing they would.

'We aren't quite sure how long we're staying in England,' Jennifer admitted, a slight flush in her cheeks. The cat back in her arms, she perched on the rather tattier sofa opposite her old boyfriend and his wife, not quite meeting their eyes. 'We might only be here a week or two. Would it be too much to ask for you to keep Ripper here until we're sure? I don't want him to get upset by being moved about too much. You know how much he hates being locked in that cat box.' She paused, biting her lip. 'I'm happy to pay whatever it costs for his continued keep ... and for any inconvenience.'

'Please, there's no need,' Hannah insisted.

Brodie was still standing in the doorway, unsure what to do. He had driven Alex and Jennifer here, but this wasn't really his business. And he had so many things on his mind, it was hard to keep smiling ...

Lizzie, jostling past him into the corridor, tugged on his sleeve. 'Go on, you sit down with Jennifer and Alex. I'm making tea and biscuits for everyone. I think there be scones too.'

'Actually, I'd like to stretch my legs if I'm not needed.' He caught a surprised look on Alex's face, and grimaced. 'Bit of a headache this morning,' he added, probably unconvincingly. 'A quick walk along the cliff should blow away the cobwebs.'

Alex frowned, but said nothing.

Jennifer, lost in her cat's hungry eyes, did not even look up.

'Make sure you don't get blown away with 'em,' Raphael grunted from the depths of the big blue sofa, his flat cap pulled down again. 'There's a strong wind out there today.'

'I'll be careful,' Brodie said, and excused himself.

To his relief, it had not yet started raining again, though the leaden skies looked cloudier and more turbulent than ever.

Outside the house, Brodie stuck his hands deep in his coat pockets, and walked head-on into the blustering wind, making his way round the cliff-side of the property. He remembered from his last visit being shown the meandering path that ran through fields and along the clifftop between Kernow House and Raphael Tregar's own farm, a little further down the coast.

He fancied walking the cliff path properly this time; not just the short stretch he'd tried before, aware of the others waiting for him back at the house, but a good mile or two. However far it took to shake this feeling of doom that had been hanging over him all morning, he thought grimly. It was likely that Alex and Jennifer would be there at least an hour before he'd be expected to drive them back to Porro Park.

It was dangerous in the strong wind, as Raphael had pointed out. Even before he reached the edge, he could feel the wind snatch at him with jealous fingers. But what the hell ... Risking a walk along the precarious tightrope of the cliffs, wind howling in his ears and the Atlantic tide tossing up white spray against the rocks below, seemed appropriate to his mood.

He was not sure what had come over him recently. It wasn't connected to Jennifer's pregnancy. This strange sense of unease predated her revelations yesterday. It also predated their decision to fly back to England for a short stay. There hadn't been a single event that had provoked it, either.

One day, back in the States, he had woken up early one morning and realised he was no longer happy. That he hadn't been happy in a long time, in fact. As simple as that. But why he was unhappy, and what he ought to do about it ... Those were questions he'd been wrestling with ever since, and he was no nearer to finding the answers. Perhaps he never would.

He reached the edge of the cliff, and glanced down as he walked. The tide was coming in or going out, he wasn't sure which. The roar and crash of waves was almost deafening, and he could taste salt spray on his face, even this high up. A violent gust of wind made him stagger sideways, but he braced against its force and soon recovered his balance.

He had left the army years ago to work for Alex, and had never regretted that decision, not even when he lost his leg. He still kept himself fit and honed, swimming and pumping iron most days, determined not to let his amputation hinder his physical fitness. It was as though he were in a constant state of readiness, like a soldier waiting for the call to action. But the only call he ever got these days was from Alex, needing him to liaise with a producer or drive him somewhere.

He had enjoyed his job at first. The sheer glamour of it, and the unpredictability too, jetting around the world at a moment's notice. He had accompanied Alex to exotic locations for meetings or filming, and guarded him from hordes of star-struck fans or anonymous death threats – it was bizarre how strongly some people felt about his best-known action film character, Cheetham – and nursed him through the post-traumatic stress Alex had suffered for over a year after the hotel bombing. The long nights he'd sat up with Alex, reassuring his friend as he wept and clawed at his face, and never mentioned his own suffering . . .

Was that it? Did he feel neglected in some way?

God, he hoped not. That would be so bloody pathetic and embarrassing. He didn't want or need anyone's pity.

Yes, okay, he too had suffered mentally after the bombing. And still woke some nights, drenched in sweat, pitched back into that moment of utter blackness when he'd come to after the explosion, and known something was wrong with his leg. Terribly, appallingly wrong.

But none of that meant he needed professional help or attention. It was nothing he couldn't cope with alone.

Besides, he hated the idea of opening his heart to a stranger, of 'letting it all out'. He had even refused the course of therapy offered him after he left hospital, preferring to get back to work as soon as possible. And at the time he'd felt that was the right decision.

But had it been a mistake?

It had been over three years since he'd lost his leg, along with a good friend, Paula, their camerawoman. He could still remember her smiling face, showing them a photo of her son on her phone. That was the last time he'd seen Paula alive. They'd been crossing the brightly lit hotel lobby in a small group, laughing and joking, on their way to a party, when suddenly he'd been lifted into the air on a furious wave of heat and light.

Beyond that moment, all he remembered of the aftermath of the bombing were dreamlike flashes of memory, tiny glimpses into hell. Smoke, thick dust in his lungs, fires burning everywhere, and people screaming in the darkness. He had felt no pain at first, only a curious numbness in his lower regions. And then Alex had found him among the wreckage, a blood-stained face leaning over him, calling his name, and he had blacked out again.

The path wove precariously close to the cliff edge again. Brodie stopped, shoulders hunched against the wind, and stared out to sea.

The ocean heaved and swelled like a sick body, ripples cracking the grey-green surface here and there under the long whip of the wind. His gaze dropped to the rock-strewn beach at his feet, where the tide now appeared to be coming in, further up the pebbly shingle than it had been before. There was a cluster of sharp black rocks hundreds of feet below, the ocean smashing itself against them time and again, running off in white rivulets, lacy foam everywhere . . .

He took a few steps closer to the edge and leant over for a proper look.

It was a pretty long drop, he thought, scanning the cliff face below, and not much to break it if someone fell from here. Stones, grasses, a tangle of bramble, the odd jutting rock. Then the pebbles far below. That would make a nasty mess, for certain.

A grey-backed gull burst out of hiding somewhere below, shrieking at him as it soared on the thermals, wings fighting the strong gusts.

Brodie stepped back, his heart thudding hard. Awkwardly, he turned to watch the bird fly on inland, its mournful cry soon lost on the wind.

Had he really just contemplated jumping?

With an effort, he shook himself and hurried back towards the farmhouse. But he knew he was in trouble. Ever since Alex's marriage, he had started to feel lonely again, as though his friend's full life had highlighted his own sense of emptiness. Maybe his depression was coming back. He didn't think he could bear to go through that darkness again.

Was it time to get therapy at last?

He couldn't imagine that conversation with Alex. And didn't want to. Between the two of them, he had always been the rock, the friend who survived, no matter what. To admit that he was having difficulties would be an admission of weakness, and there was no way that was going to happen.

No, whatever it took, he had to get through this on his own.

On returning to Kernow House, he found Alex and Jennifer just leaving, politely saying their goodbyes to Hannah and Raphael, with an excitable Lizzie already hovering beside the car, holding some kind of wicker box partially covered with an old blanket. From the violent shudders and growling emanating from the box, it was clear there was a cat inside it.

'What's this?' Brodie fished the car keys out of his pocket and unlocked the door for Lizzie to place the cat carrier inside. 'I thought Ripper was staying with you guys.'

'Not any more,' Lizzie said cheerfully, and with his help, arranged the wicker cat basket on the back seat.

A low, melancholy yowl, only slightly muffled by the blanket, indicated that the occupant of the box was far from happy.

'Don't worry, Ripper, it's not a long journey.' Brodie shut the rear door as gently as he could and then walked round the other side of the car, frowning. 'I don't understand,' he said, opening the front passenger door for a smiling Jennifer. She's practically glowing, he thought. He glanced in at the cat basket again, and alarm bells rang in his head. Too loudly to be ignored. 'So Ripper's coming home with us now?'

'That's right.' Without further explanation, Jennifer climbed into the front seat, a satisfied look on her face.

'I'll drive back to Porro Park,' Alex said, surprising him.

Brodie handed over the keys, and got in beside the cat box in the back of the four-door sports car. The cat yowled again, and the wicker basket shook violently as she attempted to escape. Jennifer turned, saying something soothing to her pet, while Brodie lifted the blanket to check the cat hadn't actually achieved his goal.

Ripper growled and spat at him, his eyes twin points of pure fury, and he hurriedly dropped the blanket. He wouldn't put it past that animal to draw blood even while in captivity.

Alex drove slowly out of the yard and on to the bumpy lane back to the main road, waving goodbye to Lizzie and the Tregars out of his open window. 'Well,' he said, with a short laugh, 'that didn't quite go as planned.'

'No kidding.' Brodie sat forward, leaning his arm on the back of Jennifer's seat. 'I thought you two had decided not to bring the cat home, given it's only to be a short stay.'

'Erm, yes.' Alex glanced at his wife. 'Slight change of plan.'

'My fault entirely,' Jennifer said, turning to Brodie with an awkward smile. 'We would have consulted you, but it all happened rather fast. As soon as I set eyes on Ripper, I knew I couldn't leave him there. Not that Lizzie wasn't looking after him properly. In fact, he's never looked so well-fed and pampered. But I just couldn't spend another day without him. So I asked Lizzie to find the cat carrier and his favourite toys and . . .' She hesitated, looking away. 'The thing is, I told Alex I was bringing Ripper home for good, and that was that.'

'I beg your pardon?'

'It was a three-line whip,' Alex told him drily, 'I didn't have much choice in the matter.' He switched on the wind-screen wipers as rain started to pour at last, the skies glowering as he turned out of the narrow, muddy lane in the direction of Pethporro. 'Basically, Jenny doesn't want to live abroad any more. Turns out she's missing her roots. So she's decided to stay and have this baby in Cornwall. And wherever Jenny goes, that's where I go too.'

In the back, Ripper yowled again, a lonely, plaintive sound this time.

Brodie felt like joining him.

'Sorry, mate.' Alex glanced at Brodie in the mirror, and shrugged. 'I know we had a few films lined up. But that's going to have to change. We're not going back to the States.'

CHAPTER TEN

Dumping her shopping in the kitchen, Caroline grimaced as she began to put the chilled food away in the fridge. Bloody Savannah and Malcolm had their sound system on at top volume again, blasting out some kind of rave music. People could probably hear the insistent thumping beat on the other side of Pethporro. She glanced at the clock. It was only four o'clock in the afternoon. Not exactly party time. And on a weekday too. But no doubt they had their reasons. Just as she would have her reasons when she went round there with a frying pan and intent to cause grievous bodily harm.

Her mobile screen lit up as it rang.

It was Jennifer.

Caroline answered the call, clamping the phone between her ear and one shoulder, and covering her other ear so she had a reasonable chance of hearing her sister.

'Hello?' she yelled, still putting her shopping away. 'Rave Central.'

'Oh my God, what on earth is that racket?'

'Savannah and Malcolm. Entertaining us all for free. I

may kill them. Is it possible to plead temporary insanity caused by loud music?'

'You have to get out of there, Caro.'

'Ooh, are you inviting me to dinner? Because that would save me from life imprisonment.' She glanced at the limp ready-made salad she'd grabbed from the mini-market in Pethporro where Jenny had dropped her earlier. Shopping had seemed like a good idea at the time, given her empty fridge and unsettled state of mind. A bit of retail therapy. But her neighbours' loud music had taken away her appetite.

'Yes, come to dinner at our place,' Jenny said, and laughed a little wildly. 'I have something to tell you.'

'What does that mean?' When her sister didn't reply, Caroline shut the fridge and stood waiting, a frown on her face. 'Jenny, what's up? Come on, spill.'

'Not on the phone. Let's talk over dinner.'

'Okay, give me time to change and I'll drive straight over. It started raining after you dropped me in town and I got a bit damp, mooching around the shops.' She peered out of the window at the dismal weather. 'Actually, it's raining again now. Such cheerful weather.'

'You can pack a bag while you're changing. Or two bags.' Jennifer paused. 'Sod it, bring the whole damn house.'

'What on earth are you talking about?'

Jennifer gave a weary moan. 'What does it sound like? I'm asking you to come and stay with me at Porro Park.'

'What? Why?'

'Just come, will you? I need you.'

'I can only stay a few days. I've got work on Monday. I have to be back home by then, because I'll be on call.'

'We'll talk about that, okay? Just be here for seven o'clock sharp. Brodie and Alex are cooking.'

'They're what?'

'It's Françoise's night off. She's gone to the Rebel Cinema with her girlfriend. You remember Marie?'

'Of course I remember her. But why are the men cooking? Why not send out for pizza or something?'

'It's a bonding ritual. Or an apology. I'm not sure which.'

Caroline blinked. 'You're not making any sense.'

'Look, I have to go. Alex is shouting something about anchovies.' Jennifer paused. 'Please come. I need to talk to you.'

'About what?'

'You'll see,' her sister said mysteriously.

Caroline ended the call, and went back to unpacking her shopping. But her brain was whirring feverishly. She was so distracted that she barely noticed the music had switched off next door, and she could hear shouting instead. More arguing, no doubt. At least she'd get to escape it for a few hours. Or even longer, perhaps. Until Monday, potentially.

Pack a bag while you're changing. Or two bags.

Jennifer was behaving very oddly, she decided, and not just because she was in her first trimester, though that probably had some bearing on it. As for the guys cooking dinner tonight ... Well, even something inedible with anchovies at Porro Park was preferable to sitting down to a shop-made salad on her own. But what did Jennifer want to talk to her about? Something to do with the baby, perhaps.

She was just heading upstairs to change when her doorbell rang.

It was her mother, clearly visible through the glass-panelled front door.

Topaz!

And behind her, both of them angry-looking and red-faced, were her next-door neighbours, Savannah and Malcolm.

The late afternoon was thick with dark, almost mauve rain clouds, dusk falling more rapidly than usual due to the unsettled weather. The sky had a malevolent feel to it, despite the street lamps that had only recently come on, misty halos about each one as the rain drizzled down.

'What on earth?' Caroline opened the door and stared at the three of them. 'Sorry, did I miss something?'

Topaz was looking unhappy, a flush in her cheeks. A wide-brimmed hat was squashed down over her blonde curls, so she wasn't as damp as the other two. 'Can I come in?'

'I suppose.' Caroline stood aside.

Topaz threw her a grateful look, wiping her feet on the doormat before sidling past into the warm interior.

'Is that your mother?' Savannah demanded in a shrill voice, arms folded across her black top, her green hair sparkling with raindrops, thick goth make-up starting to run.

Caroline looked from Topaz to Savannah, and then on to Malcolm, who was standing beside the teenager, his expression equally furious.

'Erm, probably.'

'What do you mean, *probably*? She's either your mother or she isn't.' Malcolm shook his head in disbelief. He was wearing a T-shirt, despite the rain, perhaps to show off his bulging biceps covered in lurid tattoos. They were certainly impressive. 'What kind of answer is that?'

'Whoever the bloody hell she is,' Savannah said sharply, 'she owes us a fibreglass Bast.'

Caroline blinked. 'A what?'

'My decking ornament.' Savannah's eyes flashed. 'A four-foot fibreglass statue of the Egyptian cat goddess, Bast. It cost Malcolm seventy-five quid. That woman kicked it with her great big hobnail boots and now it's broken.'

Bemused, Caroline looked round at Topaz, who shrugged and shook her head, as though disavowing all knowledge of the breakage. She was still wearing the red Doc Martens though. Not hobnail, but certainly sturdy enough to do serious damage to any fibreglass ornaments in her way.

'I don't understand,' Caroline began, but Malcolm interrupted her.

'It's simple.' He pointed past her at Topaz, who had removed her hat and was sitting on her sofa, looking agitated. 'That woman, who claims to be your mother, except apparently you're not sure if she is, came banging on our front door a few minutes ago, ordering us to turn our music down, because it was driving *you* mad.'

Caroline's eyes widened in shock. Speechless, she looked round at Topaz again. During lunch, she'd mentioned in passing where she lived, and described her annoying neighbours with their loud music and constant arguing. But she'd never dreamt that Topaz would turn up on the doorstep a few hours later and start sorting out her private life.

How embarrassing!

But she wasn't about to let Savannah and Malcolm bully her mother. Especially as she was secretly glad that some-one had finally told them to their faces how annoying and antisocial their behaviour was. She just wished that person hadn't been Topaz. Or that she hadn't seemingly destroyed an expensive ornamental cat in the process.

'Well, I didn't send her round to you,' she said. 'So you can stop yelling at me, for starters.'

'And our fibreglass cat?'

'Perhaps it was an accident. Have you considered that?'

She started trying to shut the door, and heard Malcolm shout, 'That's it, I'm calling the police!'

Furious now, Caroline yanked the door open again and stared at her neighbour with cold dislike. 'You do that. You call the police.'

'I bloody will!'

'And when they arrive, you can explain to them why I can smell marijuana from your place most evenings. Because it's not me smoking it, and I'm guessing it's not old Mrs O'Brien on the other side of me. Though you never know these days.' She clucked her tongue, pretending to be shocked. 'She's a lollipop lady too. I hope they don't mind her turning up to the school crossing every day, stoned out of her mind. What do you think?'

Malcolm said nothing, but glared back at her, clearly livid. Savannah swore under her breath, then grabbed her partner's muscular, tattooed arm and dragged him back next door.

'Forget it, Mal,' she said, throwing a last furious look back at Caroline. 'Stupid cow. Her and her mad old mum. They're not worth bothering about.'

Caroline shut the door and turned to face her mother, who had collapsed sideways on her sofa in an exhausted fashion and now looked as though she never planned to leave again. But she was wrong about that.

'Bravo!' Topaz said, abruptly sitting up and clapping her hands. 'Such nasty people.'

'Did you break their cat statue?'

'Yes, but not deliberately.' Topaz looked contrite. 'Honestly, the decking was wet and I slipped, and my foot just kind of caught it, accidentally, like you said. It must already have been cracked, because it disintegrated in front of my eyes. It really wasn't my fault at all.'

It was not hard to see why Topaz's relationship with Caroline's quiet-spoken, conservative father had broken up, despite the bond of having a child together. They must have been like chalk and cheese, she thought, wholly unsuited to each other.

'Thank you for trying to sort out my neighbour problem,' she said, and sat down opposite her. 'But I'm afraid you may have made things worse.'

'I'm so sorry, darling. I didn't mean for that to happen.'

Caroline smiled. 'I'm sure you didn't.'

'But you have a lovely house.' Topaz glanced about the room, which was rather spartanly furnished, adding politely, 'It looks easy to clean too.'

'You can't stay,' Caroline told her apologetically. 'I was just about to go out.'

'Oh no, must you?'

'My sister Jenny has asked me to visit her for a few days. At Porro Park, you remember?'

'That huge house out in the countryside? But how marvellous for you, darling.' Topaz took her hands. 'Well, in that case, you must go. Don't let me stop you. I think it's lovely that you're so close to your sister.'

'You do?'

'She's family, and family is important.' Topaz gave her a sad smile. 'I think we both learned that lesson the hard way.'

Caroline felt like crying. 'Yes.'

'So I'll get out of your way at once.' Topaz got up and went to the door, peering out at the rain. 'Now I know you're busy, I'll grab something to eat in town and go back to my friend's house instead.'

'You're sure?'

'Of course, darling. Don't bother your head about me.'

'We're going shopping in Boscastle soon, remember? I'll give you a ring to fix a date, like we arranged.' Caroline gave her a hug at the door. 'Thank you for trying to help with those idiots next door. But I doubt it will do any good.'

Even as she said that, the rave music started up again next door. Though it was noticeably reduced in volume now.

Topaz shook her head in disgust. 'You should call the council.'

'I already did. The council don't care. Not until it's been going on for years, and only so long as I keep a detailed record of every time they break the decibel level. And who does that?'

Topaz kissed her on each cheek, then settled her wide-brimmed hat back on her head and slipped reluctantly back out into the rain.

Her truck was parked a little down the road under a street lamp, a large hairy dog visible behind the wheel, rain glistening on the windscreen.

'Don't forget to ring me, darling,' Topaz called back over her shoulder, her voice wavering, as though worried Caroline wouldn't keep her word. 'I've only just found you again. I couldn't bear to lose you a second time.'

CHAPTER ELEVEN

'But how did she find out where you lived?' Jennifer asked Caroline, then smiled up at Brodie, who had brought in the coffee tray and was placing it on the sideboard. 'Thanks, you're a superstar.'

Ripper was curled up beside his mistress on the sofa opposite, purring deep in his throat. The night had grown stormy, and all the lights were on in the large living room at Porro Park, the burgundy floor-length curtains drawn across the windows to keep out the cold. It was a world away from her cramped and chilly tenancy in Pethporro, Caroline thought, kicking off her slippers with a sense of luxury and drawing her feet up on to the generous armchair.

Brodie smiled back at her. 'Fancy a cup, Jenny? It's a Brazilian blend.'

'Please.'

'Caroline?' he asked over his shoulder, pouring a cup of coffee for Jennifer and adding a dash of cream.

'Yes, thank you. It smells delicious. Black, no sugar.' Caroline turned back to her sister. 'I told her over lunch where

I lived, just in passing, but Topaz obviously took a note and decided to come calling afterwards.'

'That's kind of creepy.'

'Do you think so?' Caroline knitted her brow, considering it. Then she caught Brodie's careful gaze on her face, and found herself defending Topaz's behaviour, even though she'd been unsettled by her mother's appearance herself. 'I'm not sure. Perhaps she was worried our lunch would be a one-off, and thought turning up at my door would show how much she cares.'

'I suppose that's possible.' Jennifer sounded a little doubtful. 'But to go round and pick a fight with your *neighbours*? Smashing one of their garden ornaments . . . I know those two have been driving you crazy, but all the same, that's pretty extreme behaviour.'

'I have to admit, I was a little . . . shocked.'

'I've been thinking that maybe you should ring Dad anyway, even though I haven't told him about the baby yet.' Jennifer grimaced, stroking Ripper's head as the Siamese cat looked up at her adoringly. 'He'll flip when he finds out Topaz has resurfaced. Her name was barely mentioned when we were growing up, and when it was, Dad wasn't exactly complimentary about her.'

'We already discussed this. I don't want to spoil your good news.'

'I know,' Jennifer said slowly, 'that's why I've decided to see Mum and Dad as soon as possible. I miss them so much. We talked on the phone most weeks while I was in the States, but I haven't seen him and Mum in person since the wedding.'

'Well, that's easily fixed. We'll do what you suggested and take a drive up to St Ives one day, and pop into their new gallery. You and Alex can tell them about the baby, and then ... then I suppose I'll have to tell Dad about Topaz.'

'It doesn't sound like you're looking forward to that conversation.'

'I'm not.'

Her sister looked at her searchingly. 'And how do you feel about having your mum back in your life? Be honest.'

'I don't know. A bit off-balance, I guess.'

'I'm not surprised.' Jennifer gave her a sympathetic smile. 'And you're sure she's come back to get to know you again? Not for ... any other reason?'

Caroline wasn't sure how to answer that.

'Here, drink this.' With a dry smile, Brodie handed Caroline her coffee in a delicate white-and-gold china cup. 'Hope it's okay.'

'Thank you, it looks fine,' Caroline told him, turning back to her sister. 'What other reason could she possibly have to come back now?'

'Forget it, it's not important.' Jennifer shrugged casually, but Caroline wasn't deceived.

What was going on? She sensed Brodie hovering beside her chair, while Alex, previously stretched out on one of the other sofas for a rest, seemed to be listening intently to their conversation. Everyone's attention was centred on her, and it was making her feel uncomfortable.

'Be straight with me, would you? What are you saying?'

'Don't bite my head off,' her sister said, a flash of impatience in her face. 'I'm not alone in being worried about you, you know.' She nodded to Alex and Brodie. 'We're all concerned.'

'But what on earth for?'

'Okay, since you've asked . . . Don't you think it's a bit strange, Topaz suddenly deciding to come here to Porro Park in search of you?'

'It wasn't *sudden*. She saw an old celeb magazine feature about you and Alex getting married, and it mentioned me, and . . .' Caroline tailed off, aware of Alex's stillness and the knowing look in Brodie's face. 'What?'

Jennifer gave a frustrated groan. 'I knew you'd start getting defensive about this. But I'm just trying to look out for you. I want to be sure Topaz is on the level. That she isn't here because Alex is famous and wealthy, and she . . .'

'Is what?'

'Looking for a meal ticket.'

'For God's sake!'

'Caro, I've seen it before. It's stomach-turning. People are all over me at Hollywood parties, and not because I'm interesting in my own right. Simply because I married a celebrity.'

'Jenny,' Alex said warningly. 'We talked about this.'

'Fine,' Jennifer said hotly, glaring at her husband. 'I'm not saying that's definitely what she's up to. I'm just throwing out a possibility, that's all.' She reached across to touch Caroline's hand, her eyes shiny with unshed tears. 'Please don't get me wrong. I haven't met Topaz, so this is all conjecture. She's probably a really nice woman at heart, if a little eccentric in her behaviour. All I'm saying is, you need to be careful.'

Caroline was taken aback by the concern throbbing in her sister's voice. But Jennifer was brimful of hormones, of course, still adjusting to the strange new reality of being pregnant. And she had seen enough newly pregnant women come through her clinic to know how tough that transition could feel sometimes. It was a deeply emotional time, and for new fathers too.

'I am being careful,' she insisted. 'I'm listening to her and getting to know her. But that's as far as it will go until I've had a chance to talk to Dad face to face.'

'That's fine.' Jennifer sat back, smiling faintly. 'That's all I wanted to hear. And I'm sure when you tell Dad, he'll explain the difference between their two stories. Because there'll be a reason. Trust me.'

Caroline felt less sure, having believed Topaz implicitly when she told her tale of unhappiness and neglect. But Jennifer meant well, she knew that.

'Time to change the subject, perhaps,' Alex said softly.

'Good idea.' Caroline smiled at him gratefully. 'Now look, please don't think I'm ungrateful to you both for rescuing me from my noisy neighbours, but how long am I staying at Porro Park? I've got work on Monday, and it's a bit of a commute into town. Besides which, I'll be on call, which could mean leaving in the middle of the night sometimes. Babies do love to arrive at the most inconvenient moments.' She saw Jennifer's face change, and added hurriedly, 'I want to see you as often as possible while you're back in Pethporro. But after Monday, I'd be better off at home.'

'Caro, there's something I need to tell you,' Jennifer began hesitantly, then blurted out, 'I've changed my mind. Me and Alex . . . we're not going back to the States.'

'Sorry?' Caroline was astonished.

'I've decided to have this baby here, not in California.' Jennifer spoke lightly and quickly, as though afraid of interruption. 'I know it's going to be complicated. Alex will have to fly back to the States in the new year to get all our house packed up and sort things out there. He may even stay in Hollywood without me and do some filming. But I've made my mind up. I know it's early days, but I'm not leaving Cornwall again until after the baby is born.' She looked pleadingly at her sister. 'You don't think I'm making a mistake, do you?'

Caroline looked over her shoulder at Brodie, then hurriedly away. He was not looking surprised. No doubt they had already told him. But she could guess from his terse expression what he was thinking. That everything he'd worried about was coming true. This baby would change everything for Alex and Jennifer. Particularly for Alex, whose relaunched career was at stake.

'No,' Caroline told her, though deep down she was uncertain. 'I suppose not. If you're sure this is what you want. And that it's best for both of you.'

Jennifer sipped her coffee, looking uncomfortable. 'Is it for the best? For me, yes. Perhaps not for Alex.' She stared into her cup. 'I don't know; I can't think straight right now. It feels like I'm in a fog.'

'Pregnancy haze,' Caroline said promptly. 'It's very common. Down to hormonal changes, mainly. Though it doesn't usually set in until the second trimester.'

'See? You know about this stuff. Babies, trimesters, hormones.' Jennifer begged Caroline with her eyes. 'I *need* you.'

'You've got me. Until Monday, at any rate.'

'I don't mean just for a few days!' There was a note of panic in Jennifer's voice now. 'I need you here the whole time, Caro.'

'What?'

'I need you to keep an eye on me, make sure everything's okay with the pregnancy, and then see me through the birth itself.' Jennifer rolled her eyes. 'I'm not looking forward to *that*, I can tell you. Plus, I'll also need you on hand after the birth while I get used to being a new mum. Those first few months are going to be tough. I mean, there's nappies, and breastfeeding, and sleepless nights . . .' She gave a shaky laugh. 'Basically, you're the expert on all that, and I don't think I could cope without you by my side.'

Caroline was shocked. '*The whole time?* You mean, from now until after the birth? I'm sorry, but I can't do that. My job . . .'

'We'd pay you a monthly salary,' Jennifer said eagerly, putting down her coffee. 'Twice as much as you get for being a midwife. Three times as much, if you like. You'd live here for free, of course. Everything paid for, all your meals, electricity, internet. And you'd have plenty of time off to do your own thing. I wouldn't expect you to be here twenty-four seven.' She leant across and touched Caroline's hand. 'What do you say? Will you move in here with us and be my personal assistant-slash-midwife for the next year?'

'Jenny, be serious. Are you pulling my leg?'

'Three times pay, swear to God.'

Caroline felt like she was in a dream. Give up her job? Move into this rock star palace? Okay, Porro Park would be a fabulous place to live, with its huge grounds and its own gym and swimming pool, but the estate was also fortified against intruders, with high fences everywhere and a security patrol. And once the news of Jennifer's pregnancy got out, the media would go crazy. Did she really want to run the gauntlet of reporters every time she came and went?

Besides, she absolutely adored her work, looking after pregnant women and delivering their babies. It gave her life meaning.

Jennifer was still looking at her expectantly, her smile encouraging.

How could she turn her own sister down?

'I . . . I don't know what to say,' Caroline began, but was interrupted.

'Say yes.'

'But this is huge.'

'I know you love your job. But I really need you, Caro. And who knows? This could be a chance for you to slow down that mad pace you live at, and do something different with your life.' Jennifer smiled shyly. 'Plus, you'd get to spend more time with me, if that's not too horrific a thought.'

'I need to think about it.'

'Of course, there's no big hurry. Let's change the subject. You look like I've blown your mind.'

Caroline gave a shaky laugh. 'You have a bit.'

'Tell me more about this pregnancy haze. So, it's a hormonal thing?' Jennifer sat back, a hopeful light in her face. 'How long does it last?'

Slowly, they started to talk about pregnancy and babies again, as though nothing unusual had happened. But secretly, Caroline was still stunned. She couldn't get Jennifer's incredible offer out of her head. Give up her beloved job to look after only one pregnant woman? Move into Porro Park with them permanently?

She stole a quick look at Brodie, but his back was turned. She wondered briefly what Alex's PA thought of her living under the same roof, and then shook the question away.

What on earth did it matter what Brodie thought? This was between her and Jennifer and Alex, nobody else.

Struggling to suppress his feelings of frustration, Brodie bent to pour another cup of coffee, this time adding plenty of cream and one lump of sugar.

He hadn't known about Jennifer's startling plan to move her sister in with them at Porro Park. Not for anything up to a year, anyway. A few days' stay, he'd been told initially, during their 'council of war' before Caroline turned up tonight. Now it seemed she was to be a permanent fixture in their lives, assuming she accepted that very generous offer of three times her normal pay as a midwife. And who wouldn't?

Things were moving fast now that Jennifer was expecting a baby, he thought. Too fast for comfort.

Alex had crashed out on one of the other sofas, his feet up on the armrest, his black hoody pulled over his face in full teenager-mode. He often got like this when he was under stress, Brodie thought, and frowned as he set the sweet cup of coffee down next to him.

'Feeling rough?' he asked.

'You have no idea.' Alex tweaked the hoody to one side and peered up at him, bleary-eyed. 'Baby talk all last night. I barely got a wink of sleep. And then having to make polite conversation this afternoon with Jenny's ex . . .' He groaned. 'I'm exhausted.'

'You're sure this is the best thing to do for your career? Ground yourself here in Cornwall for the next twelve months?'

'I'm working on a plan, trust me,' Alex said mysteriously, and pulled the hoody across his face again. 'I'm going to make some phone calls. Set up some meetings. But first, I need a bit of shut-eye.' His voice was muffled. 'Sit down, have a coffee. Relax.'

Brodie straightened, his hands in his jeans pockets, and glanced about the room. The two women were still chatting. He didn't help himself to a cup of coffee. He didn't sit down. He was too restless.

He headed for the door, needing to do something to take

his mind off the situation. 'Caroline, do you need me to carry your bags up?'

She looked up at him blankly. 'My bags?'

'To your bedroom. I saw you'd left them in the hall.' Brodie could not read her expression. He could read most people like a book, but Caroline had an unfathomable quality that was quite baffling to him. Another source of frustration too. 'Françoise has gone out for the evening, but I made up one of the guest rooms for you. I hope it will be comfortable.'

'That's very kind of you.'

'Don't worry about it. It sounds like you've got your hands full at the moment.' He paused, then added nonchalantly, 'By the way, if you intend to meet your birth mother again, I can tag along if you like. Sounds like you could do with some back-up.'

Now Caroline was staring. 'Let me get this straight. You want to come with me next time I meet Topaz?'

'Only if you need some moral support.'

Jennifer was smiling, studying him with approval. 'That's an excellent suggestion, Brodie, thank you.' She reached across to touch Caroline's hand. 'I'd go with you myself, but you didn't want me there last time I tried to come along.'

'I'm sorry if that upset you. I just . . .' Caroline looked pained. 'I know you're suspicious of her, that's all.'

'Then take Brodie. At least you won't be alone with her.'

Caroline looked dubious. She darted a look at Brodie. 'Yes,' she said awkwardly. 'Okay, thanks.'

'Yes to me carrying your bags upstairs?' Brodie asked.

'Or yes to me tagging along next time you meet your birth mother?'

'Both, I suppose.' Caroline sat back and sipped at her black coffee as though the matter was now closed. A sensual look crossed her face, her lips turning up with sheer pleasure. 'Mmm, this Brazilian coffee is heavenly. Just what I needed after such a difficult day. Thank you, Brodie.'

Brodie cleared his throat, muttered something inane like, 'No problem,' and headed out to collect her bags.

He stood for a moment in the hall, staring down at her bags and suitcase. His heart was beating unusually fast, and he was finding it difficult to focus on the task in hand. He could not believe the sudden, fierce stab of sexual desire he'd felt just then, for a woman he barely knew.

That dreamy look on Caroline's face as she sipped her coffee . . .

It had been a long time since he'd felt anything even remotely resembling sexual desire. After the bombing, he'd been too intent on healing and getting used to walking with a prosthetic limb to think about relationships. Later, his fears over Alex's depression had taken precedence over his own concerns. But even once Alex had settled down happily with Jennifer, he had only met one woman who had interested him like that. And that woman had at first not been available, then had told him plainly she wasn't interested. So he had retreated into celibacy, and not been too bothered by it.

He was well aware that he was deliberately shying away from contact with women. There was always this fear at the back of his mind that no woman would find him attractive now. Ridiculous, he knew. Through support groups and during physical therapy, Brodie had met plenty of other amputees who were happily married or in fulfilling relationships.

But it was so long since he'd been to bed with anyone, he was unsure of his ability to act on that desire. After more than three years of monk-like living, he no longer dared put his masculinity to the test. Even though he despised himself for that refusal.

Grimacing, Brodie seized the suitcase, tucked one bag under his arm and scooped up the larger one, then made for the staircase.

He'd felt an intense attraction for Thelma at one stage, he remembered. Alex's sister had seemed so vulnerable and unhappy in her failing marriage, and something in him had responded to her wide-eyed desperation. But Thelma had fallen pregnant by her husband, and Brodie had hurriedly backed off.

It was only later that he realised how cleverly Thelma had manipulated his feelings, encouraging him while he was useful to her. She'd marked him out as an ex-military man, someone who could keep her estranged husband Stuart at bay, and then shooed him away without compunction as soon as she felt herself safe.

Caroline Enys was a very different proposition.

Tall, blonde, willowy, Caroline was superficially attractive in the same way as many of the models and film stars Alex had courted before falling for Jennifer. But underneath her cool, blonde looks was an earthy drive that excited him far more, and a practicality that Jennifer completely lacked. Caroline had a strong, independent spirit. She didn't need a man in her life, and she made that clear with every word she spoke. Yet the way she looked at him sometimes . . .

Brodie put the bags down in the guest bedroom and did a quick check to ensure the place was ready for her. He stuck his head round the door of the en-suite bathroom, but it looked spotless, soft white towels warming on the towel rail and a delicate fragrance about the place.

Back in the bedroom, he limped to the window and closed the curtains to shut out the wild and windy night.

If only he could shut out the clamouring of his own instincts as easily, he thought grimly. A woman like Caroline would expect him to be sexually active, to sleep with her if they dated. And he'd grown accustomed to celibacy. So bloody accustomed, he wasn't even sure it would be possible to break the habit.

Even looking twice at a woman like that could be dangerous. It would involve too much risk. For the sake of his sanity, he ought to steer clear of her. Except he had opened his mouth and invited himself along to meet her mother. Like the fool he was.

But he'd handled that godawful mess with Thelma.

He could handle this.

CHAPTER TWELVE

Driving home from work the following week, Caroline found herself turning into her old road in Pethporro in her tiredness, before suddenly remembering that she lived at her sister's house now.

'For goodness' sake . . .' she muttered under her breath before turning her hatchback slowly in the road, and heading out of town towards Porro Park instead.

Everything had been moving at lightning speed, Caroline thought, not entirely happy with the way her whole life had been derailed by her sister's pregnancy.

She'd given the local health authority a month's notice to quit her job, and although Jennifer had tried to persuade her otherwise, had insisted on working her notice. 'I want to be able to see my patients face to face,' she had explained. 'I need to tell them myself that I'm leaving, and introduce them to my replacement. Continuity of care is important during a pregnancy, and it wouldn't feel right to leave without a proper handover period.'

Her 'replacement' would probably be Martha, the other

midwife on call for Pethporro, at least until they'd hired someone new.

She'd also given notice to quit her rented house in town, and had even started packing up her things in the odd hours when she wasn't at work. The furniture had come with the house, so only her own possessions needed to go into boxes. Her bedroom at Porro Park was large and luxurious, but it wouldn't house all her accumulated stuff. However, Jennifer had allocated her a heated outbuilding as storage space for her packing boxes, and a date had been arranged for a removal firm to come round and collect it all.

Caroline hadn't seen Savannah and Malcolm, except very briefly in passing, but she wouldn't miss her neighbours from hell.

That was one blessing, at least.

And she'd arranged to meet her birth mother in Boscastle that weekend, and Brodie was insisting on going with her.

They would all be going to St Ives in December for Christmas drinks with Mum and Dad. Jennifer had arranged it over the phone one evening.

Caroline felt a little apprehensive about this Christmas meetup with their parents. Her father wouldn't be pleased that her mother had made contact after all these years, especially once he realised she had given a very different – and damning – account of their separation.

But perhaps when she'd spent a little more time with Topaz, she would feel happier talking to Dad about her.

But why did Brodie have to come along?

There was something about him that made her uneasy. And it was obvious he didn't like *her*. According to him, she was 'hard work' and 'self-obsessed'. That was what Brodie had told her, anyway.

Well, straight back at you, she thought crossly. With an attitude like that, he had no business being so tall and lean and sexy-looking. Not when he was always so aloof with everyone. Even when he smiled, the smile never reached his eyes. And he was forever watching people. Watching her, at any rate, with an unreadable expression. It was unnerving.

But work was so hectic that week, it wasn't until the weekend that she even had time to think about her trip to Boscastle.

Several women had gone into labour that week, including one of the clinic doctors, Amanda, who was expecting her third child and had opted for a water birth at home. But she was found to have a breech presentation, so ended up being rushed to hospital at Truro instead, with Caroline following as her friend as well as her midwife. It hadn't gone smoothly.

Being a doctor herself, Amanda had been horribly prickly about being examined and diagnosed by the consultant obstetrician, who'd dropped into the labour suite halfway through and insisted on an emergency C-section. It had taken the consultant's and Caroline's combined persuasive powers to get her to agree to the procedure, following which Baby Seamus had been born within half an hour, with no ill effects.

Once she was sure mother and baby were both doing fine, Caroline had driven home in a daze at about four o'clock in the morning, and fallen into bed without even taking her uniform off.

So, she'd reached Saturday, and her proposed trip to Boscastle with Topaz, having barely thought about it at all.

At ten forty-five on Saturday morning, Brodie was already sitting outside the house in the car, tapping gloved fingers on the wheel as he waited for her. He was looking very masculine in jeans and a deep blue fisherman's jumper under a black leather jacket. If only his personality could match his charismatic looks, she thought.

'Ready?' he asked unnecessarily as she climbed in beside him. His gaze moved over her outfit, long lashes hiding his expression, then he started the engine. 'You look very nice.'

She stared at him, surprised by the unexpected compliment. She had chosen a cream woollen dress with a coral cardigan and knee-length leather boots. Perfect for the chilly weather forecast for that weekend. 'Thank you,' she said, adding impulsively, 'So do you.'

Brodie shot her an ironic look, but said nothing.

So do you.

She wanted to curl up in embarrassment. And what had she meant by that, anyway? It wasn't as though she found him attractive. Not in that way, at any rate. She didn't want him to think she was making a pass, for God's sake.

To her relief, not much was said between them on the drive to Boscastle. She tried to relax, looking out at the damp green fields on either side, and the sea in the near-distance. It was still breezy, but the sky was brighter this morning, with cheering hints of sun peeking through fast-moving clouds. Perhaps her knee-length dress wouldn't be too cold after all.

'Do you miss California?' she asked impulsively.

'Not really.'

'What does that mean? I thought you were keen to get Alex back there,' she said, frowning. 'Back to Hollywood.'

'I'm keen to keep his career on track. Where he does it is less important. But Hollywood is the place to be when you work in films, there's no getting round that fact.'

'So you aren't pining for the West Coast?'

'This *is* the west coast.'

'Of America, not Cornwall.' She saw his grin, and said sharply, 'Oh, you know what I meant. Stop laughing at me.'

His smile vanished. 'I wasn't.'

'Do you think they'll miss being in the States if they stay here? Alex and Jenny, I mean.'

Brodie's face showed no change of expression, but his gloved hands tightened on the steering wheel. He looked out, studying the road ahead, the sky, the sea, the rolling Cornish hills, before answering.

'Not at first, perhaps. They're deeply in love, and so they want to be together, wherever that happens to be. But they may regret it later, when . . .' He stopped.

'When it's too late to change their minds?' she finished for him.

'If you like.'

Caroline played with the buttons on her cardigan and tried to imagine living anywhere else than rural Cornwall. She simply couldn't manage it. Perhaps she was too parochial, a country girl at heart. All she knew was that, although summer holidays somewhere hot and sunny were always welcome, she would never want to leave the Duchy. Not for good, at any rate.

Cornwall was where she had been born, and where she had always lived. Her parents might have moved further down the coast to St Ives, but she wasn't going anywhere. She belonged in Pethporro.

She'd always thought that Jennifer felt the same about the place. Until she'd met and married Alex, she'd been a deep-rooted Pethporro native, pale and unusual, an eccentric dresser, steeped in local folklore and traditions. Now her sister was smoothly tanned and more smartly dressed than Caroline herself, a sophisticated West Coaster and soon-to-be mother, expecting Alex's child.

Love did funny things to people, she considered. Falling in love could change the habits of a lifetime almost overnight, and transform a person right to the core, leaving them barely recognisable.

It was dangerous stuff, love.

'I know a few people who could help you,' Brodie said unexpectedly. 'With your mother, I mean.'

'Sorry?'

'It might be a good idea to run a check on her background. Make sure she's who she says.'

'Good God, seriously?' Caroline stared at him. 'Topaz is my birth mother. Not a serial killer.'

'How do you know?'

An image popped inadvertently into her head, of Topaz smiling as she described how she'd 'accidentally' smashed her neighbours' garden ornament to pieces.

'Don't be ridiculous,' she said, but her voice lacked conviction.

'I can make a few phone calls. Get you a full history on Topaz. Including any criminal convictions.'

Criminal convictions?

'That's a bit extreme, isn't it? The woman's completely harmless. Just a little unconventional, that's all.'

'Is that why you wanted me to come with you today? Because she's completely harmless?'

Caroline was speechless for a moment, not knowing how to answer that without admitting her insecurity about Topaz. Her immediate impulse was to reject any suggestion her mother might have an ulterior motive for getting to know her again. But deep down, she was beginning to worry that something wasn't quite right. The way Topaz had tracked her down at home had been unnerving, especially when she blew up at her noisy neighbours in such an exaggerated fashion.

But perhaps what the two of them really needed was time. Time to get properly acquainted, perhaps even become friends.

Until then, any suspicions she might harbour about Topaz's authenticity had to be pushed aside. She needed to look at her mother with kinder eyes, not start questioning her actions.

Realising that Brodie was still waiting for an answer, she said, 'Thanks for the offer, but I don't need you to investigate my mother, okay? Your company is appreciated though.'

'Fine.'

There was a wealth of sinister meaning in that one word, she thought, trying to read his face. But he was otherwise occupied now, slowing to a crawl as they entered the harbour town of Boscastle. There were plenty of visitors milling about the narrow streets, peering into shop windows strung with fairy lights and tinsel, and occasionally plunging into the road with their shopping bags, seemingly oblivious to passing traffic.

Brodie headed for the car park beside the river and found a parking space someone had just vacated.

'Ready?' he said, turning off the engine.

'Of course.' Caroline checked her make-up and tidied her hair in the sun visor pull-down mirror. She was looking pale, she thought. But it was winter, and she'd been working hard lately. 'It's only Christmas shopping. Not murder and mayhem.'

The ghost of a smile flickered on his lips. 'Empty shopping bags are in the back,' was all he said though. 'Remember the environment.'

They made their way along the main shopping street

past quaint shops and cafés, all cheerful and lit up with winking Christmas lights.

Topaz was waiting for them on the bridge. She waved as soon as she saw them, calling out, 'Over here, darling!'

People's heads turned among the shoppers, and Caroline sucked in her breath, trying not to cringe.

Topaz certainly had unusual dress sense, she thought, and even more so than Jennifer in her witchy phase. Today, she was wearing multicoloured harem-style trousers with a baggy black jumper, a woollen hat dragged down over her blonde curls, red Doc Martens still on her feet. Her earrings, she realised, were tiny Christmas trees.

She ran across the road ahead of Brodie, and hugged her mother. 'Good to see you again, Topaz. I love your earrings. Very festive!'

'Thank you,' Topaz said, beaming. She turned to Brodie. 'I remember you. The gatekeeper.' Her gaze dropped to his legs. 'You're limping. You were limping the other day too. Have you hurt your leg?'

Brodie looked at her steadily. 'No.'

'What is it, then?'

'None of your business,' he said curtly.

Topaz blinked. 'Sorry, I'm sure. I was only trying to make conversation.'

'Shall we shop first or go for lunch?' Caroline looped her arm through her mother's as she tried to change the subject. 'Which do you prefer?' She flashed Brodie an apologetic look while Topaz was looking the other way, and mouthed, 'Sorry,' with a quick grimace.

He didn't respond, his face grim and shuttered.

But while they went round the Boscastle shops before lunch, admiring all the beautiful gifts through the windows or going inside charming boutiques to see their Christmas goods close-up, she noticed how Brodie stuck close and was constantly looking around as though to check who else was nearby. She even spotted him checking out the restaurant interior, as though scanning for possible assailants, before they went inside for lunch.

Brodie was *shadowing* her, Caroline realised, like a proper bodyguard would. Which was ridiculous. She wasn't even remotely important. Why on earth would someone like her need protecting while out Christmas shopping? He was probably just used to protecting Alex everywhere they went, she decided, and now couldn't get out of the habit.

He certainly took himself very seriously.

Too seriously.

'I'll sit against the wall,' he said abruptly as Topaz tried to take that seat, and snatched the chair away before she could sit on it.

'You're not very polite, are you?' Topaz told him icily, but he ignored her. She made a face at him and then sat next to Caroline instead, asking in a piercing whisper, 'Is he your boyfriend, darling?'

Caroline saw his mouth twitch, and winced inwardly. 'No, Brodie's just . . . a friend.'

'Good, because otherwise I would have advised you to dump him. He doesn't appear to have any manners at all.'

Feeling decidedly awkward, Caroline tried to lighten the mood by listing the Christmas gifts she had bought for Alex and Jennifer, and for some of her colleagues at work. Only then did she realise that she had several bags under the table, and Topaz had none, except her handbag.

'You didn't buy anything?' she asked, curious.

'I didn't see anything I liked,' Topaz replied with a casual shrug, and reached for a menu. 'Maybe I'll find something worth buying after lunch.'

They ate a festive lunch of turkey and roasties together, making light conversation while Brodie – who had refused any food – stared stonily out at the street, sitting bolt upright as though expecting the SAS to come charging in at any moment, guns blazing.

He was making Caroline uncomfortable.

Having finished their coffee and mince pies, they decided to take one more look about the shops. The waitress brought the bill on a small platter, and Brodie took some notes out of his wallet to pay for his drink, with a little extra as a service tip, placing them on the platter too.

There was a difficult moment as Topaz looked at the bill with a distracted air. Hurriedly, Caroline told her not to worry about the cost of the meal, and looked round to summon the waitress over with the card machine. It was quite expensive but nothing she couldn't handle. Especially now that she would no longer be paying rent after this month.

Topaz shook her head at once, looking almost cross. 'Of

course I must pay my share. Don't be silly, darling.' But, rummaging about in her shoulder bag for her purse, she gave a cry of dismay.

Brodie's head turned towards her. 'What is it?' he said sharply.

'My purse,' she said, her eyes wide. 'It's gone!'

CHAPTER THIRTEEN

That's a lie, Brodie thought instinctively, looking into those panicked blue eyes. As with much of what she'd said during the course of the meal, even in casual conversation, she wasn't telling them the truth. Topaz hadn't lost her purse. In fact, he was willing to bet she hadn't even brought it with her today, or if she had, it had been left deliberately in the car. He'd not once seen her take a purse out of her handbag the whole time they'd been out together shopping, and her odd excuse of not having seen anything worth buying had sounded a little thin to his ears.

But why pretend?

It didn't make much sense, unless Topaz was broke and too embarrassed to admit it. Though Caroline would happily have paid for lunch if that were the case. She was obviously very keen to make friends with her estranged mother.

No, there was something else going on here. He didn't know what. But he was suspicious.

Brodie had long ago learned to trust his gut about people, as it invariably turned out to be right. And his gut was telling him Topaz was trouble: serious, deep-down trouble, the kind that could be difficult to get rid of once entrenched in your life.

But if the woman genuinely was Caroline's mother, there wasn't much he could do to prevent that relationship. Nor was it any of his business, of course.

But that didn't mean he needed to fall for her lies.

The problem was, he'd met women like Topaz before. Several were high-powered film executives, others well-known actresses, while most were obsessive fans who made Alex's life a misery from time to time, constantly leaving messages or unwanted gifts for him, or spreading malicious gossip about him on social media simply because he'd failed to acknowledge a tweet, or something similarly petty. And they had their male counterparts too. Men who were born narcissists or control freaks, or who enjoyed tormenting people for the sheer pleasure of watching them react in shock or dismay.

'Where did you last see it?' he asked her crisply. 'Did you use it to pay for anything in the shops?'

Topaz ignored him, head bent as she hunted through her red leather shoulder bag. It was an old handbag, well-creased and a bit tatty. But it was clear there wasn't much inside it.

'How awful for you.' Caroline was looking concerned. She did not seem to think there was anything wrong. But then, this was her mother; she was bound to trust her. 'What does it look like?'

'Erm, it's red. Red leather. To match this bag.'

Caroline peered under the table, moving the shopping bags with her foot. 'I don't see anything red down here. Brodie, can you see it?'

Topaz glared at them both. 'I haven't dropped it!'

'Sorry, of course not. I just thought—'

'I need to get back to Pethporro. To my friend's house. Right away.' Topaz jumped up so abruptly that she knocked her chair backwards, which narrowly missed another diner as it fell. The man behind stared round in astonishment, but she paid him no attention, seemingly oblivious to what had happened. 'I need to block all my cards and report this to the police.'

'Please wait before you do that,' Caroline said, also getting up in a hurry. 'Brodie's right. You need to think when you last took it out of your bag. Maybe you left it beside a till somewhere. The shop owners are very honest here; I'm sure they'd keep any lost purses behind the till in case someone returns for them. Let's retrace our steps.'

'No, no . . . I can't think straight.' Topaz shook her head vehemently, a high flush in her cheeks. 'I must go home.'

'That's okay, I remember perfectly which shops we went into,' Caroline said helpfully. 'Come on, let's walk back along the street and ask in each shop if a purse has been found or handed in. If we find it, you won't need to report it missing.'

'But—'

'Honestly, this will only take fifteen minutes and could save you tons of bother. Afterwards, if we don't find it, I'll help you ring the card helplines myself.' Caroline was good at handling difficult people, Brodie thought, watching her link arms with her mother, her voice calm and level. 'Now, which shop did we go in last?' She pointed through the restaurant window. 'The little gift shop with all the crystalware, wasn't it? Let's start there.'

Topaz made a face, her lips pursed, her shoulder bag clamped tightly to her body, but did not resist.

Before they set off, Caroline looked back at Brodie over her shoulder. 'Sorry about this. Can you wait? We won't be long, I'm sure.'

'I'll pay for the meal,' he told her, straightening the fallen chair with a quick apology to the diners at the next table, 'and carry your shopping back to the car. Then I'll come and find you.'

'Thank you,' she said, and steered her mother out of the door.

The waitress came over, staring after the two women with a worried expression. 'Is everything all right?'

'Fine,' he said coolly, giving nothing away, and got out his wallet again. 'I'll be paying by card, if you have a machine.'

Once he'd paid for their meal and put the bags in the back of the car, Brodie walked back towards the shops, grimacing a little. His leg had started troubling him, his limp more pronounced than usual. And he had a good hunch why. It was ridiculous to let someone like Topaz upset him, but he couldn't help it. On the bridge earlier, she'd made him deeply uncomfortable about his prosthesis in front of

Caroline, and her words had been irking him throughout the meal.

Some people could be insensitive about disabilities, as he knew only too well; he usually dismissed such idiots with a shrug. But he'd got the distinct impression earlier that Topaz had said those things deliberately, as though intending to humiliate him in front of her daughter, while pretending to be innocently unaware.

It had not been a pleasant moment.

Plus, he'd been wearing the prosthesis since before breakfast now, and after sitting for long periods of time – in the car, and again at lunch – it had begun to feel almost painful. He usually grabbed a few hours during the day to remove it and stretch out on his bed or the sofa for a quick rest.

But since Caroline had moved into Porro Park with them, he had been keeping his prosthetic limb on longer than usual, and even sometimes wearing trousers about the house instead of shorts. Jennifer and Alex were used to seeing him without the leg, of course, since he always took it off to swim, and he felt no embarrassment with them. But although Caroline knew about his missing lower limb, and had seen him in shorts before, somehow he still felt awkward about it.

Fool, he told himself.

He caught up with them both near the National Trust shop, alongside the river. They came out, Caroline still holding Topaz's arm, but with an odd expression on her face.

'No joy?' he asked.

'Nobody's seen her purse,' Caroline told him flatly. 'I think that's the last shop we went into. So unless someone's stolen it, or she dropped it out here . . .'

'I shall have to report the cards as missing,' Topaz said, glaring up and down the road as though suspecting every other Christmas shopper of being a thief. 'I had cash in my purse too. Quite a bit of it. Now I've got nothing. Whatever shall I do?'

'I can lend you some cash.' Caroline pulled her own purse out of her bag and opened it. 'How much do you need?'

'Oh, I couldn't possibly—'

'How much?'

Topaz turned to her with a fond smile. 'You're such a sweetheart. But please, you mustn't worry. I'll manage somehow. I always do.'

'I have fifty pounds. Here, take it.'

'Oh no, no.'

'You can let me have it back when this is sorted out. Come on, I insist.' Caroline handed her some folded notes, then took her phone out too. 'Now, do you know the number to call to report your bank and credit cards missing? I can look it up if you like.'

'I won't report them yet. I have the numbers back at my friend's house. I'll drive back and sort it out there.'

'Honestly, it's no trouble.' Caroline was still holding out her phone.

Brodie cleared his throat and said, 'Topaz, at the very least, you should let your bank know straight away. Then you won't be liable for any fraudulent use.'

Topaz looked irritated by his interference. Her blue eyes flicked to Brodie and then away, as though dismissing him as irrelevant, just as she had done on the bridge earlier.

'I'd much rather wait until I'm somewhere comfortable. I hate making phone calls. Especially nasty ones like that.' There was a slight tremor in her voice now, giving the impression of vulnerability. 'Thank you so much for that loan, Caroline. I'll let you have it back as soon as I possibly can.'

'There's no hurry.'

'What a marvellous person you are.' Topaz's mouth trembled; it looked almost as though she might cry. 'I've really enjoyed today. I knew we would get on well together, mother and daughter. Maybe we could see each other again soon?'

Caroline hesitated a microsecond. 'I'd like that, yes.'

'Darling girl!'

Topaz gave her a hug, and then air-kissed her noisily on each cheek, not quite making contact. Pulling down her woollen cap, she swung her bag over her shoulder in a determined fashion and thrust a hand deep into one of the copious pockets of her multicoloured trousers.

'Perhaps I could come and see you at Porro Park next time? I'd love so much to meet Jennifer. She sounds like the perfect sister.' Her smile looked fake, Brodie thought. Too fixed, as though it had been painted on. 'And Alex too, of course. I haven't seen any of his films. But I bet he's lovely too.'

'That may not be possible,' Brodie told her. 'Jennifer and Alex guard their privacy very carefully.'

'Oh nonsense, I'm family. I'm sure that doesn't apply to me.' Topaz was still smiling, but the look she gave him was venomous. 'You'll talk to them on my behalf, won't you, Caroline?'

Caroline blinked. 'Erm, I can try.'

'Thank you, I knew you wouldn't let me down. We've been parted all these years, but we won't let anyone come between us again, will we?'

With that, Topaz blew her daughter another kiss and strode off down the street in the direction of the car park.

Caroline watched her go, her face carefully blank, not meeting his eyes. Once Topaz was out of sight though, she groaned and sagged against the wall of the National Trust building.

'I'm so sorry,' she said, covering her eyes.

'Sorry?' He frowned. 'For what?'

'About my mother. What she said about ...' Caroline hesitated, dropping her hand to glance at him uncertainly. 'About your leg. The way you walk. I'm really sorry, I feel awful.'

Brodie felt sick inside and didn't know what to say.

The way you walk.

He knew she meant well, but wished she hadn't mentioned it again. That had been an uncomfortable moment, yes, but he'd got through it. As usual, he'd pretended not to notice or care. Neither of which was true.

But it helped him cope, pushing painful thoughts aside and focusing instead on what was next, on what he could still change in his life.

Not what he couldn't change.

Caroline gave an abrupt little gasp and stalked away,

back along the river towards the harbour. Her head was thrown back, blonde hair lifting on the breeze as she strode out in her high-heeled, knee-length boots.

He watched her go, and felt that curious stab of desire again. Which was insane. Caroline Enys wasn't his type. Not that he had a type, any more. It had been so long. But back in the day, he would probably have been drawn to someone a lot more dramatic and showy. Someone like Thelma, in fact. Someone who was exotic and wild, someone who presented him with a real challenge, someone who was hard to handle.

Though he'd told Caroline exactly that, hadn't he?

You're pretty hard work, Caroline. Did anyone ever tell you that?

The realisation shocked him. Jennifer's sister was attractive enough, even sexy in her way. But she wasn't glamorous and ostentatious like Thelma. Yet she was equally difficult, if not more so, catching a man unawares with her independence and her fiery tongue.

Still frowning, Brodie caught up with her, matching her pace despite the pain in his leg. 'Where are you going now?'

She turned to glare at him, rubbing at her cheeks, and Brodie was bewildered to see that she'd been crying, her face blotchy, eyes wet with tears.

'Caroline, what on earth's wrong?' he demanded, hating to see her so upset. 'Is there something I can do to help?'

'What you said before, about making some phone calls and investigating Topaz ... Were you serious? Can you really do that?'

He nodded, waiting.

'Then please, make the calls.' Caroline put a hand to her mouth, looking shaky. 'I want to trust Topaz, I really do. But there's something off about this whole situation.'

'I agree,' he said promptly. 'But why not simply ask your dad about her? You could phone him right now.'

Caroline shook her head vehemently. 'I don't want to spoil Jenny's news. Not before she's had a chance to tell him in person about the baby.'

'I think Jennifer would understand.' He frowned when she hesitated. 'Your sister certainly wouldn't want to see you so unhappy.'

'Oh God, I don't know what to do.'

'Then you should do whatever feels right.' Brodie shoved his hands into his jacket pockets, resisting the urge to make some kind of comforting gesture. He badly wanted to touch her, to give her a hug. But he feared she might take it the wrong way. 'I'll make those calls for you, don't worry. But your dad ought to know what's going on. Right now he doesn't have a clue that Topaz is back in your life. It's only fair you tell him.'

She looked at him, clearly torn. Then pulled out her phone again and found her dad's number. 'I shouldn't be doing this,' she whispered, putting the phone to her ear as it began to ring.

He heard her father answer, his voice cheerful, presumably having seen his daughter's name flash up on his phone screen.

'Hi Dad,' she said into the phone with what he suspected

was forced cheeriness. 'Yes, I know. It's been too long since I called.' Caroline gave a wan smile. 'And yes, I'm looking forward to seeing you and Mum too. Jenny's arranging the whole thing. We're coming to see you at the gallery, then having lunch out in St Ives.' She nodded, listening to him talk on the other end. 'I can't wait either.'

Brodie took a few steps away as the conversation continued, not wanting to intrude on such a personal call, but reluctant to move too far. She might feel he was abandoning her.

'Look, Dad,' she said at last, 'I've got something to tell you. Something you might not like.' He heard the nervousness in her voice. 'It's about . . . Topaz.'

CHAPTER FOURTEEN

Brodie frowned. 'You want to start your own film company?'

'That's my plan, yes.' Alex paced restlessly about his study, hands clasped behind his back. 'It will be based initially here at Porro Park, but with the potential for expansion to other locations within Cornwall once we're up and running. We'll need to start work straight away on converting some of the outbuildings into studios for filming, sound and post-production.' He stopped to gaze out of the window, as though imagining how the place would look once Porro Park had been converted to a film studio. 'I'll put in most of the capital required for the start-up myself, with help from a few good friends. But beyond that we'll need proper investment, which will take a lot of hard work and persuasion.'

'Good God, you're serious.'

Alex stopped pacing at last and turned, winter sunlight hitting the side of his face. His study overlooked the lawn, stately beech trees reaching towards the sky in the background.

His look pierced Brodie's skull, or so it felt.

'Of course I'm serious. Jenny isn't planning to return to the States, and I'm certainly not leaving her to have this baby alone, so here we are, grounded in Cornwall for maybe the next year. This is me making the best of a bad job. Or maybe,' Alex added, running a hand over his face, 'this is me doing something I've always secretly wanted, moving past being an actor to running the whole show. Yes, it's a challenge, and yes, we might lose our shirts.' His smile was lopsided. 'But hell, I'm willing to give it a shot.'

'And you want me to come in with you on this project?'

'Not investment, I know that's not going to be your strength. But I'd like to shift your duties from personal assistant to admin and logistics,' Alex said, watching him intently. 'Basically, I need you to sort out the basics while I'm wooing investors. Find out what else is going on film-wise in Cornwall, check out the buildings we have on site, get quotes on conversion costs, and look out for any other good locations.'

'It would be good to have somewhere nearer the A30.' That was the main route into Cornwall from the rest of the country; having a studio in mid-Cornwall would make transport quicker and easier, especially for those who were London-based. Their current location was too far north and west to be close to any transport hubs. 'Maybe some-where on Bodmin Moor?'

'Atmospheric.' Alex nodded. 'I like that idea.'

'I'll look into it.'

'Though don't forget the airport at Newquay. And we could get a new helicopter if you think it's worth it.'

Brodie made a quick note.

'I'll get on to these straight away.'

'Thanks, Brodie, I really appreciate it.' Alex met his gaze, a guilty look about him. 'I know this isn't what you signed up to.'

'Yes, where are the beach beauties I was promised ... Bodyguard to a film star, you said first. Then I ended up handling phone calls and making dinner reservations. Then house-hunting for you. Now this ...' Brodie grinned to show he was only joking. 'It's a real education, working for Alex Delgardo.'

'Hey, if you want a pay raise—'

'Can you afford one?'

'Probably not,' Alex admitted, grimacing at the reminder that he could be materially damaging his career with this sideways move. 'Look, once things start happening, if you want to take an active role in sourcing scripts, actors, locations, maybe even producing your own film one day, I'm happy to facilitate that. But only if film-making is something that genuinely interests you. I want you fully on board, not just tagging along for the ride.'

Brodie, who had been standing beside Alex's mahogany, leather-covered desk, straight-backed as a soldier on parade, relaxed his stance somewhat.

He was tempted by the idea of getting involved in films himself. Not as an actor, of course. He didn't have any talents in that line. But he'd often watched Alex while he was filming, and had privately thought he could do a better job than some of the producers and directors he'd seen. But thinking and doing were two different things.

Could he really make such a bold leap?

'You seem to have put an incredible amount of thought into this project,' he said, intrigued. 'When exactly did you come up with the idea?'

Alex's mouth quirked in a smile. 'A few years back, when I first bought Porro Park to be nearer my grandmother.' He fell silent for a moment, perhaps remembering Nelly and her eccentric, vivacious personality, and then sighed. 'But after she got sick, I put it aside. It would have taken too much hard work, and Nan needed me on hand daily. But I still had some of the numbers sketched out on paper. So when Jenny told me she was expecting a baby, and it became clear we wouldn't be heading back to Hollywood any time soon, I reactivated the idea.'

'Who have you called so far?'

'There's a list on the desk. Actors, directors, producers, sound and camera people, plus some heavyweight inves-tors. Not all of them on this side of the Atlantic. I've put ticks next to the ones who've said they're interested, and crossed out anyone who gave me a flat no. The others either haven't been contacted yet or are still thinking about it.'

'Well,' Brodie said, frowning as he picked up the list, 'it looks like this is really happening.' He read through some of the names, his brows raised. 'John said yes? You're kidding!'

'I know!' Alex gave a short bark of laughter. 'And after I was so rude about his last film, too.'

Chuckling, Brodie studied the list properly. There were some impressive names with ticks beside them. People willing to invest in their venture, either financially or by providing their talents. So they were definitely staying in Cornwall, and not just that, but starting a film company here. And he was being offered a chance to do something in films, rather than always being on the periphery, a mere observer.

It would be exciting to take this project on.

A challenge.

Plus, there were other, more personal things to consider. He and Alex were close, of course; they'd been friends for years, ever since they'd met and served together in the army. But Alex was his boss too. This new venture might help to even things out between them.

'Listen, Brodie, if you really feel this is something you can get behind,' Alex said abruptly, 'then I'd want you to come in as a director of the company with Jennifer and me.'

Brodie stared at his old friend, emotion churning inside him. Exhilaration, he decided. With a touch of fear, only kept at bay by an upsurge in adrenalin. He'd experienced the combination before, mostly in combat situations. But also when he'd managed his first few steps with his prosthetic limb.

'A director?'

'Sure, why not? The three of us, working together as a team.' Alex was smiling, hugely confident, as always. Yet he was fidgeting slightly, one foot tapping, arms folded tightly across his chest. His whole posture betrayed his uncertainty. It was clear the success of this project meant a great deal to him, as did Brodie's involvement. 'I think we'd be unstoppable. Don't you?'

Brodie put down the list. 'Okay, Alex,' he said with a grin, 'you've sold me. Where do I sign?'

CHAPTER FIFTEEN

'Are you sure you'll be warm enough in that outfit?' Caroline asked, pulling her own jacket tight with a grimace as she got out of the car.

Her sister's designer jeans and boots were perfect for walking, she thought, and that pink beret looked very snug indeed. But her elegant cashmere sweater was on the thin side.

Though if the paparazzi spotted them, at least Jennifer wouldn't have to worry about her appearance. Unlike Caroline, who had not thought to bring any headgear on this spontaneous expedition, and whose hair was already whisking about her face in disarray.

'Warm enough for a quick ten-minute walk on the beach,' Jennifer insisted, locking the car. 'So you can stop fussing.'

'I thought that was why you wanted me around? To fuss over you?'

'I've got Alex when I want someone to tell me off for not wearing a coat in these Cornish winds. You're here so I can be sure the baby's growing properly and I'm eating the right diet.'

'You hardly need me around twenty-four seven for that.'

'Maybe not.' Jennifer grinned and took her arm, pulling her close as they began to cross the rocky sands together. 'But it's more fun with you here. Alex is too busy right now to keep me company, and let's face it, now that I've married a celeb, I can hardly go out and join a knitting club. Someone from the press would be bound to find out, and they'd pursue me relentlessly.'

'I suppose you're right.'

It was late afternoon, within about half an hour of sunset, and there was hardly anybody else on Pethporro beach. A few people walking their dogs, that was all, plus one middle-aged woman jogging steadily along, listening to her headphones. The winter sun dipping low on the horizon cast an orange hue over the beach and rocky cliffs at that end of the bay, and would have made everything feel almost summery if it hadn't been for a sharp wind blowing in off the sea.

The rush and drag of the tide over sandy shingle grew louder as they made for the water's edge, its lacy fringe delicate and frothy, always running just ahead of the glittering shallows.

'Isn't this gorgeous?' Jennifer stopped and faced the sunset to the west. She inhaled the tangy salt air, a dreamy look on her upturned face. 'I missed this place so much when I was in California. The weather there is incredible, of course. Every day is a beach day. But the light here in Pethporro ... the crisp cold of a Cornish winter's day ... Some days out there I woke up to blue skies and dazzling heat, and just wished I could be back home instead.'

Caroline, who held Cornwall dear to her heart, could quite understand her nostalgia. She had to agree, Pethporro beach was a beautiful place. Still, she'd often walked along the sands here on her own during Jennifer's long absence, staring out to sea and wondering if she'd made the right choices in life.

Despite youthful dreams of travelling the world, she had chosen to never leave the quiet Cornish backwater where she'd grown up. She wasn't unhappy in Pethporro, of course. But was it possible she might have been happier somewhere else? She'd often wondered if there was something missing in her life, in a vague, low-level way. Leaving her job and moving into Porro Park with her sister had brought that feeling into sharp relief, she realised.

'Well, next time, I'll go to Hollywood and you can stay here. We have rain too, remember. Lots of it. I bet you didn't miss that.'

'I did, actually. I love rainy days in Cornwall. I love everything about this place. It's my home.' Jennifer closed her eyes, sighing. 'It will always be my home.'

'I'm glad to hear it.' Belatedly, Caroline remembered a lecture she'd intended to give her sister this morning. 'Though about last night, staying up past midnight to look at the stars with Alex—'

'It was incredibly romantic. There's hardly any pollution here, so you can see the night sky clearly. Venus was as big as my thumb.' Jennifer held up her thumb to the sky, and then laughed. 'Well, you know what I mean.'

'But you need to stop with the late nights. Now you've got a passenger on board, a good night's sleep is really important.'

Jennifer made a face. 'Oh, that.'

'Hey, watch out,' Caroline warned her, disentangling her arm a little too late. 'The tide—'

'Oops!'

Her sister jumped back as the foaming sea sloshed over her boots, but only laughed, even though the expensive leather looked soaked through.

'Perhaps we'd better head back,' Caroline said.

'Not a chance, sis.' Jennifer captured her arm again, dragging her close, and they continued to walk slowly along the water's edge together, this time keeping a good distance from the frothing tide. 'Not until you've told me what Dad said on the phone.'

'Oh.' Caroline looked out to sea, suddenly nervous.

'You didn't tell him about the baby?'

'Of course not.'

'Okay.' Jennifer peered into her face. 'So come on, what did he say about Topaz? Did he admit to having had an affair, or did he deny it?'

She had told Jennifer about her meet-up with Topaz soon after returning from Boscastle, plus the lost purse and the loan of fifty pounds, and the subsequent call to their father. But she hadn't elaborated on what Dad had said about Topaz, as it had all felt too raw at the time.

Now Jennifer wanted answers. And she couldn't blame her.

'He refused to talk about it,' Caroline said unhappily.

'He did *what*?'

'I told him everything Topaz had said. Even about the affair. Though it was so embarrassing, I could scarcely get the words out.'

'I bet.'

'First, he went very quiet. I actually thought he'd hung up. Then he said he needed some time to think about it.'

Jennifer came to a halt again, shock in her face. 'What is there to think about, for God's sake? Either he had an affair or he didn't. It's a simple binary choice.'

'I know.'

'You didn't press him for an answer?'

'Of course not.'

Jennifer shook her head, as though disapproving. 'I would have done,' she said starkly, and started walking again. 'So, how much time does he need to take? When's he going to ring you back?'

'He isn't.'

'Are you serious?'

'He wants to talk to me about it in person,' Caroline explained carefully, and steered her sister back up the beach again. The setting sun had almost vanished now, and the wind off the sea was decidedly chilly. 'When we all meet up in St Ives for lunch, probably. I guess he doesn't feel comfortable having that kind of conversation over the phone.'

'Hmm.' Jennifer mulled it over for a moment, then shrugged. 'I suppose that's wise. On the phone, you never quite know who's listening. And besides, some things should only be said face to face, if possible. That's why I want to tell them about the pregnancy in person. So I can see their faces. Enjoy the moment.'

'I'm sorry, this can't be much fun for you. Your big moment.'

'No, it's fine.' Jennifer gave her arm a squeeze. 'This thing with Topaz needs to be sorted out, and I know how difficult it's been for you. But maybe you should talk to Dad about her after we've had lunch, rather than before.' She grimaced. 'In case it all blows up in our faces, and we end up having chips on the beach at St Ives instead.'

Caroline smiled, though it wasn't that funny. She still recalled the shiver that had gone through her when her dad went silent on the phone. Her birth mother had always seemed like a taboo subject when she was young. Anyway, it had felt really uncomfortable, talking to him about her.

'I won't bring it up,' she promised. 'I'll let him choose the moment.'

'That's a good idea.' Jennifer frowned, nodding up the beach in surprise. 'Who on earth is that? Some woman waving at us . . . And is that her dog?'

Caroline followed her stare and froze. 'Oh my God.'

'What's the matter? Who is it?'

The huge, hairy dog bounding excitably towards them across the sands was Bouncer, her mother's dog. And a few hundred yards behind him . . .

'It's her,' she said hoarsely, her eyes on a woman in lurid

pink jogging bottoms and matching hoody, zipped up against the wind off the Atlantic.

'Her?'

'My birth mother.'

Jennifer stared at the woman, her eyes widening. '*That* is Topaz?'

Topaz was waving now as she ran towards them, both arms above her head, shouting something across the wind-swept strand. Her blonde hair had been tied up in a ponytail, and there was a fluffy pink sweatband across her forehead.

Tongue lolling cheerfully, Bouncer reached them but did not stop, running in a wide looping circle about them, and then galloping back towards his mistress.

Caroline's heart began to thump. 'Please don't say anything to her, okay?'

She felt guilty, aware that her mother had tried ringing since the lunch in Boscastle and she had declined her calls. But only because she was still struggling to work things out in her head and wasn't sure what to say to her. She needed more time.

'Sorry? You want me to ignore her?'

'No, I mean, don't tell her about my phone call to Dad. The whole St Ives trip.'

'I wouldn't dream of it.'

'I don't want her to think I've been checking up on her story.'

'She must know you'll tell Dad sooner or later.'

'Of course, but . . . it's embarrassing, that's all.'

'I bet.' Jennifer lowered her voice. 'Odd-looking creature, isn't she? That pink sweatband is horrific. And what on earth is she shouting?'

They didn't have to wait long to find out.

'Darling!' Topaz came jogging up to them, smiling broadly at Caroline. 'What a surprise,' she said breathlessly. 'I've been trying to call you. Then I suddenly decided to go out jogging, and who do I see across the beach? My own daughter. Such a fabulous coincidence.' She gave Caroline a tight hug. 'It must be fate. The universe obviously wants us to be together.'

'It does seem so.' Caroline felt again the tug of longing in her heart. This was her mum, after all. 'How are you?'

'Oh, I'm marvellous. Couldn't be better, especially now I've caught up with you again.' Topaz turned her curious gaze on her sister. 'Hullo! It's Jenny, isn't it? I recognise you from your picture in the magazines ... I'm Topaz, Caroline's mother.' She stuck out her hand. 'How lovely to meet you at last!'

'You too.' Jenny shook her hand.

'You're every bit as stunning in real life. I hope you don't mind me saying so. I've read so much about you and your talented husband, I feel like we already know each other.' The dog reappeared, jumping up at Jenny with wet, sandy paws, and she broke off to reprimand him. 'Down, boy! Naughty dog. I'm sorry, he usually has better manners than that. I hope he hasn't dirtied your jeans.'

'Don't worry, I can put them in the wash,' Jennifer insisted, seemingly fascinated by Topaz. 'What a big dog.'

'Huge, isn't he? I couldn't survive without him, being on my own. He keeps me safe.' There was that sad note in her voice again. The vulnerability that Caroline had noticed before. Topaz turned to her wistfully. 'But enough about me. How are you, darling? I'm so glad I spotted you. Though you look pale. Are you unwell?'

Caroline shook her head. 'I'm fine. Just a bit cold.'

'Oh, you should try jogging. Keeps the blood pumping, whatever the weather. Look, about that money I owe you—'

'It doesn't matter.'

'Of course it matters.' Topaz drew a ten-pound note from a pocket in her jogging bottoms. 'Here, take this now, and I can give you the rest next time we meet. All my money's back at the place where I'm staying.'

'Where's that?' Jennifer asked quickly.

'Oh, just a friend's flat.' Topaz flapped a hand vaguely back towards the promenade with its row of quaint old fishermen's cottages, all whitewashed with blue-framed windows, such a draw for the tourists. 'It's up in Pethporro, near the centre of town.'

'Please, keep the money.' Caroline felt horribly embarrassed. 'I don't want it back.'

'Well, I'll keep it for now. But you will get it back, and that's a promise.' She gave Caroline a pleading look. 'I don't want to disturb your walk, darling, but . . . maybe we could all go for a coffee before you go back to Porro Park? There's still so much catching up to do.'

'I . . .' Caroline hesitated.

'I'd love to chat to Jenny about her husband too.' Topaz

adjusted her ponytail, her wide-eyed gaze flicking towards Jenny. 'Alex Delgardo. A film star. He sounds *fascinating*.'

Caroline was torn. She still wanted to get to know her mother properly, as she'd always dreamt of being able to do. And with Jennifer by her side, she would probably feel more relaxed.

But, at the same time, she badly needed to be sure she could trust Topaz, that what she'd told Caroline so far about why she'd left the family home was the truth. Caroline kept thinking back to how her father had fallen so ominously silent on the phone when she'd mentioned Topaz. Clearly, he had not wanted to discuss her real mother. Not even in passing. But did that demonstrate guilt or something else?

Then there was what Brodie had said, and Jennifer's gentle warnings . . .

Could they be right?

'I'm sorry, Topaz, but I think Caroline's busy today.' Jennifer gave an apologetic smile. 'Most of this week, in fact. We've got plans. But maybe some other time?'

Topaz looked past her at Caroline, as though hoping she would contradict her sister. 'Darling?'

Caroline licked her lips. 'Jenny's right, I'm afraid. We are kind of booked solid for the next week or so. The run up to Christmas, you know? Everything's manic at this time of year.'

She caught a deepening look of unhappiness in her mother's face, and instantly wished she could unsay that. But Jennifer had thrown her a lifeline. And a few days' grace might be enough to clear her mind.

'I'll ring you as soon as I'm free, I promise, and we can have coffee.' Caroline wrapped her arms tightly about herself, shivering in the wind blasting off the ocean. 'Assuming you're still in Pethporro, that is.'

'Oh, I'm not going anywhere,' Topaz said lightly. She turned to whistle for Bouncer, who had run halfway across the beach in pursuit of a smaller dog, and he came lolloping reluctantly back towards them. 'Don't worry about that, darling.'

CHAPTER SIXTEEN

Despite Brodie and Alex working hard to put their plans into action as swiftly as possible, more than a fortnight passed before things really began to move on the new film company, which, after some deliberation, had been christened Delgardo Films. But there was no doubt it was going to happen.

Alex took himself off to London to speak to some investors, and then to his bank, always with a lawyer in tow, and came back with official company documents to be signed by all three of them in the presence of a witness, and promises of investment steep enough to make Brodie whistle soundlessly.

Brodie found a rickety old farmhouse on the fringes of Bodmin Moor which would be fantastic for their purposes, he felt, once transformed into a working studio and film set.

It needed some serious renovations, but had three sizeable outbuildings and enough acreage for large-scale outdoor shoots. It was also far enough from other buildings and main roads to be almost completely silent, apart from the winds that tore across the moors in poor weather. Yet it was near enough to the A30 main route into Cornwall to make it easy to bus crews and actors on and off the set at speed.

Plus, the overseas owner had swiftly accepted their offer and was happy to exchange contracts immediately, as the place had already been standing empty for more than a year.

Jennifer seemed excited by the idea too, though she'd pointed out that she was pregnant and therefore would have to stop working at some stage, and also that she knew next to nothing about films and film-making in general.

'I could make lots of tea, I suppose,' she said, with a shrug. 'And tell folk tales between shoots to keep everyone happy.'

Jennifer was a professional storyteller and folklorist, among her other skills. Though she hadn't worked in that capacity since her marriage to Alex.

'I'm writing another book about Cornish magic,' was what Jennifer always said in response to queries about her work. And she did spend long hours in the small upstairs room she'd designated as her office now they were back in Cornwall, surrounded by books and odd items, like her old row of jars containing odd potions and spell ingredients. She claimed the newts' eyes were just lentils, but Brodie was never quite convinced, even after examining them close up . . .

'We'll bring in caterers for tea-making,' Alex reassured his wife. 'You're a sleeping partner. So you don't need to do anything at all if you don't want to.'

'But I do want to,' Jennifer insisted.

Alex smiled and kissed her, his arm around her waist. 'That's what I love about you. You always have to be involved.' He thought for a moment. 'Then you can do other things. There'll be plenty of work to go round, trust me. Maybe look at scripts that come in? Or fact-check. You're a great researcher.'

'I'll do whatever it takes to help you make this film company a success,' she said, and smiled fondly at her husband.

Brodie's phone went, and he excused himself, walking out of the room to answer it, having recognised the caller's name. 'Hey, Sean, how's it going?'

'Can you talk?'

He wandered casually into the atrium-style hallway, mobile to his ear, and stood looking out across the lawns to the nearby woods.

'Yeah, go ahead. What have you got for me?'

Pixie Cottage lay that way, the place Jennifer had been renting from the estate when she and Alex met; it was roughly a ten-minute walk from Porro Park and couldn't be seen through the trees, but it was frequently on Brodie's mind at the moment. The cottage was standing empty, and he'd been toying with the idea of jazzing it up to house visiting actors once the company was actively working on a film.

'You remember I've been looking into that background information for you?' Sean sounded cagey, obviously unwilling to say much down a phone line. Force of habit, probably. He was another ex-army pal, and had since moved on to work for the British government in some undisclosed capacity. 'Sorry it's taken so much time, but I've been working on another case. A politician and her husband.'

'Sounds fun.'

'You have no idea what some of these people get up to.'

'I can imagine.'

'I'm not sure you can. Not with these two.' Sean laughed. 'Look, Brodie, I'm about ready to send through my preliminary report. Email okay for you?'

'Is it bad?'

Sean hesitated. 'There's a criminal record.'

Brodie froze, still staring across at the darkening woodlands. It was getting on for late afternoon and dusk was swiftly approaching, the temperature dropping as the light thickened and grew dim.

'What kind?'

'Fraud. And one count of assault. Nothing more serious than that. But it makes lurid reading.' Sean cleared his throat. 'What's this about, anyway? You said it was for a friend. Or was that a euphemism?'

'Not entirely,' Brodie said, dropping his voice and checking over his shoulder as he heard footsteps up above. Sure enough, Caroline was standing at the top of the stairs, looking down at him. He turned back to his surveyance of the lawn. 'Sorry, I have to go. Email it to me, would you?'

'No problem.'

'Will there be more?'

'I always do a follow-up. Besides, not all the info has come in yet.'

'Well, don't forget to attach the invoice.'

'About that,' Sean said hurriedly, a cheeky note in his voice. 'You said there might be a Christmas party down there in Cornwall. Is that still going ahead?'

'It might be.'

Alex had in fact set a date for a Christmas party only a few days before, but they were waiting to see if his sister Thelma, who lived in London, and Jennifer's parents in St Ives could make that date before going ahead with the final arrangements. No doubt he would also be inviting people who had expressed an interest in Delgardo Films or were actively investing in the project. Alex never missed a trick when it came to wooing the right people, and Porro Park's unusual architecture and attractive grounds, with the silver-blue ocean as its backdrop, made it the perfect venue to highlight Cornwall as a world-class location for making films.

'I never met Alex Delgardo when we were in the army. It's on my bucket list. Wrangle me a party invite and you can forget the invoice.'

'Okay, you're on.' Brodie grinned and quickly ended the call, aware of Caroline behind him.

She was wearing her blue, knee-length uniform. It was tight-fitting, he couldn't help noticing. He tried not to stare, but not even her plain black shoes could detract from the power of that uniform to raise his blood pressure.

'Sorry, did I disturb you?' she asked, both arms raised as she twirled her blonde hair into a short ponytail.

Brodie counted mentally to five before answering, the

temptation to say, 'Yes,' almost too much to resist. 'Not at all,' he said smoothly. He looked her up and down, and then glanced at the car keys in her hand. 'I thought you were having dinner with us tonight. I take it you've been called out instead?'

'Yes, better give my apologies to Françoise. Tell her to pop dinner in the fridge for me and I'll reheat it when I get home. It's not a problem, I'm used to missing meals in this job.'

She didn't look as reluctant to be heading out on a call as she was making out, he thought. But she loved her work, that was obvious. Brodie wondered how she would cope once Jennifer was her only patient. Would she get bored? It seemed likely.

'It was supposed to be my evening off,' Caroline continued, dragging on a deep blue overcoat to protect against the cold weather. They were almost into December now, and although Cornwall was quite mild compared to the rest of the country, the frequent rain showers this past week had turned increasingly icy. 'I think they're making the most of me while they still have me. Anyway, it can't be helped. One of my ladies has gone into labour slightly prematurely. Shouldn't be too tough, except Baby wasn't in quite the right position last time I checked her.'

'That sounds tricky. I hope it goes well.'

'Thank you.' Caroline headed for the front door, her shoes loud on the marbled flooring. Before she got there, she stopped and said over her shoulder, 'Any news from that friend of yours, by the way?'

'Sorry?'

'You said you knew someone who could find things out about my mother. That you'd contact them.'

'I've received nothing back yet. I'll let you know.'

Caroline walked out without further comment, and soon he heard her car start up and spin away over the gravel drive.

Brodie closed his eyes, disappointed in himself. Why had he lied to her in that ridiculous way? Why hadn't he told her what Sean had discovered?

It wasn't a complete lie, of course. He hadn't read Sean's email yet. But he did know there was something unpleasant in Topaz's past. A criminal record, Sean had said. She'd been found guilty of fraud. Assault too, which was worrying. And that was only the preliminary report. What else might his friend yet uncover about Caroline's birth mother?

He'd lied to protect her from getting hurt. Which was pointless, because she'd have to learn the truth about her mother's past sooner or later. Regardless of how much pain it caused.

CHAPTER SEVENTEEN

'Now, remember, don't push yet,' Caroline said calmly, and gave Simone an encouraging smile over the edge of the birthing pool that was currently the centrepiece of the accountant's living room, sofa pushed up against the wall and plastic matting down to contain floods and spills. 'You could tear if you push too soon, and we don't want that, do we?'

Simone panted in an exaggerated manner, rolling her eyes in Caroline's direction. 'But . . . I need . . . to push!'

'It's hard, I know,' she said soothingly, 'but try to resist the urge. You're doing great. Only a few more minutes and you'll be holding your baby.'

A phone rang shrilly over the calming whale music that Simone had chosen to accompany her birth.

'Oops, sorry, that's mine.' Caroline glanced at Simone's partner, Edward, who was looking anxious, and nodded for him to take her place beside the paddling pool. 'I'd better take it outside. Keep panting, Simone, quick and shallow breaths, to stop yourself from pushing. That's the way.' She slipped her shoes back on, grabbed her jacket, with the phone in its pocket, and made a dash for the back door. 'Back soon, won't be a jiffy.'

It was nearly midnight, she realised. Outside, the air was sharp and cold. She stamped her feet to keep warm.

'Hello, Pammy?' She had seen the caller display and felt her heart sink. Not another premature labour, surely? 'What can I do for you?'

'I'm sorry to ring so late, Caroline,' a deep voice said, definitely not Pammy's voice but her partner's, Tobias. 'But Pammy's been having pains all day. We put it down to indigestion at first. I mean, she's not due for another three and a half weeks. But they're getting stronger and closer together, and she's in a fair bit of discomfort.' He paused. 'What should we do?'

'Right, erm . . . Let me think.'

Caroline closed her eyes, pushing away her nagging fatigue to focus on this new problem.

Last time she'd checked, Pammy's baby had been breech. But often babies moved around into the correct head-down position in the last stages of pregnancy, so she hadn't got to the point yet where she was worried. But if she'd gone into early labour with Baby in the wrong place, that could mean a trip to hospital instead of a home delivery.

'I'll call in as soon as I can. Do you think Pammy can hang on a little longer for an examination? Maybe as long as another couple of hours?' She hesitated. 'Or I could ask Martha to check in on you. It's her day off, but she is on call.'

'No, no, we'll wait for you.' She could hear the smile in Tobias' voice. 'Pammy likes you best out of the team. As do

I, of course. We were both sad to hear you'd be leaving soon, and worried in case you left before James arrived.'

A couple in their late thirties, they knew from tests which sex their baby was, and had already picked out James for his name, which had been Pammy's late father's name. Tobias was a calm, smiling man, but Pammy, who was a drama teacher, was a little highly strung, and this was their first child.

'Thank you, that's very kind of you both.' Caroline checked her watch again, making a mental note of the time. 'I should be with you by two o'clock, at a guess. If her pains subside before then, or if they get substantially worse, give me another call, okay?'

Ringing off, she took a moment to get herself composed again, then went back inside, smiling broadly as though the call had been nothing to worry about. There was no hurrying a labour, and she didn't want Simone's birthing experience to be marred by knowing another woman needed Caroline's help as soon as she was finished.

'Everything okay?' Edward asked, his shirt front soaked from leaning over the paddling pool to hold Simone's hand.

'Perfect.' Caroline knelt on the other side of the paddling pool and smiled warmly at Simone, who was looking tense and wild-eyed. This was her second child, but her first had been born seven years ago, so it had taken her a while to feel confident about giving birth again. 'Shall we check Baby's position again, see if you're ready to push yet?'

'I'm ready now,' Simone muttered through gritted teeth.

A little over an hour later, with baby Amelia weighed and wrapped up in a blanket in her mother's arms, little woollen cap keeping her head warm, Caroline bid the couple goodnight and headed out into the dark. It had been quite an easy delivery, all things considered, and she was satisfied that Amelia was healthy and breathing normally, no undue signs of stress from labour. But then, she'd observed that water-birth babies often seemed calmer than those born under the harsher lights of a hospital labour room, however much they installed dimmer switches and provided 'normal' beds rather than trolley beds, or birthing balls and other calming equipment.

The ground was frosty underfoot, her breath steaming, and the night sky was a dark, velvety blue-black, studded with creamy whirls of tiny stars, far enough from any sources of pollution to be crystal clear. One of the perks of living in rural Cornwall, she thought happily, gazing up at the heavens. And little baby Amelia had been born under those stars tonight . . .

But there was still another potential baby alert on her patch tonight, so no time to delay. Caroline unlocked her hatchback and threw her delivery kitbag in the back seat, then hurriedly jumped inside. She was already shivering in the chilly air after hours spent in the warmth of Simone and Edward's very comfortable home.

But when she turned the key in the ignition, nothing happened.

'What the hell . . . ?'

She tried again. Still nothing.

Caroline exhaled and counted silently to ten. Then she gave her biggest, brightest smile to nobody in particular. The stars above, perhaps. Or the universe in general. 'Come on, come on, come on,' she said out loud.

Then she turned the key for a third time.

Nothing.

The car was dead.

She groaned under her breath, then gave all the usual spot checks a cursory run-through. Could she have flooded the engine? Unlikely; she hadn't even heard it turn over the first time. Had she run out of fuel? But no, she'd only filled up the tank a day before. Which, with her limited experience with car maintenance, only left the battery.

Had she left the lights on in her hurry to get inside to examine Simone? But that was a no, too. Everything was turned off, or seemed to be.

She glanced back at the house. But she couldn't ask Edward for a lift to the next patient. He needed to be with his wife and child.

She toyed with her mobile, not sure what to do. She would ordinarily call for back-up. But Martha was the only other team member on call tonight, and was probably fast asleep, and in any case she would be at her boyfriend's house tonight in Launceston, a good hour's drive away. There was no way she would be troubling an ambulance for this, either. Not unless she got there and found it was a real emergency, of course. That would change matters.

Hurriedly, she found the local taxi firm number. Pethporro

had two firms, but one only worked the summer season. So it was George's Taxis she rang.

'Sorry, love,' George's wife mumbled, half-asleep, 'you've just missed him. He's on his way back with a fare from Newquay Airport. One of the night staff whose car broke down.'

'I know the feeling,' Caroline said, making a face.

'Can you wait an hour?'

'I'm afraid not. Don't worry, I'll find someone.'

She rang off and sat with her head bowed, feeling exhausted. She could ring Jennifer, she thought. But she had only recently instructed her pregnant sister to go to bed earlier and get more sleep, for the baby's sake. It would then be pretty rich to disturb her at this time of night, asking for a lift . . .

So her sister was out of the question.

There was Alex, of course.

'Oh, good idea,' she told herself sarcastically, disturbing the silence, 'call up a global film star in the middle of the night and ask him to come and chauffeur you around, like he has nothing better to do. How to be the world's most annoying sister-in-law.'

That only left one person to ring.

Caroline groaned.

Grimacing, she found Brodie's number.

The last person she wanted to see right now was Brodie. There was something about the man these days that made her nerves jangle and her skin grow hot, as though he naturally gave off some low-level vibration that messed with her body chemistry. Yet he was also probably the only person she could ask for help in this situation.

He answered almost immediately with an abrupt, 'Brodie here,' sounding wide awake. Her eyebrows shot up. Did the man never sleep?

'I'm really sorry to disturb you,' Caroline faltered.

'I wasn't asleep. What's wrong?'

Embarrassed, she explained the situation as succinctly as she could, half expecting him to sound annoyed when he realised he would need to get up and traipse out into the cold night to rescue her. But again, to her surprise, there was no emotion in his voice. Just a matter-of-factness that she found deeply reassuring. Not that she would ever have told him that.

'What's the postcode? I'll be there as soon as I can.'

'Thank you,' she said, and gave him the details, then ended the call and sat waiting. She rang Tobias with a few words of reassurance, asking for an update on Pammy's condition.

'Her waters broke a few minutes ago, and her contractions are definitely closer together than they were an hour ago.' His normally placid voice sounded a little ruffled now. 'I was just mopping up when you called.' Tobias paused. 'Are you on your way?'

Caroline stared out at the darkness, trying not to let frustration get the better of her. If Pammy's waters had broken and her contractions were increasing, labour was well and truly underway. With a first baby, the birth itself might not happen until much later in the day. But she couldn't count on that, especially now the waters had broken. Sometimes a first baby could surprise everyone by arriving at top speed.

'I'll be there as soon as I can, Tobias. Try not to worry. How is Pammy coping?'

'She's not,' he said flatly. 'She's stressing out.'

'Try to keep her calm, and remind her the waiting's nearly over. She'll soon have lovely James in her arms.'

That usually worked.

She decided not to mention her transport issues. The poor man already had his hands full with Pammy; he certainly didn't need something else to worry about. She just hoped that Brodie would be able to find her. He might have the postcode, but Edward and Simone lived in the middle of nowhere, their road part of a bewildering network of single-track lanes with high hedges that all looked the same, especially in the dark. One error could cost a driver precious minutes just finding somewhere to turn around and go back.

But to her surprise, Brodie pulled up beside her in the Land Rover less than twenty minutes later, looking dark and forbidding in a roll-neck black sweater and leather jacket. He must have been fully dressed, she thought, staring. She could not believe he'd had time to change out of pyjamas as well as navigate here through unfamiliar territory.

Still, he had been in the army for a number of years. That might account for his almost ruthless efficiency at practically everything.

Caroline grabbed her delivery kit from the back seat and locked her car. 'I've got the satnav coordinates for the address,' she told him, climbing in beside him. 'I'll key them in while you turn round. We need to be on the main road back towards Pethporro. I could shout out directions, but I've only been there a couple of times myself and I'm already running late, so it's probably safer to let the satnav get us there.'

'Not a problem,' he said, meeting her eyes briefly before backing up and turning around in the tight space.

Once the satnav was guiding them to their destination, Caroline said, 'Thank you for coming out. Especially in the middle of the night.'

'Happy to help.'

'Well, it's still very good of you.' She felt flustered, which was ridiculous, and put it down to simple fatigue. It had been a long night, and promised to be even longer. 'I tried calling the Pethporro taxi firm, but—'

'There's no need to explain, Caroline. You needed a lift. I wasn't doing anything in particular. So here I am.'

Curious, she looked at his profile in the faint light from the headlights ahead. She was weary, she knew. Her back ached from leaning over the birthing pool for hours, and there was a faint ringing in her ears. Though she knew a strong cup of coffee and a burst of adrenalin when she reached her next patient would soon get her moving again.

Brodie didn't look tired, she thought, studying him with a tiny touch of resentment. On the contrary, he looked perfectly alert, his voice crisp, his movements decisive.

Was he made of steel?

'You hadn't gone to bed, then?' She checked her watch, incredulous. 'It's nearly two o'clock.'

'I'm a night owl,' he said tersely.

'Me too, in general.' Caroline had been slumped in the passenger seat, yawning under cover of darkness, but she sat up straight when his head turned towards her. She shook off her heavy-lidded tiredness, trying to gather her thoughts and sound coherent. 'Though part of that is training. I need to be able to stay up all night in this job. Babies don't appear on a nine-to-five schedule.'

'It was the same in the army. Years of unsociable hours and night-time manoeuvres. That can be a hard habit to unpick when you get back to civvie street.'

'Civvie street?' she queried, then realised in the same breath what he meant. 'Being out of the army, in other words?'

'That's right.' Brodie shrugged, gripping the steering wheel with gloved hands as he slowed for a left-hand turn at the invitation of the satnav. 'On top of that, when we were out in Los Angeles and Hollywood, there were so many parties and night shoots, sometimes I didn't get to bed at all. Even now, I'm still partly in that time zone mentally. I find it hard to go to sleep at a normal time, so I often sit up late and read, listen to music, maybe watch a film.' He glanced at her wryly. 'Or drive Cornish midwives about the countryside, hunting for babies to deliver.'

Caroline laughed, genuinely amused, and looked sideways at him again. Against her will, she was feeling a strange kinship with him. Maybe it was just the late hour, or her weariness, but she had suddenly realised he was okay company. More than okay, if she was honest.

And yet she knew Brodie still disapproved of her sister's pregnancy, and as someone who spent every day talking to women about babies, she couldn't find it in herself to forgive that. Jennifer might be a film star's wife, with all the complications that brought, but she was also a normal woman, and she didn't need to hear disapproval from anyone about this baby; what Jennifer needed was love and support.

Besides, Caroline was uncomfortably aware that a certain attraction for Brodie had started to work its way into her thought processes.

He was a damn sexy man, she could no longer deny that, try as she might. There was an air of mystery about him too, which she found irresistible. But he had issues, that was also clear. And she had issues too. One of which was the need to avoid the complication of a relationship for as long as possible.

Perhaps even forever.

She used to love dating, trying different types of boyfriends almost at random as though looking for the best fit, but rarely sticking with any one man for longer than a few weeks. Commitment was highly overrated, in her view. If her mum and dad's relationship was anything to go by, a long-term relationship only led to boredom and arguments over who should take the bins out. To avoid that dreary fate, she had quite deliberately avoided dating anyone who might potentially be a keeper. Jennifer had mocked her in the past for a string of one-night stands or short-term affairs that she'd nearly always ended herself, swiftly bored by Jack or Ben or Grant, or whichever boyfriend was on speed-dial that month.

Yet, for some reason, she hadn't thought about asking anyone out for ages. And indeed hadn't accepted any invitations either, though there had been a few interested parties. Especially as they rocked towards the festive season, when there were always parties in and around Pethporro, and plenty of fish willing to be dragged out of the sea for a passionate kiss or two under the mistletoe, only to be thrown back the next day without regret.

'Stop there,' she said suddenly, pointing ahead to the detached bungalow decked out in flashing Christmas lights, complete with Santa climbing a ladder up the house wall and a group of reindeer with glowing red noses in the front garden. 'This is the place.'

Obediently, Brodie slowed to a crawl and parked parallel to the herd of glowing reindeer. 'I'll wait for you,' he said, eyeing the flashing decorations dubiously.

'No,' she insisted, gathering her bag and delivery kit together. 'Thank you, but you should go home now. Get some sleep. This could take hours. Anyway, I can call a taxi afterwards.' He looked at her stubbornly, as though about to refuse, and she sighed. 'Okay, I'll ring you when I'm finished. How's that?'

She watched him drive away, vaguely aware of Tobias opening the front door behind her, light streaming out across the dark lawn.

She had to shake off this feeling, Caroline told herself firmly. Work had been her priority for years now, and she had no intention of changing. She was still getting to know her real mother – though Topaz's odd behaviour disturbed her at times, it was true – and supporting Jennifer in her pregnancy. There was no room for anything else in her life right now. So this prickling awareness of Brodie Mattieson was far from welcome and could simply get lost.

'Right,' she told the father-to-be cheerfully, charging up the garden path towards Tobias with a fresh burst of energy, 'let's see how Pammy is getting on, shall we?'

CHAPTER EIGHTEEN

Caroline finished work the following week, and woke up the morning after her big leaving party with a throbbing hangover and a feeling of unease. Too much pink gin and not enough tonic, she thought, sitting up and blearily picking the remains of blue streamers out of her hair. That had been one hell of a party! She had a vague memory of drunkenly kissing several of the doctors, and possibly even Martha, perhaps by accident, perhaps deliberately. And now it felt as though someone had bashed the back of her skull with a mallet while she was sleeping.

Groping in her bedside drawer for some fast-acting headache pills, Caroline popped two out of the packet and downed them with last night's still-full glass of water that she'd been too squiffy to drink.

So she'd left her job. What now? she kept thinking.

But her aching brain was empty of ideas, and she couldn't seem to come up with any answers. Or not any that immediately made sense. Her future was a tangle of vague possibilities and maybes.

One simple fact kept her sane.

She could still return to work as a midwife once Jennifer's baby had been born and the first few postnatal months successfully navigated. This didn't have to spell the end of her career as a midwife.

At the same time, though, this could be the moment to look at what else was out there for her. Yes, Caroline would miss the glow of expectant mothers and that breathless anticipation that always accompanied labour and birth, whether at home or in the hospital delivery suite. But perhaps something new would eventually take their place.

There was a knock at her bedroom door.

Caroline staggered off the bed, and dragged on a dressing gown. Her head was thudding violently and she felt a bit queasy. 'Erm, come in,' she called out in a wavering voice, hoping to goodness it wasn't Brodie. 'It's not locked.'

It was Jennifer. 'Good grief, you look dreadful.'

'Thanks.' But Caroline peered at herself in the mirror opposite, and realised her sister was right. She hadn't removed her make-up last night before collapsing into bed – she hadn't committed that sin since her teenage years – and she looked a fright. 'I was just about to jump in the shower.'

'Once you've done that, come downstairs for a pick-me-up. We've got lots to talk about.' Jennifer grinned at her expression. 'First day of your new job!'

'Right.'

'Hey, don't sound too keen, will you?'

'Sorry, I've got the mother of all hangovers. Don't mind me.' She suddenly realised her sister was clutching a letter. 'What's that?'

Jennifer grinned. 'A new ultrasound scan date.' She hadn't been feeling well on the date of her first scan appointment, so had decided to cancel it and had been waiting impatiently for a new date ever since. 'It's next Tuesday afternoon.'

'At last!'

'Will you come with me and Alex?'

'Are you kidding? Of course I'll be there. I'm your doula, aren't I?'

'My what?'

'Your doula. That's a birth assistant who sort of becomes your best friend during your pregnancy too.' Caroline groaned, her head thumping horribly again. 'By the way, did we ever discuss working hours? Or days off?' Caroline shot her sister a crafty look, wondering how far she could push it. 'Apart from the scan appointment, maybe I could start working for you after Christmas? I'm feeling a bit delicate right now.'

'And whose fault is that?'

Caroline threw a pillow at her, and her sister ducked, laughing.

'Seriously though,' Jennifer added, 'you should do that. It would be good for you to have a few weeks to yourself. Plus, you could get some proper Christmas shopping done without rushing round the shops last minute like you do most years.'

Surprised, Caroline blinked. 'Thanks.'

That was easy, she thought.

'You can start the new job in the new year,' Jennifer said cheerily. 'That makes sense. But I still need to talk to you about something special.' She gave her a mysterious smile, the one that meant trouble and usually ended up with Caroline being forced into doing something she had absolutely no desire to do. 'Come downstairs when you're ready, okay?'

Once she'd left, Caroline headed into her gorgeous en-suite bathroom, moving very slowly as though afraid bits of her might fall off if she hurried. She soon felt better under the sting of blissfully hot needles in the power shower, washing all traces of last night's streamers and debauchery out of her hair. But her mind was ticking.

What was Jennifer up to now?

As she crossed the landing to head downstairs, she saw Brodie's bedroom door open, on the other side of the large staircase. It was all quiet, so she tiptoed across, unable to resist a peek inside his room. It was rather utilitarian, with just a bed, a desk and a wardrobe, and plenty of space to move around between them. And a second doorway stood open into his en suite, which looked very clean too, all white-and-grey marbled tiles.

All the bedrooms at Porro Park – and she had counted at least seven of them, though there could be more – seemed to have en-suite bathrooms, so that it felt almost like a hotel at times. Though distinctly more comfortable, of course. It was an old manor house, set in long-established gardens, but Jenny said the shell had been modernised by Alex during his extensive renovations, with the huge glass atrium installed downstairs and all the bedrooms completely stripped out and redecorated, some of the smaller rooms being knocked together for more space. That was when he'd also added the gym and an indoor heated swimming pool, of course. Alex Delgardo wasn't a man to do things by halves.

The large double bed had been made since its occupant had got out of it, she noticed. It had a smooth, dove-grey bedspread with a dark oak headboard and a lush green watercolour of a Cornish landscape hanging above it. On the desk under the window, which faced the moody-looking woods, was his laptop and various documents, all neatly arranged, nothing out of place.

The bedroom of a perfectionist, she thought, gently backing out.

'Can I help you?'

She spun on her heel in the doorway, ludicrously guilty. It was Brodie, of course. And though he made no accusation, his raised eyebrow showed her exactly what he thought of guests who snuck about, peering into other people's bedrooms while they were absent.

'I'm sorry, the door was open—' She hurried away, not meeting his gaze. 'Jenny needs to see me downstairs. Catch you later.'

In the kitchen, she found the radio on and Jennifer poring over paperwork on the large pine table while Françoise mooched about in Crocs, emptying the dishwasher and whistling along to jaunty Christmas tunes. The French housekeeper glanced at her curiously, but as usual didn't say much, except 'Bonjour,' to which Caroline replied with a grim, 'Good morning.'

'Shall I turn the music down?' Jennifer asked, her lips twitching at Caroline's look of dismay.

'No, it's great. I love Christmas music.' But her expression betrayed her. Bad enough to be suffering from a hangover without having just made a fool of herself in front of Brodie, by nosing about in his room. 'I'll have my breakfast in the other room, if it's all the same to you.'

To the sound of Jennifer's laughter, Caroline trod gingerly through to the breakfast room, thankful to find a fairly hot pot of tea still on the table, along with croissants and pastries. Not that she was hungry, but it might settle her stomach to eat something.

Pushing Brodie and his raised eyebrow firmly from her thoughts, she stared out of the window. It was a cold, bright December day outside, and she could see Ripper stalking some unfortunate creature hidden in the undergrowth on the other side of the back lawn. She wondered how drama teacher Pammy and her husband Tobias were getting on with their newborn son, who had arrived in a perfectly ordinary way after all her fears about the baby's position. She'd called in on them just before the end of her notice, to check on Baby James' progress one last time, and been brought to tears when they gave her a leather-bound edition of *The Complete Works of Shakespeare* for having looked after Pammy 'so brilliantly', as Tobias put it.

She would miss her lovely patients, and particularly miss meeting the babies who were still in their mothers' wombs, the unborn children whose galloping heartbeats she had listened to and whose growth she had monitored all these months. Someone would deliver those babies safely into the world, she was sure. But it would not be her.

Caroline stared blindly out of the breakfast room window without reaching for anything to eat or drink, a sad and wistful ache in her heart.

A few minutes later, Françoise came in carrying a toast rack full of fresh toast and took the teapot away to refresh it. Just as Caroline was finishing her second slice of toast and marmalade, Jennifer came in and sat opposite her, that mysterious smile back on her face.

'What are you doing on Friday?' her sister asked.

'Nuttin,' Caroline mumbled indistinctly through a mouthful of toast, and hurriedly swallowed before taking a sip of tea. 'Why do you ask?'

'I've arranged for us to see Mum and Dad in St Ives for Friday lunch.'

'Sounds great,' Caroline said, feeling relieved.

'I'll confirm that with Mum, then.' Jennifer paused, eyeing her speculatively. 'This means you can speak to Dad at last. Have you seen Topaz since that day on the beach?'

Caroline shook her head. 'But she's sent me a few texts, asking to meet.'

'And what are you going to do?'

'Meet her, of course. I can't put her off forever. But at least speaking to Dad should finally get all this sorted out.'

'Agreed.' Jennifer hesitated. 'I didn't want to upset you by saying so at the time, but when I met Topaz, I thought she was a bit odd myself.'

'Just because she's an eccentric dresser—'

'I don't mean her clothes. I mean she seems shifty. Untrustworthy.' Jennifer tipped her head to one side, watching her. 'I don't want you to get hurt.'

'What are you trying to say?'

'Only that she was very keen to get to know me, and especially Alex. Surely she ought to have been focused on you, not us. But you can speak to Dad about her after the lunch in St Ives.' Jennifer frowned. 'Not in front of Mum, though.'

'How are we going to manage that?'

'I'll try dragging her away for a few minutes with Alex. You take Dad off on his own, and get him to admit if there's anything in that story Topaz told you.' Jennifer gave her an encouraging smile. 'Listen, there's a Christmas party at Belinda's house on Friday evening and she's invited us. So if it all goes pear-shaped, at least you can get roaring drunk later and forget all about it.'

'Belinda Basildon?' Belinda was a rising star in the British television industry, having cut her teeth on a soap before going on to star in several hugely successful mini-series, and she lived near St Ives. 'A party at her house? But I don't have anything suitable to wear.' Panic rose inside her at the thought of being on show in that kind of celebrity world. 'Maybe the dress I wore to your wedding reception would do, at a pinch. Though it's satin, far too bridesmaidy for a Christmas party. No, I couldn't wear that.'

'Stop fretting.'

'Easy for you to say. You've got a wardrobe full of designer clobber.'

Jennifer raised her eyebrows. 'You always look spectacu-lar, Caro, whatever you wear. And this party will be a great excuse to show off your figure.'

'Meaning?'

'I know for a fact you haven't been out with anyone in ages.'

Caroline felt quite aggrieved. 'I haven't had time for dat-ing. I've been rushed off my feet at work for months. What on earth do you expect?'

'You always used to have a boyfriend on the go.'

'When I was younger, yes. Maybe I'm just pickier now.'

'Fair enough. I only want what's best for you. Besides, this will be my last Christmas before becoming a mother. So we should both make an extra-special effort for this party.' Jennifer gave her a warm smile. 'I think you need cheering up after all this business with Topaz. Let's get our hair cut and styled for this party together, shall we? Like we used to in the old days.'

'In Pethporro?' Caroline was dubious.

'Truro,' Jennifer said. 'I know a chic little salon there. Very exclusive, very discreet. They do nails too.'

'Okay, thanks, if you're sure.' Caroline was beginning to feel excited at the prospect of this celeb party. 'But what about an outfit?'

'It will be quite a dressy affair, if I know Belinda. All glitz and sparkle, anything goes. So borrow whatever you want of mine if you don't have anything suitable to wear in your wardrobe.' Jennifer sighed, glancing down at herself.

'Though you might need to take some of the dresses in. I've filled out a bit since I left Cornwall.'

'I wasn't going to say anything,' Caroline said drily.

'Shut up!'

'Jenny, you look far better now than you did before you met Alex. You were skinny as a pipe-cleaner back then, and it didn't suit you.' Caroline leant forward, her mind racing through the possibilities. 'Okay, so we'll have our hair done for this party, and get glammed up. Wild horses wouldn't keep me away. But we still have to meet Mum and Dad for lunch first. Where will we change into our glad rags and do our make-up?'

'I thought maybe we could book a suite or two at one of the big local hotels.' Jennifer beamed. 'Staying locally will save us having to drive back in the early hours. If you're happy with the idea, I'll get the booking arranged and make sure Brodie is willing to drive us there and back.'

'Brodie's going?'

'He always goes to parties with us. He's Alex's best friend. It wouldn't be a party without Brodie there.' Jennifer looked at her innocently. 'Why?'

Caroline thought back over some of her sister's more barbed comments, frowning. A suspicion began to form in her head.

'Jenny, you wouldn't be trying to set me up with Brodie, would you?'

'Sorry?'

'Double-dating. You and Alex, me and Brodie.'

'Don't be ridiculous.' Jennifer got up quickly and bustled

hurriedly away, not meeting her gaze. 'I'll get everything arranged. It'll be a great night out, you'll see.'

Caroline pushed away the last of her toast and watched her sister go, feeling strangely vulnerable.

When Jennifer had first started shutting out the world on account of her failed love affair with Raphael Tregar, Caroline had tried several times to set her up with a blind date, a double date with her and her latest boyfriend and whichever reasonable male happened to be free that night.

But Jennifer had always managed to wriggle free, either by not turning up or by coming along but behaving so badly, she was sure of never being asked out again. Was it Jennifer's time to drive Caroline crazy with similar date night set-ups?

It would be funny if the date in question didn't also happen to be Brodie, whom she found attractive but was certain didn't return the compliment.

She'd been vaguely aware of her renewed interest in Brodie these past few weeks, yet had buried herself in work instead of trying to attract his attention, acting out of character. If she did make an effort for this Christmas party, could simply styling her hair and dolling herself up make any difference? Would it make Brodie's head turn at this party, for instance?

The problem was, she couldn't decide if she genuinely wanted Brodie to notice her, or if she would prefer to be left alone. A committed relationship wasn't the answer to everything. Yet over the last few years, despite a few fun affairs that had started with a glorious bang and then run their course as always, Caroline had started to notice a curious emptiness inside.

She'd dismissed the emptiness at first as broodiness: her biological clock was ticking, and that was something she could ignore, still in her early thirties and not even sure she wanted kids. But gradually, the ticking had grown louder and the sensation of emptiness more pressing, until there was a gaping hole in her life that she couldn't ignore and that no amount of girls' nights out or disastrous blind dates could satisfy. A space where something truly special ought to be.

Could that thing turn out to be love?

CHAPTER NINETEEN

In swimming shorts, a white towel slung over his bare shoulder, Brodie made his way through the empty gym to the heated swimming pool beyond. He enjoyed swimming in the mornings, especially in winter, when he could be alone in the blissfully warm water and tune out the voices in his head. Voices that mocked him for not living a fuller life, for not taking more risks ... But he had already taken all the risks he was likely to take, and couldn't stomach the thought of more pain. At least in the pool, he could forget his disability, and swim freely, or just float with his eyes closed, lost in the past.

The pool room overlooked the lawns and the woodlands beyond, the rectangular swimming pool itself sunk a little below ground level, so hiding swimmers from any passers-by.

He liked that extra privacy, since various components in his prosthetic leg were not completely waterproof, meaning that he needed to remove it before entering the pool to avoid damage.

But today, someone had got there before him, and was swimming.

A sleek blonde head emerged from the water, and Caroline Enys looked round at him, startled.

'Good morning,' he said, and saw her eyes widen, looking him over.

'Hello,' she replied.

Brodie hesitated beside the pool, suddenly more conscious of his prosthetic limb than he could ever remember being. He felt a rush of impatience. The woman had seen him in shorts before, what was the problem? But maybe it was the setting that was making a difference, the moist heat in the air, the intimacy of them both wearing next to nothing . . .

'You don't mind me swimming, do you?' she asked when he failed to move. 'I had an early workout in the gym, and after my shower, the water just looked so inviting.'

'Of course I don't mind. Why on earth should I mind?'

Except he did mind. This was his private place in the mornings. His sanctuary.

But he was being selfish.

'The pool is for everyone,' he said calmly, draping his towel over the back of a poolside chair and sitting down.

It was all part of his ritual. He would hang up his towel to keep it dry and sit beside the pool in this chair. Then, ordinarily, he would bend to remove the prosthesis before swimming. Only she was right there in the water, looking straight at him.

He sat there for a few minutes, unmoving. His heart

began to thump and he could feel his chest rising and falling, as though he'd been doing something strenuous, like pumping iron.

Caroline swam a little way down the pool and then back again, flicking a curious glance at him from time to time. She was wearing a white bikini that showed off her figure.

God, it was hot in here, he thought, and wiped his brow.

'Aren't you coming in?' she asked.

'Maybe in a bit.' He grimaced, realising how ridiculous that must have sounded, and stood abruptly. 'Actually, I've just remembered something. An urgent phone call I forgot to make. Excuse me.' He picked up his towel again and threw it over his shoulder. 'Enjoy your swim.'

Back in the safety of his bedroom, Brodie shut the door and leant his forehead against the wood, groaning.

Why on earth had he done that? If it had been anyone else, he would have gone through with his routine, removed his leg, and let himself down into the pool as usual. He had never experienced any qualms about Jennifer or Alex seeing him remove it, or not for a long time now.

For some reason, he couldn't face the idea of Caroline Enys seeing him without his prosthetic limb.

'Get a bloody grip,' he growled angrily. 'She's not interested in you, so what's the point in trying to preserve your dignity in front of her?' He limped across the room and started dragging clothes out of his drawers, ready for the day ahead. 'You fool, a woman like that is never going to look twice at you. Just face it.'

It wasn't a disaster. He doubted she had even noticed anything wrong. And this problem could be dealt with by careful planning.

While Caroline was living under this roof, he would simply reschedule his swims for times when she was unlikely to be in the pool herself. Or he would not swim at all.

CHAPTER TWENTY

Days had passed since that embarrassing encounter in the pool, and Brodie knew he had to get past his nerves and speak to Caroline alone. That bloody email from Sean was burning a hole in his conscience.

Yet every time he spotted a chance to take her aside for a private chat, he found some equally pressing reason not to do so.

Coward, he told himself grimly. Just tell her the bad news. Get it over with. But deep down, he knew what the problem was. He liked her, and didn't want her to be upset.

No, correction. He found Caroline Enys attractive. Powerfully attractive. And the temptation to ask her out was growing stronger every day.

The only way to control it was to stay away from her. Which he had been doing, assiduously. Until now.

He stood at the top of the front steps at Porro Park, hands in his pockets, and studied the cool December sky.

Today, they were all driving down the Cornish coast to the picturesque seaside resort of St Ives. They would be staying the night at one of the bigger local hotels, and driving back after lunch the following day. Jennifer had asked him to book a prestige suite for her and Alex, and two luxury en-suite bedrooms for him and Caroline.

'It's going to be a lovely weekend,' Jennifer had announced early that morning, handing him her overnight bag for the back of the Land Rover. Her glossy dark hair had been slightly trimmed, he realised, and shone with delicate highlights. 'St Ives is so gorgeous at Christmas, and I haven't seen Mum and Dad for ages.'

'Your hair looks amazing,' Brodie told her, smiling.

'Thank you.' Jennifer gave him a secretive glance from under long eyelashes. 'How about you, Brodie? All ready for the party this evening?'

'Of course,' he'd said smoothly, and carried her bag out to the car.

Except that wasn't strictly the truth, was it?

Tonight, he'd be expected to attend the party at Belinda Basildon's large and stylish home, which was situated a few miles outside St Ives. They'd been there a few times before, mostly for dinner parties or drinks, and she had come to the wedding, of course.

In her early thirties, Belinda was a curvaceous blonde with outspoken political opinions, whose name was currently dominating British television drama. She lived in London most of the year, but often came back to her second home in Cornwall for the festive season. He imagined the typical showbiz crowd would be there, with all the sparkle of Christmas, and there would be much drinking and dancing, and gossip.

Normally, he would attend such parties with utter disinterest, only there to keep an eye out for Alex and Jennifer, and not engage too much in conversation with the 'luvvies' of that world.

But things had changed. He was no longer merely an assistant-slash-bodyguard to a film star and his wife. He was now one of the three directors of Delgardo Films, and as such, he would be expected to take an active role in recruiting talent and attracting potential investors. Which meant he could no longer stand in a corner with a non-alcoholic drink and watch the goings-on with a jaundiced eye. He would have to engage with people. Speak to them. Maybe dance with someone. Maybe even someone like Caroline . . .

With difficulty, he pushed that disturbing thought away.

A tiny sound behind him brought him round.

His eyes widened.

It was Caroline, but she looked very different to the Caroline he'd seen yesterday afternoon. He'd taken the evening off and gone for a drive last night, stopping by the coast in the chilly dark and staring out over the barely visible expanse of the Atlantic, hearing rather than seeing it shifting inexorably under the cloudy heavens. He had been wrestling with something inside himself, some restless unhappiness that he couldn't name or fathom.

And so he'd missed Caroline and Jennifer returning from their day trip to Truro. They'd gone Christmas shopping, he'd been told. But what they hadn't mentioned was that a joint trip to the hairdressers would form part of the excursion.

Her shoulder-length ash-blonde hair had been ruthlessly cut and styled, its fine layers now feathered about her cheekbones, accentuating the delicacy of her features. She was wearing only a light amount of make-up, barely-there foundation with soft pink lipstick and a silvery hint to her eyelids. Far less than he was used to seeing on actors, in fact. Yet, being accustomed to her face devoid of make-up apart from the odd, hurried dash of lipstick in the mornings on her way out to work, the transformation was remarkable. Her fingernails too had been shaped and smoothly painted, giving her a more polished, sophisticated air.

And for lunch she'd chosen to wear a figure-hugging, sky-blue woollen dress that stopped tantalisingly mid-thigh, worn with black tights and knee-length boots like something out of the swinging sixties.

In short, she was once more like the hot, flirtatious blonde he'd first met, though her tentative smile suggested she felt less confident than she looked.

'You had your hair cut too,' he said, struggling not to gape at her.

'And doesn't she look stunning?' Jennifer said brightly from behind her sister, and suddenly Alex was there too, shrugging into his jacket as they all emerged from the house.

'For God's sake, Jenny!' her husband muttered.

Brodie swallowed. 'Yes, she absolutely does.'

Caroline hurriedly looked away.

'Alex loves Caro's hair too.' Jennifer seemed not to have noticed her sister's discomfort, continuing blithely as she shouldered her new Prada bag. 'That style suits her perfectly. Almost pixie-like around the face, but with length too, so it's versatile.'

Brodie locked up the house, and they all bundled into the car together. He was driving, and Alex took the passenger seat, while the two women sat in the back. Alex had offered Jennifer and then Caroline the front seat, only for both women to decline, apparently preferring to sit together.

'We want to gossip about you,' Jennifer insisted, laughing at her husband's expression, 'literally behind your backs.'

'When are you getting the goats back?' Caroline asked as they headed south-west towards St Ives.

Brodie glanced at Alex, but he was busy scrolling through screens on his smartphone. 'Lizzie says it would be best not to move them until spring. Winters outside can be quite tough on goats, apparently, and they have custom-made shelters where they are now.'

'Such a shame,' Jennifer said, and Brodie saw her indulgent smile in the rear-view mirror. 'I miss Baby.'

Baby was the smallest goat, of course, and the one that had brought her and Alex together, or so the story always went, more lovingly embellished with every telling. Jennifer even swore that Nelly had told the goat to come and fetch her from Pixie Cottage. But nobody really believed that. Though, remembering Nelly's almost supernatural gift for knowing things before anyone else, and her ability to change the atmosphere with just a smile or a soft word, he wouldn't have put anything past the old lady. Jennifer might not be a practising witch these days, but she and Nelly had certainly had much in common when they first met and bonded over a stray goat . . .

'I can arrange for you to visit them next week, if you like,' Brodie offered. 'I don't think the shelter closes for the Christmas break until the 22nd.'

'Could you? That would be wonderful.' Jennifer looked ecstatic, turning to her sister. 'Come with me, Caro. It'll be fun. You remember Lizzie?'

'Who could possibly forget her?'

'She's been so kind, taking on all Nelly's goats. And she took such great care of Ripper. I still feel bad about that. It was obvious she didn't want to part with him.'

'Lizzie actually liked Ripper?' Caroline sounded disbelieving.

'What does that mean?'

Jennifer's voice was suddenly haughty. Her obsessive, overprotective love for her crazy Siamese had been part of the reason Alex had fallen so hard for her. His wildly eccentric grandmother had felt the same about her seven goats, from whom she had stoutly refused to be parted even when she was dying.

'Oh, only that I dare not go within a few feet of your mad cat, in case he attacks me for having dared breathe in his vicinity.' Caroline wisely did not press the point though, adding drily, 'You and he are well-suited on that front. Which, I'm sure, is why he never unsheathes his claws for *you*. You're soulmates, you and Ripper.'

'Huh,' Jennifer said, but it was clear she was secretly pleased.

Brodie smiled.

'How far to St Ives?' Alex asked, looking up from his phone at last. He looked rough this morning, his hair unruly, his designer stubble a little longer than usual. 'I'm going to need to make some calls before lunchtime, and my mobile signal keeps coming and going.'

Alex had been up most of the night, apparently, exchanging emails over the purchase of the Bodmin Moor property they were acquiring for Delgardo Films, and also trying to persuade a few famous names to come and visit them once the company was fully established.

'Only an hour and a half,' Brodie reassured him. 'But I can stop at a service station if it's urgent.'

'No, it can wait,' Alex said, stuffing his phone in his jacket pocket and turning to look out of the car window instead. He drew in a deep breath and then exhaled slowly. 'God, this place is so beautiful. I'd forgotten how *green* Cornwall is. It's like some gigantic . . . cabbage.'

Brodie met Caroline's gaze in the rear-view mirror, and had to bite his lip to stop himself from laughing.

'Cabbage?' Jennifer sounded outraged. She leant forward between the seats to glare at her husband. 'Excuse me? If you haven't forgotten, I'm a Cornishwoman born, and I deeply resent the land of my birth being compared to a cruciferous vegetable.'

'C'mon, sweetheart, you know what I mean.'

While the couple squabbled, Brodie glanced in the

mirror again, and saw that Caroline too was gazing out of the window at the lush Cornish countryside. But her expression was sombre again, all traces of laughter abruptly gone. Despite her new hairstyle and subtle, flattering make-up, she looked almost sad today, he thought.

Was she worrying about Topaz, he wondered? Or did her wounds, like his own, go deeper?

He had to stop thinking about her, Brodie decided. It was doing neither of them any good and, given his inability to form relationships since the bombing, could only lead to trouble and heartache. He would tell Caroline what he'd learnt about Topaz at the party tonight, he decided. The news would go down better after a few gin and tonics. And once that was done, he could steer clear of her for good. For both their sakes.

CHAPTER TWENTY-ONE

Caroline felt the strangest sensation when she saw her mother and father – her stepmother and father, she corrected herself mentally – waiting for them in the doorway. Their art gallery stood on a corner of one of St Ives' tiny, narrow, winding streets that always seemed to bend back on themselves, leading further and deeper into the town's maze of low, whitewashed shops and houses with Regency-style bow windows and overhanging second storeys. Not a large space, but rather a neat and compact gallery, the art for sale on the stark white walls was all sea-themed, huge canvases of stormy seascapes or boats in cramped, Cornish harbours or bobbing at anchor on wide, sunny waters. But she barely noticed the paintings or small statuettes on plinths; her focus was fixed completely on her parents.

She was no longer sure how much she really knew about how they had first met and married, after listening to Topaz's very different account of her relationship breakdown with Caroline's father. Which was a shame, as she loved them both deeply. It was also a pity that she saw them so rarely, she thought, warmly embracing her step-mother first, then her father.

'I'm sorry it's taken me so long to come and visit,' she said, releasing her dad. 'Life's been mad, I suppose.'

She met Brodie's glance over her father's shoulder, and felt again that odd jolt in her psyche. She no longer trusted her father as implicitly as she had once done.

'How are you, Caroline?' her father asked, somehow a weight of meaning behind that innocent question.

'I'm fine. How are you, Dad?'

Her father hesitated, searching her face. There was a slight frown in his eyes, and she knew instinctively that he was thinking about her meeting with Topaz. Everything she'd told him on the phone in Boscastle. Her birth moth-er's accusations about him, the real reason why she had left all those years ago, abandoning her partner and her child . . .

Yet he didn't mention any of that.

'I'm fighting fit,' he said with a cheerful tone. 'Never better.' He turned to Alex and Jenny. 'Welcome to the gal-lery. And thank you again for helping us buy it.'

'It was no problem, Dad. Please stop thanking us.'

Debbie beamed round at them all. 'Your father and I have been looking forward to this visit all week. It's wonderful to see you all again.' She touched Caroline's shoulder, her eyes widening. 'Goodness, you cut your hair. I love it.'

'I cut mine too,' Jenny said quickly.

'I see that,' her mother said, laughing. 'You girls both look amazing. We're very proud of you.'

Her parents began to show Jenny and Alex around the gallery, since they had never actually seen the place in real life, only viewed it over the internet.

Despite describing himself as 'never better', her dad seemed less robust than she remembered, his hair thinning and definitely greyer on top. And her stepmother had a shuffle to her walk that made her appear older than she was, her smile somehow forced.

Had Dad told her about Topaz reappearing? Caroline wondered. Or were they simply nervous about this lunch? More nervous than her?

Alex would be there, it was true.

Sometimes she had to remind herself that Alex was a famous actor; he had become her brother-in-law in her mind. Just another member of the family, in other words, not an international celebrity. But Mum and Dad had only met Alex on a handful of occasions, so it probably felt a lot stranger to them, having this living, breathing film star wandering about their gallery in St Ives.

'I love these larger canvases,' Alex was saying to her father, pointing to one of the huge stormscapes that dominated the far wall.

Jennifer was admiring a statuette of a hare standing almost upright on its hind legs, her smile appreciative, while Mum told her about the artist, a young local man whose work always featured wild animals.

'It's very witchy and feminine,' Jennifer said, accepting a glass of orange juice from the tray of drinks Mum had brought out from the back room. 'I love it. It's exactly the kind of piece I'd acquire myself. The hare is an ancient symbol of fertility, of course ...' She paused, including their father in what she was saying. 'In fact, there's something I need to tell you both.'

Caroline caught Jennifer's glance, and realised what her sister was slowly leading up to ... Telling their parents that she and Alex were expecting a child.

Suddenly, she felt horribly in the way and desperate to escape.

This was their moment, not hers.

And maybe she was a teensy bit envious too. All those babies she'd delivered, all those pregnant women she'd cared for, and yet she'd never been pregnant herself, or even tried to be.

Not that she really wanted to be a mother. All that hard work, all those sleepless nights! But there was no denying it was occasionally an attractive idea. As a midwife, she'd seen the contented glow of a woman contemplating her own bump hundreds of times over the years, and knew she was unlikely ever to experience that contentment herself.

By choice, yes. But somehow it still stung.

'I'm just popping across the road,' Caroline said awkwardly, aware of the way her father turned to stare, a frown drawing his brows together. 'I need something from the newsagents. You carry on, don't mind me. I'll be back in a jiffy.'

Without waiting to hear their reaction, Caroline hurried out of the gallery and blundered across the narrow, windy street without looking left or right. Luckily, there were no cars coming, as driving in the centre of St Ives was heavily discouraged, even in the winter, so she survived, reaching the other side intact.

It was good to be out of the overheated gallery, drawing sharp wintry air into her lungs, feeling the sea winds gnaw at her through her fleece-lined jacket. No doubt her parents would think she was crazy, dashing out into the street like that. But Caroline couldn't help that. She had been listening to Jennifer and watching the loving pride on Alex's face, and suddenly needed to be out of there, to be alone.

Only she wasn't alone, she realised, looking back with a start.

Brodie had followed her.

He was becoming dangerously fascinated by her, Brodie thought, limping across the narrow Cornish street behind her.

When he'd first met Caroline, he'd made various assumptions about her – mainly that she was the opposite of Jennifer, whose interest in the esoteric arts had instantly marked her out as wild and extraordinary, even if she didn't keep a broomstick by the door, as he'd half hoped. By contrast, Caroline had seemed down-to-earth, practical, almost ordinary, apart from those elegant good looks. But he'd been wrong. She might appear smooth and no-nonsense on the surface, but beneath that facade she was as elemental, in her own way, as her sister, though she kept all her wildness inside, only letting it flare out at odd moments. Such as just now, a moment ago in the gallery, when Jennifer had opened her mouth to tell her parents she was pregnant.

He had been watching Caroline intently, otherwise he might have missed the wide-eyed, almost fearful expression on her face as she muttered some excuse and fled the place as though it were on fire.

What on earth had left her so unhappy that she couldn't stay to listen to her sister's good news? Especially given her career as a midwife. She ought to have been there at Jennifer's side, offering expert insights on the pregnancy, and looking every bit as smug as the parents-to-be themselves.

But perhaps it was her authoritative air and neat blue midwife's uniform that had deceived him. All he knew was that Caroline Enys was very different at heart from the way she appeared to the world. Though maybe some of that was down to her birth mother's disappearance at a tender age. It was well known that early trauma could leave an indelible mark on a personality.

Had the emotional turmoil brought about by Topaz abruptly leaving her life and Debbie entering it made Caroline afraid to show her true self in public? Or taught her that people you love can suddenly leave when you least expect it?

Once, he would have dismissed such questions as psychobabble. But after his own and Alex's complicated responses to being caught up in the appalling bombing of that hotel, he knew the human mind was both more fragile and more adaptable than most people realised. It could be left deeply wounded, and yet find strange and inventive ways to circumvent that hurt.

Was her birth mother's absence the wound that drove Caroline to invite friendship with one hand and reject it with the other?

'I don't need a babysitter,' Caroline said angrily as he reached her. There was a cross, defensive look on her face, her arms folded across her chest. 'I'm not famous, I can shop on my own.'

He raised his eyebrows at her tone. 'Nobody said you couldn't.'

'Then why follow me?'

'Who's following you? I was desperate for fresh air. It was so stuffy in that gallery; they must have the heating cranked up to full.' He paused, trying for a lighter tone. 'Besides, I wanted to grab a newspaper.'

'Oh.'

'And maybe a packet of mints.'

She looked him up and down suspiciously. 'You like mints?'

'Dreadful, isn't it? My secret sin.' He smiled at her. 'Don't tell Alex, will you? All that sugar . . . I'd never hear the last of it.'

He led the way into the newsagents and pretended to be browsing the local and national newspapers. She stood a little away from him, shoulders hunched in her flying-style jacket, also pretending to be looking through the women's magazines section. But he could tell she wasn't really studying the covers, stealing little sidelong glances at him every now and then instead.

'Do you fancy a walk down to the seafront?' Brodie asked casually, not looking at her, though an image of her in that mid-thigh dress and those sexy boots was probably imprinted on his memory forever. 'I don't know St Ives very well, though it's supposed to be one of the most popular coastal towns in this part of Cornwall. It would be good to get a better feel for the place.'

'But Jennifer and Alex . . .'

'We can meet them at the restaurant. I'll send Alex a text. It's near the seafront, anyway.' He picked up a newspaper he wasn't even remotely interested in reading, and a packet of mints from the adjacent display, and carried them to the till. 'I don't imagine anyone will mind if we escape for a bit. They'll have plenty to talk about, don't you think?'

He saw the flash in her eyes, and knew he had not been mistaken earlier. She was definitely upset about something. Jennifer's pregnancy? Or seeing her parents again? Perhaps she wasn't as close to them as her sister was.

But why come down to St Ives at all, then? Unless it was just for tonight's big showbiz party. She had certainly made an effort with her hair and make-up, so maybe that had been the draw.

Or was he missing the point?

'Yes, all right. Let's take a walk.' Caroline gave him a swift, professional smile and bought a packet of tissues from the middle-aged man behind the till while Brodie waited.

That smile chilled him. This was going to be difficult. She didn't want to spend any time with him. And she certainly wouldn't want to hear what he had to say. She was only buying tissues because she didn't want to admit her visit to the newsagents had merely been a ruse, an excuse to escape. Like his own newspaper and packet of mints. They were both playing games here, acting and putting on masks. It was rather dispiriting.

'It's probably downhill to the seafront,' Brodie said, standing outside on the street and pointing down through the crowded buildings to a space where the sky had a rougher, emptier feel. 'Do you know St Ives?'

'I've been here maybe half a dozen times.' She didn't sound very comfortable around him, he thought, noting the way she kept glancing anxiously back at the gallery as though poised to change her mind. 'And yes, the sea is that way. Not very far.'

He tried to sound cheerful. 'Lead on, then.'

As they walked downhill in a headlong, bracing wind, seagulls dancing above them on the cold air, he tapped out a brief text to Alex.

Going for a walk with Caroline. See you at the restaurant in fifteen.

Less than a minute later, Alex's reply popped up on the screen.

Copy that.

The road grew even narrower, the buildings on either side not much more than a few feet apart, until he could scarcely believe cars could get down there without scraping their wing mirrors on *both* walls.

They passed the restaurant where he had booked a table

for one o'clock for six people, and abruptly there were no more buildings, and they were facing an expanse of open water. Painted boats bobbed in the distance, wires slapped against masts, and seagulls cried above them.

Caroline stopped. 'You know something about my mother, don't you, Brodie? Something bad. That's why you've been avoiding me.'

Brodie looked at her, unsure what to say.

'Tell me,' she said firmly, staring out to sea rather than at him. The wind ruffled her new hairstyle and flapped at her coat, but she paid no attention. 'I want to know everything.'

CHAPTER TWENTY-TWO

Caroline ignored the clenching fear in her stomach and stared doggedly out to sea, her eyes fixed on the far horizon, that vanishing line that was misty grey today, somewhere on the way to America.

She didn't really want to hear whatever he'd discovered about Topaz. Maybe it wouldn't be so very bad, of course. But there was something. She'd seen it in his eyes lately, and the way he kept slipping out of a room as soon as she entered it; Brodie had heard back from his contact, yet had decided not to share the information with her. Which could only mean one thing . . .

She was not going to like it.

'I don't think this is a good time for that, frankly,' Brodie told her. 'What I have to say might upset you, and you still have to sit through lunch with your parents.'

Caroline turned, staring at him in disbelief. 'Not a good time?' she lashed back at him. 'This is important to me.'

He raised his eyebrows at her. 'More important than your sister's big day, telling your folks she's expecting their first grandchild?'

Caroline drew in a sharp breath, ready to argue the point, and then slowly let it go, acknowledging the simple truth of what he'd said.

This was Jennifer's day. She didn't have the right to spoil it with her own mini-drama. And she didn't want to.

'I suppose not,' she agreed reluctantly.

'I'll tell you everything you need to know later tonight.' He spoke with infuriating calm. 'But only once we're at the party.'

'Won't be much of a party then, will it?'

'On the contrary, a party is the perfect place to hear difficult news. Where better to drown your sorrows? Besides, if I tell you now, there'll be a scene. And I don't think you want that.'

'I still need to talk to my father after lunch,' she told him doggedly. 'He said he would answer my questions today. But only face to face.'

'About Topaz?'

Caroline nodded.

'Well,' Brodie said, 'go ahead and talk to him today as planned. But let me hold on to my information until this evening. It's probably best you wait to hear what your father has to say before learning what my friend found out. That way, if the two stories don't match up, you'll be less inclined to call him a liar to his face.'

'You think he would lie to me?' she demanded hotly.

'I think he's your father, and you love him.'

She looked away, silenced by that.

They stood there a while without speaking, both gazing

out to sea. She wondered what he was thinking. Then he put a hand under her elbow.

'Come on,' Brodie said gently. 'Time to go to lunch. They'll be waiting.'

Her parents were delighted by the news that they were going to become grandparents. At lunch, her father ordered two bottles of champagne, that he insisted on being allowed to pay for, and everyone had a few glassfuls – except for Jennifer, who was sticking determinedly to orange juice.

'To parenthood,' her dad said proudly, holding up his champagne flute in a toast.

'And grandparenthood,' Alex added with a grin.

Everyone drank.

'I'm so thrilled for you both,' Debbie told the parents-to-be, her face flushed and happy. 'And it's wonderful that your own sister will be looking after you and the baby. Caroline's an experienced midwife, and to have her there twenty-four seven . . . I think it's an absolutely marvellous idea.'

'It's given me real peace of mind.' Jenny knocked back her orange juice with an envious glance at the empty champagne bottle. 'And it's helped Caro out too.'

'How's that?' Debbie asked, curious.

'Her neighbours in Pethporro were awful.' Jenny explained briefly about the dreaded Malcolm and Savannah, their love of loud music and their screaming matches in the early hours. 'Now she's free of them.'

'So you're living full-time at Porro Park now, Caro? That must be nice.' Her father had turned towards her, though she noticed he did not quite meet her gaze. 'I remember admiring that indoor heated swimming pool. And the gym. Such a luxury in the winter months, when it's too cold and damp to exercise outside.' He made a wry face. 'We just about have room for a rowing machine in our conservatory.'

'In that case, you must come and stay with us in the New Year,' Alex told him, taking the hint. 'Do you ever give yourselves a break from running the gallery?'

'I wish!' Her mum glanced at her dad, a look of entreaty on her face. 'Jim keeps insisting we need to stay open twelve months of the year. But I don't see the point. Footfall will drop off massively once the Christmas rush and New Year sales are over.'

'February, then.' Jenny gave their father a coaxing smile. 'How about it? We'd love to have you both for a week or two early in the year, if you can bear to close the gallery for that long. We've got plenty of room at Porro Park, and you could use the time to revisit old friends in the area.'

Her dad's smile faltered, but only for a second. 'If Debbie has her heart set on it, who am I to say no? And I would like to try out your gym again. Not to mention the pool.'

'That's settled, then,' Alex said.

Their hors d'oeuvres arrived.

Caroline eyed her avocado toast with little enthusiasm. It smelt delicious but she had no appetite today. Not knowing that she was going to be talking to her father about Topaz after the meal.

Debbie leant across the table and took Jenny's hand, smiling mistily. Mother and daughter, they looked so alike,

Caroline thought, recalling how she and Topaz looked uncannily similar too. Her heart ached and she looked away, wishing life could be simple.

'I'm so proud of you, sweetheart,' Debbie was telling her daughter. 'We both are. And it's marvellous to see you so happy . . . We were worried for you a couple of years back. That awful Raphael business.' She shook her head. 'But it worked out all right in the end, didn't it? Like one of your old fairy stories, only in real life.'

Jenny's grin was crooked. 'Actually, Mum, most of my fairy stories have pretty gruesome endings. But I know what you mean.' She winked at Alex beside her, who was busily tucking into his smoked salmon. 'I had to kiss a few frogs, including Raphael Tregar, before I found my prince.'

Alex waggled his eyebrows at her, and everybody laughed.

After they'd finished lunch, Jennifer lured her mother away as arranged for a walk through St Ives with Alex and Brodie.

Which left Caroline alone with her dad.

'Shall we go back to the gallery for a coffee?' her father suggested as they left the restaurant. 'I'd like to open up again now lunch is over. It's best to stick to regular opening hours, I find, or we lose customers. Plus, I have a delivery of miniature seascapes to unpack.' He paused. 'If you don't mind me working while we chat.'

'Of course not.'

But she was a little worried by his casual air. Was her dad trying to distract her from questioning him about Topaz?

Back at the gallery, her worst suspicions were confirmed.

He made them both a mug of coffee, and then stood by the counter unpacking boxes of artwork and sculpture, newly arrived for last-minute Christmas shopping, as though any conversation they had would be unimportant.

Her nerves almost got the better of her. But Caroline forced herself to broach the subject, her heart thumping erratically.

'Dad,' she said, interrupting his lengthy description of a bronze sculpture he had sold the week before, 'I'm sorry, but I really need to talk to you about Topaz. You said that you weren't happy discussing the past over the phone. I suppose you didn't want Mum to overhear.' She put down her mug of coffee. 'Well, I'm here now and we're alone.'

Frowning, he stared down at the seascape he was unearthing from the packing case. 'Topaz,' he repeated, as though reminding himself who she was. 'Yes, you told me she'd come to see you. An odd thing to do.'

Something about his tone nettled her. 'She's my birth mother. Not so strange that she'd want to meet me, is it?'

He quirked an eyebrow, considering that question. 'On the face of it, no. But Topaz never showed any interest in finding you before now, did she?'

'Actually, she told me that she wanted to come back to Pethporro years ago, but she was too nervous to make contact.' She had almost said 'scared' but decided against it. There was no point getting him upset. 'Look, I'm not here to pick her behaviour apart. I just want to know the truth.'

Her father sighed, and put the seascape back into the packing case. 'Go on then, ask your question.'

'I told you on the phone what she'd said about you. That you'd had an affair.' When he didn't respond, she pressed him. 'Dad? Is that true?'

Her father turned away, pushing his hands into his trouser pockets and staring out of the front window of the gallery. For a while, he said nothing, apparently deep in thought. Then he asked, 'You like spending time with Topaz? You get on well with your mother?'

'What's that got to do with it?'

'I always found her difficult company, myself. After the first few years together, that is. Topaz can be very ... demanding.'

'Please tell me the truth, Dad.' Caroline felt like she was going mad. 'Did you have an affair with another woman?'

Her father glanced round at her. 'It was partly my fault, I suppose. The reason we split up. I handled the relationship badly.'

'Is that an admission of guilt?'

'All I'm admitting to is a near total lack of experience with women. I was still young then. Topaz was my first serious girlfriend. Then you came along, and I was over the moon. I thought that was it. That we'd be together forever, like my own parents.' He gave a harsh laugh. 'I was an idiot.'

'For straying? Yes, I think you were.'

Her father sucked in his breath at her reprimand, but said nothing.

'And afterwards?' she continued, struggling to understand his behaviour. 'When she was so unhappy that she tried to commit suicide? Why did you let her get so depressed? Why didn't you look after her?'

He frowned, looking down at the floor. 'I told you, I got it all wrong with Topaz. And paid the price.'

'It sounds to me like it was Topaz who paid the price. Not you.' Caroline stared at him; she couldn't believe his uncaring attitude. 'You didn't answer any of her letters, Dad. You didn't even let her see me. Her own child.'

He said nothing, his face still averted.

She had not intended to lose her temper, but his refusal to speak plainly was infuriating. 'What I really don't understand is why you chose not to tell me any of this before. You cruelly let me believe that Topaz just walked out on us, that my own mother didn't care enough to take me with her. When in fact she'd been locked up for her own safety in an institution, and wasn't even allowed to see me.' She swallowed, her heart squeezed by an old pain. 'Do you have any idea what it did to me, thinking for all those years that she'd abandoned me?'

'I have some idea, yes.' He looked round at her awkwardly. 'Debbie and I tried to shield you from that by showing you how much we both loved you.'

'You still should have told me.'

'It wasn't a suitable tale for a child's ears.'

'And when I grew up?'

He ran a hand over his forehead. 'Look, I decided long ago to put the past behind me, and that includes Topaz. Your real mother ... Well, she has mental health issues, let's put it like that.'

'Sorry?'

'That suicide attempt . . .' He grimaced. 'Well, she's clearly an unstable person. I can see you like Topaz, but you can't necessarily trust everything she says.' He drew breath to say more, then shook his head. 'I'd rather not talk about this any more, if you don't mind.'

'Dad, you can't just leave it at that.'

He shot her a strained smile. 'I love you, Caroline, so please just trust me on this. I've always tried to do what was best for you. But if getting to know your mother is making you happy, then I'm really glad she's back in your life. And I wouldn't interfere with that for the world.'

'But—'

'No, I'm sorry, that's it. End of discussion.'

Her father turned back to his work without another word, and Caroline realised that this brief and unsatisfying exchange was all she was ever likely to get out of him on the subject of Topaz.

But there was still Brodie, she thought grimly. She hated having to drag him into this upsetting family secret. But if he could shed some light on why her father was so reluctant to talk about the past, it would be worth it.

CHAPTER TWENTY-THREE

The party at Belinda Basildon's house was in full swing when they finally rolled up the drive, music booming out of every downstairs room, the whole house illuminated by flashing, coloured fairy lights, flaming torches set at intervals along the broad gravelled drive. Photographers and journalists were thronging the road outside her house – though mansion would be a better description, Brodie thought – with flashes going off as they rolled past and through the gates. There was barely anywhere to park, despite the large grounds, but Brodie was directed by a man in a high-vis jacket on to the double tennis courts and managed to squeeze the Land Rover into a gap between the wire fence and a glossy new Rolls Royce.

'I told you we should have left the hotel sooner,' Alex muttered from the passenger seat, eyeing the narrow space between his door and the wire fencing, but was ignored.

He and Brodie had been dressed and ready on time, but had stood about in the hotel lobby for nearly an hour, waiting for the two sisters to descend. They had been changing into their party frocks together in Caroline's room.

At last, the lift had opened and they had emerged arm-in-arm, laughing and sauntering on high heels, both immaculately made-up and with beautifully styled hair, Jennifer dark and mysterious as always, Caroline giving off blonde Swedish model vibes. It was a startling combination.

With their sequinned dresses glittering, lavish jewellery catching the light as they walked, Brodie thought they looked like a couple of Christmas trees. Though he wisely kept that observation to himself.

Jennifer seemed genuinely happy to be going out to a Christmas party, but Caroline's mood was wild. She smiled too much and laughed too loudly, and there was a savage look in her eyes when she wasn't pretending to be enjoying herself.

Maybe her father had told her something unpleasant about Topaz's past when they spoke at the gallery this afternoon. Caroline had certainly been looking unhappy when they all got back from their walk through St Ives. But if so, she hadn't said a word to him about it afterwards . . .

Belinda Basildon herself was at the front door, still greeting latecomers. Blonde, busty and long-legged, she was wearing silver and red spangles tonight with thigh-high red leather boots, and elaborate gold earrings that brushed her neck.

She was a beautiful woman in the prime of her life, and she knew it.

'Darling, fantastic to see you again,' she said warmly, kissing Alex several times like he was her long-lost lover, then spotting Jennifer's brooding stare and hurriedly releasing him. 'And your lovely wife too! How marvellous that you could both come. And Brodie, of course. Wherever Alex goes, Brodie's never far behind.' Belinda kissed him, leaning in close, her perfume enticing and expensive. Then her gaze moved to Caroline. 'And, erm . . .'

Jennifer said baldly, 'This is my sister, Caroline.'

'Your sister, how wonderful! Welcome, welcome!' Belinda shook Caroline's hand with vague enthusiasm, and then turned to smile broadly at the couple coming in behind them, one of whom was an up-and-coming young television director whose name Brodie couldn't remember. 'Darlings! I'm so glad you could make it to my little party. I hope it wasn't too long a drive.'

The house was packed with partygoers. They found drinks in an adjacent room, and then funnelled through the crowds, stopping every few minutes so somebody could kiss Alex or shake his hand, and whisper things in his ear, while he smiled and nodded.

Brodie caught Jennifer's eye. 'Quite a lot of people here,' he said loudly over the music.

'Ridiculously rammed. I can hardly move.' She tugged on his sleeve and he bent his head closer. 'Hey, ask Caro to dance, would you? She's been thoroughly wired all evening. I asked her what Dad said about Topaz, but she refused to go into detail. So it can't have been anything good. Look at that face!' She frowned, clearly worried about her sister. 'See if you can get her to relax, would you?'

To his surprise, he experienced a wave of frustration, and struggled not to show it. He'd thought they were getting on to more of an equal footing, the three of them, now that he was a company director. But it seemed he was still there to be ordered about and treated like the hired help.

'Maybe she doesn't want to dance,' he suggested.

'Of course she does!' Jennifer rolled her eyes. 'This is Caroline we're talking about. She always wants to dance.' She nudged him towards her sister. 'Go on, they're dancing through there. See?'

His jaw clenched.

It was half in Brodie's mind to refuse and walk away. He knew quite a number of people here. He could easily strike up a conversation with someone else and ignore Jennifer's matchmaking. But if he made a fuss, Jennifer would get suspicious and start to think he had something to hide. Like his attraction to her sister.

Besides, it was clear that Caroline had caught some of their conversation, because she was now standing stiffly, her face averted.

If he walked away now, she would be hurt.

That would never have bothered him in the past. He was used to protecting himself or Alex from difficult situations, regardless of who got upset. But Caroline was different. He didn't stop to interrogate himself on why or how she was different. She just was.

So much for staying away from her tonight, he thought grimly.

He moved towards Caroline, a smile on his face, half hoping she would refuse. 'Shall we go and watch the dancing?' he asked her. 'Jenny's waiting for Alex to finish chewing the fat with Billy Temple. Film talk, I imagine, but it could take a while. No point standing here like a couple of lemons.'

Caroline glanced past him at Jennifer, then gave a terse nod.

Don't look too keen, Brodie thought irritably, but made no comment. He took her arm and led her through to where the dancing was happening.

A dance floor had been set up in the largest of the downstairs rooms, exactly like the last time he'd attended a big party at Belinda's house, with a rig of whirling disco lights overhead. A live band at one end of the room was playing fairly generic pop music covers, and the room was already pulsing with people dancing and swaying together, glittering under the lights. He and Caroline moved slowly about the periphery of the dance floor, watching bodies gyrate under a sudden welter of strobe lights. It was a young crowd, mostly early- to mid-twenties, but there were a few middle-aged people there too, getting down to the music. He watched them in amusement for a few minutes before realising that Caroline was glaring at him.

'What's the matter?' he said into her ear, though he was fairly certain he knew what the answer would be.

'You promised you would tell me about Topaz tonight,' Caroline said in a loud voice, and gulped at her tall glass of gin and tonic. 'Why are you holding back on me?'

'I thought you already knew the worst,' he told her frankly. 'You've been giving me daggers ever since we arrived. I assumed that meant your father gave you the bad news at the gallery earlier.'

'What bad news?'

He was surprised. 'He didn't tell you?' He hesitated. 'Maybe I shouldn't either, then. Not tonight, anyway. This probably isn't the best time—'

'Oh, it's never the right time for the *truth*, is it?'

He caught her arm as she spun away, sloshing gin everywhere, including down his arm. 'Careful, for God's sake,' he muttered.

She had consumed rather a lot of wine at lunch, he had noticed, and later Jennifer had ordered drinks and snacks up to the suite while they were changing for the party. Non-alcoholic drinks for Jenny, of course, because of the baby. But he suspected Caroline had not done the same.

'Why don't you put that drink down,' he said, helping her do just that, 'and come outside with me?'

Her look was belligerent. 'Why would I want to come outside with you?'

'Because I'm going to tell you what I discovered about Topaz,' he said in her ear, 'and I don't want any of the other guests to overhear us. Now, are you coming or not?'

Her eyes widened, and she nodded slowly.

Brodie led Caroline through the heaving crowd to the kitchen, then out on to the back patio. There were a few people outside, drinking and looking up at the stars, so he drew her along the path beside the outdoor swimming pool and through a narrow archway into a secluded garden.

It was cold, but he took off his jacket and put it round her shoulders as they walked through the dark garden, its shrubs and trees lit by soft glow torches stuck into the earth at intervals.

'You were right,' he admitted once they were safely out of earshot of the other guests, 'I did get an email back from that friend of mine. He found out some interesting things about your mother. It's not wonderful news though, I'm afraid.' Brodie studied her face with misgiving. 'Are you sure you want to hear this tonight?'

'Tell me,' she said flatly. 'I'm sick of being lied to.'

'Fair enough.' He shrugged. 'The story starts before you were even born,' he said softly. 'But I guess it only became clear to your dad once he'd asked Topaz to marry him.'

Caroline had been studying a ghostly statue at the far end of the path, but now twisted her head round to stare at him.

'He did *what*?'

'Oh, he was definitely planning to marry her. That's where the trouble started. She said yes, and they even went so far as to book a date with the registrar. Only she suddenly changed her mind about tying the knot. I imagine that's when he started to get suspicious.'

'I don't understand.'

'I didn't either at first. But I'm guessing he searched through her things and found some details that didn't add up, because he hired a private investigator a few months after she called off the wedding.'

Caroline put a hand to her mouth, looking as though she might be sick. 'Are you serious? He hired a private investigator?'

'You want me to go on?'

She nodded silently.

'This guy came up with the goods,' Brodie continued, watching her carefully. 'My friend spoke to the investigator, though he's retired now. It turned out she was already married.'

Her relief was obvious. 'Is that all?'

'Twice over.'

'Sorry?'

'Your mother was already bigamously married to two other men while she was considering a third marriage to your father.'

CHAPTER TWENTY-FOUR

Caroline turned away and made for a stone bench a little further along the dark path. Shakily, she sank on to it, her head buzzing. Why the hell had she drunk so much?

'But I . . . I spoke to Dad at the gallery today,' she muttered. 'We talked about Topaz. He never mentioned any of this. Not a thing.' She made a face. 'Except for telling me that my mother has mental health issues and I shouldn't trust her. Which is just charming.'

'Maybe he's trying to protect you.'

'By lying to me?'

He shrugged. 'It's a complicated tale. And not a very pleasant one. Perhaps he didn't feel up to talking about it.'

'I don't care; I want to hear it.' She dragged his jacket closer, suddenly glad of its warmth. 'Please.'

He nodded, coming to stand before her. 'Her first husband had emigrated to Australia. She'd gone with him initially, but then flew back alone. I guess a life down under didn't appeal.'

'But she didn't get a divorce?'

'Apparently not. Maybe he refused, or she just pretended it hadn't happened.'

Somehow, Caroline could imagine Topaz doing that. Just moving on without considering the legal implications . . .

'The next husband lived in Scotland,' he continued, 'up in the Highlands. She was only with him about six months. At some point after that, she came down to Cornwall, perhaps for somewhere quiet to hide, and met your father. They had a whirlwind romance, by all accounts, that ended in her falling pregnant. It worked for a while, playing house with him here in Pethporro. Until your dad foolishly decided to make an honest woman of her.' He shrugged. 'I guess it was beyond even her skills at deception to manage the same trick a third time.'

Music pumped out from the lit-up house behind him, and she could hear a woman laughing hysterically at the poolside.

His jacket half slid off her shoulders and she fumbled to catch it. 'So she was a . . . a bigamist,' she said in a hollow voice. 'But bigamy is illegal, isn't it?'

'Very.'

'Did Topaz get into trouble with the law for that?' Caroline tried to piece it together. 'Or was she too worried about getting caught to stay with my dad? Is that why she left me behind? To avoid being found out?'

He looked away, and she peered at his averted face, trying in vain to read his expression. But it was too dark in the little walled garden.

'What is it?' she asked, frustrated and uneasy. A sudden breeze gusted, tearing at his jacket, and she shivered. 'Brodie? What are you not telling me?'

'She left because she was wanted for fraud,' he told her flatly.

Caroline did not understand. 'Wanted?'

'Topaz was a fraudster. She'd been happy to hide out down here for a few years, knowing the police force in Cornwall was too stretched to be a threat. She'd burnt her boats with her former surnames. But, as Mrs Enys, she would have looked squeaky clean to the authorities. So I imagine she jumped at the chance to marry your father.'

'Oh God, poor Dad.'

'Unfortunately for her, it proved harder to fool the local registrar than the previous one, and she quickly gave up the effort. But, by then, it was too late. Her sudden change of heart had sent your father off on a quest to find out what she was hiding. And he found more than he'd bargained for.'

'But fraud?' She was bewildered, unable to take it in. Her brain was reeling. 'Wh-What does that even mean? What on earth did she do?'

'She ripped off her second husband. He was some big businessman with his own company up in Scotland. Only it didn't work out. Six months later, he wanted a divorce after she'd been caught with some other man, and was refusing to give her a penny.' He shrugged. 'Topaz must have known she wouldn't pass muster with his lawyers if she demanded a big divorce settlement. They would have found out about the bigamy.'

'But you said she ripped him off?'

'She pretended to leave of her own accord, claiming she hated him. Then she waited until he was away on a business trip and broke back into the house, cleaned out his safe, his various money stashes, took all his most valuable possessions ...'

Caroline groaned. 'I feel like I'm going mad. Please tell me this is a joke.' She stared up at his face. 'A sick joke.'

'I'm afraid it's not.' Brodie hesitated. 'And there's more.'

'No, no.' She closed her eyes.

'You want me to stop?'

She forced her eyes open again, swallowing hard. 'No, better tell me everything,' she said faintly. 'Go on. What else?'

'Your father got the report back from the private investigator. But he didn't immediately go to the police as he should have done.'

'He helped Topaz escape? Is that why she disappeared?'

He shook his head. 'Not quite. Your father confronted her, and she attacked him before fleeing the scene. Made quite a mess of him, I believe.'

Caroline was horrified. 'Poor dad.'

'Not surprisingly, he called the police at that point and they eventually caught up with her.' His jaw clenched. 'Topaz was charged with bigamy, fraud and assault, and refused bail as a flight risk. But before her case came up, she tried to hang herself in her cell.'

'God, no!'

'After that, she was sectioned for her own protection,

and put in a plea of insanity at her court case, which meant she spent her sentence in an institution instead of a prison.'

Deeply shaken, Caroline dropped her head into her hands, going back through everything he'd said, piecing it together with her mother's story and her father's even patchier account of what had happened between them.

'Did my dad really have an affair, though? Was that part of her story true, at least?'

'I'm not sure. I guess we'll never know.'

Caroline groaned. 'Half-truths and exaggerations. Though one thing was true,' she added, her heart hurting at the realisation. 'She didn't abandon me.'

'No.'

'They locked her up instead, and that's why she never came back for me.' She pushed aside the possibility that Topaz would never have come back for her. She wanted to think better of her, even knowing the rest wasn't true. 'She must have been so unhappy . . . Poor woman.'

Brodie said nothing, watching her.

'But why didn't my father tell me all this when I asked?' Caroline demanded. 'And not just today, but years ago. I spent my childhood thinking I must have done something wrong to deserve being abandoned. I thought my mother must have hated me. Why did he lie?'

She buried her face in her hands.

She wished Brodie didn't know these things about her birth mother. It was humiliating. What must he be thinking about her family?

'Go back and ask him,' he suggested.

'I can't.' She shook her head vehemently and stood up, too agitated to sit still a moment longer. 'He's done something worse than Topaz, if you ask me. She lied because it was in her nature. But my dad . . .'

'Loves you,' he finished for her softly.

Caroline handed back his jacket, hurt and unconvinced. 'I'm cold,' she told him, not meeting his gaze. She couldn't think straight. Not standing here in the dark with him as though they were lovers. It was too confusing. 'Let's go back inside.'

'You want to leave?'

'Not a chance. I'm not a quitter.' She threw her head back defiantly, still a little bit drunk but determined not to let all this shit drag her down. Not tonight. The music was playing and her head was pleasantly muzzy. Tomorrow would be soon enough to figure out what to do. 'I want to dance.'

CHAPTER TWENTY-FIVE

'Dance with me,' she told him as soon as they got back inside, an unsteady note in her voice. 'I've never been so miserable in all my life. And I don't want to spoil Jenny's evening by telling her what you told me. So this is the least you can do to make up for it.'

Brodie's lips twitched. 'Whatever you say.'

He followed Caroline between gyrating couples on the dance floor until they found a small space under a spinning red disco light. He started to dance with her there, trying to match her movements and ignore the death ray of her furious glare.

At first, it was exciting and unusual. The way she moved her body was mesmerising. But soon, he was uncomfortable and wished he could stop without hurting her feelings. He didn't know why he'd agreed to dance with her. He hated dancing. Not merely since he'd lost his leg and learned to adjust to a prosthesis, but even before that, as a youth at school discos, feeling like a fool in front of the girls.

Girls, plural, because he'd been far more of a player as a young man. And he'd often got dates too, because his looks weren't bad; he'd known that then, and he knew it now. It was the rest of him that had been shot to hell.

Was she enjoying dancing with him?

She looked at him and then away. Her face was flushed, the glittering sequins on her dress lighting up her throat and face like thousands of tiny flames under the red light.

Abruptly, the music changed pace, becoming slower, less frenetic. The lead singer's voice dropped, husky and romantic in tone.

Brodie tried to match his movements to the slower beat. Covertly, he studied Caroline's movements, mesmerised by the rhythmic sway of her hips, the way she had thrown her head back, her eyes closed as she danced, each step somehow sultry and enticing.

'Tired yet?' he asked her.

'Sorry?'

The music was too loud; she hadn't heard him.

He leant forward, their faces so close now they were almost touching. 'We don't have to keep dancing if you'd rather not. I don't mind.'

'No, I want to dance.' Caroline surprised him by putting her arms about his neck, her body suddenly close to his. He could smell her perfume, her soft hair brushing his cheek. 'It helps me forget all that other stuff.'

He couldn't blame her for drinking or for seeking a little comfort. Today, she'd discovered that her estranged birth mother, whom she'd only just met again, was a bigamist and fraudster who had been incarcerated for her crimes. And that her father had been lying about it her entire life.

She just needed some reassurance, that was all.

He could do that without compromising himself. He could be a friend to her, couldn't he? Just for these first few hours while she was feeling so fragile and didn't want to look to her sister for support . . .

Brodie closed his eyes and circled with her leaning on his chest, both of them swaying to the hypnotic rhythm of the song.

Alarms were ringing in his head but he ignored them.

'I like this song,' she said dreamily.

She stumbled and he caught her more tightly against him. His hand steadied her back, moving slowly down her spine.

'Mmm,' she said, both arms still looped about his neck.

Brodie drew in a sharp breath as her fingers played with the short hairs on the nape of his neck. 'Caroline,' he said in a low voice, every nerve in his body tingling. 'For God's sake . . .'

Suddenly, there was a tap on his shoulder.

He turned, surprised.

It was Alex, a frown on his face. 'Jenny wants to leave early,' he said, speaking into his ear rather than raising his voice above the music. 'She's not feeling well. She was fine, then she ate something off the cheeseboard and now she's got a tummy ache.'

'That sounds bad.' Brodie hurriedly disentangled himself from a drowsy, protesting Caroline. 'I'll get the car.'

'No, don't bother.' Alex looked past him at Caroline, his brows raised. 'It looks like someone's enjoying the party, even if Jenny isn't.'

Caroline waved at him sleepily. 'Hello, Alex!'

'You look great,' Alex told her, grinning, then said into Brodie's ear again, 'I've called a taxi for me and Jenny. You bring Caro back to the hotel when she's ready.' When Brodie started to speak, he shook his head. 'No, I insist. Jenny would be furious if we dragged her sister off early just because she's not feeling a hundred per cent.'

'You're sure Jenny's going to be okay?'

'Absolutely.' Alex clapped him on the back. 'Look, you two have fun. I'll see you in the morning.'

When he'd gone, Brodie studied Caroline. She was stretching, yawning slightly.

'What did Alex want?' she asked.

'He and Jenny are leaving early,' he told her. 'You want to stay or go back to the hotel with them?'

'Stay, stay, stay,' Caroline chanted, and started dancing again as the music changed tempo, moving her hips to a faster beat. 'Oh, I love this one.' Her gaze challenged him. 'Don't you?'

It was nearly two in the morning when Brodie eventually persuaded Caroline to leave the party, and although she had not drunk much more, she was still tipsy and cling-ing. He steered her slowly into the lift, under the watchful gaze of the night concierge, and then towards her hotel room, opening it one-handed while supporting her with his other arm.

'Here we are,' he said softly, not wanting to wake the other guests at the hotel, including Alex and Jenny, whose prestige suite was at the far end of the corridor. 'Time for bed.'

'Not yet,' she said, far too loudly. 'Come in, let's have a nightcap. Jenny left a bottle of . . .' She hiccupped. 'A bottle of turquoise gin. There's probably soda water left too.'

'You've had enough,' he said, shushing her.

But she refused to be shushed. 'What's the matter?' Caroline demanded, swaying on the threshold of her room. 'Don't you want to have a drink with me, Brodie? Am I not good enough now you know my mum's a . . . a . . . criminal?' Her voice broke, and she buried her face in her hands. 'Why did nobody tell me? Why didn't Dad tell me?' she gasped. 'Everything he told me was a lie. My whole life's been a lie.'

Grimacing, Brodie helped her inside the bedroom and closed the door. 'Try to calm down,' he told her, but wasn't sure she was even listening.

It was dark inside, only a faint glimmer of starlight threading through a gap in the curtains. He fumbled about for the light switch, but she pushed him against the wall, still breathing like she'd been running.

'Hey, what are you doing?' he said sharply.

'Help me,' she pleaded with him. 'I'm so lost, Brodie. I don't know who I am any more. Will you . . . will you help me?'

Her arms came up around his neck in the darkness, her perfumed body warm and soft against his, just as it had been when they were slow-dancing together.

'Caroline, no,' he said patiently, suppressing the flicker of panic inside. But he was struggling not to acknowledge his attraction to her. She was standing so close, and they were alone in her bedroom at night, wrapped in warm intimacy. 'I don't want to hurt your feelings. But it's late and I need to get to bed.'

'Yes,' she agreed, stroking the back of his neck with delicate fingers. 'That's a good idea. We should both go to bed.'

'Caro, please.'

Gently, he tried to unpick her fingers, but she raised her face blindly in the darkness, finding his mouth.

'Brodie,' she whispered.

Her lips met his, and his heartbeat took off at once, the heat that he had been fighting to ignore suddenly raging inside him, barely controllable.

This was what he had been afraid of. It had been too long since he'd allowed himself to kiss a woman, to hold her, to feel anything like this heady rush of desire. Too unbearably long. And Caroline was molten in his arms, all that smooth elegance falling away as their bodies came hungrily together, two pairs of hands stroking and exploring.

Had she always been like this, underneath her cool, nononsense facade? He had a sudden vision of Caroline in her fitted blue uniform, delivery kit in hand, a bare minimum of make-up on, hair sternly controlled, and could not believe this was the same woman.

He did not know how long they were kissing for, but he

was abruptly aware that things had somehow graduated to her bed.

Alarm surged through him.

Caroline was dragging at his shirt, tugging on his buttons. He rolled on to his back, breathing hard. 'No,' he said again, and knew he had to get out of there before he did something they would both regret. 'Not like this . . .'

'But I need to,' she insisted, a hoarse urgency in her voice as she stroked a hand down from his chest to his belt. He raised his head to stare at her, and could almost feel the waves of fear and unhappiness coming off her. 'And I know you do too.'

'No,' he repeated, and sat up.

Caroline watched him grope his way to the light switch, and blinked at the brightness, groaning as she fell back on the bed, covering her face.

'I'm sorry,' he said, and left the room.

Reaching his own room across the corridor, he got inside and then stood against the locked door, willing his heart rate to slow, his ragged breathing to return to normal.

Brodie shut his eyes, trying not to remember what had almost happened between them. How the hell had things between them escalated so bloody quickly?

He was furious with himself. Knowing how attractive he found Caroline, he should never have gone into her room in the first place, let alone kissed her back. It had been one of the stupidest, most reckless things he'd done . . .

She'd been consenting, of course. There was no doubt in his mind about that. But Caroline had also been drinking, and it wouldn't have been right to take advantage of that. Nor her vulnerability following the shocking news about her mother's bigamy.

Though even if Caroline had been stone-cold sober, he wasn't ready for that level of intimacy. Not nearly ready.

CHAPTER TWENTY-SIX

Caroline squeezed Jennifer's hand as they sat next to each other in a small side room in the ultrasound department of the Royal Cornwall Hospital at Treliske, waiting to be called.

She had wrangled a private room from Jane, the receptionist and a long-time friend of hers, explaining that if Jenny and Alex didn't get one, they could end up being mobbed by fans or the paparazzi.

'Not in my hospital,' Jane had said firmly, and steered them away from the busy public area before asking them to wait, with one last admiring glance at Alex from under her lashes.

That had been over half an hour ago, and she could tell that Jenny was getting more and more nervous as the minutes ticked by.

Alex, sitting at his wife's side, lifted her hand to his mouth and kissed it. 'Everything will be fine with the baby,' he told her, not for the first time. His smile was warm and loving, quite unlike the taciturn action hero he played in his most popular films. 'You're fit and healthy, Jenny, you're in the absolute prime of life. So stop worrying so much.'

Jennifer tried to smile in return, but only succeeded in looking more tense. 'I can't help it,' she muttered. 'I had any number of drinks before I realised I was expecting. All those Hollywood parties . . .'

'Hey, you're not exactly a lush,' Caroline pointed out. 'Listen to Alex. He's making sense. The baby will be fine. All this is routine.'

'To you, maybe,' Jennifer said, her eyebrows rising steeply. 'Not to me.'

At last, the sonographer appeared in the doorway, clipboard in hand, looking confused. 'Jennifer Delgardo?'

All three of them got up and shuffled over together in a pack.

'Sorry about the delay, I've been looking for you. Not quite sure why you were shown in here. I'm Priti, I'll be taking your scan today.' The sonographer cast Caroline a puzzled look as well. 'Hello, what are you doing here?'

'Jenny's my sister.' Caroline knew Priti from occasional stints at the hospital. 'I'm her birthing assistant. It's her first baby and she wants me to sit in on the scan too. Is that okay?'

'Sure, come along.' The sonographer smiled and ushered them into the cosy ultrasound room. 'There's not much room, I'm afraid. But you should be able to squeeze in, if you don't mind—'

She stopped talking, her jaw dropping as she finally recognised Alex. 'Delgardo,' she repeated, taking a step back to look at him properly. 'Oh my. Are you . . . Alex Delgardo? Like, the real Alex Delgardo? Alex Delgardo from all those big movies? Bang, you're dead, Alex Delgardo?'

'That's me,' Alex said calmly, and sat on a stool next to the trolley where Caroline was already arranging Jennifer, ready for her ultrasound scan. 'Nice to meet you, Priti.'

'Well, goodness.' Priti, clearly flustered, took a few minutes to get over having a film star in her ultrasound clinic. Then she drew up her stool, turned the machine slightly towards Jennifer, whose belly was now on show, and started asking the usual set of questions in a careful, methodical manner. 'So, Jennifer, when was your last period? Would you say your cycle is regular or irregular? What kind of symptoms have you been noticing?'

Caroline was only half listening, already knowing most of the answers, as she and Jennifer had been through them weeks ago. Her mind began to creep back towards their trip to St Ives, though she'd promised herself she wouldn't dwell on what happened there. Not that she was sure precisely what had happened, only that she had made a fool of herself with Brodie.

She had woken up with a terrific hangover the morning after the party at Belinda Basildon's house, feeling horribly unwell.

'I'm not surprised you're a bit queasy,' Jennifer had told her over breakfast in her and Alex's suite that day. 'I've never seen you drink so much in one afternoon.' She paused, looking at her sympathetically. 'And you've barely said a word about your chat with Dad yesterday. I thought maybe it had gone badly so I didn't pry. Are you okay?'

'It's not just that,' Caroline had muttered, getting up from the breakfast table, unable to face any food. 'Dad more or less confirmed what Topaz had said, though without any details. It wasn't what I'd been hoping to hear. But then later, Brodie . . .'

'What's the matter? Did Brodie upset you?'

'No,' Caroline had snapped, and then bitten her lip. 'Sorry.'

'It's okay, I get the point. You don't want us interfering. But this Topaz business sounds horribly complicated, Caro. You don't need to deal with it on your own.'

'You've got enough on your plate.'

'But I've always got time for my sister.' Jennifer had got up to give her a quick hug. 'So Dad didn't deny it?'

'Not in so many words.'

'That's insane. I can't believe he would have an affair behind her back, then dump her and disappear. I know they weren't married, but she was the mother of his child, for goodness' sake. And according to Topaz, losing you both like that nearly killed her.' Jennifer had sounded suspicious, her brows drawn sharply together. 'I don't know . . . It seems so out of character for Dad. He'd bend over backwards to avoid upsetting someone.'

'There's more,' she'd admitted, and told her sister the rough outline of what Brodie had found out about Topaz's past.

'Good God,' Jennifer had gasped, sinking back on to her chair. 'A bigamist? And she assaulted Dad?'

'I keep hoping it's not true.'

'Sweetheart, if that's what Brodie says happened, then it must be true. I've never known him to get something like that wrong. Alex and I trust him completely.' Jennifer had jumped up again and thrown her arms about Caroline, breathless with anguish. 'You poor thing. To find your birth mother again after all these years apart, only to discover what she did, what she is . . . What will you do now? Will you agree to see her again?'

'I don't know.'

And that was the truth. Caroline wasn't sure she wanted to see Topaz again. Not even to confront her with what she knew about her past.

But most days her mother sent a dozen or so manic texts, and kept trying to call, even though Caroline didn't feel ready to talk to her yet and had set her phone on diversion to voicemail.

It was disturbing.

But perhaps not as disturbing as knowing she'd got insanely drunk and tried to rip Brodie's clothes off after the party.

She only had the vaguest memory of those few wretched moments in her room before he walked out, leaving her to sleep it off, still in her make-up and party frock. But what she could remember was enough to have made her fiercely avoid all contact with Brodie over the three days that had elapsed since the party. Luckily, he seemed as keen to avoid her company as she was to avoid his, so they hadn't been in the same room together for more than a few minutes since getting back from St Ives.

Caroline blushed, haunted by her embarrassing behaviour that night. She remembered kissing Brodie like a sex-starved idiot, and didn't think she would ever be able to look him in the eye again.

What must he think of her?

Not much, given that he'd barely spoken to her on the drive back from St Ives and had made himself scarce since then. Alex had not commented on his absence today, but had driven them to the scan appointment himself. As far as she knew, neither Alex nor Jennifer knew what had happened between them, and she hoped it would stay that way. But she still squirmed inwardly whenever Brodie's name came up, wishing she could just run away to her little house in Pethporro and hide there for a few years, until these feelings of deep humiliation had worn off. She'd given up her rented house though several weeks back now; there was no longer any escape possible.

Priti had started the dating scan at last, moving the scanner slowly over the barely rounded tummy, and Jennifer almost sat up, gasping, at the first blurry outlines of her baby. 'Oh Alex, look at that!'

'I see it.' His smile was rapturous.

Caroline also studied the ultrasound screen, pushing her embarrassment aside as she tried to summon some professionalism instead.

That looks odd, she thought, tilting her head to one side.

'Is that . . . is that a foot?' Jennifer stared at the faint moving images, clearly mesmerised. 'Oh my God, is that its heart beating? It's the cutest thing ever!' She turned to beam at Caroline, and abruptly stopped smiling. 'Wh- What is it? Caro, what's the matter?'

'Nothing,' Caroline said quickly.

'Don't lie, I always know when you're lying.' No, you don't, Caroline thought, but kept that observation to herself. 'You've seen something wrong, haven't you?' Jenny looked from Caroline's neutral expression to the sonographer's attentive study of the screen, getting nothing from either of them. 'For God's sake, please tell me. You're frightening me.'

Alex stirred. 'Priti, what's that?' He pointed to the left of the image of the baby, and his unease too was clear. 'That's not part of the baby, is it?'

'Yes, and no,' Priti said, and glanced at Caroline, her eyebrows raised. 'Do you want to tell them, or shall I?'

'Tell us what?' Jennifer's voice had risen in alarm.

'*This* is a baby,' Caroline said, leaning forward to point at the screen where Jennifer had seen the unmistakeable pulse of a tiny heart, beating fast. 'And *that*,' she continued, pointed at the blurrier line Alex had noticed on the far side, 'is another baby.'

'I don't understand,' Jennifer said.

Alex blinked but said nothing. He stared at the screen in disbelief, still holding Jennifer's hand.

'You're expecting twins, Mr and Mrs Delgardo,' Priti told them, smiling joyfully at the parents-to-be. She turned comfortably back to the screen and set about marking up the two foetuses' measurements to help establish a due date, while Caroline watched her deft, expert clicks. 'Two babies for the price of one. Isn't that wonderful?'

'I don't believe it. *Identical twins?*'

Alex laughed at Brodie's stunned expression, his own face glowing with happiness. 'That's what it looks like. Though we'll need to wait a little longer to be certain they're sharing a placenta. Non-identical twins each get their own placenta, I'm told. But there are definitely two babies in there.'

'That's marvellous,' Brodie told him, thrilled for his friend. 'You saw them both on the screen?'

'Yes. Two hearts, beating strongly. And Jennifer's got pictures to prove it. She's taking a nap at the moment, but I'll ask her to show them to you later.'

'I'd love that.'

'Twins . . .' Alex was clearly still coming to terms with their discovery. 'Isn't it the most amazing thing? Not that we intended to have a baby at all. But having two at once is rather impressive.' His smile broadened. 'I'm still not quite sure how we managed it, though I have some theories.'

'What does that mean?'

They were standing outside on the lawn, watching as the gardener Alex had recently hired sorted out heaps of fallen leaves with a large and very noisy hand-held leaf blower. There'd been some strong winds recently and most of the deciduous trees about the grounds were now stark and bare, their branches denuded. But some were still jealously guarding a few last leaves as the year turned towards Christmas.

'Oh, you know. I'm just a twin-making machine.'

'I see.' Brodie shook his head at his friend's smug expression. 'You're taking all the credit for this, then.'

'Of course.'

'So, when these two are teenagers and kicking up merry hell, Jennifer will remind you of that, and blame you for everything.'

Alex looked shocked. 'Teenagers? Good God, they're barely out of the first trimester. Let's not look that far ahead. It makes me feel old.'

'Just as well you decided to launch Delgardo Films though,' Brodie said slowly, considering the situation. 'You'll have even less time available for big film roles when the twins are born.'

'Yeah, I know you disapprove. But it'll happen to you one day, Brodie, and believe me, you'll understand.'

Unbidden, a heated memory of Caroline kissing him with fierce abandon sprang into his mind. Bloody hell! Brodie ran a hand through his hair, thrusting that image back where it came from.

'I doubt it.'

'You don't want kids? You don't want to settle down, start a family?'

'Maybe I'm not a family man.'

'That's not it.' Alex studied him, suddenly frowning. 'You don't think anyone will have you, do you? That's what this is about.'

'I beg your pardon?'

'Because of your leg. You think nobody's ever going to want to take you on, that you'll be alone forever.'

'What the . . . ?'

Alex shook his head, raising a hand when Brodie swore

at him under his breath. 'Yeah, okay, I'm sorry I said that. But you are definitely a family man, Brodie. So don't feed me that old line. And I'm sorry about your leg too. Really sorry. You know that better than anyone.'

Alex was talking about his breakdown, of course, when he'd blamed himself for Brodie's injuries in the bombing, suffering terrible nightmares and flashbacks. Jennifer had brought him out of that hell and on to the road to recovery. But there would be no ministering angel to save Brodie. Nobody could ever restore his leg or bridge the dark abyss in his head, the place he went when he was alone and hurting.

'But you can't live in the past forever,' Alex finished. 'Especially when the future could be so much better.'

'Great pep talk, Dr Alex. Thanks for that.'

'For God's sake . . .'

Brodie's mouth tightened. But he refused to lose his temper with Alex. They were still best friends, after everything they'd been through together, including the terrorist bombing, and he wanted to keep it that way. Even if it meant swallowing some of Alex's well-intentioned advice occasionally.

'Look, Alex, I know this is excruciatingly bad timing,' Brodie said roughly, shoving his hands into his jeans pockets and hunching his shoulders, 'what with Christmas coming, and the new company launch too . . .' He stopped, suddenly too awkward to continue. There would be questions asked, and he wasn't sure he was ready to give answers. Or not honest answers, at any rate. And he disliked having to lie to this man. Better, perhaps, to say nothing.

'But?'

'But . . . I need to ask a favour.'

Alex raised his eyebrows. 'Whatever you want, mate. You only have to ask. You know that.'

'I'd like to move into Pixie Cottage,' Brodie said quickly, before he could change his mind about asking. 'To live there rather than here at the house.'

His friend looked at him steadily, and Brodie could almost see his brain ticking through the possibilities. There was a difficult moment of silence.

'Why?'

'The cottage has been standing empty for a while now. I know we talked about using it for visiting actors or producers, but that's unlikely to happen anytime soon, and . . . I just feel like some time alone, you know?' Brodie carefully avoided Alex's searching gaze, ending his request with a shrug. 'Though if you'd rather I stay at the house, it's not a problem.'

'Of course you can move into Pixie Cottage. Take it, it's yours.'

'It's just temporary.'

'Stay as long as you like. There've been a lot of changes recently, I expect you've got a lot to think about. And we've been living out of each other's pockets for years now. It makes perfect sense, you wanting some private space, a place to call your own.'

'Thanks, Alex.'

They shook hands on it, as though sealing a deal. Brodie felt a bit better, though he was uncomfortably aware that he hadn't revealed his true reason for wanting to leave the main house. A light rain began to fall, and they turned to head back indoors, the flat-capped gardener continuing with his work without even looking up.

'Something happened between you and Caroline at the party the other night, didn't it?' Alex asked, with a casual air that didn't fool Brodie for one minute. As he had clearly not fooled Alex either, he thought bitterly, opening his mouth to deny it. 'No, don't say anything. It's obvious from the way you two haven't spoken to each other since. What happened?'

'Nothing,' Brodie muttered, looking away. 'A misunderstanding.'

'Got drunk, did she? Made a pass at you?'

Brodie stopped and stared at him, feeling winded. 'Has . . . has Caroline been speaking to Jenny about it?'

'Of course not. She hasn't said a word to either of us. Probably too embarrassed, like you.'

Alex laughed at his stunned expression and continued to walk on as the rain grew heavier. Behind them, even the sound of the leaf blower had stopped now. Brodie caught up with him after a short hesitation, deeply unsettled, not sure what to think or how to react.

A cream-coloured cat detached himself from the shrubbery and ran for the door too, no doubt sensing an opportunity to get out of the rain.

'Look,' Alex told him coolly, 'don't worry about it. From

what Jenny's told me, it sounds like typical Caroline-at-a-party behaviour. She's always been the same. Any port in a storm. Her flings don't mean anything though. Jenny says they never last.'

Alex threw open the side door into the house and they bustled inside, both wiping their feet. Uninterested in them except as door-openers, Ripper padded silently past on damp paws, probably in search of somewhere warm to sleep.

'So if you're moving out of Porro Park because of that, don't bother,' Alex continued, his voice echoing along the corridor. 'I'm sure it'll all blow over in a few days.'

'I'm not moving out because of anyone,' Brodie insisted, keeping his voice down. 'I want to live at the cottage because . . .'

Brodie fell silent, unable to give his fear a name. All he knew was that he needed to be alone for a while, to confront whatever he was feeling and get the hell past it. And he couldn't do that while aware that Caroline was sleeping a few hundred feet from his own bedroom. It was becoming hard enough to sleep at night without having to wrestle with that temptation.

'Because you need some head space away from this circus. Yeah, I get it, no need to explain yourself.' Alex gave him a reluctant smile. 'I can't say I'm overjoyed about the arrangement. But Pixie Cottage is only a few minutes' walk through the woods, and you'll always be on the end of a phone if there's an emergency. Plus it's almost Christmas so we ought to be taking a break about now, anyway. In

other words, I guess I'm cool with it.' His friend hesitated.
'You'll still come here to work when you're needed?'

'Absolutely.'

'And you'll join us for Christmas Day lunch?'

'Who's cooking? You?'

'Françoise.'

'In that case,' Brodie said with a grin, 'I accept.'

CHAPTER TWENTY-SEVEN

Caroline was helping Jennifer decorate the massive Christmas tree in the atrium. It was an eight-foot spruce with thick lush branches curling with fragrant greenery. Now that all the flashing lights and silver tinsel had been wound about its sturdy frame, the baubles and ornaments needed to be attached. Jennifer handled the baubles while Caroline hooked beautiful white ornaments here and there, trying to get the spread right. The box of ornaments held sparkling reindeer, angels, little children praying, stars of all styles and sizes. But they were quite fiddly to attach, so that Jennifer had finished with her baubles long before Caroline hooked the last shiny star on the tree.

Both sisters stood back to admire the effect.

'Gorgeous,' a deep voice said from behind them. 'But I think you've forgotten something.' It was Alex, and he was holding out the large, handmade angel destined for the top of the tree. 'Allow me.'

He moved the stepladder into position and climbed up, placing the pretty gilt angel as straight as possible on the topmost spur.

'What do you think?'

Her halo and broad, featherlike wings glittered under the atrium lights, wide white skirts slightly translucent, fairy lights flashing through them.

'Perfect,' Jennifer whispered, clasping both hands together, her face radiant with happiness. 'Absolutely perfect.' Then her smile faltered and she looked round wistfully at her husband, a note of pleading in her voice. 'I only wish Brodie were here to see it.'

'He'll be here for Christmas drinks tonight as arranged,' Alex said soothingly. 'And Christmas Day lunch too, of course. He's just taking a few days out for the holidays, you know that. Come January, it'll be work as usual.'

'But he won't move back here in January, will he?'

'No, he's determined to stay at Pixie Cottage for the fore-seeable future.' Alex paused. 'I guess he has some issues to work through.'

'But what does that mean? What kind of issues?'

Alex glanced at Caroline, then away. He shrugged. 'No idea. He didn't share. And frankly, it's none of our business.'

'It's our business if we did something to upset him.'

Alex shook his head. 'Brodie wants some time on his own, that's all. Let's leave the man alone, shall we?'

'Caro, what do you think? Should we walk over to the cottage and ask Brodie to move back in over Christmas, at least?' Jennifer smiled at her encouragingly. 'I miss him about the place, don't you? And nobody should be alone at Christmas. It's not right.'

Caroline muttered, 'I expect Alex is right, we should

leave well alone,' and bent to collect the empty ornament box. 'And speak for yourself, Jenny. I don't miss him.'

'Caro!'

Her sister sounded stunned, staring wide-eyed.

Aware of a slight flush in her cheeks, Caroline hurriedly carried the box back down to the cellar where she'd found it, and stood there in semi-darkness for a few minutes, gathering enough composure to be able to face them again.

Did she miss Brodie?

She'd lied to her sister. He'd only been gone a few days, but the house seemed almost bare without him. Ridiculous, really. And she kept feverishly going over that bloody party in her mind, and what had followed. The way she'd danced with him, and then later kissed him, trying to undress the man, for God's sake!

Small wonder he had fled to the relative seclusion of Pixie Cottage, where his boss's sex-mad sister couldn't pursue him. No doubt he had been disgusted by her behaviour. Disgusted and repulsed.

She put her hands to her hot cheeks, wishing she could just live down here in the cellar and never be seen again.

It was horrible to imagine what he was thinking now, how appalling he must find her. She had never thought of herself as a sex pest. But what else could she take away from the fact that Brodie had almost immediately packed his things after that night in St Ives, moving instead into the old cottage beyond the woods where Jennifer had once been a tenant? She was not fooled for a minute by Alex's reassurances that his friend had 'issues' to work through.

He had chosen to leave this very comfortable and luxurious house, at Christmas time no less, and camp out in a damp old building that hadn't been lived in for several years, though Alex had insisted it was clean and would soon warm up after a good fire. Nobody would make that choice without a damn good reason.

And she was the reason he had left.

Her, Caroline Enys.

She moaned softly, hating herself.

Whatever else happened, she must try never to even *look* at him again. Even if they had to sit in the same room together, which was almost certainly going to happen at some point. There was a drinks party tonight, of course. But it was easy to avoid someone at a party. However, the logistics of never looking at him again if the four of them had to spend Christmas Day together, including sitting down to lunch in the dining room, would probably defeat her. But she was determined not to give Brodie any reason to call her behaviour into question again.

She wondered if she owned any truly chaste-looking clothes that she could wear at Christmas lunch. Maybe a roll-top sweater and floor-length skirt. Something suitably nun-like.

'You all right down there?' Alex called down the stairs.

Jumping guiltily, she started back up the cellar stairs at once. 'Sorry, I was just, erm, rearranging some things.'

She needn't have worried that Alex would find her behaviour strange. He was looking distracted, a frown on his face.

'Jenny wants you to go out with her, if you're free.'

'Sure.' Caroline put on a fierce, bright smile. 'Free all day!'

'That's great. She wants to take Brodie some of Françoise's home-baked Christmas goodies, and it's obvious she won't be happy until she's done it.' He paused. 'I need to make some calls, but I don't like the idea of her walking through the woods alone. Can you walk with her?'

Her smile felt frozen, pinned in place but unreal. 'She's going to Pixie Cottage? This morning?'

He patted her shoulder, nodding his thanks, and strode off to his office without another word, tonight's drinks party no doubt on his mind. Several investors and other business acquaintances had agreed to come, and they had a team of caterers and an event organiser arriving mid-afternoon to start setting out tables of food and drinks, and getting Porro Park ready to receive party guests.

Meanwhile, she was going to walk through the woods to visit Brodie with a basket of goodies. Talk about Little Red Riding Hood! Only the wolf would be more scared than she was.

Caroline wanted to scream her frustration.

Jenny came downstairs, already in her new faux fur-lined boots and suitably wrapped up against the cold. She spotted Caroline and smiled. 'Did Alex tell you? Come out with me, I'm taking Brodie some of Françoise's delicious gingerbread biscuits. And a few other things, of course. Tinsel, spare decorations, a bottle of crème de menthe to keep him warm.' She laughed, making for the other box of decorations, which was still half-full of shiny, glittering objects. 'I bet he hasn't even bothered making the cottage look festive. Won't he be surprised when we turn up?'

'Jenny, I don't think it's a very good idea,' Caroline told her earnestly.

'Why ever not?'

'Barging in there unannounced ... Brodie wants privacy, doesn't he? I doubt he'll be happy to see us.'

'Nonsense.' But Jennifer was frowning. She stopped rummaging through the other box of decorations and looked up at her. 'Has something happened between you and Brodie? He was fine until we left the two of you together at Belinda's party. Alex mentioned something about it but I didn't believe him. Now though ...' Her voice tailed off at Caroline's unhappy expression. 'Oh my God, was Alex right? What on earth happened?'

'I was a bit pissed, that's all. Nothing to get excited about.'

Her sister's eyes narrowed on her face. 'Then you won't mind coming with me to see Brodie.' It was a statement of fact, not a question. 'You'd better get a coat on. I know it looks sunny, but there's a sharp wind.'

Caroline knew she had to put her foot down. Yes, Jennifer was paying her to be her companion-slash-live-in-midwife, but she had agreed that the job wouldn't start formally until after the New Year. And surely her work didn't include tailing about everywhere after Jennifer, according to her sister's every whim. It simply wasn't reasonable.

Plus, she had no desire to see Brodie again. Tonight at the drinks party would be quite soon enough, thank you. And it would be easy to ignore him at a gathering. Not quite so easy when she was face to face with the man in a tiny bloody cottage.

'I'm sorry,' she said, trying to sound calm, 'but I'd rather not go over there right now. Why not ...' Caroline hesitated, racking her brains for a suitable alternative. 'Why not hand over the gingerbread biscuits and decorations when he comes round tonight?'

'Because I want to see him,' Jennifer said unhappily, and folded her arms across her chest. 'I want to check he's okay. He's a good friend and I'm worried about him. And you should be too.'

Guilt flooded her. Brodie had left Porro Park because of her, she was sure of it. But Jennifer seemed to think he was upset, when he was far more likely to be in hiding, taking care not to spend more time in Caroline's company than was absolutely necessary.

'I don't understand. Why are you so worried?'

'Because it's not like Brodie to suddenly disappear. I've never known him to do something like this before, and neither has Alex. Something has to be badly wrong.' Jennifer gave her a searching look. 'And I think you know more about this than you're telling.'

'Don't be silly.'

'Then why won't you come with me?'

Caroline was saved from having to answer by the steady buzzing of her phone. She fished it out of the back pocket of her jeans.

It was a call.

From Topaz. Yet again.

Her heart sped up at once and she felt unmistakeable signs of panic: sweaty palms, and a violent desire to throw her phone across the atrium.

'Who is it?' Jennifer asked, curious.

'Doesn't matter.'

Caroline turned away and forced herself to let the phone ring out, then sucked in a breath as it chimed with a new notification. A voice message.

Gingerly, she called her service and listened.

It was Topaz, of course.

'Darling, it's Mummy. I've been trying to get in touch. Is your phone on the blink or have you lost it?' A peal of fake-sounding laughter. 'Anyway, look, this is about the hundredth voice message I've left. And I've lost count of all the texts I've sent. I need to make sure you're okay, so I'm coming over. I'll be there about midday, and I hope the gate will be open this time. Love you, darling!'

Caroline closed her eyes in horror. When her mother had said, 'I hope the gate will be open this time,' there had been a note of steely threat in her voice.

Coming to a swift decision, she turned back to Jennifer with a smile. 'Actually,' she said brightly, and saw Jennifer's eyes narrow again in suspicion, 'I do rather fancy a walk, if you're sure you feel up to it. Something to shake off the winter blues. And Brodie loves those gingerbread biscuits, doesn't he?' She hurried towards the stairs. 'Give me a minute to wrap up properly, and I'll be right with you.'

CHAPTER TWENTY-EIGHT

Pixie Cottage lay just beyond the woods, its low white-washed walls and gently smoking chimney overshadowed by the trees. It was pretty, the kind of cottage you might find pictured on a jigsaw puzzle box, and with a flower-bright garden to match in the summer. During the winter months, the garden was bare and damp, its dark soil empty of green shoots. Ivy clung to the trunks of the nearest trees, and in places to the stone-topped garden walls, lending greenery to the scene. A vast holly bush dominated one corner of the garden, with gorgeous red berries in abundance, a feast for the birds that hopped or flew quickly out of view as soon as Caroline and Jennifer swung open the garden gate.

'I remember this place so well,' Jennifer said softly, taking a few steps down the garden path. She stopped, turning on her heel to gaze about herself at the enclosed garden and the cottage before them, the words Pixie Cottage carved into a piece of driftwood attached to the wall, along with an image of a cheeky-looking Cornish piskie.

'Well,' Caroline said reluctantly, nodding to the chimney, 'at least we know he's in. There's a fire lit.'

'To keep out the damp. Very wise. This place had a damp problem when I was living here. Though Alex soon had it fixed.'

'I seem to recall you having to move in with Alex at Porro Park while the work was being done,' Caroline reminded her, and laughed when her sister looked away, smiling shyly at the memory of those early days of their courtship. Teasingly, she added, 'I can't imagine how on earth you whiled away the lonely hours, stuck in a mansion with an international film star.'

'Oh God, the boredom!'

'Not to mention his seven bloody goats.'

'Well, his grandmother mostly took care of the goats . . .' Jennifer's smile faded and her voice tailed off. 'I miss her so much. Dear Nelly. I wish she could have seen us married. It would have made her so happy.'

'Maybe she did see it.'

Jennifer cast her a long, considering look. 'I didn't think you believed in that kind of thing.'

' "There are more things in heaven and earth," ' Caroline quoted. 'Yes, I'll never be that heavily into . . . Well, witchy things. Not like you. But I guess I'm open to the concept of some form of consciousness after death. Especially with something like that. Besides, it's a comfort to people, isn't it?'

Jennifer nodded sombrely.

The door to the cottage opened.

Brodie stood there, looking grim and a little underdressed in shorts and a vest top, considering the chilly December weather. She noticed his brawny muscles first, strong shoulders still tanned from the Californian sun, and his enticingly broad chest. Then belatedly, she glanced at his bare leg beside the prosthetic limb, again with thigh muscles prominent. He was drying his hands on a towel, staring at them without saying a word.

Jennifer nudged her. 'Shut your mouth, you're drooling,' she whispered.

'Excuse me?'

'Merry Christmas!' her sister said more loudly, going up the garden path with her arms full of presents. 'Been working out, Brodie? Looking pretty buff there.'

Brodie nodded. 'I brought my weight rig over from the house. It's not the same as using your gym, but it keeps me out of trouble.' He hesitated, looking at the box she was carrying. 'For me?'

'I see your psychic powers have improved after spending time in my old cottage.' Jennifer grinned. 'Those old walls have seen a lot of magic, of course. Some of it must have rubbed off.'

Brodie gave her a dry look. 'Well, you'd better come in.' He slung the towel over his shoulder and stood aside, adding belatedly, 'Merry Christmas.'

He had not met her gaze, Caroline thought miserably.

'I brought stuff too,' she said lamely, carrying it inside, and then stopped, staring. 'Gosh.'

The cottage looked very different from when Jennifer had been living there, she thought, turning to look about the downstairs in surprise. Gone were all the jars of witchy ingredients and strange posters detailing moon phases and other esoteric information. The comfortable old sofa had been pushed back against the wall and Brodie's weights rig had taken its place, steel and shiny chrome glinting under the wall spotlights, alongside a state-of-the-art rowing machine. A few intellectual-looking books were stacked up on the coffee table, alongside a *Financial Times* and a copy of the *New Scientist*. There was an espresso machine standing beside a large new microwave on the kitchen surface, and the rugs had been removed to leave well-polished bare boards underfoot. The deeply feminine feel to the cottage during Jennifer's tenancy had given way to a hard-edged, even brooding masculine vibe.

'Wow . . . You've really made some changes.' Jennifer set her box of Christmas goodies in the small kitchen area, a slight note of disapproval in her voice. She was also studying the place, no doubt noting the differences since her own residence at Pixie Cottage. 'I mean, if this is what you want, that's fine. But it's a bit of a come-down after living at Porro Park, isn't it? And don't you get lonely out here?'

'I felt like some time on my own, that's all.'

Brodie sounded defensive and perhaps a little annoyed too. Probably because Caroline had turned up on his doorstep after he had gone to all this trouble to avoid her.

Caroline set down her own gift bag and looked curiously at the weights and rower. She wondered if he missed having constant access to the gym at Porro Park; she had seen him in there more than once, looking impressively muscular and pumping iron.

'I totally know what that's like,' Jennifer agreed, and laid a hand on his arm. 'That's why I moved here too, remember? But you're always welcome with us. Nobody should be alone at this time of year.' She paused, frowning. 'I certainly hope it wasn't something we did. Please tell me we didn't drive you away, because that would be awful.'

'It was my decision. Nothing to do with you. Honestly.' Brodie managed a smile, though Caroline was aware that he had still barely glanced in her direction. 'Now look, can I get you two a drink? I've got coffee, tea, or you might prefer something more festive.'

'Nothing alcoholic for me,' Jennifer said promptly. 'Tea would be great. Though let me make it. I know my way about, remember?'

With obvious reluctance, Brodie moved aside, letting Jennifer bustle about the tiny kitchen space instead, cheerfully pulling mugs out of cupboards and filling the kettle.

'What about you, Caroline?' he said, turning to address her at last. 'Can I tempt you?' His gaze met hers, and she felt a jolt run through her. There was such a look of searing honesty in his face, it was hard not to flinch from it. 'To a drink, that is.'

Brodie felt almost winded by her presence. He could not believe the damage it had done to his mood, having Caroline in his private space, standing only a few feet away. He had been working out with free weights before the two women arrived, focused on his body, each muscle contracting and relaxing, the steady rhythm taking him to a place where he could be calm and centred. Then he had heard voices out in the garden, and instantly recognised hers, its husky feminine pitch. And he had dropped the weight he'd been working out with, though not particularly heavy, his newfound calm deserting him at once.

Peering out of the window, he had seen her with Jennifer, gloved and hatted, but with the winter sun lighting up her blonde strands so that it seemed at first glance as though she were glowing.

'Bloody hell,' he'd muttered, glancing down at himself in shorts and sweaty vest top, but it had been too late to do much more than grab a towel and dry himself off.

Brodie felt ludicrously vulnerable and exposed in front of Caroline. He felt more acutely than ever the physical disadvantage of his prosthetic limb, how the absence of his left leg marked him out as different from other men. It shouldn't be an issue, he knew, and the others at his support group would surely leap to attack that attitude if he was ever stupid enough to mention it to them.

But ever since he'd made the mistake of kissing her, and discovered that his attraction to Caroline ran deeper than a Christmas party fling, things had become skewed in his mind.

Now, he couldn't help fearing what she might think of him.

Of *it*.

'Bit early for me.' Caroline smiled, but her mouth looked stiff. Like she was forcing herself to seem friendly. 'I'll be fine with tea, thank you.'

She was offended, of course, and he could hardly blame her. Caroline had been in the mood for more than a kiss and cuddle after that bloody party, and at first he had shown willing, and then abruptly walked out on her. She must feel rejected. That's how he would feel in the same position. Rejected and angry, his pride hurt. And he could see it in her face.

'You need to pace yourselves for tonight's drinks party,' Jennifer threw over her shoulder as she waited for the kettle to boil. Her look was pure mischief. 'You don't want a rerun of St Ives, do you?'

Caroline looked daggers at her sister, but did not respond, merely stalking to the window and gazing out at the wintry garden and woods beyond.

Brodie knew how she felt.

Grimacing, he snatched a flyer off the table and held it up. Time to change the subject. 'Did you get one of these, by the way?' He handed it to Jennifer, since Caroline had not looked round. 'I saw it at the newsagents in Pethporro the other day, but forgot to mention it to Alex. It's an advertisement for the Boxing Day pageant. You used to run that event, didn't you?'

'Yes, once upon a distant memory. I wonder who's running it this year?' Jennifer's eyebrows raised as she scanned the colourful flyer. 'Hey, this looks rather fun.' She read out, *'Morris dancers. Pony Rides. Banishing the Midwinter Dark Ritual. Torchlit Carnival Procession to the Beach,'* then added with a knowing smile, 'They have a great refreshments tent too. This year they've got a whole range of local beers, a roast pig on a spit, plus the usual Pethporro pasties.' She looked at him, and then glanced towards Caroline. 'Shall we all go together? It would make a great day out.'

Caroline said nothing, her back still turned.

Although he hadn't actually intended to go to the pageant, having very little interest either in the food or the local beers on offer or even the famous torchlit procession to the beach, Brodie heard himself say, 'Count me in, I'd be happy to go,' and was rewarded with an approving smile from Jennifer.

'Caroline?'

With obvious reluctance, Caroline looked round. 'I'll be there,' she agreed. 'The midwifery team always goes, unless there's a call-out. I was invited too. But I'll go with you and hook up with my friends at some point.'

Their eyes met fleetingly, but all he saw in her face was coolness and distance. An ice-cold goddess, perfect in this wintry setting.

Brodie had a sudden urge to shout, 'Stop hating me!' Or kiss her wildly. Or apologise for being an idiot. Perhaps all of them at once. Yes, he was seriously messed-up, but he'd been dealing with it, trying to regain control over his emotions before this damn drinks party tonight. The last thing he'd needed was having to deal with his weakness for Caroline before he felt completely ready . . .

A sudden noise from above the house made him stiffen in surprise, looking up as though he could see through the rafters.

What the hell?

There was a crazed yowling at the half-open door, then a slim cream flash tore across the cottage and into his mistress's arms.

'Oh, Ripper!' Jennifer exclaimed, cradling the Siamese cat and rubbing her forehead against his fur as he yowled and arched his back. 'Don't panic, you silly thing. It's only a helicopter.'

Brodie strode to the door and out into the garden just in time to see the whirring rotor blades and dark blue body of a helicopter above the treetops, seconds before the pilot began to descend, presumably to the helipad on the lawns at Porro Park.

Emotion stirred in him: a primitive excitement at the idea of flying again, in all likelihood. He remembered looking down at the bright patchwork of England's fields, the helicopter's shadow running beneath them. He'd missed the sheer adrenalin of flying a helicopter at speed, that was for certain. Of being in control of all that raw power.

But that was yet another desire he had to stifle. The helicopter was not his. It belonged to Delgardo Films. And despite initially embracing the idea of being a film company director, he was no longer sure about staying on with Alex.

He still didn't know how he would take to this new role, after all. Being in charge for once, not obeying an order without question but giving the orders himself – and facing the consequences if he called it wrong. That was another reason he had come out here to the peace and quiet of Pixie Cottage. So he could meditate on his future, undisturbed by constantly bumping into Caroline Enys.

As soon as she was under the same roof as him, his brain refused to work and all he could think about was . . .

He pushed that crazy impulse away with difficulty.

'Alex asked them to deliver the new helicopter before Christmas.' Jennifer had come to the door, a shivering cat still in her arms. 'Will you go up with Alex in it sometime over the holidays? He'll be eager to check it out.'

Alex had taken his pilot's licence in the States and had insisted on buying a new chopper now they were permanently settled in Cornwall. And it was true that a helicopter was the fastest way to get about the north of the Duchy, with its winding roads and lack of train line. But he was a less experienced helicopter pilot than Brodie, who had trained to fly soon after leaving the army.

'Of course.' Brodie came back inside and closed the door. Caroline had sat down on the sofa during his absence, her long legs crossed, her face still averted. 'It would be my pleasure.'

There had been a time, Brodie thought, when Alex had been unable to bear even the sound of a helicopter's blades. It had reminded him of the terrorist bombing they'd both endured; helicopters had been used afterwards to ferry them to hospital, miles across the desert. Even after he'd returned to Cornwall, the sound of a passing helicopter had triggered an attack once that left Alex battered and horrified by his own reaction.

Nothing so dramatic in Brodie's case, of course. His own

triggers since the bombing were far more subtle. But they still existed.

'You've never been up in a chopper, have you, Caroline?' His tone was deceptively casual. He knew she didn't like flying.

'No,' Caroline said sharply. Her gaze jolted against his, then she glared down at the backs of her hands instead, as though offended by them. 'Nasty, unnatural machines. I'm happy in a car, thank you, even if it takes five times longer to get anywhere.'

He said nothing, watching her.

Jennifer handed out the steaming mugs, looking from her sister's flushed face to Brodie's calm exterior.

'Well, Merry Christmas, everyone,' she said, her smile ironic.

CHAPTER TWENTY-NINE

To Caroline's relief, moving with a smile among the guests, the Christmas drinks party seemed to be passing off without a single hitch. They had managed to keep the paparazzi firmly outside the gates, though flashes had gone off every time a car turned in and swept up the drive, and apart from one intrepid photographer found wandering in the shrubbery, nobody who wasn't on the very exclusive guest list had turned up. And despite repeated text messages from Topaz demanding entrance, which had got Caroline a little agitated earlier in the evening, so far nothing had happened to spoil the party.

On the minus side, Brodie had barely looked at her all evening, so that she regretted having worn a rather decorous cream satin sheath dress when she might as well have chosen the slinkiest outfit in her wardrobe. But at least there was a long slit at one side of her dress, not visible unless she lengthened her stride, but there all the same. A kind of unconscious nod towards the turmoil inside her, the electricity she could feel building . . .

Not that her appearance mattered. The most important

investors spent most of the time clustered about Alex, while Jennifer wowed the visiting actors and Ripper prowled about the downstairs rooms, alternately charming guests with his looks and ripping their hands to shreds with one vicious swipe.

The atmosphere was mellow and relaxed rather than festive, despite the sparkling Christmas tree and the lavish decorations that adorned every available space. Françoise and her partner Marie joined them towards the end, her work done, while the hired catering staff continued to circulate with trays of champagne and canapés. A pianist-vocalist called David played soft background music in the atrium, looking rather dashing in a dress shirt and fitted black dinner jacket.

Brodie had a friend visiting. Some guy called Sean, whom he introduced to her briefly as an ex-army buddy, had come down from London specially for the party. The two men stood drinking and chatting together most of the evening, until Brodie took him over to talk to Alex and a group of film people, and left him there. But Caroline noted that he still didn't come over to talk to her afterwards, but disappeared among the guests.

Almost as though she didn't exist, she thought bitterly.

They were all standing in the atrium as the clock was striking midnight, listening to the vocalist sing 'In the Bleak Midwinter' to an appreciative crowd, when Françoise suddenly detached herself from Marie and headed unsteadily in her direction.

Taking Caroline by surprise, Françoise took her aside

and hissed, 'Miss Enys, tell your mother to stop coming to the gate, *hein*? I am under strict instructions from Mr Delgardo not to let her in, and she does not like hearing that. Nor do I like repeating it until I am nauseous.' Her fierce gaze seemed to pierce Caroline's skull as she grabbed her arm. *'Tu comprends?'*

'Oui,' Caroline said crossly, pulling her arm free so violently she spilt some of the bubbly in her champagne flute. 'Yes, I understand. But I don't know why you're blaming me. I can hardly stop Topaz from visiting.'

'She told me you were *expecting* her.'

Caroline blushed. 'Oh.'

It was true that Topaz had warned her she would come to Porro Park if Caroline kept ignoring her texts, and she had paid no attention. But it was also true that she couldn't control her mother's choices.

Topaz wanted something, clearly, and wouldn't be content until she got it. Caroline was afraid that something was money, and since she had none herself, it seemed likely that Topaz would be hoping to lean on Jennifer and Alex instead. Or more worryingly, pressure Caroline to do the leaning.

Which she would absolutely refuse to do, of course.

'I thought as much.' Françoise nodded grimly, then weaved back to her partner's side, throwing a menacing, 'Perhaps next time I call the police!' over her shoulder.

Marie gave her an apologetic smile. 'She's been drinking,' she mouthed.

Her face hot with embarrassment, Caroline turned and

hurried blindly down the corridor to the kitchen before anyone could see her mortified expression and start asking questions.

Call the police?

She barged blindly into a side pantry and stood there in the darkness, cringing in horror at the thought of the police getting involved.

Her phone beeped with a message. She took it out, checking the screen unwillingly. All her texts from the past few days had been from Topaz. And the longer she left them unanswered, the more unpleasant they became.

This one was no different.

Why don't you ever reply to me? Or answer your phone? I never thought my own daughter would turn out to be such a bitch.

Caroline groaned.

Topaz was her mother, for God's sake! And it didn't bear thinking about the scandal she could unleash on their family with a few choice words to a reporter . . .

But perhaps the nasty texts were deliberate, she thought. Topaz might suspect that Alex would offer her money if she threatened to sell her story to the newspapers. He was a celebrity, after all, and some people might pay to read about his sister-in-law's dodgy mother.

She had promised Topaz twice now that she would meet her for lunch again, but only after the Christmas break. It would be for the last time. She owed her mother that, to tell her face to face there was no longer any point lying, she knew all about her past. And to say goodbye.

But apparently, making Topaz wait until after Christmas

to see her was not good enough. So the angry texts had started to flood in.

'Is everything all right?' A husky voice brought her head up in alarm. 'Caroline?'

It was Brodie, standing in the darkened doorway. Who else? she thought, cursing her luck. He must have spotted her leaving the party and followed her down here. Unless he'd been doing a security sweep. Which would be typical of him. Even now he was no longer Alex's bodyguard-cum-assistant, he was still acting the part.

She hesitated over the latest text from Topaz, then placed her phone face down on the counter. It was too embarrassing to admit she was being harassed by her own mother.

'I'm fine,' Caroline threw at him. She knocked back the last of her champagne. 'I just needed some air.'

'In a pantry?'

'All those flashing Christmas lights were doing my head in. It's cool and dark in here.' She paused, then added defiantly, 'And peaceful, until you came along.'

She was a teensy bit tipsy, she realised, hearing the high pitch of her voice and the silly things she was saying. All the same, she raised her chin, glaring at his shadowy outline as though blaming him for everything. Which seemed like a good idea, right now.

'So, what's your excuse?' Caroline continued, unable to control her urge to needle him.

'Sorry?'

'Shouldn't you be at the party? Mingling with the bigwigs?' She set her empty champagne flute on the counter next to her phone. 'You're a company director now. You should be schmoozing.'

His face hardened. 'I'm not very good at ... What did you call it?'

'Schmoozing.'

'That's right, schmoozing.' His sarcastic tone showed what he thought of *that* idea. 'I tend to leave that kind of thing to Alex and Jennifer. They're far better at socialising than I am.'

'Remind me, what is your role in this new film company? What exactly do you bring to the table, Brodie?'

Apart from all that undeniable sexiness and heat, she thought wildly, feeling her heartbeat accelerate as he took a couple of steps into the pantry. With the light behind him, she couldn't see his face clearly. But his presence seemed forbidding, his eyes glittering in the darkness.

She waited, but he didn't reply.

Instinctively, Caroline edged further away, swaying on her high heels. 'You can't get by forever on your lone wolf image.'

'My *what*?'

'Lone wolf. Knight errant.' She gesticulated wildly, reaching for sense and not quite getting there. 'Hermit ... dude.'

'Exactly how drunk are you?'

'For God's sake, Brodie, you should be out there with the other guests, introducing yourself, giving them confidence in Delgardo Films. Instead, you're wandering about on your own in the dark. You don't even have a drink in your hand.' She looked him up and down in the immaculate, tight-fitting black tuxedo. 'You look more like . . . like hired security than the man in charge.'

She didn't know why she was taunting him like this, only that just looking at the man made her angry. Or not angry, but disturbed and unhappy. Like everything inside her was churned up, her stomach fluttering in part-nerves, part-excitement. It felt like fury. But deep down, she knew it wasn't, and hated herself for being so weak.

Temper whipped up inside her as she stared at him. 'I mean, why did you even bother turning up tonight?'

'Because it's my duty, and I owe it to Alex and Jenny to be here.' His voice was tight, his face still unreadable in shadow. 'Besides, it sounds like you've had enough to drink for the both of us.'

'Oh, shut up!' Furious, Caroline tried to barge past him, but he caught her by the arm. 'What are you doing? Let go of me!'

'I wish I could,' he said thickly, and drew her closer.

Before she really knew what was happening, Brodie was kissing her. She ought to have pushed him away, of course. But she didn't. She could feel heat coming off him in waves, and it wasn't just physical. She was so deeply attracted to him, it actually hurt to be this close.

His lips were harder than she remembered, his kiss more forceful. And his arms about her felt so right, it was hard to protest.

He made a noise under his breath, and then kicked the pantry door shut behind him, locking them in darkness together.

In one smooth move that she didn't see coming, Brodie shifted her back against the wall, their lips still clamped together, kissing desperately as though their lives depended on it. With barely any effort at all, he lifted her until the slit in her silky dress fell away, exposing her thigh, and she found herself wrapping both legs about his hips in an act of pure instinct. One hand slid hungrily down her side in the satin dress, warm and searching, until it rounded her hip and cupped her buttock.

She gasped, 'Yes,' against his mouth, and he groaned as though in answer.

Their kiss deepened impossibly.

She could feel how aroused he was, and felt herself begin to tremble, her skin running with heat, unable to control her own desire. Certainly she was making zero effort to stop him.

She shouldn't feel anything for him, of course. She ought to be fighting this. Fighting him. But why the hell should she? She'd been eager to sleep with Brodie after the party at St Ives too, and in her heart she knew it hadn't just been too much booze fuelling her desire. All the drink had done was strip away her inhibitions. She was genuinely attracted to this man, and she couldn't deny it any longer: not to herself, not to anyone. It was reaching the point of an unhealthy obsession. And perhaps if she got the urge out of her system, if she scratched that itch just once, she would be free of it.

He was stroking her bare thigh with a restless hand, his warm lips buried in her throat. 'Caro, Caro . . .'

'Mmm,' she hummed in her throat, half-dizzy with pleasure.

Yes, it was official.

She wanted him.

But not here in her sister's pantry, for God's sake. Not with a few dozen famous and influential guests milling about a few hundred yards from their hiding place. And if Françoise or one of the hired catering staff were to come in search of extra food . . .

Some dim memory of common sense intruded on her excitement, and she put a hand on his chest, trying to push him away.

'Not here,' she whispered. 'Brodie, stop. We can't.'

To his credit, Brodie released her without argument, but did not raise his head, still nuzzling her hair, her throat. It felt good. Too damn good.

'Not here,' she repeated, hoping she could get through to him before his kisses destroyed her ability to think straight. 'Upstairs. My . . . my bedroom.'

'The cottage,' he said indistinctly, still kissing her throat.

Pixie Cottage?

It meant a walk through the woods in the dark. And the temperature had dropped recently, threatening frost and perhaps even snow. Though they could drive round instead. Spitting gravel in their hurry. People would surely notice that. Especially Jennifer, who wasn't drinking during her pregnancy. How her sister would grin tomorrow!

Still, the privacy of Pixie Cottage was an appealing thought.

But she was saved from having to make that decision. Or the universe decided to spoil her fun. In her fuzzy state, she couldn't decide which, but glared instead at her mobile, its dark shape moving about as it buzzed crazily on the counter.

It was probably Topaz again.

'Don't answer it,' Brodie said, his palm cupping her cheek.

She tried to ignore it, but the mobile kept buzzing, now perilously close to falling off the counter.

'Oh, for God's sake,' she muttered, unable to resist, and grabbed up the phone, not looking at him. Perhaps this was for the best, she thought hazily. One last chance to avoid a truly stupid mistake. Brodie had already rejected her once. He would certainly reject her again.

Tonight might have been sublime, yes.

But tomorrow morning would have been too horrible to countenance. She couldn't allow her life to be thrown off-balance like this.

'Topaz?' Her voice was shaky and unfamiliar. She cleared her throat and tried again, reality slowly intruding. 'Topaz, you can't keep ringing me like this.'

'I'm afraid this isn't Topaz,' a male voice said on the other end of the phone. 'This is PC Whaley from the Devon and Cornwall Police. Am I speaking to Miss Caroline Enys?'

Caroline felt herself go cold, and not just because Brodie had finally taken a step back, his luscious body heat removed.

'Yes, I'm Caroline Enys.'

'Could you just confirm how you are related to the owner of this mobile?'

'Topaz? She's my ... my mother.' Alarm rose in her. 'What's this about? What's happened? Why are you ringing me on my mother's mobile?'

Brodie opened the pantry door and light flooded in from outside, along with the sound of piano music, guests chatting and laughing, and the chink of glasses. She blinked, looking away, horribly off-balance.

'I'm sorry to tell you this, but your mother has been hurt.'

'Oh my God, is she all right?' Slowly, the police officer's words filtered through to her champagne-hazy brain. 'Sorry, how was she hurt? Some kind of accident?'

'It would probably be best to talk to you in person about—'

'Please, just tell me!'

Suddenly, she couldn't bear to have Brodie see her, listen to her. This was too raw, too personal. She turned her back on him, bending her head as she listened to the police officer's apologetic reply.

'Well, at the moment, it looks as though she may have attempted to take her own life. We can't confirm that yet, as she's not in a fit state to answer questions.'

'*What*?'

'Your mother's at the Royal Cornwall Hospital in Truro, Miss Enys.' The police officer paused. 'And she's asking for you.'

CHAPTER THIRTY

Caroline had been standing beside the open ward doors, out of sight of anyone inside, for several minutes, her face and body frozen. It didn't take any psychic powers to know that she was going through hell, but Brodie cleared his throat all the same, aware that the male nurse who had already walked past them several times was on his way over to ask if he could help.

'You okay?' Brodie hesitated. 'You want me to go in with you?'

She looked round at him, her face distraught. 'I don't know. Maybe, yes. Or no, she wouldn't like that. But . . .'

'I'll go in with you.'

She nodded, not arguing.

The male nurse, whose name badge said Graham, stopped in front of them with a friendly smile. 'Here for visiting time? It's a little early.'

Caroline bit her lip, saying nothing.

'Yes,' Brodie said shortly, not giving much away.

'Which ward do you need? Do you know?' Graham glanced briefly over his shoulder at the sound of a bell ringing somewhere further along the corridor, then looked from Brodie's face to Caroline's. 'Who are you visiting?'

'Her name's Topaz,' Caroline said, almost in a whisper.

'Ah, Topaz.' His smile was hurriedly replaced by a more sombre expression. 'Is she expecting you?'

'I think so, yes.'

'Family?' The male nurse shot Brodie a dubious look.

'I'm her d-daughter.' Caroline stumbled over the word, then took a deep breath and tried again. 'I couldn't come last night,' she said more firmly. 'But I'm here now. I know it's still early, but—'

'No, it's fine. Follow me.'

Graham headed off into the ward, and Caroline followed him, Brodie a few steps behind, not really sure what his role was here, except to make sure she stayed safe.

He had promised Jennifer that before they'd left the house that morning, aware of her fears for her sister.

'I won't let anything happen to Caroline,' he had tried to reassure her, and nodded to Alex before escorting a rather shaky Caroline out to the Land Rover. He could have taken her to the hospital in the chopper, but he hadn't yet had a chance to run safety checks on their brand-new acquisition, and it wouldn't have been safe.

Jennifer had come along soon after the call. Finding Caroline in a distressed state, she had become fierce, demanding to know who or what had upset her sister. Brodie suspected some of her ire was aimed at him, as though she thought the two of them had argued. Then Alex had been summoned from the party, and Caroline, haltingly and with obvious reluctance, had told the couple about her mother's latest suicide attempt.

'I don't like the sound of this situation,' Alex had told Brodie later, when they were alone at the end of the party, locking up the house. He was frowning. 'It's not my business if Caroline is determined to get close to this woman, but all the same, I don't want to see her get hurt.'

'Me neither.'

Alex looked at him closely. 'About you and Caroline . . . Tell me to mind my own business, but—'

'Mind your own business,' Brodie growled.

'Okay.' Alex grimaced, but gave it up. 'Back to Topaz, then. You think this is a genuine suicide attempt?'

'I'm not sure.'

'But Topaz may be after money? You reckon that's why she's been hanging around in Pethporro all this time?'

'It seems logical. But she's asked for Caroline, and Caroline's determined to go.'

'You'll go with her.' It had been a statement, not a question.

'Try and stop me,' Brodie had muttered.

Now he was less sure about that decision. Caroline had hardly spoken to him on the drive over, her face averted. The gorgeous, seductive woman from last night had vanished, and a grim-faced Caroline had taken her place, sombre in black jeans and a fitted black jumper.

They were two days away from Christmas, but neither of them seemed to be in a particularly festive mood. The party had gone well, so Alex and Jennifer were happy at least. But what had he been thinking, kissing Caroline again?

He'd gone back to his cottage afterwards and banged his head on the wall in sheer bloody frustration. He seemed to enjoy giving himself pain. Because rejection and humiliation were the only possible outcomes of a fling between him and Caroline Enys, and the only person who didn't seem to understand that was him.

Caroline had never seen her mother looking so messed-up. Topaz was sitting up in bed at the end of the ward, white-blonde hair lank and uncombed, her skin ashen, eyes bloodshot and red-rimmed as though she had been crying. But she smiled wanly as the nurse left Caroline and Brodie at the bedside, putting aside the magazine she had been reading.

'Darling,' Topaz said in a hoarse whisper, and held out a hand that trembled. 'You came. I knew you would.' Her smile was proud. 'I knew my own daughter wouldn't abandon me, even if the rest of the world has.'

Caroline leant over the bed and kissed Topaz on the cheek. Her mother's skin felt chilly, despite the suffocating heat on the ward, and there was a distinct whiff of stale alcohol about her.

'How are you? The police told me you tried to hurt yourself.' Caroline studied her mother, trying desperately to read her expression. 'Please tell me that's not true.'

A few steps behind her, Brodie cleared his throat and turned away, as though to give them some more privacy.

He hadn't mentioned their stupid clinch on the drive here this morning. Not one word, thank goodness. But every now and then she caught him looking at her sideways, and knew it wasn't over. She couldn't deal with Brodie now though. This thing with Topaz was more important.

'Oh, darling. I wish I could tell you that.' Topaz's large eyes brimmed with sudden tears. 'But what was I supposed to do? Here I am, come down to Cornwall especially to be with you at Christmas, and you won't even see me. Or answer any of my calls. How many times have I texted you this week? I've lost count. But you didn't reply. Not once.'

'That's not true,' Caroline said, her heart hurting at the accusation in her mother's voice. 'I texted you back to say we could meet up after Christmas. And I begged you to stop messaging me. I'm sorry if that came across as cruel. But I felt . . . overwhelmed.'

'Overwhelmed? By your own mother?'

'Yes.' Caroline took a deep breath, trying to express herself both clearly and without unkindness. 'I'm sorry if I hurt your feelings, Topaz.'

'Call me Mum, please.'

Caroline hesitated, then continued doggedly, 'But your behaviour has been a little odd. It's unusual to text someone dozens of times every day. And some of your texts yesterday were quite unpleasant, you must admit that. To be honest, I didn't know what to think.'

Her mother's lip trembled. 'The only thing you should have thought was that I'm your mother, Caroline. Your *mother!*'

'I know.'

'You only get one mother.'

Caroline thought rather disloyally of Debbie, her calm and eminently sensible stepmother, but said nothing.

'You were ignoring me. Refusing to let me see you, and at Christmas too. The time when families should be together. Also, that nasty French woman spoke to me through the intercom yesterday as though I were nobody.'

'I'm really sorry about that.' Caroline felt bad and did not know what to say to fix things. She had indeed left Françoise to deal with the situation, unable to cope with Topaz's persistent and intrusive attempts to get into Porro Park. 'But it's not my house, you see, and hardly anyone is allowed in. Alex is a very private person.'

'Private? That didn't stop him having a big swanky party last night. To which I was not invited.' When Caroline did not reply, deeply embarrassed, Topaz nodded, glaring up at both her and Brodie. 'I saw all the posh cars arriving and the photographers with their long lenses. I even tried to get in myself but the security guards on the gate were nasty to me. They said nobody could come in without an invitation, whoever they were. Vile little bullies!'

'They shouldn't have been rude to you.'

'I told them who I was, but they told me to get lost.' Her chest swelled with outrage, and a hint of colour came back into her pale cheeks. 'Me! Your own mother!'

Caroline dragged off her jacket and sank into the plastic chair beside the bed, feeling quite sick. Her heart was thumping too. She was overheating in this bloody hospital, that was the problem. Not to mention that she felt trapped in a nightmare.

She had finally met her true birth mother, and thought they could be friends. But then Topaz had begun to behave strangely and unpleasantly, and Caroline had dreaded meeting up with her again.

Now this . . .

What on earth was she to do?

Brodie was standing at the foot of the bed, arms folded across his chest, watching her without expression. His gaze was somehow steadying. She met his eyes and took several deep breaths, trying to calm down.

'Topaz,' she said slowly, and looked up at her mother, 'what exactly happened to you last night? I mean, after you left Porro Park?'

Her mother gave an angry shrug. 'What do you care?'

'I care, honestly.'

'I had some old sleeping pills left,' Topaz said dismissively. 'Nine or ten of them. I took the lot with some whisky. That's all.'

'And who found you?'

Topaz looked confused. 'Nobody found me. I called an ambulance straight afterwards.'

'You called for an ambulance?'

'Of course.' Topaz looked at her as though she was mad. 'Pills and whisky? I could have died!'

'I'm sorry if I'm being insensitive, but if you took all those pills, I have to assume you did so deliberately.'

'I was unhappy, I wanted to die. Only I changed my

mind, didn't I? Called an ambulance and they got me sorted. Pumped my stomach, gave me a bed for the night.' Her smile was somehow both dazzling and unnerving. 'Otherwise, how could I have seen my lovely daughter at Christmas?'

Caroline stared at her, horrified and speechless.

'And here you are at my bedside,' Topaz continued, a look almost of triumph on her face. 'So everything worked out perfectly, didn't it?'

No longer sure what was real and what was false, and unable to listen for a moment longer, Caroline jumped up and made for the ward door.

'Caroline?' her mother cried. 'Where are you going?'

She stopped, and turned.

Topaz was looking after her, her eyes already full of tears again. She seemed able to cry on order.

Brodie had followed her to the door. 'You okay, Caro?'

She hated the pity in his eyes. He must think her such a soft touch, falling for another of her mother's sob stories. Yet what could she have done differently? The police had informed her that Topaz had tried to kill herself and was in hospital, asking to see her. She could hardly have ignored her mother's cry for help and carried on with Christmas as though nothing had happened.

'Fine,' she said shortly, and stalked past him to her mother's bedside again. 'Topaz—'

Her mother's smile flashed out again, so charming it was hard to resist. 'Mum,' she corrected her softly. 'Or Mummy. I'd love you to call me that.'

'Topaz,' she said with deliberate emphasis, 'let's draw the curtains round the bed. I think we need a little privacy.' As she did so, shutting out Brodie, she caught a sudden wariness in her mother's face. But she continued nonetheless, perching on the edge of the hospital bed, determined not to back down. 'Look, I need you to tell me something. And try to be truthful, please.'

'Darling, you're hurting my feelings. I'm always truthful.'

'You didn't always tell my father the truth though, did you?' Caroline paused, holding her gaze. 'Or the other men you married.'

Topaz's face stiffened. 'There's no law against—'

'Bigamously,' Caroline added softly, aware of other women in the beds around them.

Her mother said nothing.

This was not a conversation she had ever wanted to have in public. But what choice did she have? She'd left it too late to do this privately, and she couldn't walk away from her mother – as her mother had walked away from her, decades ago – without saying face to face what needed to be said.

'I've heard stories about your life before you met Dad,' Caroline continued, 'and what happened afterwards. I haven't heard your side, though.' She hesitated. 'Or why you did any of it in the first place.'

Topaz sat a moment in silence, looking bitterly at the blue curtains about the bed, making no effort to meet Caroline's gaze. 'I suppose you think I'm wicked.'

'I think you're a liar.'

Topaz's gaze flashed angrily to Caroline's face, then. 'How dare you? You have no idea what my life was like in those days. What it's like now, in fact. The things I've had to do in order to survive.'

'So tell me.'

Her mother shrugged, her tone defensive. 'I married Ted while I was still married to Charles. But what the heart doesn't know the eye can't grieve over. And he would never have given me a divorce. Never! I couldn't afford to wait or hire a lawyer. I had to be free to marry Ted before . . .'

'Before?'

'Before he changed his mind. Ted was a lovely man, but volatile. I had to catch him while I could. So I told a little fib. So what?'

'Bigamy is against the law.'

'Oh, who cares about the law?'

'But you were arrested for theft as well as bigamy.' Caroline leant close to her mother so nobody else in the ward could hear what was being said behind the closed curtains. 'You stole from one of your husbands too. Maybe from both of them. Do you deny it?' There was no response. 'Please, Topaz, tell me what happened. Maybe your husband kept your things when you left and you were just taking back what was yours?'

Ever since Brodie told her about Topaz's past, Caroline had been hoping she had some reasonable explanation for some of that behaviour. That perhaps that man had taken her possessions and she'd been forced to steal them back. But Topaz merely looked at her sullenly.

Caroline wanted to walk away. But she had to ask one last question. 'Did you try to steal from Dad too?'

'Steal from your bloody father? Don't make me laugh.'

'Sorry?'

'He never had a damn thing worth stealing!' Topaz hissed.

Caroline looked at her mother pityingly, seeing the damage in her face. The fury too, bubbling under the surface. There was something perilously close to madness there.

What had made Topaz the way she was?

Sympathy tugged at her. 'You must have been so afraid when you were arrested. You had nobody to turn to, did you?'

'I see what you want.' Topaz glared at her. 'You want me to tell you some soppy nonsense about being lost and alone, and that's why I tried to kill myself in prison. Well, you can forget that.' Her eyes were hard as stone. 'My lawyer told me they'd go easier on me if they thought I was suicidal. So I put on a show for them.'

'I don't believe that.'

'You always were stupid. Ordinary-looking too. Nothing like me.' Her gaze focused on Caroline's hair. 'Except the hair. You had my hair. But the rest . . . No, you'll never be my match.'

Caroline stood up, trembling. 'So what was last night about?'

'I just wanted to teach you a lesson, mother to daughter. You thought you could push me away and nothing would happen. Yet here you are, weeping at my bedside.'

'I'm not weeping.'

'Not yet.' Topaz leant back against the pillows, her face alight with sudden malicious intent. 'You're interested in Brodie, aren't you? Don't waste your time. A bit of fun, that's all you are to him. I've seen that look in a man's eyes a thousand times, and it never lasts.' Topaz paused, and gave a cruel smile as a tear spilt down Caroline's cheek at last. 'Aww, diddums, what's the matter? I thought you wanted the truth.'

'I'm leaving now.'

'Doesn't bother me what you do, darling. I only got back in touch with you because of Alex Delgardo. That big expensive house and all his Hollywood friends ... I've always wanted to be in films. But you couldn't even do that right, could you?' Topaz waved a dismissive hand at her. 'You're no use to me now, you might as well get lost. Bouncer and I will be leaving Pethporro as soon as I get out of this bed, and good riddance to the lot of you.'

Caroline dashed away that stupid tear and fumbled her way out through the blue curtains to find Brodie standing there, looking grim.

He must have heard every bloody word, she thought, ready to curl up and die with intense embarrassment. She didn't crumble though. The other patients in the ward were staring too, some openly, others pretending not to be looking, but clearly fascinated. No doubt they'd been treated to some of Topaz's high-handed behaviour already today. And her years of training as a midwife allowed her to remain professional even at the worst of times.

'Don't listen to her,' he began, but she held up a hand.

'Not now, please. Let's just get out of here.'

In her heart, she'd hoped what Brodie had told her about Topaz would turn out to be a misunderstanding. Or a miscarriage of justice, at least.

She hadn't wanted to believe that her mother was a liar and a cheat.

Caroline scrubbed angrily at her wet eyes, hearing Brodie behind her but not looking back as she headed for the hospital car park.

If only she had never agreed to meet Topaz and get to know her. Her father had tried to warn her, of course, mentioning her mental health issues, but rather too late. Caroline had survived just fine for more than two decades without her birth mother. Yet just a few weeks of 'getting to know' Topaz, and here she was, reduced to a pathetic, weeping blob of emotion.

But had she really been 'fine' all those years? Surviving wasn't the same as thriving. And today, she felt as cold inside as the December sky above.

Bitterly cold, and more alone than ever.

CHAPTER THIRTY-ONE

On the morning of Christmas Day, Brodie showered and shaved, pulled on some smart-casual trousers and a sweater, and headed through the trees to Porro Park. It was a cold, crisp day in the woods, no hint of the mist that had clung to ivy-smothered trunks on previous mornings. Birds sang in the bare branches, or scavenged in the tangled undergrowth, and the sky opened up above the woods with a blue so pale it was almost white.

It was cold enough to snow, Brodie thought, glad of the thick overcoat he had donned on top of his sweater.

Snow rarely fell in Cornwall at Christmas. But it was possible that icy weather might be on the way as the new year beckoned. After all, they had passed the winter solstice now, as Jennifer had reminded them all by going out mysteriously on that evening in a witchy-looking cloak and boots, refusing everyone's company as she tramped the frosty grounds alone, chanting and singing, or whatever it was she usually did to honour the turn of the year.

As he approached the house, crossing the lawn, he caught

sight of a face at an upper window, and his pace slowed instinctively.

Caroline.

She turned away as soon as she realised Brodie had spotted her. But not before he'd seen the look of angst on her face.

That bloody mother of hers!

He had known Topaz was trouble the instant he laid eyes on her. But at least the truth of why her mother had left was out in the open now, and Caroline could put it all behind her. A cliché, perhaps, but he felt it was better to face a difficult truth and deal with it, however painful, rather than live a comfortable lie.

To her credit, on returning to Porro Park, she had sat down and told Alex and Jennifer everything her mother had said, though leaving out her unpleasant remarks about Brodie.

Alex had sat silent and grim-faced throughout the whole sorry tale, then got up and hugged Caroline. 'I can imagine how that feels,' he had told her. 'Mothers can be difficult. For what it's worth, you have my full support. Whatever you need, just let me know and it's yours.'

Jennifer had let out a shriek of outrage when Caroline described Topaz's parting words in the hospital. 'I'm so sorry she hurt you like that. But at least she's out of your life now.' She too had held Caroline tight and even kissed her on the cheek, something the two sisters rarely did. 'We may not be blood relatives but we're still your family . . . me, Alex and Brodie. And we love you.'

Brodie had slipped away from the big house a short while later, and made his way home without saying goodbye.

His cottage had felt cold and lonely. But peaceful too.

There was so much confusion in his head at the moment. Desire and confusion. But he tried to block it out. Happiness and romance were not for him, Brodie decided. He'd lost that chance on the night of the bombing. Not that he was bitter about it; merely pragmatic.

From now on, he needed to decide what to do with his life instead. How to deal with this pent-up energy and determination and . . . Oh God, all the love he felt inside.

He hadn't come up with any ideas yet.

Though retreating to a monastery somewhere suitably remote and starkly furnished was high on his list of possibilities.

Now it was Christmas Day. He entered the house, whistling and smiling. 'Merry Christmas!' he called out to nobody in particular. The cat, perhaps, who lay watching him with slitty eyes beneath the Christmas tree, a red bauble swaying gently above his head. 'Merry Christmas, Ripper! Now don't pull that tree over again, will you? Remember what happened last time . . .'

The cat yawned, displaying sharp white teeth.

Brodie set his bag of presents down beside the tree and began to unpack them. He had wrapped an assortment of gifts for his friends: an ornately carved chess set for Alex, who loved the game; a box of fragrant, handmade soaps for Jennifer, purchased while they were still in the States; and a beautiful, iridescent blue silk scarf for Caroline that

BETH GOOD | 326

would match her eyes perfectly. He had also bought a box of brandy-filled French chocolates for Françoise and Marie, and a studded collar for Ripper.

He enjoyed giving gifts. But it had felt strange, not waking up under the same roof as the others on Christmas Day for once. Not bad-strange, he decided, but good-strange. As though a demarcation line had been drawn between him and Alex. About time too, he thought; they had been best buddies for years, and always would be, but now that Alex and Jenny were expecting twins it was time to stop living on top of each other.

'Brodie!' Jennifer appeared from the dining room and gave him an affectionate kiss. 'Merry Christmas! Oh goodness, so many presents. We'll open them after lunch, shall we?'

Jennifer was barefoot, and wearing a flowing dark green chiffon dress with satin panels. He could see a small bump now, where before her tummy had been flat. She really was quite beautiful as a pregnant woman, he thought.

Alex appeared then, giving him a bear hug. 'Glad you agreed to come over for lunch. It's not Christmas without you, mate.'

They drifted from the atrium into the vast dining room, where Françoise had been busy, laying the long table with a white linen damask tablecloth and napkins, crystal glassware and shining silver cutlery. There were Christmas crackers too, at every place setting, and a red-and-gold flower arrangement as the centrepiece, with a large red candle rising from it, already lit with a flickering flame. Alex opened a bottle of champagne that had been sitting in an ice bucket, and poured him a glass, then handed Jennifer an innocent-looking orange and mango juice instead of alcohol.

'Merry Christmas,' Brodie repeated, raising the glass to his lips, smiling round at his hosts.

'Merry Christmas,' someone echoed from the door.

His heart was already hammering before he had even turned to smile at Caroline too. The smile felt frozen in place, utterly fake. But she seemed to fall for it.

Caroline looked stunning as ever in a tight-fitting blue dress and heels, a sparkling bracelet her only jewellery. But it was her face that captured his attention, her skin oddly pale, eyes wide, something ethereal about her today, as though she had not slept well. Not just last night but for days.

If so, he knew exactly how she felt. Empty and hollow inside, everything scraped too thin. Running on reserves.

'You came,' she said unnecessarily, and accepted a glass of champagne from Alex with murmured thanks. 'It's good to see you.'

Brodie did not reply, but continued to smile. He felt like a fool. Apparently, he was unable even to make polite conversation with her.

Lunch passed in a daze, the festive food of little interest to him, though he helped carve the turkey, praised Françoise's cooking skills along with the others, and joked and laughed as usual. Later, he and Alex joined forces to wash the larger pots and pans, and stack the dishwasher with dirty dishes, while Françoise and Marie enjoyed a well-earned drink with the others in the lounge.

When they finally joined them, the two men brought in a tray of coffee along with bowls of steaming Christmas puddings with cream. Brodie drank his coffee black, standing up by the window, trying to avoid the temptation to sit next to Caroline on the sofa.

Once dessert and coffee were finished, they wandered out into the atrium, where large cushions had been strewn about, and opened the gifts heaped under the Christmas tree.

Brodie knew a moment of intense pleasure when Caroline opened her gold-wrapped parcel and drew out the shimmering blue scarf, her eyes lighting up. 'Thank you so much,' she told him huskily, lifting her head, and for an instant their eyes met. He felt the jolt of that contact strike through him like lightning. 'It's gorgeous, I love it.'

He held his breath, nodding without a word.

Jennifer leant over to admire the scarf too. 'Oh, goodness. That shade matches your eyes so perfectly.' Her smile was knowing. 'Clever of Brodie to find it.'

Alex glanced at him, but Brodie focused on the shiny present he had been unwrapping. He was too afraid what might be glimpsed in his face at that moment.

He checked the smart gift tag. It was from Caroline, of course. And she was watching.

It was an old leather box, worn with age, with a pair of antique binoculars inside. He held them up to his eyes and marvelled at the sharp focus, looking through the atrium windows to the lawns and woodlands beyond, easily settling on a robin perched on a fence. The bird's eye shone darkly as its head tilted, listening to some sound, then suddenly the robin startled and was gone.

'Thank you,' he told Caroline, and hesitated, wanting so badly to express himself properly, to make her see how deeply pleased he was with this unusual gift, yet somehow tongue-tied. 'Really, it's . . . Thank you.'

Caroline flashed him the briefest of smiles, then turned back to the others, looking to see what they were unwrapping.

He slipped the antique binoculars back into their leather case, pretending not to have noticed how offhand Caroline was being with him. But his heart thudded dully in his chest, heavy and hurting. She couldn't have made her 'Stay away from me!' message more obvious if she'd written it in neon above her head. If only he hadn't been so stupid, giving into the dangerous temptation to kiss her at the drinks party. She had looked at him with such vulnerability in her eyes though, and kissed him back with so much passion.

Alcohol-fuelled passion, he realised now, only too aware that Caroline had been treating him with cool dismissiveness ever since.

At the time, it had felt so real . . .

Brodie wished that he could find some excuse to leave and return to the quiet solitude of Pixie Cottage. To run away, basically.

But he knew Alex would want a game of chess later on his ornate new board, and he didn't want to draw attention to himself. It didn't help that Alex and Jennifer kept eyeing them both with expectant looks and smiles. He had too much respect for his friends to tell them to get lost. But their clumsy attempts at matchmaking were driving him crazy.

Given his own way, he would have spent today peacefully on his own, grounding himself with exercise and meditation. Not drinking too much champagne and struggling to take his eyes off the most beautiful woman in the world, who seemed to find his presence at Porro Park almost as painful as he did.

CHAPTER THIRTY-TWO

Dusk was slowly falling over the Pethporro annual Boxing Day pageant, as the torchlit procession finally wound its way through narrow streets and between whitewashed buildings hung with fairy lights and glinting decorations, heading for the tide-streaked strand. Musicians played as they walked ahead of the crowd, drummers and flutists together, with two fiddlers dressed as Cornish piskies following; behind them came a group of primary school children in red-and-gold costumes, singing a traditional Christmas song in high-pitched voices.

The Lord of Misrule, in beaked mask and ragged black cloak, whirled among them all with his stick, calling out words in Cornish which Caroline couldn't understand, though she imagined some there would.

And of course there was Lizzie near the front, grey hair bound up with brightly coloured ribbons, leading a goat also adorned with ribbons, its hoofs clacking across the uneven cobbles.

Caroline had spent some time with Alex and Jenny in the refreshments tent, talking to local dignitaries and feeling a little out of her depth, before being tapped on the shoulder by her former colleague, Martha.

With a sense of relief, she'd gone off to drink with her old friends from the midwifery unit instead, sharing a vast dish of hot roast pork with them and catching up on all the gossip from her old workplace – which babies had been born since she'd left, and how those mums and babies were doing, and which women had fallen pregnant.

Caroline had no idea where Brodie was or if he had even turned up. He'd promised Jennifer days ago that he would come with them to the famous Pethporro pageant. But he hadn't answered his phone earlier, even after several tries, so they had eventually made the hard decision to go without him, Alex leaving a voice message to explain where they'd be.

For the past two hours, she had smiled and laughed with her friends, and talked cheerfully about Alex and Jenny without giving any secrets away, and all the time her gaze had moved restlessly around the bustling crowd of tourists and locals, hunting for one face.

She was *obsessed*.

That's what this was, she decided bitterly. A sad, embarrassing obsession. And over a man who could kiss her until she was close to bursting into flames, and then barely string two words together afterwards, so desperate was he to avoid any further contact.

And thank goodness for that, she told herself fiercely.

She was not in the market for a boyfriend.

Not even close.

She had her whole bloody life to live before settling down with one man. And perhaps she would never settle down. Perhaps her mother's wanderlust had infected her too, and she would become a kind of nomad as she got older, wearing outrageous clothes and dying her hair unlikely colours, drifting from place to place, always searching for the one who got away . . .

Caroline wanted to scream at herself, *stop thinking about Brodie!* Instead, she just smiled more widely and laughed more loudly. Now she was dancing in the torchlit procession, dressed in forest-green leggings and a floaty green top with long sleeves to keep out the cold, and a green cap.

'Caroline, what on earth are you going to the pageant as?' Alex had asked that morning, wrinkling his nose in confusion at her costume.

'I'm an elf.' Caroline had given him a twirl.

'But . . . your ears . . .'

'Oh well, who cares? I did my best.'

She hadn't bothered giving herself big ears, merely jamming her cap down over her hair so that it stuck out roughly where her outsized elfin ears would have been.

But of course Jennifer had tutted, and insisted on taking her upstairs to her bedroom to make fake elfin ears out of cardboard, sticking them with difficulty to her cap.

'If you're going to be an elf,' her sister had said sternly, frowning at her in the dressing table mirror, 'at least make it believable.'

'There's nothing believable about an elf.'

'Sorry?'

'Elves don't exist. Didn't you get the memo?'

'Hush, I refuse to listen to your anti-elfist propaganda!' Jenny had grinned and shaken a fist at her before sweeping down the stairs in her old storytelling costume. 'Come on, quick. Or we'll be late for the opening ceremony.'

Alex had sent away to London for his pageant costume, and was dressed as a wizard, complete with drooping black hat and a large, heavily carved staff with a fake jewel flashing at the top.

He and Jennifer had given an impromptu free storytelling session for the crowds after the mayor had opened proceedings, much to everyone's delight, Jennifer telling a story about an old Cornish wizard and Alex acting the part himself, stamping about furiously and raising his staff to the cloudy skies every so often. The applause afterwards had been rapturous.

Hannah and Raphael Tregar had been among the crowd too, laughing and mingling with the local dignitaries. Later, she'd seen them join the torchlit procession towards the beach, Raphael carrying little Santos on his shoulders, who looked to be enjoying himself.

Caroline had heard on the grapevine that Hannah Tregar was pregnant again, but since she was no longer her midwife, Caroline had resisted the urge to go and enquire about the pregnancy. It was none of her business now. Though she could see that Hannah had a little telltale bump. Four or five months gone, at a rough guess. She imagined Raphael must be over the moon about it.

The Tregars weren't alone at the pageant either, but

were hanging out with Bailey and Penny, old friends of Hannah's from her first days in Cornwall. Bailey and Penny were a couple, and had a child together, little Tommy, now an active toddler, sitting up bright-eyed in his pushchair. Bailey had given birth to him after undergoing IVF treatment, and though Caroline hadn't been her midwife during labour, she knew the young woman had done extraordinarily well, somehow producing her son after only a three-hour labour.

It seemed everyone was here today, enjoying themselves.

And even she was dancing now, she thought dizzily, having somehow got separated from the others, looking helplessly about for Alex or Jennifer.

One of her ears had come unstuck, she realised, patting the place where it had been. Suddenly, a hand appeared out of the crowd.

'Your ear, I believe.'

She turned, her heart leaping. It was Brodie.

'Th-Thank you,' she stammered, and accepted the slightly misshapen cardboard ear, clutching it as she stared at him. He was wearing all black, his hair slicked back in a sinister way, brows somehow darker than usual, his expression forbidding. 'I thought . . . that is, we all thought you weren't coming to the pageant.' She paused. 'Are you wearing make-up?'

'A little,' he admitted, and touched his face self-consciously. 'I'm a devil. I only had black clothing though. I needed better . . . devil features. I got to the house too late, but luckily Françoise was still there and she helped me.'

'She did a good job. You look suitably . . . demonic.'

'Thank you.' He looked her up and down. 'And you look very elf-like. I saw you dancing before.' His smile disturbed her. 'Beautiful.'

She did not know what to say.

Ahead, the flames from the torches fluttered in the breeze, reflecting off the wet sands as the leaders turned off the promenade and down the causeway on to the foreshore.

The procession followed more slowly, heading across the beach towards the water's edge. At the front of the pack, the black-cloaked Lord of Misrule could be seen dancing wildly and erratically back and forth like a mad crow. There were the Tregars again with Bailey and Penny, and baby Tommy in the pushchair, Penny pushing it determinedly across the wet sands. And Lizzie was skipping with her goat, while the school kids broke into a trot beside her, giggling and singing as they ran.

'Where are Alex and Jenny?' Brodie asked, frowning as he searched the people's faces around them.

'Somewhere at the back, I expect, with the mayor and the other local bigwigs. I was with some friends.' She glanced about too. 'But we got separated once the procession started.'

The crowd began to unravel as they reached the foreshore, spreading out from one long ribbon of people into a looser gathering, getting into position for the closing ceremony.

Caroline glimpsed a few familiar faces as people shuffled on to the sands, holding their torches aloft, but chose not to call out to them. She didn't really go in for supernatural belief, despite her sister's own peculiar practices in that area; even so, there was an odd formality about the moment, with the dark drawing in across the land behind them, and the first stars winking above them. She didn't want to spoil the atmosphere.

Brodie drew Caroline off to one side, turning to watch for Alex and Jennifer as those at the end of the procession trailed past.

She tried not to stare, but he was so attractive, the last faint rays of light gilding his dark profile . . . *Stop looking at him*, she told herself crossly, and stared down at the damp sands instead, then realised that was stupid too. It was ridiculous, feeling this jittery with him. Why couldn't she just say what was on her mind?

Because you're afraid, an inner voice jeered at her.

Afraid of what, though?

'Why were you so late, by the way?' she asked him, her voice falsely bright. 'We waited for you for ages, then we had to leave.'

'Didn't you get my message? I left a voicemail on Jenny's phone.'

'She probably didn't take it with her. No pockets in her costume.'

'Right, of course.'

'Alex tried to call you though.'

'Yeah,' Brodie said casually, shrugging. 'I got his message later. I was probably in a signal blind spot at the time. I had to drive out to meet someone who needed a lift to the pageant. Their car had broken down.'

Her heart thumped jealously. 'Someone?'

'Yes.' His hooded eyes met hers, and suddenly he did indeed look demonic. 'A very special someone.'

Caroline bent her head again. *A very special someone.*

So what?

It was nothing to do with her. She didn't want to get involved with this man, anyway. He might say no. As he'd already done, for God's sake. And even if he didn't, she was perfectly happy being single. She was a modern, independent woman. She didn't need a man to complete her.

But it might be nice to have someone there, a friend to talk to at the end of the day, a lover to keep her warm while she slept . . .

'Ah, there they are at last.' Brodie lifted his hand. 'Alex? Jenny?' His raised voice sounded loud and intrusive in the quiet, shimmering dusk. Heads turned curiously, some disapproving. 'We're over here!'

'Hush,' she said instinctively.

'Sorry.'

'The ceremony is beginning.' She nodded towards the foreshore where they were starting to lay wreaths in the rippling tide as it rushed in, foaming white in the twilight. The mayor was there now too, and someone was intoning a poem in Cornish. 'Shouldn't we go down there and—'

Her voice died away as she realised that Alex and Jennifer were not alone. They joined her and Brodie, bringing two more smiling figures with them.

'Debbie? Dad?' Her voice was a squeak as her stepmother gave her a quick hug, wishing her a Merry Christmas. 'Merry Christmas to you too. But what are you doing here?

This is a surprise.' She glanced at Jennifer, and saw an anxious look on her sister's face. 'Is everything okay?'

Her dad embraced her. 'Stop panicking. Nothing's wrong. Jenny gave me a call earlier and asked if I'd come down for the pageant, that's all. We'd have been here sooner, but the car broke down. Brodie came out to help us.' His expression grew sombre as he studied her face. 'Jenny said you might need another private word with me.'

'Did she?' Caroline threw a look at her sister that promised a stern word later, though she knew Jenny meant well. 'Yes, it's probably a good idea for us to talk.'

'Then let's talk.' He smiled at Brodie, who had reached over to shake his hand. 'Thanks again for the lift, Brodie. Merry Christmas.'

'And to you too, Mr Enys.'

'Jim, please.'

Brodie smiled in return, shot her an unreadable glance, and then melted away into the crowd, taking the others with him. Even Debbie, who seemed suddenly fascinated by the traditional year's end ceremony of blessing the sea and asking it to bless the land in return.

'Right.' Her dad linked his arm with Caroline's, pointing out a quiet, rocky stretch not too far down the darkening beach. 'Shall we take a walk together?'

'Erm, okay.'

As they walked at a slow pace, roughly parallel to those crowded along the water's edge, her dad gave her a reassuring smile. 'You make a good elf. Though one of your ears is a bit wonky.'

She laughed shakily. 'At least it's not missing.'

The deep orange of the sunset faded out gently to the west. The shadows about them lengthened to the accompaniment of the rushing whisper of the tide coming in, and the sound of applause and cheers behind them as the ceremony came to an end.

'So,' he said at last, 'what did you want to talk about?'

Gradually, in a faltering voice at first, growing stronger when he did not interrupt her or show any sign of anger, Caroline told him about Topaz's badgering behaviour, and then her apparent suicide attempt – which she still wasn't sure about – leading to that appalling scene in the hospital.

'I'm so sorry,' he said, looking distressed.

'I know you didn't tell me the truth about why Topaz left us. Brodie asked a private investigator to find out for me. When I heard the truth about the bigamy, the fraud, and the way she assaulted you ... I was quite angry at first. Because I felt I deserved to know the truth.'

'I didn't want to hurt you, Caroline. You were just an innocent child; you didn't need the weight of that knowledge on your shoulders.'

'I understand that. But once I was an adult, and especially after she came back into my life ...' Impatiently, Caroline dashed away a tear. 'You ought to have told me the whole thing when I came to see you in St Ives, Dad. Instead, you kept to your story, like I was still a child, and refused to elaborate even when I pushed you. Why?'

He was quiet for a moment, then said slowly, 'I was embarrassed. I've always felt it was my fault, what happened with

Topaz. And I wanted to believe that she might have changed over the years. Become a better person.' He shook his head sadly. 'You seemed to be making friends with her. It would have been cruel to ruin that for you.'

Her father had been staring ahead as he spoke, his steps taken almost on automatic, though the beach was getting too dark really for walking. Now he stopped, and looked back the way they'd come, his face cast in shadow. The main crowd had started to disperse. A few wreaths were still caught in the surf, being dragged to and fro, white flowers lit up by the torch flames of those still at the water's edge.

He gave a heavy sigh, then turned, looking into her face. 'Yes, I lied to you. To you and Debbie as well. Even your stepmother still doesn't know the whole truth about Topaz. I just couldn't face explaining . . .' He grimaced, abruptly releasing her to run a hand over his face. 'You can't imagine the horror of discovering her crimes, perhaps. The humiliation of it all. I'd asked her to marry me. We had a child together, for God's sake.'

'But Topaz backed out.'

'Yes,' he agreed unhappily. 'We went to see the registrar. But Topaz didn't have any documents and the registrar said he couldn't proceed without them. Suddenly, she changed her mind about getting married. The mask slipped and for a moment, I saw what kind of person she really was. That's when I hired someone to check out her background.' He shook his head. 'I couldn't believe what the guy found, that she was already married and wanted by the police. I begged Topaz for an explanation, I was sure there had to be one.

But she just flew at me. She was like a wild thing, all claws and teeth and kicking feet. One of our neighbours called the police, but when they arrived, she ran away.'

'That must have been awful.'

'She'd been hiding down here in Pethporro, hoping nobody would connect her with that other woman, the one up north who'd committed all those crimes.' He lifted a shoulder wearily, staring out over the dark tide as it crept higher up the beach. 'I was amazed when they put her in an institution instead of sending her to prison.'

'Do you think that was because she tried to kill herself?'

'I expect so,' he agreed. 'At her trial, the medical experts insisted she was unbalanced and so couldn't be held entirely responsible for what she'd done.' He sighed. 'But I feel responsible for the way she's hurt you. If I'd told you everything that first time you rang and said she was back in Pethporro . . .'

'It's okay, Dad.' Caroline felt like crying. But also like comforting him. She kissed him on the cheek. 'I understand why you didn't want to.'

'Thank you.'

'Perhaps if you had told me, I wouldn't have seen her again. But I'm glad I got to know her, even if only for a short time. It's eaten away at me for years, not understanding why my mother left. Now I know the truth, I can stop living in the past, always wondering about her . . .'

'I'm sorry.' His voice shook slightly, and she could see the glint of tears in his eyes. 'None of this was ever your fault, Caroline.'

'I know,' she said.

'If it's anyone's fault, it's mine. But I was afraid you might try to find her when you got older, and that it would hurt you too deeply to discover what kind of creature she was, your own flesh and blood.'

'It's not important, it's over now.'

'You're so forgiving,' he said wonderingly. 'I don't deserve it.'

'Come on, it's getting cold.' Feeling curiously lighter now, as though released from a burden, Caroline started to walk back towards the others, spotting their shadowy figures waiting beside the causeway. 'I'm glad you came to Pethporro today. That we had this talk.'

'Me too,' he said, but she heard the strain in his voice and knew it would take her father a long while to get over such a difficult conversation.

She felt shaken too, and was glad when Jennifer and Alex walked ahead with her dad and Debbie on the way back. The narrow streets of Pethporro were still crowded, pubs heaving with locals and visitors. But with all the emotions churning inside her, what she really wanted to do was run home to Porro Park and hide in her bedroom.

Brodie dropped back to walk beside her, his face hard to read. 'You okay?' he asked gently.

'More or less.'

'You talked about Topaz, I take it?'

'Yes, Dad told me . . .' Her voice grew thick, her throat clogged up with tears. 'He said it wasn't my fault.'

Brodie glanced at her sharply in the semi-darkness, then

suddenly a warm palm brushed against hers. She looked down numbly, too surprised to say a word. Their fingers laced together almost instinctively, and she found it impossible to pull away, though she was bewildered too, her heart hurting, struggling to understand the gesture.

Abruptly, he dropped her hand, and stuck his hand in his pockets instead. 'Well, he's right,' he said indistinctly, and looked away. 'It's not your fault.'

Caroline stared at him blankly. She suddenly understood why Brodie had taken her hand like that, and why he'd released it too. And she realised in the same second why she had automatically interlaced her fingers with his, and why her heart was aching so badly . . .

She had to be the stupidest woman alive.

CHAPTER THIRTY-THREE

On the morning of New Year's Eve, Brodie was surprised when Alex came to find him at Pixie Cottage, his friend looking happier and more relaxed than he'd done in weeks. 'Hey, buddy,' he said on the doorstep, looking Brodie up and down before mock-punching his arm, 'still in your PJs? It's gone ten o'clock. Aren't you usually working out by now?'

Brodie raised his eyebrows. 'Today's a holiday, isn't it?'

'It certainly is.' Alex grinned at some secret joke. 'Hey, you still coming over for a drink tonight? Françoise and Marie have got the night off, so it will just be us for once. Jenny's on the fruit juice, of course. But you and I can share a few bottles. And Caro will be there too.'

Brodie stiffened at her name.

He had been avoiding Caroline for the past week, spending as little time at Porro Park as he could manage, and keeping his conversations deliberately short whenever he bumped into her.

Some things simply weren't meant to be. He had known that for sure when he had tried to hold her hand after the

Boxing Day pageant, and she had stared at him with such a startled expression, he had felt sick inside and dropped her hand like he'd been stung.

He wasn't just failing to attract Caroline Enys, as he had feared previously; he was now actively repelling her.

It was on the tip of his tongue to cry off, find some excuse not to celebrate the New Year with his friends. But then he realised how cowardly that would be. Caroline had him hooked, even if her interest in him had only ever been fleeting at best. But that didn't mean she had him beaten.

'Of course I'll be there,' he said with forced cheerfulness. 'Is that why you came over?'

'Not quite. I've got some good news. Can you guess what?'

'My mind's a blank.' Brodie stood aside to let him into the cottage. 'Coffee, by the way? I've just brewed some fresh.'

'Thanks, smells delicious.' Alex leant against the fridge and watched as Brodie poured them both a mug of coffee. 'We've finally agreed a date for the builders to start work on Delgardo Studios – first week of April, assuming all permissions are in place by then.'

Delgardo Studios was the name they had decided on for the Bodmin Moor property.

Brodie was impressed with the speed at which everything was progressing. 'That's great news.'

'It gives us three months to get the preparatory work done. I'm driving over to look at the place again today. To check measurements and specs before we give the architects our final instructions next week.'

'I'll come with you.' Brodie handed him a coffee and winced with sudden pain. 'Damn it.'

Alex looked concerned. 'You okay?'

'Nothing a couple of painkillers and some gentle stretching won't solve.'

'Sure?'

Brodie gave him a rueful smile. 'Just a little stiffness. Like you said, I'm usually working out by now. Anyway, why all the sudden concern? Since when have you worried about my health? You know me, I'm tough as old boots.'

'Oh, it was just something Jenny said the other day.'

Brodie stilled. 'And what was that?'

'Something and nothing. You know what women are like. Jenny thought you were looking unhappy.'

Brodie swore under his breath.

'Hey, don't blame me, mate.' Alex threw up his hands. 'I didn't say it, she did. As far as I'm concerned, your unhappiness is your own business.'

'I'm not unhappy.' Brodie gritted his teeth. 'Just focused on work. There's a difference.'

'Sure,' Alex said, a steely flick of irony in his voice. 'That's why you're still hiding out here at Pixie Cottage, though you said it was only temporary.'

'I'm not hiding either.'

'Yeah, you said. You're just focused on the work.' Alex hesitated, clearly reluctant to say more, then rolled his eyes. 'We've been friends a long time, haven't we? We don't have many secrets from each other. And you helped me through that rough patch after the bombing, when I was acting like a maniac and nearly threw away my chance to marry Jennifer. You were always there for me, even though I behaved like a total dick at times.'

'I would never have said so to your face.'

Alex laughed. 'Quite right too. But Jenny keeps pointing out to me that you're going through a rough patch too, and I ought to repay the favour.'

'I'm not going through a rough patch,' he protested.

'Of course not. Hence your monk-like retreat at this damp little cottage in the woods. Rice and spinach for dinner every night, no doubt, and a hundred press-ups before bedtime. And before breakfast too. With no visitors allowed. Perfectly normal behaviour for a film company director.'

'It's not damp.'

Alex sighed. 'Listen, if you don't want to share, that's fine. It's your business how you live your life.'

'Damn straight.'

'But if you change your mind,' he continued, 'whatever's bothering you, you can tell me. I'm here for you. Jenny and I, we're both here for you. Message received?'

Brodie shifted awkwardly. 'Copy that.'

'Well, thank God that's over.' Alex clapped him on the back, a relieved laughter in his eyes. 'It's been weighing on my mind ever since Jennifer first broached the subject. She insisted I speak to you, to check you're okay, but I've been putting it off, as you can imagine.' He made a face, pretending to mop his brow. 'Now I can honestly tell her I've made the offer and been rejected.'

'I know the feeling,' Brodie muttered.

'Sorry?'

'Nothing.' Shrugging briskly into his jacket, Brodie bent to turn off his computer. 'Let's head over to the studio site, shall we? Am I driving?'

'Ah,' Alex said apologetically, holding up a hand, 'that's where I need to stop you. I promised Jennifer I'd take her out today. Not you.'

Brodie stared at him, puzzled.

'Apparently, I've been so busy with work lately, I've been neglecting my wife. So this is her treat. A leisurely drive over to Bodmin to check over the property, lunch at one of those quaint little pubs on the moor, and then back in time for dinner and a few New Year drinks before the bells.' He glanced at his watch. 'And I'm running late.'

Brodie took off his jacket, grinning at the thought of Jennifer scolding her huge, bear-like husband for neglecting her.

'Fine,' he said mildly, and accompanied Alex to the cottage door. 'Have a good time. I've got some paperwork to finish anyway.'

'Hey, it's a holiday, remember?'

'I won't work too hard.'

Alex hesitated. 'The reason I came over is ... Do you mind if I take the Land Rover? The Aston Martin's not right for that kind of terrain. Besides, the temperature's been dipping for days. I think it might snow later, and snow on the moors sounds like Land Rover weather.'

'Of course,' Brodie said easily, and bent to fish his keys

out of his jacket pocket. It was a company car anyway, and the only reason he tended to use it more than Alex was because Jennifer preferred the Aston Martin. 'See you both for drinks later.'

'Come round about eight o'clock. I think Jenny's making pizza.'

Brodie changed out of his pyjamas and started his morning workout as soon as Alex had gone. But his mind wasn't focused on his exercise routine. He kept going back over what his friend had said, his brow furrowed.

You're going through a rough patch too.

Alex had been comparing his decision to move out of Porro Park and into the seclusion of Pixie Cottage to his own wild behaviour the year he met Jennifer, when all the psychological horror of the bombing had come back to haunt him.

On more than one occasion, Brodie had found himself fixing Alex's hurts after some violent outburst. Once, Alex had smashed up his hands while trying to dismantle a drystone wall, so that he had to walk about swathed in bandages for days, to everyone else's mystification. Yet he'd denied there was anything wrong, still resistant to Brodie's suggestion of going back into therapy.

Alex had lost himself so deeply in the past, he'd even gone crazy here at the cottage, dreaming himself back there in the bombed-out hotel, dealing with dead bodies everywhere, including one of their own friends. He'd hurled himself about, attacking the wall and shouting at nothing. Terrified, Jennifer had rung Brodie, and he'd driven out to the cottage immediately and taken Alex back to Porro Park to calm down.

That was when Alex had finally agreed to go back into therapy, though it had almost been too late. He'd been tee-tering on the edge of another nervous breakdown by then.

Thankfully, Nelly's worsening illness and a pressing need to care for his grandmother had given Alex something to live for. Otherwise, Brodie felt sure his friend might have done something stupid in those dark, terrible days before he eventually let Jennifer into his life . . .

Your unhappiness is your own business.

Brodie gave up pretending to exercise and buried his head in his hands instead, groaning.

I'm not unhappy. I'm not hiding.

But he knew they were right. He was deeply unhappy. Worse, there was no simple way to remedy the source of his unhappiness. No amount of therapy or days off work or talking it through with his friends would fix this problem, which was as old as time itself.

He was head over heels in love with Caroline Enys. He couldn't keep denying the truth. All that achieved was to make the ache in his heart a thousand times worse, while his friends thought he was an idiot.

Caroline was beautiful, smart, elegant as hell, and yes, he wanted her desperately. She was also funny, kind and generous-hearted, a midwife who cared for other women, whatever the time of day or night, who thought nothing of labouring for long hours alongside them to bring a new soul into the world.

Beside her vocation, his own life looked empty and pointless.

Caroline was the woman of his dreams. But she was not someone who would ever reciprocate that emotion. She was independent. She didn't need a man, except when it suited her to reach for a little physical comfort. And he respected that.

But he was wounded, broken, imperfect. He couldn't offer her what she deserved: a happy man in a perfect body.

It was nearly dusk when her mobile rang, shattering the silence of her bedroom where Caroline had been reading a book. Surprised, she saw Brodie's name on the screen.

'Hello?'

Brodie sounded breathless, like he was running. 'I'm on my way over to the house. I've just had a call from Alex. They're out at the new property on Bodmin Moor, and Jenny's in trouble. It's her pregnancy ... She's refusing to go to the hospital, but he thinks something's badly wrong. I promised to get you over to her straight away.'

'Oh my God.'

'I'll be there in a few minutes. Get your stuff and meet me at the helicopter. Bring whatever you need.'

Caroline jumped up. 'Of course,' she said, her mind already racing ahead to what the problem might be and what she'd need to take in her kitbag. 'I'll be right there.'

After the call, she grabbed up her emergency bag, checked its contents, slipped on her shoes and coat, and dashed out to the helipad.

The air was freezing and there were even a few snow-flakes whirling about, though not sticking yet. The helicopter sat still and silent, shiny dark blue machinery waiting for a pilot. Caroline stood there alone in the cold evening, breathing hard and stamping her feet to keep warm. She was trying hard not to consider what might be wrong with the babies There was nothing she could do before she'd had a chance to examine Jennifer.

Dusk was not far off, she realised with a shock, looking up at the sky. The weather had been threatening sub-zero temperatures for days. But now there were dark clouds too. Was it going to snow tonight? That was an alarming thought. The last thing they needed was snow.

Finally, she saw him running out of the woods in a thick black jacket, the wind lifting his hair, and she darted forward, her heart thumping violently in her chest.

'Brodie,' she gasped, her cheeks flushed, 'at last.'

He helped her into the helicopter, then got in and showed her how to strap herself in. 'Got everything you need?'

'It's all in my bag. But don't you think they should have called an ambulance instead? We could be wasting precious time.'

'Alex said it would take too long, because the house is so remote, right on the high moors. He says we need to bring the helicopter. Then I can fly Jenny straight to a private hospital if necessary once you've examined her.'

'Yes, that makes sense. Quick, please hurry.'

Caroline did not like travelling by helicopter. As the

rotor blades began to gather speed, she tried not to worry or fret about the journey ahead of them. That could do no good and would only make her panic. Instead, she imagined her sister out there on the darkening moors, hoping for a small black speck in the sky to grow larger and larger until finally the helicopter was in sight . . .

CHAPTER THIRTY-FOUR

With surprising swiftness, it only took the helicopter a few minutes to reach the vast, shadowy emptiness that was Bodmin Moor.

Thankfully, Brodie had already studied the maps to see the best approach by air, and found the place even in the gathering dusk, using the headlights of traffic moving fast on the A30 main route into Cornwall as a visual guide. From there, it was an easy approach across the moors to where the property they had acquired was nestled in a kind of natural shelter, a dip situated only a short distance from a rocky outcrop that blocked the icy winds that came whistling across the moors in winter.

He pointed, shouting, 'Over there!' above the noise of the rotor blades, and saw Caroline's head turn.

She had not yet been out to visit the moorland farmhouse, he realised, so was seeing the place for the first time. Though at dusk, it was not possible to make out much beyond a vague outline of roofs and buildings surrounded by wilderness.

He landed the helicopter in the spot they had agreed

would be marked out later as a helipad, a vaguely level area of grassland about five hundred yards from the first outbuilding, and turned off the engine.

Snowflakes dashed themselves against the glass as he looked out, hoping to see lights in the house, but seeing nothing.

'Wait for the blades to slow down,' he warned Caroline, who was not used to travelling by helicopter and had looked very nervous throughout the short trip. Though perhaps she was just scared for her sister, not of flying. Now she was fumbling with her belt, not looking at him, her face a pale oval in the dark interior of the helicopter. He released himself and then leant over to help her with her safety belt. 'Here, let me.'

Their heads were so close, he could smell her light fragrance and almost feel the heat off her skin. Or was he simply imagining that?

'I'm sure she'll be fine,' he said, hoping to reassure her, but aware that those were empty words. He wasn't sure of anything at all.

But Caroline nodded. 'Probably.'

'I'll be ready to take off again at a moment's notice though,' he told her, 'just in case she needs to go to hospital.'

'Thanks,' she muttered, picking up her bag, and then opening the door the way he had shown her before take-off.

As they ran through the rough, ankle-high grasses together, he was relieved to see a door open in the house ahead, light pouring across the unpromising backyard.

Alex stood in the doorway, a powerful torch in his hand

lighting up their path towards the house. 'Over here!' Snowflakes danced wildly in the beam of light. 'Thank God you've arrived. Jenny's through there,' he told Caroline, pointing her towards the snug downstairs room, once a sitting room, that had been designated as a meet-and-greet area once renovations had taken place.

Brodie closed the door, dusting snow off his coat, and turned to find Alex looking guilty. Caroline had already disappeared into the sitting room, and he could hear Jennifer's low tones responding to her questions. She did not sound in too much pain, thankfully.

'How is she?' he asked, not sure if he should unbutton his coat or leave it on, in case he had to fly Jenny to the hospital.

'Much better, actually,' Alex said, and grimaced. 'Sorry to have called you out in this weather. I think it was a false alarm.'

'Well, best to make sure. Caroline knows her business. I'm sure she'll soon let us know how the babies are doing.'

Brodie gave him a reassuring smile, relieved that it didn't seem as serious a situation as he had feared. The last thing Alex needed in his life was another tragedy; his friend had only recently started to put the horrors of the bombing behind him, and relax into married life and his celebrity.

Alex had been lucky, of course, in attracting the love of a woman like Jennifer. She had drawn him out of that dark place, and shown him the light waiting just beyond it. Not everyone was that fortunate, Brodie thought, but pushed the bitterness away as soon as he tasted it. It was his fate to be alone, and he had to learn to accept that.

'Yeah, you're probably right.' Alex glanced nervously over his shoulder though. The door to the sitting room was ajar, and they could hear the two sisters talking, the sound just audible in the quiet house.

'Shall we?' Brodie suggested, and since Alex didn't raise any objection, he poked his head round the sitting room door.

Jennifer was lying on the sofa, one arm thrown over her eyes as though the overhead light was hurting her. Standing beside the sofa, Caroline was stooping to put away a hand-held ultrasound device in her emergency midwifery bag. She was frowning.

Jennifer struggled up at his entrance, turning to smile at him. She looked a little weary, but that was hardly surprising, given her condition and the fact that she'd been out since quite early that morning.

'Thank you for coming out so promptly,' she said, hurriedly coming towards him, and gave Brodie a clumsy hug. 'It was really sweet of you. I didn't think you'd come at all, but Alex was sure you would.'

'Of course I came,' he said, surprised. 'But how are you?' He glanced down at her small baby bump. 'What did Caroline say?'

'Oh, the babies are fine. Heartbeats as strong as ever.'

'A false alarm, like I thought.' Alex put an arm around his wife. 'I'm glad you're okay though, sweetheart.'

Jennifer touched Brodie's arm. 'I've apologised to Caroline

for making a fuss about nothing. Now I need to apologise to you. I'm sorry you made all this effort for no reason. And on New Year's Eve too.'

Brodie shook his head. 'It's not a problem.'

'But I feel so guilty,' she insisted. 'I probably had too much caffeine at lunch today or something silly like that.'

'Honestly, Jenny, don't worry. I was happy to help.'

'All the same, I'd better stay off the coffee from now on. It'll save a fortune in helicopter fuel, not to mention being better for the environment.' Jennifer laughed in an odd way, and glanced past him at Alex. Some kind of message seemed to pass between them, a look that made Brodie suspicious there was something here that he'd missed. 'Erm, can I have a word, Alex? I need to tell you something. In private.'

Looking awkward, Alex turned to Brodie. 'Sorry, do you mind? Maybe you could wait in here with Caroline for a few minutes? Most of the rooms are still empty. But we've had the fire going for a while, so at least it's not too cold in here. And there are snacks on the coffee table.'

'Sure,' Brodie said, though he was still suspicious. He smiled at Jennifer. 'I forgot to eat lunch today, so I'm quite peckish.'

They left the room, closing the door behind them.

Brodie looked round for Caroline, but she had dropped into an armchair near the open fire and was staring silently into the flames that licked about a heap of crackling logs.

'Help yourself,' Caroline said, a glass of red wine in her hand, not looking round at him.

'I can't drink and fly,' he reminded her.

'There's juice.'

She was right, he realised. There were several glasses, a jug of fruit juice, and some bottles of wine on the coffee table, along with various heaped bowls of snacks. Which was strange, Brodie thought. But perhaps Alex and Jennifer had changed their minds about coming home for drinks tonight and had been planning a romantic New Year's Eve party out here, just the two of them, when she'd been taken ill.

Why more than two glasses, though?

'Maybe in a minute.' He stood looking at the fire, suddenly a little overheated in his thick coat. 'Well, this is cosy.'

'Yes, isn't it?'

'So you examined Jenny and there was nothing wrong?'

'She's fine. The babies too, as far as I can tell.' She took a gulp of wine, not looking at him but at the fire again. 'Nothing wrong at all.'

'That's a relief.'

She didn't answer, her head still turned away.

The logs popped and crackled loudly in the silence, the heat undeniably appreciated after the bitter cold of the helicopter ride. Across the room, the curtainless window showed blackness unrelieved by any lights, the farmhouse being too far from civilization, but punctuated by an increasing number of white flecks that no longer melted as soon as they touched the glass.

The snow was still falling, and more heavily now. The

forecast for the coast had been occasional snow and sleet showers. But they were on the high moors now, and getting marooned was a real possibility if the weather continued like this.

Thank goodness they had the helicopter and could be away from here in a matter of minutes. Hopefully, Alex and Jennifer would be finished soon with their 'private' conversation, whatever that was about. Jennifer had insisted there was nothing wrong with the babies, and Caroline had confirmed that too. So why all the covert behaviour?

Brodie heard a familiar sound above the noise of the fire and the whistling wind, and stiffened, frowning. 'What the hell?'

Caroline looked round at last, surprise in her face.

He tore out of the room and across the narrow hallway to the door they had come in through.

It was locked.

Swearing under his breath, he cast about for a key, but couldn't find one. Then he remembered the back door which led off the kitchen, and headed that way instead, breathing hard. The back door was bolted but not locked. He drew back the bolt, flung the door open on a whirling sea of white, and dashed out into the cold evening.

The helicopter was already in the air, its lights picking out snowflakes. In the cockpit, he could see Alex at the controls.

'Hey!' Brodie shouted, waving his arms about wildly. 'Hey, what the hell are you doing?'

Looking down briefly, his friend raised a hand, half salute, half apology, and then turned back to the controls.

The helicopter turned and rose even higher before moving on, its faint lights fading westwards, presumably beginning its journey back to the coast and Pethporro.

Brodie's first response was fear. For his friend, who had only got his flying licence last year in the States, and for the pregnant woman by his side. But he knew in his heart that Alex was a perfectly competent pilot and that the snow might complicate the journey, but on such a short run was unlikely to cause real problems.

Then he knew a moment of utter bewilderment.

He trod heavily back inside, shut the kitchen door and bolted it again, to find Caroline staring up into the night sky.

'What's going on?' she demanded, looking round at him.

'They've gone, in case you didn't hear the helicopter,' he said angrily. 'Alex and Jenny. They've taken the chopper and left us here. Why?'

'I don't know.' There was a look of panic on her face.

'Well, they may have taken the helicopter, but there's always the Land Rover. They drove here, didn't they?'

'But it's snowing,' she began, tailing off when he turned on his heel, leaving the room.

'It's a Land Rover, it won't mind a bit of snow.'

After a few minutes of bitterly cold hunting, snow in his face, the wind tearing at his clothes, he found the Land Rover under cover in one of the barns. But the car was locked. Had Alex taken the car keys with him?

Belatedly, he took out his mobile and tried calling Porro Park. He could speak to Françoise at least and leave a message. Then he would call a local taxi firm and . . .

There was no phone signal.

Of course not. They were on the moors. He stared down at the 'No Signal' message in dismay. Why had they not thought of that when purchasing the property? What kind of film studio had no mobile phone signal?

Brodie swore loudly, staring at the useless vehicle.

That was when he began to understand what was going on. Alex, his closest friend, had lied to him tonight. As had Jennifer, with her pretended innocence and awkward hug, and no obvious signs of distress. They had lured him and Caroline out here on false pretences. It was likely that Alex had driven out somewhere with a signal just to make that initial call. Then they'd flown away in the helicopter and left him alone there with Caroline.

The only thing he didn't know was why.

Brodie went back to the house, struggling to control his temper, and impatiently stamped the snow off his boots before going inside.

The house was dark and silent, except for a soft glow shining through the half-open door into the sitting room.

His leg was aching in the cold, the prosthesis rubbing after a long, hard day at a desk, followed by too much sudden running about on uneven ground. If he had been at home, back at Pixie Cottage, he would have removed the prosthesis and taken a long hot bath before falling thankfully into bed. But he wasn't at home, and didn't even know if this place had hot running water, let alone somewhere to sleep.

Caroline was standing by the window in her coat, only a

little wine left in her glass now. When he came in, she turned, hurriedly gulping the last of it.

'If we leave now,' she said, 'it shouldn't be too bad. The snow isn't falling heavily, even though we're quite high up here.'

'We're not going anywhere,' he said flatly.

Her eyes widened. 'What do you mean?'

'The car's locked and I'm pretty certain Alex has taken the key with him. So we're stranded.'

'We can phone for a taxi. Or maybe I could ask a friend to come and pick us up. I know it's New Year's Eve, but ...' She tailed off when he shook his head. 'Why not?'

'No signal,' he said, and held up his mobile phone with its non-existent signal bars. 'Like I said, we're stranded.'

'I don't understand.'

'Oh, I think you do,' he said grimly. 'And I do too.'

Caroline put down her wine glass and crossed the room towards him, her eyes intent, fixed on his face. He was very aware of how alone they were up here on the desolate moors, in this large empty house, their friends probably already back at Porro Park by now and laughing at him, no doubt.

'What do you mean?' she asked softly. 'What are you talking about?'

Desire flooded him at the husky note in her voice. Desire and suspicion. 'I'm saying this whole thing has been a charade,' he said, 'designed to throw us together for the night. And I think you were in on it.'

'Me? Why in God's name would I agree to ...?' A faint

flush came into her face as his words sank in. 'Oh my God, I get it. You think this is a seduction. You think I wanted to spend New Year's Eve stranded with you on Bodmin Moor, in the bloody snow ...' Her chest was heaving. 'You must be out of your mind, Brodie Mattieson.'

CHAPTER THIRTY-FIVE

To her relief, he seemed to believe her.

Though even as she'd said that, furious that he could suspect her of something so underhand, she'd realised it sounded like the perfect opportunity to make things right between them.

Jennifer must have known that too. And Alex.

That was why they'd stranded them here together. To see if they could fix this broken thing between them.

But was it really broken? Or non-existent?

Brodie had held her hand on the beach at Pethporro, and looked at her in the light of the flaming torches, and she had . . . What had she done?

She tried to unpick that moment, struggling against fear and self-doubt. Brodie had taken her hand, and she had felt something deep inside, known something intuitively that could not be understood except in the heart, and seen something in his eyes, an answering desire . . .

No, not desire. But maybe love.

She had thought him immune to her. And herself immune to him. She had made wild assumptions based on a lifestyle that had suited her for years, a lifestyle that had stopped her getting too close to anyone, and quite deliberately. She had not wanted to be tied down, to be married or in a partnership, to be one of two, part of a couple, never free but always bound to another human being. Yet her heart had ached and looked for exactly that bond, without her even wanting it to or being aware of its secret intention.

And her heart had found Brodie Mattieson.

But had he found her in return?

His brief touch on the beach, and the interlacing of their fingers, had told her with some degree of certainty that, yes, Brodie felt the same. That he too had got himself caught up in whatever this was. Desire. Love. Infatuation. An inner yearning she dared not name. That he was as helplessly attracted as she was, and in just as deep.

Now though, inches away from him, the two of them completely alone in a desolate place, she felt assailed by the most horrific panic. The next few hours could determine the rest of her life. Or destroy her completely.

'So Alex and Jenny planned this little stunt together?' he asked, and she could not read his expression. 'You weren't a part of it.'

'Not even remotely.'

His gaze became troubled. 'I see.' He looked away, frowning. 'In that case, I apologise. We've both been duped.'

'So what do we do?'

'Drink the wine, see in the New Year, go to sleep.' He jerked his head towards the sofa. 'This is the warmest room. You take the sofa. I'll take the armchair. Wrap myself in my coat.'

'I can take the armchair.'

'No,' he said, grimacing. 'You, sofa. Me, armchair. No more discussion.'

She felt like saluting. 'Yes, sergeant.'

He shot her a look, but didn't comment, picking up the opened bottle of red wine and pouring himself a large glass.

'Happy New Year,' he said sardonically, raising his glass to her, and then took a large swallow.

This would be the loneliest New Year's Eve of her life, she thought sadly, and went to fetch her wine glass. He refilled it for her, and for a few minutes they stood before the crackling fire together, drinking wine and avoiding each other's eyes.

Damn Jenny. She was sure her sister must have been the mastermind of this embarrassing little scheme. All totally pointless, of course. Because it now seemed she'd been mistaken on the beach at Pethporro; Brodie didn't want her after all. Caroline wanted him, but a seduction only worked when both parties were into each other.

She dragged off her coat and threw it aside, then continued drinking her wine. God, it was overheated in this room.

He glanced at her over the rim of his wine glass, and away again. He was looking flushed, she realised. The heat of the fire, perhaps. Or the wine, starting to warm them both up.

'I'm sorry,' he muttered.

'About what?'

'Accusing you of planning this. I realise now you didn't, that you're not ... I shouldn't have said it.' His voice was stilted. 'Please forgive me.'

'That I'm not ... what?'

'Not interested.'

She downed some more wine. Her cheeks felt hot. Her chest was rising and falling very rapidly too, like she was panting, which was weird.

'Say that I am—'

'That you're what?'

'Interested.' She realised her glass was empty and put it down. Daringly, she added, 'Would that make any difference? I mean, to the whole sofa, armchair thing?'

He stared at her, his glass stilled on its way to his mouth. 'Interested,' he repeated slowly. 'In me?'

'In you,' she agreed.

His eyes locked with hers. 'What does that entail, exactly? By way of specifics. A one-night stand? Or something ... more?'

She wanted him so badly, it was an ache deep inside. It was dark outside and they were alone together. There was wine and a fire and a comfortable sofa. And he was at least discussing the prospect.

Perhaps Jenny was not to be damned after all.

But he was not an easy catch.

'Can't we just make it up as we go along?' Caroline moved a little closer to him. His pupils were dilated, she realised. Not exactly a sign of disinterest. 'Do we have to draw up a three-point plan or sign everything in triplicate beforehand?'

'I'm not sure,' he said, putting his glass down.

Ugh, this was far harder than Caroline had thought it would be. She must have imagined this seduction at least a dozen times in the privacy of her head. Though in her much-rehearsed fantasy, he had simply swept her off her feet and carried her off to bed . . .

Instead, they were still talking. And going in circles.

'Do I need to spell this out to you, Brodie?' She was frustrated now, self-doubt giving way to a desire to kiss the confusion off his face. 'I want you.'

'You want me,' he echoed.

'Yes.' She stared into his eyes, willing him to understand and to take the initiative. 'Like at the Christmas drinks party. Only without the unwanted interruptions. Or the wall behind me instead of somewhere more comfortable.'

His eyes widened, no doubt remembering that passionate clinch they'd shared in the pantry at Porro Park.

'I didn't plan this evening,' she continued. 'We're both victims of Alex and Jenny's little hoax. But now we're here, it would be a shame to waste a perfect opportunity. No phone calls, no people to burst in, no interruptions . . . Just you and me, getting to know each other properly.'

His gaze searched her face. 'Getting to know each other?'

'That was a euphemism,' she whispered.

Caroline leant forward and put her lips against his. Brodie stood statue-still, and for a terrible moment she feared that she had miscalculated. He didn't want her at all, all this had been her imagination. But then his lips began to move against hers, and his arms came up to grasp her back, and finally they were kissing.

She felt her heartbeat accelerate, heat burning in her cheeks as his hands stroked down her back, moulding her against his body. Standing up, the fire still crackling behind them, they kissed for what felt like ages, but was probably only five minutes. His breathing became more ragged, and his heart raced too. She cupped his face with both hands, a burning deep inside her that would not be satisfied with mere kisses.

But this was when something had always gone wrong before, she recalled. Kissing had never been the issue. It had been getting beyond the kissing stage that always seemed to run into a snag.

As if on cue, Brodie pulled away. 'I can't, I . . .' He took a deep breath. 'You don't know me. You don't understand.'

'Don't understand what?'

'I'm not . . .' He groaned again, his eyes tormented. 'I haven't . . . done this.'

'Ever?' She was shocked.

His laughter was husky. 'No, of course not. I meant, since the bombing. I haven't been to bed with anyone since then.'

'And?'

'I . . . I may be rusty.'

'Don't worry, I'll be happy to give you a few pointers. But I'm sure you won't need any. It's the kind of thing you never forget.' She smiled at his uncertainty, and began to unbutton his jacket. 'Let me help you with this. You look overheated.'

Still frowning, Brodie let her take the jacket off him, then he dragged his own sweater off, his gaze fixed on her as she kicked off her boots.

'Are you sure about this?' he said softly.

'Of course.'

'Because I'll understand if you ... if you change your mind.'

Standing before him barefoot, Caroline paused midway through removing her jumper, bewildered by his hesitancy.

'Brodie, what on earth are you talking about?' she asked, unable to stay patient with him any longer. So he hadn't been sexually active since the bombing. So what? She had suspected as much, anyway, and it was hardly a deal-breaker for her. It was rather cute, actually. 'I'm lost.'

A faint tinge of red came into his face. 'My leg,' he said thickly, looking away at last. 'You remember I lost mine in the bombing. I have a ... a prosthetic limb.'

'I know. I've seen it.'

'But you've never seen me without it.' He ran a hand through his hair, looking almost savage. 'I don't think I could bear it if ...'

What on earth ...?

'Hang on, let me get this straight.' Her hands dropped to her hips in sheer frustration at his stupidity. 'You think I'm going to shriek in horror and run away at the sight of you with only half a leg?'

His jaw clenched. 'Maybe.'

'Seriously? Is this why you've been holding back? Because you're afraid how I might react to seeing you *naked*?'

'It's not that simple,' he began, but she didn't let him finish.

'Brodie Mattieson, you drop those jeans right now.' Caroline glared at him, no longer even joking. 'Come on, get 'em off!'

'Sorry?'

'I'm a nurse, Brodie.' Her head was seething at what he'd put her through over the past couple of months without ever once bothering to explain the real issue. 'Of course I know you lost your bloody leg. And I've seen your artificial limb before. You do wear shorts occasionally. Like that time you came down to the pool when I was swimming, remember?'

'But you haven't seen me *without* it,' he said doggedly.

She blinked. 'Is that why you didn't get into the pool that day? Because you didn't want me to see you taking it off?'

He said nothing, but a muscle jerked in his cheek.

'I think I'm beginning to understand.' Caroline folded her arms angrily and nodded to his bottom half. 'Right, let's sort this out, once and for all. Get those jeans off, and then lose your prosthesis. I want to have a long hard look at you,' she added crossly, 'before I kick you out into the snow.'

He stared, and for one awful moment she thought he was going to refuse. That would be the worst thing imaginable, she thought, holding her breath.

But this . . .

This thing with Brodie was something she could change,

if she handled it right. And shouting, 'Get your jeans off!' had probably not been the most sensitive thing to do, under the circumstances.

'Please,' she added softly, and unfolded her arms, wishing she didn't have such an impulsive nature. 'I'm sorry I raised my voice to you, Brodie. I didn't mean to, I was just so mad that you could even think that about me.' She bit her lip, willing him to understand. 'But I really do want to see you without the prosthesis. If only to prove you wrong.'

CHAPTER THIRTY-SIX

Brodie felt like he was in some bizarre dream. Or nightmare, to be more precise. He heard his own breathing as though from a distance, rough and uneven. What did she want? What had she asked him to do? To take off his jeans, and then his prosthesis, to show her what he looked like without the artificial limb?

Caroline was baiting him, he decided. She had discovered his greatest fear and now she was tormenting him with it.

He should leave. But where would he go?

Snow beat at the windows, and beyond the whirl of flakes was a barren darkness, the moors under a moonless night. Not exactly hospitable.

In here, by contrast, it was warm, almost suffocatingly so. The fire was burning fiercely, and there were plenty more logs in the basket on the hearth. The bottle of red wine was still more than half full, and the large sofa was strewn with luxurious furry throws and large cushions.

He imagined pushing her back among the cushions, if

she would have him, and making love to her, and the thought almost drove him crazy.

'Well?' she said gently, still watching him.

She wanted to see him without it. She must be mad, he kept thinking, even as he bent to remove his boots first, his hands fumbling, nervous. The foot of his prosthetic limb was now clearly visible. He waited but she said nothing. Then he straightened, and his hands went to the fastening of his jeans.

She kept her eyes firmly on his face until he was finished, then she took her time looking him up and down. Her eyebrows rose slowly.

'My God,' she said huskily, 'you're in bloody good shape.'

'I do a lot of push-ups.'

'It's noticeable.' Her mouth twitched in a fleeting smile. Then she drew a deep breath and nodded to his prosthesis. 'Now that.'

'Kiss me first.'

Her eyebrows stayed high. 'Bargaining?'

'For courage.'

'Oh, in that case . . .' She came towards him, and put a hand on his bare chest. Her skin felt cold, but a good cold, giving him shivers. She smiled into his eyes, then kissed him. Delicately, her tongue played against his while she stroked that hand up and down his body until his blood sang in his ears and he felt like his body was about to turn into a human torch. 'Better?'

He could barely speak, but managed some kind of nod.

Then he sat back on the sofa, while she knelt on the rug

beside him, and methodically removed his prosthetic limb. It didn't usually take this long, but he lingered over the familiar task, his heart thumping uncomfortably.

Job done, he could barely bring himself to look at her, more anxious than he had ever been in his life – even as a soldier, even in the hospital when they'd said his lower leg would need to be amputated.

Caroline gazed at him steadily, her eyes intent in the silence between them. What was she thinking?

'Here,' she said, holding out her hands. 'I want to see.'

Brodie handed her the prosthesis, and she studied it with interest before laying it aside on the rug, and kneeling up, her smile downright seductive.

'May I?' she whispered, and he nodded.

He felt her cool hand stroke him where the prosthesis had been attached, and he groaned as though at an electric shock, collapsing back among the cushions.

'Does that feel . . . nice?'

'God, yes,' he hissed, then looked up, startled, to see her climb on to the sofa and straddle him. His hands came up automatically, supporting her. 'What . . . what are you doing?'

'Seducing you, of course.'

Somehow, he got her jeans off and watched as she pulled off her white vest top as well, revealing a crop top bra that held her snugly. Then she bent her head to kiss him, her body warm and lithe against him, and he drank in her scent, their mouths meeting passionately. He reached up to help remove her bra, first cupping her breasts gently and then kissing them in wonder.

'You're so beautiful,' he told her, feeling almost drunk at the luscious sight and feel of her nudity against him.

'So are you,' Caroline replied, and smiled when he looked up at her in astonishment. 'As beautiful as a god.'

He said nothing, but her smile had touched him to the core. His heart felt suddenly strong and powerful, beating a rhythm for them both to follow. They touched and explored each other at length, and then she got up briefly to turn the light off, so they were bathed in shadowy fire-light instead. They lay together in the deep cushions for a while, kissing and whispering as the fire burnt lower and lower.

Finally, she straddled him again, and he lifted her hips with confident hands, settling her over him, and drew her down close and tight until they were both locked in ecstasy.

Their mouths met as they made love, his skin hot and unbearably sensitive, all his doubts forgotten as they joined at last as one.

'Oh Brodie,' she gasped.

He groaned, unable to take his eyes off this complex, talented woman who had decided he was worth taking a risk on, this sexy, gorgeous, life-giving . . . goddess.

'I love you,' he said, and saw her eyes widen in shock.

He held very still against her, watching her face change, and feared those three words had been too much, that she would reject him. This was a woman who needed no man's love, after all. Why should he believe himself to be any different, that he of all men would mean something special to her?

Then Caroline bent her head to kiss his mouth, and he heard her whisper, 'I love you too, Brodie,' before his eyes closed and he was lost in the most exquisite pleasure he had ever felt.

It was daylight when Caroline finally stirred, opening her eyes on an unfamiliar ceiling. For a few seconds, she lay there, drowsy and confused, and a little bit sore in places.

What the hell?

She turned her head, and only then realised that she was lying against a strong, muscular chest, her lower limbs wrapped around a powerful body she had thoroughly explored last night. Explored, tasted and played with until they were both hot, exhausted and glowing with perspiration, despite the bleak howl of wind around the farmhouse and the snowstorm that had raged outside most of the night.

As that memory was restored, she felt herself blush. She'd had no idea how passionate Brodie could be in bed. Nor how strong and energetic . . . and interested in experimentation. Goodness, had she really done all those things with him?

Worse, had she actually told him, *I love you*?

Yes, she had.

Caroline closed her eyes in pain for a second, catching her breath, before slowly remembering that he had said it first.

I love you.

Yes, they really had said that phrase to each other while

making love. But maybe the strangest thing was, she had meant it with all her heart and soul. She felt pretty certain that he'd meant it too, and he had absolutely no reason to lie or flatter her. So it must be true, mustn't it?

She was in love with Brodie Mattieson. And she'd told him. And he hadn't laughed at her or tried to take advantage.

It was official. They were in love with each other.

Her heart soared with joy.

'Hey,' a voice rumbled next to her, and she lifted her head to find Brodie watching her with intent blue eyes. 'Awake at last, huh?'

'Just about,' she whispered back.

His smile was dry, and a touch wary. Was he worried that last night had been a one-off thing? That fear had crossed her mind too, she had to admit.

'That's good. I think my arm was beginning to go to sleep. But I didn't want to move and disturb you. Just in case you were ready to go again.' He grinned. 'Not that I'd mind that, but I'll need a comfort break first. And maybe some strong black coffee.'

Caroline smiled. She loved his sense of humour.

'No, I'm pretty much exhausted.' She laughed, sitting up slowly, and felt the cold air hit her. The fire had gone out hours ago, and when she glanced towards the windows, she saw nothing but white in every direction. The house was surrounded by snowy moorlands. 'Oh my God, it's freezing.'

She leant over and grabbed her jumper off the floor. Dragging it on, she shivered, watching as Brodie reached for his prosthetic limb, deftly locked it into place, then found his own clothes and began getting dressed.

'Looks like we're snowed in for today at least,' he said, heading for the window to stare out across Bodmin Moor, still pulling his sweater down over his muscular chest. 'Though given our lack of transport, that's hardly important.'

'I don't mind,' she admitted shyly.

'Neither do I.' He turned and came back towards her, looking lean and a little bit dangerous, his blue eyes full of laughter. 'I have to congratulate you. I was thoroughly seduced last night by a beautiful, hedonistic siren.'

'I don't recall you complaining at the time.'

'I'm not complaining now, darling.' Brodie met her eyes with a look of wry understanding. 'Trust me.'

He had called her *darling*. Her heart thudded, and she felt unsteady. *Trust me*, he'd said. Could she trust him though? Trust him with her heart, a vulnerable and fragile part of herself she had never given to anyone? Not really, not like this. Not forever.

She looked into his face, silenced and horribly unsure of herself. Like a teenager with a bad crush. She wanted to open her heart to him again, as freely and passionately as she had done while they were making love by firelight last night. But in the cold light of day, she couldn't think of anything to say that wouldn't sound needy and clinging. And she hated the idea of seeming needy or clinging.

'Did we ever say Happy New Year to each other?'

'I can't remember.'

'I'm from Scotland; we take that kind of thing very seriously.'

'I think we missed celebrating the stroke of midnight,' she said softly. 'Too busy doing other things.'

'Well, we may have missed the bells, but here's to a very happy new year indeed.' Brodie put a strong arm about her waist and pulled her close, then kissed her deeply. Their mouths met, and for a few dizzying minutes she forgot everything except how it felt to be in his arms again. Then he kissed her throat, murmuring, 'By the way, I need you to know something.'

'Mmm?'

'I meant what I said,' he told her. 'I'm madly, wildly, deeply in love with you, Caroline Enys, and last night was ... It was a dream come true. It was beyond words. Beyond anything I've ever experienced.'

Her mind reeled.

'Oh,' she whispered, suddenly breathless.

'But if you've changed your mind, then please just say so now. Will you do me that favour?' His voice had turned rough, as though he were in pain. 'Let me down now, Caro, not later. I couldn't bear to date you for a few months, then break up with you. I think that would kill me. I'd rather you were honest and told me straight out if I'm not ... not everything you'd hoped.'

'Brodie,' she said, cupping his face in her hands and staring deep into his eyes, 'you do say the stupidest things.'

'Do I?' He was frowning, trying to make light of it, but

she could see that he was hurting. 'Yes, I probably do. I guess it's my superpower.'

'Shut up and listen,' she said. 'It's taken me a while to work things out, but I had a lot of baggage to sort through first. Not just Topaz and her lies, but the men I've known in the past ... who were never quite right for me,' she added in a hurry, wanting to reassure him. 'Plus, my need to be independent, of course. I've had trouble kicking that one. And I think maybe you've had some issues to deal with too. Neither of us have been exactly honest with each other.'

He grimaced. 'I suppose not.'

'But we got here eventually, didn't we? So no, I'm not going anywhere, and I'm not giving up on this. We can work the rest out as we go along.'

'You're sure?'

'I love you, you beautiful idiot. To bits and beyond.' Tears welled up in her eyes. 'I think I've been waiting for you all my life. And now I've found you, I'm never going to let you go.'

Now it was Brodie's turn to say a breathless, 'Oh,' seemingly mesmerised by her little speech.

'Now hush,' she told him, running a finger across his lips. 'Let's get that coffee and comfort break out of the way, so we can get back to doing what we do best.'

'Arguing? Misunderstanding each other?'

'Healing each other,' Caroline whispered, and kissed him while he was still smiling.

EPILOGUE

'Only two or three more good pushes,' Caroline said encouragingly, and patted her sister's hand. Then she reached into
the trolley cart and drew out a clean set of gloves from her
delivery kit, ready for the next baby. The lights in the spa-
cious private delivery suite had been dimmed for the past
hour as Jennifer chose to leave the warm birthing pool and
set up camp on the cushioned floor for the final phase of
her fifteen-hour labour. 'I can see Nadia's head crowning.
She's ready to come out, she wants to meet you.'

'But I'm so tired . . .'

'You can do it, Jenny. Come on, baby Natalie needs her
sister too. Look at that cute little face. Are you going to
disappoint her?'

They both gazed round at the firstborn twin, wrapped
in a blanket and cradled in her father's arms. As though on
cue, the red-faced newborn girl, who had been staring at
nothing in particular, suddenly stiffened and let out a
shriek of outrage, then settled into a furious howling.

'See?' Caroline made a mock-sad face. 'Poor diddums,
she's fed up with waiting. It's been over fifteen minutes

and her sister Nadia is still inside her mummy's tummy. That's not right.'

Alex, who had been staring down at his child in silent wonder ever since Caroline had placed her in his arms, suddenly chuckled. 'You should do this for a living.'

'Hush,' Caroline said sternly, glancing up at him and suppressing an urge to giggle. Jennifer was genuinely tired and had lost her sense of humour some hours ago. 'Your role in all this is to look after your firstborn. Number Two is coming any minute now. And then we can all have a nice cup of tea.'

Jennifer groaned and stiffened as another contraction rippled through her, then blew out a short series of panting breaths before bearing down hard. The baby came out a little more, but no further.

'I need pain relief!' Jennifer grimaced. 'Now!'

Amanda, the private doctor in attendance, hurried forward to help with the gas and air. She had agreed beforehand not to interfere with Caroline's delivery of the babies unless an emergency occurred, and had been true to her word. But it had been nice to have a doctor on hand throughout, as twin births could become complicated very quickly, and Caroline had been secretly nervous in recent days, unable to sleep at night, worrying in case something went wrong during her sister's labour.

Brodie had told her not to be silly, reminding her how experienced a midwife she was, even with multiple births.

'Everything's going to be fine,' Brodie had told her only two nights before, cuddling her as they lay in bed together at Pixie Cottage after a long day. 'I can't wait to meet Natalie and Nadia. I feel like I've already seen them, with all those ultrasound pictures and listening to the heartbeats.' He'd shaken his head in wonder. 'It makes you think, doesn't it?'

'Think about what?' Caroline had asked, confused.

She had moved in with Brodie only a few weeks before, after realising that she would soon be living in a house with newborn twins, who would be waking for feeds or nappy changes at all hours, and generally making their presence felt on the eardrums.

Suddenly, the idea of Pixie Cottage's peaceful isolation was deeply appealing. And the cottage was only a few minutes' walk or drive away, if something went wrong and one or both of them was needed back at the main house.

Besides, she rather fancied that Alex and Jennifer were keen to have Porro Park to themselves for a while, as they came to terms with parenthood.

'About doing that too,' Brodie had muttered mysteriously, and nuzzled his face in the side of her throat. 'Just like Alex and Jenny.'

'Brodie, I don't understand.'

'Having a baby.'

'Oh,' she'd said breathlessly, and felt as though everything she had ever taken for granted had just turned on its head. 'A b-baby.'

'Or two.' He'd stroked her cheek. 'Or maybe three.'

Caroline had been stunned into silence by this suggestion, not sure what to say or if she should take him seriously.

Try for a baby? Or even more than one? Her and Brodie? They had only just started living together. It was ludicrous. Unthinkable. But now that he'd put the seed of that crazy idea in her head, it seemed hard to dislodge it. After all, he was clearly serious, and what else was she waiting for? Wasn't this the best possible time to become a mother, while she was still taking a break from her work as a midwife and considering what else to do with her life?

And she was heading towards her mid-thirties. If she delayed another few years, she knew from her work with pregnant women that there might not be much time left if it proved tricky to conceive or if they wanted more than one child . . .

'I'll think about it,' Caroline had said cautiously in the end, shaking her head when Brodie gave a whoop of absolute glee. Then wriggled when he hooked a powerful thigh over hers, his arms snaking expertly around her, even though they had decided on an early night. 'Hey, mister, what exactly do you think you're doing?'

'Getting some early practice in,' Brodie had said with a wink, and that wicked smile that always made her insides melt.

Now Brodie was in the waiting room outside the delivery suite with their dad and Debbie, and a vast array of flowers and balloons and pink teddy bears that had already arrived from friends and well-wishers. Somehow the word had got out that movie heart-throb Alex Delgardo's wife was in labour with twins, and apparently a few determined members of the celebrity press were camped outside the gates of the well-guarded private hospital, waiting for news or maybe a chance photograph of the star.

'Push again! And again! That's it, perfect. She's coming now!' Caroline knelt and caught the second baby with practised hands, then cut the umbilical, rubbed her with a soft towel, and carefully checked her over before bundling her into Jennifer's waiting arms. 'Say hello to Nadia.'

Two months ago, the couple had finally decided to be told the sex of the twins before the birth, and on hearing it would be two girls, had chosen their names almost immediately.

'Natalie because it sounds so wild and exotic,' Jennifer had told her sister happily. 'And Nadia because it's so delicate and beautiful. One of Alex's favourite names, apparently.' Alex had agreed, before adding that Natalie's second name would be Deborah, after Jennifer's mother, and Nadia's second name would be Paula, after the camerawoman who had died during the hotel bombing. News that Brodie had taken with sudden tears in his eyes, and a sharp nod of approval.

Now both babies were safely here, her work was almost done, Caroline thought, stepping back to remove her gloves. There were a few other tasks required, but Amanda could take care of those.

Once all the checks had been completed, and Amanda had left the room, Alex brought Natalie to a grinning, relaxed Jennifer.

'Look what we made,' he whispered.

The new mother held both babies proudly, one dainty bundle cradled in each arm, their faces uncannily identical, while Alex took photographs. Then Brodie was called in, so he could take photos of them all together, along with Dad and Debbie. For a while there was much noisy laughter and admiration, with Debbie charmed at having her name used for one of the babies' second names, and Caroline even accepting a glass of champagne from Alex, though she felt more like collapsing after not having slept in more than twenty-four hours.

'But they're so tiny,' Brodie exclaimed on first seeing the newborn babies, much to Alex's amusement, while a look of utter enchantment crossed his face when he held baby Nadia for a few rapturous moments. 'Gorgeous,' he kept saying, and locked gazes with Caroline. 'Perfect.'

'They complete me,' Alex said seriously, and put an arm about Brodie's shoulder. 'Your turn next, mate.'

Jennifer rolled her eyes at Caroline. 'Oh, pay no attention.' With their dad holding one baby, and Brodie the other, Jennifer lay back against the pillows, though her eyes were sparkling and she didn't look tired any more. Running on pure adrenalin, probably. 'Nobody expects that.' Then she saw the way Brodie and Caroline were looking at each other, and her eyes widened in astonishment. 'Unless it's what you want, of course.'

'We're thinking about it,' Caroline and Brodie said in unison, then laughed together too, Caroline blushing as everyone stared at them both.

Alex poured Brodie a glass of champagne and handed it to him as soon as Debbie had taken baby Nadia out of his arms.

'Poor devil,' Alex said, and grinned. 'Welcome to my life. You could do worse.'

THE END

ACKNOWLEDGEMENTS

Writing may be a solitary business, but publishing is not. Therefore, as ever, I'd like to thank the people around me who make it possible. Firstly, my wonderful agent, Alison Bonomi, for her thoughtful words of support and encouragement. Our mutual obsession with all things Georgette Heyer also provides us with a never-ending source of awesome things to tweet about. (If you've never read one of Heyer's romances, do it now!!!) A big thank you also to the hard-working Quercus team, and especially my editor, Emma Capron, who kept me on the straight and narrow for this latest book from Chapter One to The End. My only regret is that the scourge of coronavirus has prevented us from meeting up in person.

Thanks are also due to the *real* people of North Cornwall, my friends and neighbours, who helped me construct the fictional world of Pethporro simply by being themselves. Celebrating Christmas down here in rural Cornwall is a magical and moving event, and I highly recommend it to everyone. A special thank you to one friend in particular, whom I have promised faithfully not to name here, who currently works as a midwife and was so helpful and patient in providing me with answers to the dozens of questions I bombarded her with, despite having far better things to do with her time – such as delivering gorgeous babies! Any mistakes on the technical side of midwifery practice are my own, needless to say.

Finally, loving thanks to my husband Steve, who gently reminds me to come offline whenever I need that extra push on my book and the lures of the internet are proving too great to resist! (I encourage him to do this, otherwise I would never write a word.) And to my fab kids – Kate, Becki (now married to Gary!), Dylan, Morris and Indigo – who don't seem to mind at all that their mother is an eccentric writer who spends a goodly part of most days shuffling about in a dressing gown, talking to herself. Thanks, guys.

And lastly to my father, Richard Holland, to whom this book is dedicated. When I was about twelve years old, Dad, you read my first rambling attempt at a novel – about a time-travelling caveman! - and made copious pages of notes for me to take away and inwardly digest. I still haven't managed to avoid using too many adjectives, sorry. But I hope this latest attempt of mine makes you smile. Love you always, xxx.

All Summer with you

There's no place like home . . .

Nursing a broken heart, Jennifer Bolitho retreats to Pixie
Cottage. Her new landlord – a former soldier turned movie
heartthrob – has grounds so large, she's sure the little
house nestled in the woods will bring her solitude.

Alex Delgardo also has reasons to hide away. Seeking
refuge after a tragic incident turned his world upside
down, he knows that the most important thing
now is to care for his ailing family.

But when Jennifer enters their lives, that changes.
Because, as they both learn, you can't heal others
until you learn to heal yourself . . .

**A summer romance for fans of
Daisy James and Sarah Morgan.**

Available now in paperback and eBook.

Quercus